The

(Paradigm Book ...)

Written by:
Glenda Clemens

This is a work of fiction. Names, charters, organizations places, events, and incidents are either products of the author's imagination or are used fictitiously.

Published by Glenda Clemens through KDP, Amazon

Cover design by Glenda Clemens

Photo by David Clemens

Special Thanks

Thanks to my daughter Lorien.
She had the courage to speak up.
Her courage guided the story.

Thanks to Judy Risely and Judy Burns
My Power Partners and Okie Goddesses.

Thanks to all my family who read
The Gloriana Paradigm in it's
Roughest form
And loved it anyway.

Most special thanks and love to my husband
David, whose editing added much to the story.
He sees the Goddess in me always.

Dedication

This book is dedicated to every woman,
A Goddess in her own power.
An embodiment of love

Lady Rainier

Beauty standing morning light
Robes pink, glowing bright
Singing sunrise to all below
Praising night with her glow.

Singing echoes from darkness
Always heard in daylight
Hidden power, deep below
Praising night with her glow.

Beauty in morning light
Terrible power, her might
All will vanish below
Praising night with her glow.

Chapter 1

"A woman in harmony with her spirit
Is like a river flowing.
She goes where she will without pretense
And arrives at her destination
Prepared to be herself and only herself."
--Maya Angelou

"Fuck! I can't believe this!" Glory stood quickly and looked around the typical cube farm. *Of course, no one is paying attention! Typical. None of us pay any attention to each other while we work unless we need to. We have to keep ourselves isolated in this zoo or we can't work.*

She sat back down, hot tears coming now as she turned back to her computer. *Frankly, I am a little disappointed no one heard my outburst. Dammit, my entire world is collapsing around me and no one fucking noticed.*

Gloriana had built her adult life around marriage to Edgar and the hope for a strong loving family they would build together. Instead, he was 'cutting her loose' and through a fucking email no less! It felt as if she were adrift in this moment without rudder or sail.

She read the email again. Tears were flowing down her face and the feelings of drifting in a bottomless pit made her dizzy. Glory closed her eyes, and the sensation worsened. She put her head on her desk and tried some deep breaths. *Martha is big on deep breaths*, she thought and smiled a little. As the dizziness subsided, she could think better about what was happening.

Edgar, her husband, was leaving her. Worse yet, he was not leaving because there was another woman. *Really? I thought another woman was the cause of nearly every failing marriage. One partner found someone new is the way it usually goes.* He was leaving her, 'because life is too boring to go on this way. I'm hitting the road'.

She wiped the tears from her face. "Damn Edgar. This makes no sense!" She had begged him, for years, to go on a road trip across country. He had found reason after reason to not go on a long road trip. He said he was too busy at work; it would be too much effort just driving around the country and looking at stuff; it would be too expensive; it would be boring.

"'I'm hitting the road'." Glory shook her head. "Right. The stay-right-where-we-are-all-the-time-man is hitting the road. Unbelievable!"

Glory looked at the email. The last paragraph galled her the most, "You'll find an attached PDF of the divorce papers. If you sign them and send them to my lawyer, then we won't have to bicker and fuss. You know how I hate fuss. Really, I'm making this easy for both of us. I'm leaving you everything except my car, clothes and personal belongings which I'm taking. The house and the minivan you bought are yours to keep."

"You fucking bastard!" *I do not want to cry about this. I want to be strong.* She sat up straighter put her shoulders back and reached for a tissue. She took a sip of her coffee she had bought on the way to work this morning just like every morning. It was a luxury she allowed herself since she rarely made coffee at home. Edgar hated the smell of coffee in the house. She loved the smell of coffee anywhere. Now her coffee felt like comfort and acceptance. She wiped her eyes and face and as quietly as possible blew her nose.

It's time to quit crying and take charge of the situation. She needed to give herself some time and space to take it all in. She needed to think.

She opened a new email to send to her supervisor, Jeff Blake. The email said, "Hi, Jeff, I need to take two or three days off. I know this is short notice and it is only Monday but I'm not feeling well. Even coffee isn't helping this morning. My work is caught up. I'm sure I'll be feeling better soon. I'll be back Wednesday or Thursday if I'm feeling better."

She hit 'send' and gathered her things. She shoved her belongings into her backpack and pulled her purse from the drawer. She turned off her desk lamp and cleared her desktop of pens, notepads and the messages from today. She stood looking in the mirror. At only 5 feet tall she could see in the mirror on the five-foot cubicle wall without bending over. She had to tiptoe a bit to see over the wall, however. She was glad to see no one was looking her way or seemed to have heard any of her swearing at her husband. *I don't want to deal with anyone right now.*

Her blue eyes were a little red rimmed, but she didn't look too much like she had been crying. She ran her fingers through her long, silky, blonde hair and fluffed it around her face. *There. I don't look too bad.* She unplugged her laptop and looked down when she heard the 'ding' of incoming email. She saw Jeff had already responded to her email. "Glory, no problem. I hope you feel better soon so you can enjoy your week. You have over 6 weeks of PTO saved up. You are good to take off as much time as you need. Hope you feel better soon. Just let me know how you are doing in a day or two. Enjoy!"

She shook her head. "Enjoy. Right." She set an out-of-office message for any incoming emails then shut down and closed the laptop. She had to get out of here and get home so she could think.

I spent four years of my life married to you, Edgar Shaw! Glory knew she needed to be strong but right now all she could feel was anger, humiliation and loneliness. She wanted her mom, but she had died over three years ago. Her next best hope was Martha. With her wild, red, curly hair and dark green eyes Martha was the best friend any woman could want. *I wish Rob still lived here and not in Oklahoma. We were the three amigos in high school.*

Glory rolled her shoulders back, took a deep breath and put her laptop in her backpack. She looked at the picture frame on her desk of Edgar. "You will not ruin my life!" His dark brown hair and gray eyes seemed to see nothing. Glory picked up the photo and shoved it into her backpack too. She zipped the backpack closed and pulled it onto her shoulder.

She quickly walked to the elevator and punched the button for going down. The elevator door opened and to her relief it opened to an empty bay. She punched the button for the ground floor and quickly punched the button to close the door. She saw one of her work team friends, Megan, racing toward the elevator and calling her name. Glory could not talk to anyone right now and kept pushing the closing button until the doors slammed shut.

Megan called, "Glory! Wait! The police..." *Damn!* Thought Megan. *I don't know what is going on, but I tried to catch you Glory.*

Glory heard Megan calling her name. *I can't talk to anyone right now. Everything around here can wait.*

Jake turned on the lights as he entered the kitchen from the garage. *Where's Liz? Her car is in the garage. I don't understand why the lights aren't on. She is usually cooking dinner by this time.* He walked through the kitchen and dining room. When he entered the living room and turned on the lights, he was surprised Liz wasn't there either. *She probably went for a walk.*

He walked into the bedroom, turned on the light and heard a moan. He looked at the bed to see his wife, Liz, lying on the bed curled in a ball. "Liz? Are you all right?"

She rolled over and said, "I'm fine. Just a little tired."

"Are you sick?" he asked going to sit beside her on the bed.

"No, just tired."

She got out of bed. Jake noticed a small dark red stain on the back of her underwear. He asked, "Are you on your period?"

"No. Why would you ask?"

"There's blood on the back of your underwear."

She looked around, couldn't see the bloodstain. "Don't worry about it," she said, and went into the bathroom.

Jake followed her and watched as she pulled down her underwear and sat on the toilet. She pulled a sanitary napkin off her underwear and wrapped tissue paper around it before depositing it in the trash can beside her.

"I thought you only used tampons," Jake said. "And if you aren't on your period, why are you bleeding?"

Liz held up a hand. "Go away, Jake, please. Leave me alone."

"Why?"

"I don't feel well and just need rest," Liz answered. "Leave me alone for a few minutes. I'll come out after I clean up."

"Are you sure you are okay?"

"Yes. Just give me a few minutes."

Jake left the bathroom and went back to the kitchen. He got a beer out of the fridge and sat at the table waiting for Liz to join him. *It's not like Liz to be so evasive.* After two years of marriage he knew her and how she behaved. Tonight, she was behaving differently, and he did not know why.

He and Liz were a lot different. She liked mixed drinks; he liked beer or better yet coffee. She liked going out to eat; he liked simple food prepared at home. She liked fancy clothes and more shoes than any woman could need; he liked blue jeans and cowboy boots. She loved malls and shopping; he loved the out of doors. She wanted to live in the city; he loved living in the country. He chuckled to himself. *It's like the old sit-com, Green Acres.*

Liz walked into the kitchen. "I know you are worried about me but you need not worry. I will be fine."

"Well, I was surprised to come home, find all the lights off at seven in the evening and you in bed. It's not how things usually are. Please tell me what is going on."

Liz shook her head and went to the cupboard for a wine glass. "You really don't want to know." She opened the refrigerator, pulled out a bottle of white wine and pour some into her glass. She sat down at the table across from Jake.

"Liz," Jake said reaching out for her hand, "If something is wrong I want to know. What is wrong?"

She took a sip of her wine and pulled her hand away from Jake. "Are you sure you want to know? You will not like it."

He looked at her, surprised by her tone and words. "Liz what is going on?"

Chapter 2

"There are moments in life
when it is all turned inside out"
—*Aleksandar Hemon*

Edgar chided himself, *there is no reason to feel badly about how I handled the divorce.* The marriage had been on the rocks for a long time. Glory knew this and eventually would have come to the same conclusion. Edgar felt sure of this. He looked at himself in the rear-view mirror. He couldn't look himself in the eye, however. He let the thoughts go as soon as they entered. He said, "You did the right and best thing buddy."

He continued driving down Highway 167 heading south. If he were honest with himself, he probably should never have married Glory. *I was weak, and she was beautiful. We were in the same history class. I loved her way of thinking. Rather than just accepting what the professor said, she was the one who asked questions. They were deep questions; they were the why questions. She was smart, intuitive and graceful. I was attracted to this short, adorable, beautiful woman with her brilliant mind, head and shoulders above everyone in the class, even me. I never thought she would date me much less marry me.*

He had asked her out, and they dated for a few months. They went on long walks discussing the topics of the day, topics of history, topics of society. He had never been around a woman like Glory. That she would date him was a miracle. Then one day with little thought he asked her to marry him. He surprised himself that he asked her *the question.* He was happy when she said yes. His parents weren't happy with the marriage, but he ignored their protests. He knew he and Glory didn't have a burning passionate love, but he thought they belonged together. *We were friends but somehow it all has changed.*

He had no real expectations for the marriage other than continuing on as they had been while dating. For the first few years it was great. But as time went on, things changed. They argued about silly things. What color to paint the walls for example. She wanted a lot of different colors and he wanted the walls all to be white. It was easier for him. Glory wanted everything in the house different from how he thought was best.

Coming home to find she had painted the guest bedroom a soft peach made him furious. She said, "You never come in here. You don't have to be aware of it at all." But he was aware of it and it irritated him more and more every day.

She rearranged the furniture regularly. He hated not knowing what to expect about where a particular chair was, or the television was; whether in a different corner or a different wall all the time. Over his protests, she added bits of colorful artwork around the house. If he fussed enough, she would sometimes move it or even get rid of the artwork. Often, she said, "I like it and it stays." He would get angry, but she would ignore his protests.

Moving furniture, adding color, bringing in artwork wasn't the worst part. It was the pregnancies that broke their marriage. He had assumed she wouldn't want children, but he had to admit they had never talked about whether to have children before they married. He thought being married to a friend and an intellectual woman meant she wouldn't want to have children. *I was wrong.*

Edgar was an only child of cold and uncaring parents. He remembered early in his childhood his mother would kiss him and comfort him when he cried. *Did she actually love me?* He shook his head.

He also remembered his father chastising his mother when she would show affection. *They would fight about someone named Arthur who I didn't understand until much later was my father's brother who died. Then I learned, much, much later, Arthur was my biological father. No wonder my father hates me.*

Edgar learned Glory wanted children after the marriage. He asked her to wait and told her he wasn't sure he wanted to have children. She had cried but agreed to wait a year or two. He had thought she would give up the idea as they built their life together. He thought she would understand what a burden a child would be and how it would change everything they did together.

Then, two years later she got pregnant. He thought she had betrayed him and had stopped her birth control pills without discussing it with him. It turned out she had missed a few nights of taking the pills when she was sick with a stomach flu. She didn't realize simply restarting the pills was inadequate.

He was worried about being a parent. He nearly left her then because of his anxiety. *I would have been a terrible father. My childhood was not a loving one and the pain of a little boy who needed love was more than I could bear then. I'm afraid of being a father, of not loving my children. Children need love. What if I can't really love? I'm not sure I even love Glory, but she is my wife, and I liked being with her at first. I do not love my parents.*

Glory had a miscarriage. The miscarriage stopped him from leaving. She was emotionally fragile for those first few months after the death of their baby.

Then it happened again. She became pregnant while on antibiotics for an infection. *She was so happy and excited she even bought a minivan which I hated.* Again, she had a miscarriage leaving her grieving and him feeling at a loss for how to help her and feeling like a failure.

He remembered one day, after the second miscarriage, watching her rock in her mother's red rocking chair she had insisted on having in the living room. She was holding a baby shirt and rubbing it against her cheek. The pain of her grief was a greater burden for him than the first miscarriage.

He felt sorry for her but said nothing. *I didn't know what to say or how to say it.* Edgar remembered thinking, *Good. We avoided the turmoil of having children. It's easier than trying to be something I am not.* He had turned away from the sight of her grief and quietly walked back to their bedroom and out to the deck. He sat there watching the sunset and trying hard not to think about any of it.

I know my parents did not love me. I can't bring more pain into the world. What I know about my birth is reason enough to not have any children. One day I may talk with Glory about it but right now I need to get away.

He was driving away from the life he had for the past four years. *Maybe it was all my fault the marriage didn't work. I wanted it to work, but it didn't. We were too different from each other and wanted different things in life. I've done the right thing ending it now without muss or fuss.*

His thoughts deepened. It surprised him when he realized a few tears escaped his eyes. "Don't worry. This is just a reaction to the stress you've been under." He knew he was not being fully honest with himself, but he wasn't ready to dig deeper and wasn't sure he would ever be ready.

He didn't see the red light. He didn't hear the blaring sounds of car horns honking their warnings. He didn't see the cement truck bearing down on him. Finally, the ear-splitting noise of the truck horn and the sharp squealing of the brakes as the trucker tried to avoid hitting him, brought Edgar back to a moment of reality. He looked to his left. He saw the horrified look on the truck driver's face and in an instant thought, *I'm an idiot.*

The shocking sound of rending metal and the sharp sudden pain were the last experiences of Edgar's life.

Chapter 3

"To love and hate at the same time;
The line between the two is fine"
—Dolly Parton

The house felt different to Glory. It was too quiet. It didn't look different on the outside or the inside, but the house felt different. There was a sense of emptiness and a feeling of stuffiness in the air.

She shook her head. "Don't be silly. It's 50 degrees outside. It's early April." She checked the thermostat set on 60 degrees and nudged it up a little to 65 degrees. She couldn't believe yesterday was April Fool's Day and yet today felt like April Fool's Day.

"Happy Fucking April Fools, to you, Edgar," Glory said to the empty kitchen.

She looked around the kitchen. All the cabinets, countertops and back splash were white. She shook her head at the mundane environment. She had wanted color and had worked in small bits of color over the past few years. Edgar had wanted white and hated her attempts to add any color other than white to their home. The walls and ceilings were white and white stone covered the floor.

She put her backpack on the white-washed kitchen table, where it did not belong. She went to the cabinet and took out a wine glass, opened the refrigerator filled the glass with red wine.

"Yes, Edgar, I know. It isn't even noon yet. I'm a grown-assed, pissed off woman. I'll have a glass of wine whenever I want it."

She walked into the living room but still couldn't define what it was she was feeling other than emptiness, hurt and rage. She went back to their bedroom and looked around the room. She saw the gray bedspread Edgar picked out and the white walls with nothing to break the starkness and coldness of the room. She shook her head. "Edgar, I tried doing things how you wanted. I couldn't live with only white." The stifling quiet of the room was not the response she needed.

She looked at her bedside table where their wedding photo stood in a silver frame. It was the only decoration in the room. She walked over, picked it up. "Oh, Edgar, you look happy in this photo. When did you change? Why did you change?"

She laid the photo face down on the side table. She opened the door under the table and pulled out two red pillows she had bought but not had the courage to put on the bed. She tossed them on the bed and loved the contrast of the soft gray with the bright red. "Well, the bed looks better."

Glory opened the closet door shocked to find only her clothes in the closet and nothing of Edgar's. *He has left me this stark reminder of a house with only me and my things to occupy it.* She opened drawer after drawer in the dresser and chest of drawers finding only the vacuum Edgar had left behind. The bathroom was the same. The only signs of life remaining in the bedroom or bathroom were of Glory.

She sighed. "Well, he's gone."

Maybe it was all of his belongings being gone that left the house feeling empty. She shook her head. "I can't believe you didn't talk with me first, Edgar. This is a new low, even for you."

She sighed and walked back into the living room and looked around. The house was not her idea of a home. It was shelter and nothing more. She sat in her mother's dark red platform rocking chair. *I planned to rock my babies in this chair. My babies died and now my husband has left me.*

Edgar hated the rocking chair. He hated more when she insisted on having her mother's rocking chair in this room. She had said, "Please, Edgar. Just one thing in our home not gray, white or some off-white color. Something I choose and want in our home." *When I cried, he relented.* She loved her mother's chair and usually felt herself relax when she sat in it.

She put her feet up on the footrest and sipped her wine as she looked around the room. Everything was in its place as Edgar demanded. Nothing could be out-of-place anywhere in the house before they left for work. With a sudden need for rebellion, Glory sat her wineglass on the side table pushing the coaster out of the way. She picked up the coaster and as if tossing a frisbee lobbed it across the room. It landed on the rug in front of the entry door.

"Whew! I feel better now." It surprised her she was feeling better. "Who knew rebellion could feel so good!"

She drank her wine and stared at the ceiling wondering why she let Edgar talk her into painting everything white. She didn't like all this white. She had planned to change wall colors in a room or two, but her one color foray with the guest bedroom walls brought too much anger from Edgar. What she really liked and wanted was color. He hated colors other than muted shades of gray or white.

It doesn't really matter anymore, she thought. *He's gone and I need to figure out what to do next.*

She never liked the house even though she had high hopes for children and dogs and a life of love. She envisioned rowdy little bodies chasing through the house with dogs yipping at their heels with delighted laughter and squeals of children. There was nothing here but silence.

She did not like the house when they bought it. "I should have said more; stood my ground."

Edgar assured her after they finished remodeling the house, she would love it. He had said, "You'll especially love it when we sell it for more than we paid for it." When they finished with the remodel a year ago, he declared it was fine and they should live in this house forever.

She remembered feeling frozen and isolated at his words. *I knew then this house wasn't the forever house I had dreamed of.* She had turned and walked out of the room and into the backyard. She had walked alone, feeling the isolation of her life and the stubborn coldness of the house. "Yet, I said nothing. I went along."

She put her feet on the floor, looked up and screamed to the ceiling, "You fucking bastard!"

She sighed and shook her head. *It's my fault. I should have said no. I should have painted the fucking walls red and just made him deal with it! It's my life too and I should have said so. I don't even know what I want out of life anymore. I've forgotten how to dream about my life.*

I'll call Martha in a few minutes. Martha will help me find my way. Martha her best friend and a trainer at a big company in Bellevue was always there for Glory. She looked at her watch and saw it was only ten in the morning. Martha went to work at one in the afternoon and worked until nine in the evening training employees of two shifts for various jobs and the company policies. *I'll call her and see if she can come over.*

Glory stood and walked back to the kitchen. She reached in her purse to find her cell phone to call Martha. Martha always knew what to say or to ask to help Glory in any situation. "Boy, do I ever need help."

The front doorbell rang. She laid the phone on the kitchen table beside her purse and went to answer the front door. She opened the door surprised to see a man in a black suit holding a badge in his hand.

"Hello," she said. She noticed a woman standing behind him wearing a black skirt and jacket with a bold blue silk shirt. Glory looked to the curb in front of the house and saw a black and white police car with an officer waiting.

"Ma'am?" The man asked.

Confused she looked at the policeman. "Yes?"

"Are you Mrs. Shaw?"

"Yes."

"Ma'am I'm sorry to disturb you. I'm Detective James Summers and this is Sara Merriweather. Ms. Merriweather is a social services liaison for the police department here. May we come in?"

"I guess so. Why?" She opened the door wider to let them in.

Sara Merriweather walked inside first and bent over. She picked up the coaster and handed it to Glory. "Please call me Sara. Why don't we sit down and talk?"

"About what?" Glory asked as she took the coaster and tossed it across the living room not caring where it landed. Sara raised her eyebrows but said nothing as Glory led them into the living room.

"Let's sit down," Sara said.

Glory shrugged and sat in her mother's rocking chair. She motioned for them to sit on the sofa or other chairs or wherever they wanted. "Okay. You're here and I don't know why."

Detective Summers looked at Sara and said, "We have some bad news for you Mrs. Shaw."

"It can't be any worse than this day has already been," Glory said. "Please call me Glory. I'm not Mrs. Shaw anymore."

The detective looked confused. "I thought you said you were Mrs. Shaw."

"I was until today."

"What happened today?"

"Edgar sent divorce papers to my work email today."

Detective Summers raised his eyebrows and looked at Sara.

There were a few moments of strained silence before he turned back to Glory. "I'm sorry. It probably will not make what we have to tell you any easier and I apologize in advance."

"What could be harder than having your husband send you divorce papers by email and not having the courage to do it face-to-face?" Glory asked. She could imagine nothing worse. Of all the things Edgar might have done today, this was something she did not understand and would not have expected of him. Even on the days when they were bickering, she had thought he cared more about her than this.

Sara looked from Glory to Detective Summers. "Perhaps it will be easier if we just tell you what happened earlier this morning."

Detective Summers nodded to Sara. "Yes. Thank you, Sara. Despite all you've been through today I'm sorry to inform you, your husband died this morning," Detective Summers said.

Glory felt a sudden icy wave spread from deep inside her belly to her whole body. She sat upright in her chair, leaned forward and grabbed the arms of the chair. She shook her head. "No, he isn't dead. Just three hours ago he sent me the hateful divorce email."

"I know; I understand," the detective said. "The reality is, about two hours ago, he ran a red light out on Highway 167. An oncoming cement truck hit him broadside."

"What?"

"A cement truck hit your husband's car squarely on the driver's side of the car. His death was probably nearly instantaneous. We don't think he suffered," Detective Summers said.

"What? That makes no sense."

Sara stood up, came across the room and knelt beside Glory's chair. She reached out for Glory's hand and held it. "Your husband died in a car wreck when he ran a red light."

Glory shook her head and looked at Sara. With a trembling voice and tears rolling down her face Glory said, "He would never run a red light. He prides himself on his perfect driving and perfect driving record. He would not run a red light."

Sara patted Glory's hand. "Perhaps not before today, but today, he ran a red light. Running a red light caused his death."

Tears rolled down Glory's face. "No, it can't be. Edgar would never run a red light. He was always a careful, methodical driver. He wouldn't turn on the engine until every door was closed and everyone was buckled into their seats. He never drove through a yellow light," Glory said. "Edgar had said over and over, 'Yellow lights are for idiots who don't pay attention'."

Sara waited holding Glory's hand.

Glory leaned forward and sobbed. Sara put her arm around Glory's shoulder and quietly comforted her. After a few minutes, Glory leaned back and said, "It's too much. I don't know what to do."

"I know and I understand," Sara said, "I'm here to help you with it all."

Glory nodded. This news made her life seem all the more surreal. "This has been a terrible, horrible day."

"Yes, it seems to have been an awful day. I'm sure this news has made it more awful."

"Unreal. Terrible. Horrible," Glory said, shaking her head.

Jake said, "No matter what is going on Liz, I really want to know."

Liz stood up, picked up her glass of wine and walked across the room. "Jake, we are a lot different from each other and want different things in life. I love you but maybe we made a mistake getting married."

"How can you say we made a mistake getting married?" He stood up, and she held up her hand.

"Sit back down, please. This is hard enough as it is, but I need some distance from you."

Jake sat back down. "Come on Liz. Please quit this cat-and-mouse game or whatever it is."

She took a deep breath. "I had a miscarriage today."

Jake felt cold, deep in his belly. He felt tears stinging his eyes. "What? I didn't know you were pregnant."

Liz nodded. "I know I should have told you. I was about six weeks along and, well, I wasn't sure what I wanted to do about the pregnancy."

"What you wanted to do?" He felt tears running down his face. "I don't understand. Why you didn't tell me you were pregnant. It's like you didn't want the baby."

Liz took another drink of her wine, set the glass on the counter. "I knew you would overreact."

"Are you kidding me?" Jake stood up tears streaming down his face. "You know how much I want to have kids. You've known from the first."

Liz nodded again. "I thought, after we were married for a while either you would give up on having children or I would warm up to the idea of having children. But I still don't want to have children. I was thinking about getting an abortion but held off until I was sure about what I wanted. Today I felt nothing but relief when I had a miscarriage."

Jake shook his head. "That's not how marriage is supposed to work. You told me you wanted to wait to have a baby. You never said you didn't want children. I would not have married you if I thought you would never want to be a mother." Jake wiped more tears from his face. *This is a nightmare. This can't be happening.*

"Jake, I know you wanted lots of kids. I don't. I want to do other things with my life than be a mother."

"Like what?"

"Like work on my photography more. Like travel to exotic places around the world. Like learn new languages. Like a lot of things I can't do with kids hanging around my neck."

He wiped more tears away with his hand. He reached out and grabbed a tissue from the box on the table and blew his nose. "I don't know how to fix this Liz. I don't know what to say. I want babies. Our baby died today."

Liz nodded. "Yes, I know and I'm sorry about how you feel about the miscarriage Jake. Really. I know you are suffering now, but I'm relieved about the miscarriage. I went to the urgent care clinic earlier today when I started bleeding. They said I would be fine. They did an ultrasound and said the miscarriage was complete. I can start back on birth control immediately."

"You told me you wanted to wait, and I agreed. I didn't know you weren't on birth control but to learn you were pregnant and thinking of getting an abortion without talking to me hurts. Deeply."

Liz nodded. "I know. I'm so sorry, Jake. But I do not want to have children. When I realized how relieved I was to miscarry and to not have to decide about abortion, I knew I was right to get back on birth control."

Jake grabbed more tissues, stood up, and blew his nose as he walked out of the kitchen. He went to their bedroom and pulled a suitcase down from the top of the closet. He threw some clothes into the suitcase.

Liz walked in and asked, "What are you doing?"

"What does it look like? I'm leaving; I'm going to my sister Helen's house before I do something I'll regret."

"You aren't a violent man, Jake."

He nodded. "I never want to be one either. Right now, I am hurt and angry and sad Liz. I think I should just go." He picked up a pair of underwear from the suitcase and wiped his face blew his nose with them. He tossed the underwear back into his suitcase. Then he got more clothes and put them in the suitcase. "I am furious with you, Liz. You were pregnant and did not tell me. Our baby has died, and you act as if it is nothing more than an inconvenience for you. I don't know how I should feel or react to those facts."

"It's my body, my choice. Perhaps, I should have been more honest with you before we even married."

"Yes, it is your body. I totally agree. You are right. You damn well should have been more honest from the start." Jake wiped away more tears and tossed the clothes he had used back into the suitcase. "But it was our baby who died, yours and mine, Liz. I am hurting right now. I should have known and should have been a part of talking this through. I was not given a choice about any of it."

"Oh, Jake, honey, I hate seeing you like this. We will get through this. I know you love me and despite everything we can have a good life together."

"How Liz? For me a good life is being happy with my life. How can we be happy when I want children and you do not? That is fundamental in our relationship."

"I'm sorry, Jake. I want to help you feel better, but I do not want to be pregnant again, ever. And before you ask, I do not want to adopt children either. I want nothing to do with motherhood."

"We both could have avoided this pain. You should not have children if you do not want them. I agree with you; It is your body and your choice about whether to have a baby. But I want children. Don't you see how this difference makes the marriage impossible?"

Liz walked closer and reached out to him. He stood still as a statue. "Don't come closer Liz. Do not touch me. We are at an impasse here. We can't go back. And, as much as I love you, I can't stay married to you if we don't agree on something as basic as whether or not to have children."

She nodded and stepped back a few steps. "Okay."

"Leave me alone to gather a few things. I'll be gone in a few minutes."

Liz turned and left the room. Sitting in the living room she picked up the remote control and turned on the television. A few minutes later Jake walked from the bedroom hallway across the living room and out to the kitchen and garage. He did not look at Liz nor did he speak to her. She heard the garage door open and the sound of his beat-up old pickup truck leaving the house. *Well, that was worse than I expected. He'll be back.*

Chapter 4

"You must master a new way to think
before you can master a new way to be."
—Marianne Williamson

Glory stood in the living room after closing the door on the police. Sara had offered to stay but Glory had declined. She couldn't think with the Detective Summers and Sara Merriweather there. She needed to think. Her brain was frazzled, and she felt confused and physically and emotionally exhausted. She wasn't sure what she should do next.

"It's too much. Just too fucking much."

She went to the kitchen, grabbed a paper towel and wet it under the cool water. Wiping her face with the towel helped her feel better. She still did not know what to do next. "Martha will know what to do," she muttered. With tears still streaming down her face, Glory picked up her phone and called her best friend Martha.

Martha answered with her usual cheerful voice, "Hey Glory! It's good to hear from you. I was just getting ready to go to work."

Glory swallowed and felt as if she were choking. She asked, "Can you come over?"

"Sure. When?"

"Now. Please," Glory asked as she wept again. She slid down the kitchen wall and found herself suddenly sobbing sitting on the floor unable to do anything else. She heard Martha's distant voice on the phone laying on the floor beside her.

"I'm on my way!" Martha responded.

Glory nodded and lay down on the floor, curled in a ball, unaware of anything but the pain she felt deep in her head, her belly and her chest. Gloriana wept.

When Martha arrived, letting herself in without ringing the doorbell, she found Glory on the kitchen floor sobbing as if the world were ending. *Maybe it is,* Martha thought.

She knelt beside Glory, helped her to sit up and hugged her close.

Glory paced the living room from her chair to the entryway, crying and muttering.

Martha texted Rob: *I'm with Glory right now. Edgar sent her divorce papers by email a few hours ago. Before she could get home, he died in an automobile accident. Glory needs us. Can you come?*

Rob immediately texted back, *Yes! I'll let know when I'll arrive.*

Martha tucked the phone in her pocket and watched Glory's anguish as she paced. After a few minutes Martha said, "Glory you are driving me nuts."

"Well, I feel pretty nuts right now."

"I'm sure you do. I would feel nuts too if I'd been through what you have today. But, really, you have to quit pacing. It is making me dizzy! I'm sure it really isn't helping you either. Please come and sit down."

Glory plopped down in her chair. "Does any of what happened today make any sense at all?"

"No. Not really. But we both know these things happened today. I'm sure making sense about all that happened to your life today is a fool's errand. I'd rather just be here for whatever you need."

"Thanks, Martha. I need a friend."

"Then a friend I will be."

Glory said, "When I got his email I was so pissed and I was cursing out loud. It fucking pissed me off. I couldn't believe he would do this. AND, even though I said FUCK! Loudly. Not a single person in the office noticed."

Martha laughed. "Oops!"

"Exactly. After I got home, I was about to call you to come over and listen to me rant and rave. But the police showed up! Now I don't know what I really feel about all of this other than pissed off and sad. I feel like today is my day to get the hell beaten out of me and be dumped on a trash heap."

"I'm sorry," Martha said. "Today has been super shitty and you have every right to feel abused. The way Edgar told you about the divorce was ridiculous and awful. The manner of his death makes it all the more gruesome. He probably was not paying attention to the traffic lights in the ways he always has. I can't see Edgar willingly letting a cement truck slam into his brand-new car and dump his wet load on Edgar and his car."

Glory grinned and wiped tears from her face. "You are right. He loved his car more than just about anything else. I feel like he started out his day today to punish me for being me and not being who and what he wanted me to be. Then he finished up his day dying in in literally the LAST way imaginable — ruining his perfect driving record by running a red light and a fucking cement truck obliterated his perfect fucking car. So unbelievable, it seems like some kind of B-Movie."

Martha smiled but waited

Glory took a deep breath and sighed, "He wanted me to be perfect, so I tried repeatedly. I am not perfect. I'm not tall enough, thin enough, beautiful enough. I like things cozy and warm. He wanted them stark and minimal. I wanted lots kids to load up in my minivan. He wanted a sleek, expensive sedan to show off with absolutely no children near the car. I love fried chicken and steak and brownies. He wanted baked fish and broccoli and kale. Who even likes kale?"

Martha laughed. "No one."

Glory nodded and wiped tears off her face. "I wish I would stop fucking crying. The tears just seemed to keep on coming. I wasn't happy in the marriage either. I spent a lot of time daydreaming about the what-ifs. Hell, I even daydreamed about getting a divorce and traveling on my own but was too damn scared to try. Why did he have to die to leave me? Surely there was a better way."

"Maybe," Martha said, "But if there was, I think you would have found it."

"It is absurd. I wish he had talked in person about it. It could have been different for both of us."

Martha said, "I agree. But do you really want to talk about this right now? Wouldn't you rather eat ice cream and brownies?"

"Yes! Perfect."

They went to the kitchen and Glory opened the freezer. "Well, I have chocolate ice cream but no brownies."

"Then chocolate ice cream it is," Martha said.

They sat at the table eating ice cream out of the carton and continued talking.

Martha said. "You will get through this. I have faith in you."

"What am I going to do? I know Sara Merriweather is coming tomorrow morning at ten to help with the legal stuff."

"Good. For everything else, you will do what needs to be done. I'm here to help you get through all there is to do. It will all be one step at a time until things are more settled."

They sat quietly for a few minutes and as Glory's tears subsided again; she seemed a little calmer. Martha said, "I hope it is okay I texted Rob earlier. He will be here tonight on the last flight for Seattle from Oklahoma City."

"Great," Glory said. "I know it is selfish of me, but I really need both of you here."

"It is not selfish, Glory; it is what good friends do for each when one of them needs helps."

"Thank you, Martha."

Martha grinned. "You got it. Now, get up off your ass and let's get started."

"With what?" Glory asked.

"First there's a funeral to prepare, then…"

Glory held up her hand to stop Martha talking. "I don't think I can face a funeral. Too much has gone on in our marriage and today has left me muddled and confused. It frankly has left me so pissed I believe right now I would just toss Edgar in a hole and throw some dirt over him."

Martha laughed. "Sounds like what funeral are for. The funeral will help close this chapter of your life. Then both you and Edgar can move on."

"I can't do it." Glory shook her head. "Or more to the point I don't think I want to do it. Edgar wasn't physically abusive, but he was constantly berating me in everything. He tried to control everything about our home and me. He made fun of my mother's rocking chair every time he walked in the room and I was sitting in it. He hated when I wore blue jeans because they were too casual. I don't think I can do a funeral."

"I have faith in you. You can do it all," Martha said, "And when it is over you will feel better about things. Besides, what about his parents and family? His friends, your friends, coworkers? Won't they expect a funeral?"

"Yes, yes, yes. I know the lines of the social script. They will all expect me to be the grieving widow and have a funeral and say lovely things about him that aren't true, at least for me," Glory said. "What I really want to do is slap the shit out of Edgar."

Martha grinned. "I'd hold him still for you if he were here but he's not. Let's table the funeral talk for now. We can talk about the funeral or lack thereof again when Sara is here to help you handle the legal bits."

Liz and Jake had talked on the phone and by email a few times over the past week. Liz called Jake and asked, "Would you meet me at Lion's Park tomorrow at noon so we can talk face-to-face. I'll bring lunch."

Jake smiled knowing she hated picnics. Maybe this was a way for them to connect at least a little. "Sure. You sure you don't want me to bring something too."

"No, Jake. But, thanks for the offer. I want to talk about what we should do next, but I hope by being in the park we can have this talk without a lot of anguish."

Jake was quiet for a few moments. It didn't feel like the talk would be about making up. "I guess you're still pretty set on not having children."

"Yes, Jake I am," she said gently. "But I'm not set on being enemies with you. Can we work out details tomorrow?"

Jake wiped tears off his face and said, "Yes, we can. I'll be there tomorrow at noon."

Jake got to the park before Liz did. He went to a picnic table with some shade and stood leaning against the end of the table. *I think this will be our marriage ending talk today. It is probably the only outcome that makes any sense but I sure as hell don't want it to be the end.* He was deep in thought when Liz walked up to him. "Hi Jake."

He looked up at her and smiled. He stood and kissed her on the cheek. "Hi, Liz."

She put white plastic bags on the table and said, "Let's sit down and eat, Jake. I bought your favorite Mexican food. There's two iced teas in there."

"Sweet?"

She laughed. "Of course."

They sat down across from each other. Liz opened the bags and handed Jake his lunch and took out hers. She had a taco salad; Jake had beef enchiladas, rancho beans and rice. There were chips, salsa and creamy queso too. Jake took a drink of his tea and then said, "Thanks for doing this Liz."

She smiled. "You are welcome. I wanted to have a nice lunch together and talk things through."

He nodded his head, took a corn chip and dipped it into the queso. "Have you come to any conclusions or solutions?"

Liz nodded. "Maybe."

Jake nodded but said nothing.

They both ate a few bites of the lunch. Neither tasted their food but were aware only of the sorrow and pain between them. Finally, Liz put down her fork. "I've been doing a lot of thinking and a lot of soul searching. I went to a counselor and talked with her about what's going on."

"Did the counselor help?"

Liz smiled a little sadly. "Yes, but it didn't make me happy."

"Why?"

"I realized I had been less than honest with you from the start. I was so blown away by you and so head over heels in love with you, I was willing to do anything to spend my life with you."

Jake smiled. "I love hearing that, Liz."

"But it doesn't change the reality, Jake. I deceived you and myself our marriage could work."

Jake sat still. He could say nothing. *I think this will be very sad in the end.*

"I know you love me, and I love you. It isn't enough," Liz said.

Jake looked down at his food and sat quietly waiting and hoping to not cry or lose his temper. He was sure he could not control it all, but he damn well intended to try.

Liz continued, "I've thought of little else this past week. After a lot of journaling and counseling and thinking and pacing the floors, I know a few things for sure. First, I love you. Second, I do not want to be a mother."

Jake nodded but remained quiet.

"I know my self-understanding will not make you happy nor will it help our marriage."

"You sure children are out of the question?" Jake asked.

Liz nodded. "Yes, and a part of me is pissed as hell."

"About what?"

"About me and how I handled this whole thing. I've always been honest an honest person. At least until I fell for you. I betrayed you and myself hoping I could change your mind or my mind. I sent you off to the ranch knowing you would come home to me. I kind of hoped ranch weekends would be enough, and you'd give up on having kids."

"That will never happen, Liz."

She smiled. "I know. I knew it Memorial Day Weekend last year when I went to the ranch with you. The house is lovely and so is the setting. I might could have adjusted to living there, part time, but the bedrooms sent me running back to Norman and never returning to the ranch."

Jake was puzzled. "What was wrong with the bedrooms?"

"Nothing was wrong. There were just too damned many of them. Our house here in Norman is two bedrooms. One for us and one for guests. At the ranch those four empty bedrooms are screaming for kids to fill them up."

Jake grinned. "Well, you are right."

"I can't fill them up Jake. Not even one."

Jake and Liz both had tears rolling down their faces. She reached out and touched Jake's hand. "Is there a loving and kind way we can dissolve our marriage? I'd like to be at least kind to each other Jake but also honest."

Jake nodded. "I think it is the only thing we can do. I agree I don't want to fight anymore, and I don't want to hurt you."

Liz said, "I have to apologize before we go any further. I should have been honest with you from the beginning. I should have told you I was pregnant. I should have never married you knowing I never wanted babies, and you did. I'm so sorry I did all this to you, to me and our marriage."

"Thanks, Liz. I'm sorry I'm not the man you needed."

She smiled. "You are a wonderful man, Jake. You are the man I wanted, but you are right. You weren't the man I needed. I may never find that man. I know deep in my heart when you heal a little from this, the woman you need, and desire will stand in front of you soon."

"The same will happen for you Liz if you are clear and honest with yourself."

"Thanks Jake. You are probably right. I will continue with the counseling for a few months. Once I'm clear about what I want and the life I want to live, it will be easier to recognize the right man for me."

They finished their lunch and then Liz said, "I have a friend who works for a kind lawyer here in town. He has an opening Monday morning. I can go by myself or you can come with me."

Jake asked, "How to you want to do this, Liz?"

"Short and sweet. Can we work out the details now and be ready Monday morning to do what is right and best for both of us?"

"Sure, we can. What are your starting ideas?"

"I'd like to keep the house in Norman, my car and my belongings. I'll pay the mortgage and my car payment. I want to keep my retirement plan. I do not want or need money from you."

Jake nodded. "I want to keep my ranch and horses."

Liz laughed. "Please keep them. I'll make sure it is clearly stipulated in the divorce even though we have a prenuptial agreement about the ranch. I know you love them, and they are nice, but they aren't a house in a small city."

"No, they are not," Jake answered with a grin. "The ranch is where I feel whole and alive."

Liz reached over and patted his hand. "The ranch suits you and I'm glad you have it. I hope the ranch will help you heal in the coming months."

"Thanks, Liz. I hope so too. I'd like to have the antique mirror of my grandparents. Otherwise you can keep everything else."

"When would you like to come over and get the rest of your things?"

"Whatever works for you."

"I'm going away for the rest of the weekend. I'm meeting some of my friends in a spa in Dallas."

"Then I'll get my stuff out before you get back." Jake looked at Liz and said, "I'm sorry about how rough I was on you the other night. It shocked me but didn't give me the right to yell at you or make you feel uncomfortable or threatened."

"Thanks, Jake. I appreciate you apologizing."

"How are you feeling?"

"Good physically. Emotionally I'm getting better the more I'm clear about what I really want in life."

"What do you want in life, Liz?"

"You know I've been taking photography classes."

Jake nodded. "Yes, and you've taken some incredible photos."

She smiled. "I have some incredible photos of you with the horses in my car. I'd like to give them to you as a divorce present."

He laughed. "I've never heard of a divorce present."

"Neither have I but I decided I wanted you to have these photos. When I developed them and saw the joy on your face and the magnificence of the horses around you, I knew the ranch and everything you are doing there was right. Just not for me."

"I didn't get you anything."

Liz shook her head. "Yes, you did. You gave me a chance to start my life over without guilt or shame. I applied for an internship with a photographer in New Mexico. I leave in two weeks to go spend a month there learning more about light and natural environments. I am sure I got the internship because of the photos of you."

"I didn't know you wanted to do photography professionally."

"Neither did I until the photography class. I originally took it thinking I might be good at interior design and would need a photo portfolio. When I showed the instructor the photos of you and the horses and suggested the internship. He said I have a natural eye for motion, emotion and the out-of-doors."

"What about your job at the furniture store? What about your friends and spas?"

"I'm taking all my vacation plus two weeks without pay to do the internship. As far as friends and spas, I'm getting pretty bored with spas and shopping too. The photography feels fresh and challenging. I want to explore photography and see where it leads. I'm feeling a big need for changes in my life."

Jake reached across the table and touched her hand. "I'm happy your are reaching out and learning new things. I can't wait to see the photographs."

"Let's go to the car. I have them ready for you, frames and all. I think they'll look great in your log house at the ranch."

Chapter 5

"Friends know the
Patterns of our souls"
— Ruth Buchanan

Martha said, "I'm going home for a few minutes and pack an overnight bag
and stay here with you."

"You don't have to do stay with me."

"Yes, I do. It's in the Best Friend's Handbook of what to do when a friend
is in distress. I'll just camp out here on the sofa."

"Well," Glory laughed, "OK. I don't want to break any of the Best Friend's
Handbook rules. So yes, please, bring over some stuff to stay the night. I
could use the company and the help in figuring out what to do next. You can
sleep next to me in my bed."

Martha hugged her. "You got it. Be warned, I supposedly snore like a
freight train although I've never heard it. When Rob gets here, we can work
together as friends and get you through all this turmoil."

Glory nearly cried again but to keep from crying she hugged Martha back
and then smiled as Martha went to the door.

After Martha left, Glory got her phone and sat back down in her chair. She
rocked the chair and let herself settle and feel at ease. Glory had to do what no
one else could do for her. She dreaded it but knew she had to call Edgar's
parents and tell them what had happened.

The doorbell rang and looking through the peephole, Glory saw Martha. Her long, red curly hair caught by the wind and her green eyes made her look magical. Glory smiled at the thought. She opened the door to see Martha had two suitcases on wheels and a backpack and her big tote bag. Glory laughed and said, "So I see you are moving in."

Martha nodded and said, "For the time being. Don't think I'm doing this for you. I'm doing it for me. I realized if I weren't here with you, I'd worry about you. I've taken off work for the next two weeks to help you with the funeral and getting started on whatever comes next. I hate my job anyway. The pay is good, and it is a great company and all, but I don't like my job. It's boring teaching the same things repeatedly."

"How did you get your boss to agree to two weeks off?"

"I told him there had been a death in the family and my family needed me."

"Just like that? It worked?"

"Yep," Martha answered. "I haven't had a vacation in over two years and only 2 sick days ever. I've got so much personal paid leave I have to use some of it this year or lose it. So, he was supportive."

"Great. I'll appreciate every day you are here with me."

Martha nodded. "Also, the new trainer I've been working with is ready to be on his own. He was delighted when I called and told him I thought he was ready for the big-time." Martha laughed a little. "Sometimes even when things are grim, things just work out right."

"Then you can have a stay-cation right here with me," Glory hugged Martha and said, "Thank you for doing this."

"You're welcome but please move aside so I can quit lugging all this stuff."

"Rob called. His plane arrives about 10:30 tonight. I offered for us to pick him up. He wanted to rent a car so if there were errands, he could easily do them."

"Sounds perfect."

They went into Glory's bedroom and after they put away her things Glory said, "I ran out and bought dinner for us. I wanted fried chicken, Cole slaw, and brownies. I couldn't face cooking, and this feels like comfort food."

"You chose well and I'm getting hungry," Martha said, "I'm happy Rob is coming to be with us and help us."

They went to the kitchen and settled in to eat dinner and talk.

"I feel lucky to have you and Rob in my life. I asked him what Hugh thought about him coming out here and he said, 'Hugh, like all good husbands stands by his man'."

Martha laughed. "Sounds like our Rob. What did Edgar's parents say when you called them?"

"They were their usual cold, aloof selves."

"Well, Edgar didn't fall far from their apple tree," Martha said.

"I know and it felt really sad. Anyway, I talked with Edgar's mom and dad. She wanted me to have him cremated and send them the ashes. They wanted to have the funeral in San Diego instead of coming here. It was tempting, but I thought about what you said about Edgar's friends and coworkers."

Martha nodded. "So what are you thinking?"

Glory grinned. "When they said the funeral had to be in San Diego, I thought 'no fucking way! I'm Edgar's wife' and I said I'd have the funeral here. I invited them to come to the funeral. They declined saying he was their son, and I was just his wife. I offered they could take his ashes home with them."

"Were they good with your offer?"

Glory shook her head. "No, they were not. His mother said, 'We will not be coming to any little funeral you have in Issaquah. You may have a funeral if you wish however the real funeral will be in San Diego'. They invited me to come to the funeral there. His father said, 'If it would be meaningful for you, please come to the funeral here in San Diego. However, we do not expect your presence. You would know only us and it might be uncomfortable for everyone.' I declined to go to San Diego but said I'd send part of the ashes on to them after Edgar's funeral here in Issaquah. I agreed to send their portion of the ashes by the courier they requested."

"And they were good with that?"

Glory grinned, "No. They wanted all the ashes. I reminded them Edgar was legally my husband, and they are not legally entitled to a say in any of the funeral arrangements or Edgar's body."

"Why are you going to keep any of Edgar's ashes?"

"I don't know for sure, but I have this gut level feeling, someday, I will know how to honor Edgar's life and death. Right now, I'm pissed and want to do nothing. Being pissed isn't my usual way to be and I'm getting uncomfortable with my anger. I'm trying to rethink things a little, at least about our relationship. I can't ship off four years of my life to San Diego and feel good about it. It feels better to have the funeral and wait and see how I can close my relationship with Edgar."

"I'm impressed," Martha said. "You are not letting them run rough-shod over you and you are being kind to them. You get to close out the chapter of your life with Edgar without having to mess with them being here. It's a bonus for you and Edgar might well agree with how you are handling things. His parents really never bonded with you. Nor did they like you and Edgar being married."

"My thoughts exactly!" Glory said, "However I was surprised they wouldn't come here for a funeral for their only son. Edgar and I never lived in southern California near his parents. But I thought his life here would have meant more to them. Neither of them cried on the phone either. It was all a matter of fact with no emotion involved."

Glory continued, "Edgar's parents have always been nice to me but in a cool, aloof way. I never really felt they connected with me. In fact, they didn't seem to be connected to Edgar either."

"Then I think you have chosen the best thing for you, them and probably Edgar too."

"That's what I finally came to and in a way I'm relieved to not have to play grieving widow to their cold feelings for me," Glory said. *I'm sure their cold feelings extended to Edgar too. They never exhibited a love for him. They provided for his education. Love was never part of their equation.*

Martha grabbed her hand, pulling Glory out of her thoughts. "I think Rob is here. I heard a car pull up in the driveway."

Glory and Martha went to the front door. They waved as he got out of the car and when he saw them, he waved back. As soon as he was close to them, he dropped his carry-on to the ground and grabbed Glory and Martha both in his arms as said, "My two favorite women in my arms. What more could I ask for?"

Martha said, "Hugh in your arms?"

"You are so right."

Jake packed up his clothes, guitar and belongings and put them all in the back of his pickup truck. *Glad I brought the camper top. My stuff will stay dry and safe until I haul it all down to the ranch.*

Jake loved his ranch in the Kiamichi Mountains of southeast Oklahoma. He wished Liz had loved it the way he did. *Maybe this all would have been different if she had loved the ranch and I had loved our house in Norman. Loving each other just wasn't enough for either of us.* He wiped tears from his eyes. *I always thought love conquers all, but I guess when two people love differently the love can't hold up to the difference.*

He had bought the ranch four years before they married. Over time, he had built a large five-bedroom log house, barns, paddocks and the beginnings of a horse ranch. Liz would go off for sauna weekends with her friends and Jake would go down to the ranch. She always had society plans for her weekends and had told Jake to "go to the ranch and do manly stuff." Then she would kiss him and tell him she loved him. He begged her to go to the ranch with him.

The only time she gave in and went to the ranch was Memorial Day Weekend. The weather was warm, but in the mountains, not too hot yet. He had stocked the kitchen with her favorite foods and planned moonlight picnics. She had brought her cameras with her and taken a lot of pictures.

Until she gave him the framed photos, he had seen none of her work. *It really is good. I love the photos she gave me.* She rode horses with him one time but then said, "I enjoyed the ride but couldn't stand the smell of horses stuck in my nostrils. I really hate the smell of horses."

Jake remembered he had laughed and said, "I love the smell of horses."

Liz had said, "You love those horses more than me."

"Not a chance," he had said and took her in his arms kissing her.

She liked the bedroom although she had said, "It's pretty but too rustic for my tastes. The bathroom and closets are spectacular, though."

When he had sat with her on the bedroom balcony watching the stars after about ten minutes she said, "I'm exhausted Jake. I'm going to bed."

And she did. *I felt abandoned in the moment. I remember watching the Milky Way fade as the full moon rose in the sky. I lost a little of my heart alone watching the night and stars.*

Liz never came back to the ranch with Jake and he tried to do activities she liked to do. One weekend he wound up sitting on a bench in the mall's center while she shopped. He remembered having to work hard to not be angry. Liz laughed at him and had said, "You're a mall husband sitting out there with other men while your woman shops."

He had realized how sad it was and went back to the ranch on weekends while she hung out with her shopping buddies and went to day spas and photography classes.

She surprised me with the photographs of me and the horses. They are beautiful. I would not have believed I looked like that with the horses if she hadn't taken those pictures.

Jake had said to her, "You sure are taking a lot of pictures."

She grinned. "It is the one thing, other than you, I'm loving here at your ranch."

She spent more time with the camera during the weekend than anything else. *I'm glad she is doing the internship in New Mexico. I hope it brings her a way to express her talents. She is talented with the camera.*

He left a note for her on the kitchen table apologizing for not being the man she needed in her life. He wrote:

"I love you, but finally agree we are mismatched. I'm sorry if I caused you any pain. I want you to know I think you are a special, talented and beautiful woman. I love the photographs and can't wait to see them at the ranch. Thank you for those; they are special. I've left a check to help with the two weeks without pay during your internship. I hope you'll accept it as a divorce gift. Thank you for the gift of our time together. I wish you nothing but love and blessings always. Love, Jake.

He locked the house and pulled out of the driveway. "So long, house. So long, Liz."

Chapter 6

"Power's not given to you.
You have to take it."
- Beyoncé Knowles Carter

Glory dreamed of the smell of coffee and bacon. Edgar will be pissed at the smell of bacon when he comes home. *It's fine. Maybe he would like bacon, eggs and toast this time.* She rolled over in bed and smelled not Edgar in bed next to her but the lingering scent of lavender, hyacinth and rose. What a nice smell she thought and woke up.

She felt sadness wash over her when she woke fully. She felt a little relieved Edgar would not be coming home but also sad. She felt sorrow he never loved the smell of coffee and bacon; not because it was coffee and bacon but because it was something to be enjoyed. "You missed a lot of joy. Edgar, I hope wherever you are you learn the joy of bacon and coffee."

She got up, went to the bathroom, washed her face, brushed her teeth and headed for the kitchen. As soon as she left her bedroom, she heard voices and occasional laughter.

She stood in the kitchen doorway watching her two best friends cooking away. There was bacon and coffee but there were pancakes too.

She smiled. "So, to what occasion do we owe this feast?"

They turned around and Martha said, "You are the occasion for the feast!"

Rob grinned. He waved her to the table. "Come on in Glory. Sit down and eat. Then we'll talk about what we need to do next."

"Including," Martha said, "what we want to do next."

Glory looked around the room with its stark white cabinets, white floors and white table. "Boy could this room use color!"

Martha shrugged. "If you decide you like the house, you can make it all any color or as many colors as you like. If you decide you don't like the house, you can sell it."

Rob nodded. "Food and good cheer, first, then we talk about what to do next."

"Agreed," said Glory as she dug into pancakes with peanut butter and maple syrup and crunched on bacon. She closed her eyes, relishing the taste of her breakfast. She smiled softly then, opened her eyes. Looking at her two friends, she realized how much she loved being with these two remarkable human beings. Tears stung her eyes at little at how very much she loved them and had missed being together.

She reveled in the laughter and stories both Rob and Martha told. It helped to ease the pain and burden of the last twenty-four hours. She was eager to soak up their love. It had been a long time since Glory felt this comfortable and loved. *What about when Martha and Rob aren't around to buoy my spirits?* Glory shoved the thought aside and gave herself up to the moment she was in. It felt good.

Her memories of her marriage to Edgar crept into her mind. At first, she balked at the memories. Then she realized she really had loved him, but it had become tainted by the stark differences in their personalities.

I wonder, why I didn't notice those differences before we got married? I remember being so happy he thought me beautiful and smart. It didn't matter the sex was never great, but it wasn't bad either. What mattered were the deep conversations we shared. The meeting of minds or even the clashes in thought were so stimulating it didn't occur to me to expect more on a relationship level. Our relationship had never been one where I felt a burning desire to be with him, but I always looked forward to talking with him. Maybe if I had seen a loving marriage modeled, it would have been different for Edgar and me.

Her daydreams were always about travel, about writing, about meeting new people, about learning new things and seeing the world. *I don't understand why I feel so strongly about traveling. I never thought of travel before I met Edgar.*

Martha said, "Hey! You seem to be miles away."

"I was just thinking about the past few years. I've wanted to travel, write and meet new people. I never wanted to do those things when I was in high school or college, though."

Rob said, "Maybe you wanted or needed to get away. A change of scenery can sometimes change your outlook on life."

Martha nodded. "When things aren't great, I think it may be a natural thing to think of being someplace else."

"I don't know," Glory said. "I think it was after I watched travel shows on public television and I felt I was missing out on the entire world. I go to work in my little cubicle. I come home and do things around the house. Then I go to bed and get up and do it all over again. I'm so bored sometimes I think I'll go nuts."

"I get it," Martha said. "I sometimes feel the same way about my job. I wonder if you needed to do what Rob said, get away."

"Maybe. I feel like I want to discover. I feel like I've fallen into a safe rabbit hole, but it is a rabbit hole none the less. I want adventure in my life."

"What about the writing?" Rob asked. "Where did that come from?"

"I love reading and lately have been playing with poetry and essays. I've even thought about a blog." She chuckled. "Everyone has a blog, right?"

"I don't have a blog," Martha said. "But if you want to write, it might be a good way to get started. When the time is right, you'll know what to do next. Maybe just be open to the possibilities."

Glory smiled and nodded.

Rob held up his hand. "It's time to get busy girls. We have a lot to do today."

"What do we need to do?" Martha asked.

"Sara from the police department will be here in about twenty minutes. I'm taking charge girls so we can be ready for her. Glory, should go shower and get dressed."

"I will after we clean up this mess."

"First," Rob said, "It isn't a mess. It is the remarkable makings and leavings of a great breakfast shared by loving friends. Second, you go get ready for your visit with Sara and I'll clean up the dishes and put everything away."

"I can help," Martha said.

Rob laughed. "No. I've seen how you clean. You need to get dressed too. In case you haven't noticed, I'm all shiny and put together."

"Well, finally my lack of domestic skills pays off!" Martha said and put her arm through Glory's. "Let's go do woman stuff while we leave the man to his work."

Glory laughed at Rob and Martha. "I bet Hugh misses you when you are out of town. But I'm glad you are here."

"He misses more than my cooking and cleaning. You two scoot and leave me to my work!"

Rob watched the two women walk out of the kitchen arm-in-arm. "I'm a lucky man to know such women." He ran soapy water into the sink and cleaned the kitchen.

When Glory and Martha finished dressing, they came back to the kitchen. Glory said, "I don't know where those bright coffee mugs came from, but I love them."

"I brought them from home," Rob said. "I found them at a local gourmet kitchen store in Norman a few days before all this started. I had bought them knowing sometime soon I would need a gift for someone. On a whim, I stuffed them in my luggage. You need brightness and color right now."

Glory hugged Rob. "Thank you."

She had dressed in her old, soft blue jeans and a t-shirt with a fish riding a bicycle. The sentiment on the shirt was "A woman needs a man like a fish needs a bicycle." It made her feel independent and powerful wearing the t-shirt.

Rob pushed her away at arm's length then laughed out loud. "I've never seen you wear the t-shirt I bought you!"

"I know and I love it." She shook her head. "Edgar hated it and told me never to wear it in his presence. Now his presence isn't here, at least physically, I'm wearing the damn shirt."

Rob grinned at her and kissed her on the cheek.

Martha said, "Never, ever let a man tell you what to wear again."

Glory smiled. "Thanks, Martha. I won't. Wearing this t-shirt feels exactly right for today."

Rob said, "Well, honey, wear it in honor of him today! Bless his silly, stuffy heart!"

"From this day forward I'm living my life for me. Whoever comes along on the journey will need to accept I'm living for me."

Rob held up a piece of paper and waved it at Glory. "Well! What good news to hear. I want you to get you started on your new life. I've made a list of things we need to do to get you started on your path forward. This is when my OCD will be your fairy godmother."

Martha grinned, sat down and pulled the paper out of Rob's hand. "Let's see what you have here!" She read from the list, "Check on will and insurance, arrange for cremation, plan funeral including where and when and who to invite, what happens next for Glory, start Glory's new life. Yes, that's what I call a good list!"

Glory started to protest, and Rob held up his hand. "Don't think about this stuff too much right now. I think if we take it as it comes it will be easier. I make lists only to make sure we don't forget something. We can add to the list if we need to. We are starting with the basics."

Glory nodded. "You are right, but it still feels weird. I didn't have my head wrapped around getting a divorce before I was a widow. I know Edgar is dead, but I keep expecting him to walk in the door fussing and fidgeting about you guys being here, hating the smell of bacon and coffee, disapproving of me wearing this t-shirt. It plain old feels weird."

Rob reached over and patted her hand. "You will stop feeling weird as soon as you can let go of all the negative shit about Edgar and concentrate on the positives moving forward. You had a life together even if it wasn't always happy. You had good times with him so think about those times. Him deciding to divorce you and then dying before the divorce could even happen is monumental in anyone's book. I have faith, as time goes on, you will remember the positives."

Glory nodded. "Thanks, Rob. You are right. I'm ready to move forward so I can create the life I want to live."

"Good," Martha said. "That's exactly how I think it should go too."

The doorbell rang, interrupting further conversation. Glory went through the living room to the front door. Looking through the peephole she saw Sara Merriweather in a bright red dress with white embroidered flowers. Her short black hair and deep dark eyes seemed even more alive than they did yesterday. Glory opened the door. "Hi, Sara," she said motioning her inside. "Come on in."

Sara carried a bunch of fresh daisies and her briefcase. "I hope you like daisies," she said. "These are from the market down the street, but they called my name, and I had to buy them." She smiled and handed Glory the flowers.

"I love daisies, they are my favorite flower. They are bright and cheerful and always make me feel better."

"Good. You feeling better was my intention. I love your t-shirt," Sara pointed at Glory's t-shirt. She raised her brief case. "Are you ready to get started?"

Glory smiled. She was glad, once again, she had chosen this t-shirt for today. She was ready to be strong and live life for herself. She motioned Sara toward the kitchen. "Follow me. Rob and Martha have already made a few lists but I'm happy you are here to help guide us through the process."

Sara and Glory walked into the kitchen. Glory said, "This is Sara Merriweather. I've told you both about her."

Rob and Martha stood up and introduced themselves. Sara said, "I'm happy to meet you both and I am happy Glory has good friends to help her through all of this."

Martha smiled and hugged Glory. "We are happy to do whatever she needs. You are kind to help Glory."

Sara nodded and pulled out a chair at the table. "I do this kind of work as a community liaison with the police department here. I don't have to do this often, thankfully but sometimes it is needed. When a loved one dies suddenly, it is difficult to know what to do."

The women sat down around the table. Rob brought over more coffee and a tray of peanut butter cookies.

"Where did those come from?" Glory asked.

"I made them this morning while cooking breakfast. They are my grandmother's recipe. I knew we would need comfort food to make this whole process easier or at least tastier."

Glory took a cookie and ate a bite. "Wow, these are terrific, Rob. Thanks for making them."

"You are welcome. Hugh likes these so much they are on the dessert menu at the bowling alley cafe. We serve them with vanilla ice cream and chocolate dipping sauce."

"Who is Hugh?" Sara asked, taking a cookie.

Martha said, "Hugh is Rob's husband and also an incredible chef and physician in Norman, Oklahoma."

Rob nodded. "He cooks at the cafe sometimes when he has a free weekend. Then we have a special menu and folks have to make reservations. He's been working on teaching me how to be a better cook. I'm a good baker and a fair cook. Learning how to cook more than breakfast, cookies and cornbread is my goal in the kitchen."

Sara said, "These are wonderful cookies. If you can only make breakfast, cookies and cornbread you're a keeper."

"That's what Hugh says," Rob replied with a grin.

Glory listened to the three of them and realized she felt relaxed and even a little happy.

Rob looked at Sara. "Enough messing about. On my lists, I have the first item as let's get Edgar taken care of, so we don't have to think so much about him anymore."

Sara smiled. "Perfect. Here is the paperwork to give to whatever funeral home you choose. They will take care of transporting Edgar's remains to their facility."

"What's next?" Glory asked.

"You need to choose a funeral home."

Rob held up a slip of paper. "Here is the list I made of nearby funeral homes. You can choose which one you'd like. All of these have great ratings on-line, so I don't think it matters much which you choose."

"What about a minister or officiant, Glory?" Martha asked.

"I don't think so. Neither Edgar nor I were religious at all. In fact, we had long talks about religion. Neither of us ever wanted to be religious. We were in total agreement there at least. It might be fine for others but neither of us believed in a personal god or the need for salvation. I don't know if his parents are religious or not. My parents weren't."

"Is your mom still living?" Sara asked.

"No, she died about six months after we married. She climbed Mt. Rainier but died on the way down," Glory answered.

"Wow! What a woman she must have been."

Glory nodded thinking about how after her father died her mother had come out of her shell and worked on mountain trails as a volunteer. Later, she joined a hiking group and started mountain climbing. "Yes, she lived a lot in the years after my father died. She always said she was going to go for the gusto and do all the things she had dreamed of doing. Climbing Mt. Rainier was one of those things. She got to the top but on the way down she slipped and fell into a crevice covered by soft snow. They could not recover her body."

"I'm so sorry," Sara said.

"I'm sorry she is not here with me. I'm not sorry about how she died and where her body is," Glory said. "I miss her every day, but, when I think of her up there frozen in time, always looking down on me, always loving me, I feel she is where she should be. When she died, she was doing what she loved and had dreamed of doing."

"Beautiful," Sara said.

Martha nodded. "I loved your mom nearly as much as my mom. I feel the same way too. I know she is here lifting us all up." Everyone was quiet for a few moments then Martha said, "We need to choose a funeral home for Edgar. What about one with an officiant or minister available for services so you don't have to worry about that part?"

"Sounds perfect," Glory said.

They continued to plan the funeral. Glory still felt there was no need to have a funeral, especially for her benefit. When she said as much out loud, Rob replied, "Right now you think you do not need to do this. But later, in years to come, I want you to have no regrets. This will help you. For now, just go through the motions and let everything else wait until its own good time for deep reflection."

Sara reached out and touched Glory's arm. "Rob is right on this. I know you've been through a lot in the past twenty-four hours. Maybe the way you remember your mother's life and death, is key to helping you move forward with Edgar's death. Settling him in his next state, whatever it is, will give you the space you need to move on and to honor him. This will be true for the rest of your life regardless of anything he did for or to you."

Glory nodded. "He was a good man really. Our marriage started out with mutual attraction and understanding about a lot of things. The love we had, however, faded over time with the stress of our different approaches to life."

"I'm glad you can remember good things about Edgar," Sara said. "Have you looked at the list of funeral homes yet?"

Glory shook her head.

Martha pointed to the list of funeral homes. "This funeral home has the best ratings. It is fairly close by and has a minister on-call for funeral services. It has cremation services too."

Glory looked at the printout Martha gave here. "This is the one I want to go with. Let's see if they will let us buy two urns. I want to have them take care of splitting the ashes for Edgar's parents and me."

"Good idea," Sara said. "I have helped others who needed to do the same thing in the past. It is easier for the family in the long run."

"Good," Glory said. "It's a relief for me. On the funeral service itself, I do not want to have a speaking role at all. I think no one would appreciate a service where I get up and say, 'Fuck you, Edgar!' and then sit down dry eyed. I guess I'm still a little pissed at him."

Everyone around the table smiled at the vision of Glory doing exactly that.

Rob laughed. "Although I can see you doing exactly that, it is probably not the best idea. Maybe the minister can do all the talking and if someone of his friends wants to say something they can."

Sara nodded. "Often no one of the direct relatives speak. Sometimes it is just too hard to do and other times it is like with you Glory. Hard feelings can't be easily masked this close to the death of a spouse."

"Thank you, Sara," Glory said. "I don't want to be mean-spirited. The past twenty-four hours have shown me, my resentment is still close to the surface."

Sara nodded. "I can't imagine how awful this has been for you. Do you want to have a reception afterwards?"

"No!" both Glory and Rob shouted.

Martha laughed. "All righty then! No food or booze for the mourners."

It had been six days since Edgar's death. It felt both like it had happened a few minutes ago and a lifetime ago. Glory was uncomfortable sitting in the funeral home chapel as the funeral began.

It surprised yet pleased her, how many people came to the funeral. It was a mix of friends of Edgar's and her own friends and both their work colleagues. His parents did not show up nor had they spoken with Glory since the day of Edgar's death. She felt if they had loved their son more, they would honor all of his life, even the life here in Issaquah, Washington with her. They never wanted this part of Edgar's life to exist.

Everyone was kind to her, expressing their condolences. *Edgar, I'm so sorry I didn't love you more and our marriage became an unhappy one. I feel a little guilty about the freedom I have now. I hope you are feeling free too.* She brushed away a tear with the tissue she held in her hand. *I will let my life begin again, Edgar. I hope you don't think I'm awful but I'm moving forward. I need a life filled with love.*

Edgar's best friend, Johnathan Hurley, was giving a moving eulogy. She saw others crying and dabbing at their eyes. She herself had cried a lot. She wasn't sure how much was grief and how much was general sadness at the state of her life.

Regardless of tensions in the marriage, Edgar had another life he had not brought home. *I didn't appreciate you had a life outside our marriage, Edgar. I am happy so many of the people here liked you and called you friend. It shouldn't surprise me, I know, Edgar. I was your friend and liked you enough to marry you. I'm sorry we didn't have enough love for each other to be happy.*

She looked up when Johnathan spoke her name. He said, "Edgar didn't talk about you often, Glory, but about a month ago he said, 'She is so beautiful and much saner than I am. I really do not deserve to have such a wife.' I know Edgar loved you very much and wanted only the best for you."

Glory smiled. She appreciated what Jonathan said. *Edgar, I hope you actually, really loved me. I don't understand how you could love me and also want to divorce me, though.* All the years of living together with him, reminding her constantly to put things away, keep the countertops, tables, shelves clear, telling her how to dress, how to talk, how to behave. Those years whittled away at the love she felt for him.

She remembered looking at their wedding photo every night before sleeping. Every night she wished for a happier marriage. *I'm not the one who planned to walk away from our life together, but I had a part in things ending the way they did.*

She felt his death was a brutal ending to their marriage. *Perhaps, if I'd been able to work through the divorce and gradually ease into a new life, a new way of being I'd feel differently about it all.* It was the knowing he was divorcing her that left her feeling his death had cheated her.

The minister from the funeral home stood up and invited the gathering of Edgar's friends and family to stand. Glory stood up between Robert and Martha. Rob took her right hand and Martha her left as they bowed their heads and the minister said a quiet, short prayer.

After the prayer, the minister came and led Glory, Rob and Martha to the back of the chapel to stand. Glory dreaded this part. She didn't want to lie to the people who were kind enough to attend the funeral.

As the first mourners approached her, she felt panic rising. She wasn't sure she could do this. *Just be kind,* she told herself taking a deep breath. *Kindness will help and it won't kill you.*

One after another they came and took her hand. They expressed love or grief or sadness or touched her shoulder and wished her well. She didn't have to say much more than "thank you" to any of the mourners.

A few of her friends hugged her. Her boss was the last in line. He reached for her hand and holding it said, "You know you have a lot of time built up for personal time off and you have two weeks of paid bereavement leave from the company. I hope you will take advantage of all the time available to you and use it to take care of yourself."

Glory nodded. "Thank you. I'll take time off, but I'm not sure yet exactly how much time off I want or what I will do. I'm not clear about anything today."

"Don't worry about it. Just let me know what you decide and when you'll be coming back.

Glory nodded and when he hugged her, she could hug him back with no sobbing or copious tears. She felt relieved when he let her go and he followed the other mourners out of the chapel.

The further east he drove on Highway 9 the better Jake felt. *It is a beautiful spring day in Oklahoma and I'm ready to accept the blessings it brings.* The weather was warm and sunny with white clouds floating on a brilliant blue sky. It was Jake's favorite kind of weather in Oklahoma. Everything was brilliant and shinning and the air felt soft and gentle.

He put in his favorite Lyle Lovett CD and sang as loud as possible with every song. He always laughed while singing about riding a horse on a boat. *Man, I wish Liz had a photograph of that!*

When he got to US Highway 270, he headed south toward McAlester and then on to Wilburton. Between the loud music, and the lovely day his spirits rose. Now and again, the music moved him to tears, but he loved the tears too. *It's all part of the game of life. Love, Joy, Anger, Sadness, Grief. I want it all.*

He was eager to get back to his ranch and work on training the new horse waiting for him. There were bigger mountains in the United States, but to Jake's mind there were none prettier than the Kiamichi Mountains.

He said out loud to no one in particular, "It's just like Daddy used to say:

I'd take everything I can see right now and never let it change if it was up to me." *I totally get it Daddy. I'm doing my best to spend all my money on keeping the land free and natural.*

As he drove across the cattle guard and toward his house he said, "There's no place like home even though we are in Oklahoma, Dorothy." He grinned as he saw his house come into view. There were no dark clouds to threaten taking them all to Oz and the Emerald City. He patted the dashboard of his pickup truck and said, "Someday, Little Darlin', I'll find me a woman who loves me and loves this place as much as we do."

Chapter 7

"The big question is whether
You are going to be able
To say a hearty yes
To your adventure."
— *Joseph Campbell*

One week after Edgar's death and the day after his funeral, Glory, Martha and Rob walked from the law office of Howard Todd, Edgar's lawyer, to the parking lot.

"The will was intense," Glory said.

Rob asked, "What are you going to do with all the money Edgar left you?"

"I'm not sure, but I'm fucking pissed as hell."

Martha laughed. "What can you possibly be pissed about? You just inherited an estate worth more than twenty million dollars with a monthly income of more than forty thousand dollars. If I were in your shoes, I'd be delighted."

Glory stopped walking. "Right here, right now, I'm pissed. Money will never change the facts. Ever. Edgar was a shit to me and then he leaves me all of the money I never wanted and never asked for. I'm pissed."

Rob and Martha looked at each other. Neither knew what to say.

"I really wanted a happy marriage with Edgar. I wanted babies. I wanted to travel. I never wanted to be wealthy. The only thing I never, ever asked Edgar for he gave me. Money. Everything I wanted he denied me. Money will never make up for his selfishness."

"So," Martha said, "I want to be careful here, Glory. I don't want you pissed at me. But, what's not to like about financial security."

Glory glared at Martha. "Financial security hasn't got a fucking thing to do with real life unless you don't have shelter, food and warmth. Then is the only time financial security has a bloody damn thing to do with life."

Martha nodded. "I get it. What do you want to do now?"

"I don't know. I don't have a fucking clue about what I want now."

Rob reached out for Glory's hand and she pulled away.

"I'm going for a walk. By myself. I'll walk home."

"But," Martha said.

"No, buts. You two go back to the house. I'll see you later." Glory turned and started walking away from her two best friends.

A car horn blared at Glory. She looked up. "Fuck! I'm standing in the middle of a crosswalk and the light is red." She waved an apology to the driver and quickly jogged to the other side.

She was standing at the corner of Front Street and Alder. "There's the H&H Bar. I've never been there before." She walked to the bar and went inside. Looking around Glory knew this was exactly the kind of place she wanted to be. No food. A little dark. Not fancy. Just drinks.

She sat at the bar and told the bartender, "Four Roses, single barrel, neat." When the bartender brought her drink back, Glory laid a twenty-dollar bill on the counter, picked up her glass and said, "One more then no more."

I will not turn into a drunk like my father just because I'm pissed and a little overwhelmed. And I fucking well will not cry.

The bartender took the twenty, got her another drink and left Glory's change beside the drink. Glory smiled and said, "Thanks." She picked up her drink, left the change on the counter and walked to a table as far from everything else in the bar as she could find.

The bartender followed her with a glass of ice water. "Just in case you need this," she said.

"Thanks, I might," Glory answered.

The bartender went back to the bar and watched Glory sit and stare into space. *I'll watch and if things go south for her, I'll see what I can do to help.*

Glory sat, staring into the emptiness she felt inside. *Except it isn't emptiness. It is white, hot anger. I'm so fucking pissed at you Edgar. Why did you leave me all that money? It makes no sense. All your yammering about things being too expensive turns out to be a crock of shit. If you weren't dead, I would kill you with my bare hands and kick you to the curb.*

She took a sip of her bourbon and looked at the large manila envelope she still carried in her hand. Mr. Todd had given her the envelope before she left his office. She opened the envelop and saw the will, Edgar's bank books, copies of documents she had signed today and a white envelope with her name on it. She pulled out the white envelope and said, "Edgar this explanation had fucking well better be good."

She closed the manila envelope and tucked it back in her tote bag with her wallet and keys. She took another small sip of the bourbon and smiled. *Four Roses, single barrel was one of the few things Edgar and I had agreed upon. It was smooth and soft and a little sweet. The last time we had a drink together, Edgar, was the night before you got yourself run over by a cement truck.*

She couldn't help laughing at the image of Edgar and his beautiful, black, expensive car under a fresh load of wet cement. "I only wish it had been a load of wet horse shit! Then we could have at least hosed you off."

She picked up the glass of water and took a long drink. It helped to clear her head a little. She lifted the flap on the envelope and pulled out the letter. She could see Edgar's precise and elegant handwriting.

He told me once he worked hard at penmanship. When he was in the third grade his teacher told him, he had a promising talent with cursive writing. The teacher told him, "Work on keeping it beautiful. It is one thing no one will ever be able to take from you, Edgar." Glory smiled. I wish we had loved each other more, Edgar.

She drank the last sip of the bourbon and opened the letter. She read:

Dear Glory,

If you are reading this, I have died. It is difficult to contemplate death for me, but it was difficult for me to contemplate life. I do not know when or how I shall die. Maybe things will change in our relationship and you will never have to read this letter. I've no idea what the future holds but I know, somehow, I must make amends with you.

There is much about me you do not know. I won't go into all the painful details but want you to know some of my life so perhaps you will understand me a little better. Hopefully, this knowledge, will help you forgive my inadequacies as a husband and a man.

I was not only, an only child, I was the child of my father's brother, Arthur. He and my mother had an affair several months before I was born but after she was engaged to my father. My father's brother, Arthur, was killed in an automobile accident before my mother was aware, she was pregnant.

After my mother married my father, she realized she was pregnant. She was honest with the man I call Father. She told him she was pregnant with her husband's brother's child. All our lives might have been different if she had concealed the facts of her pregnancy. We will never know.

Father was furious and beat her nearly to death one night. She survived and so did I. They remained married but the man I knew as my father was never intimate with my mother again. Thus, I am an only child.

My mother talked with my grandfather a few weeks before you and I married. She wanted him to know my true heritage and what my father had done to her. When my grandfather found out, what had happened and what the man I knew as my father had done to my mother, he disinherited my father and left me his entire estate. My grandfather died about a week later, perhaps because of the strain of knowing the horrid truth about his sons.

Our home was not a loving one but rather three people, isolated at every level from each other. By the time I was ten years old I was in boarding school full time and saw my parents on holidays only.

It was a very strict and regimented childhood which perhaps added to my inability to love anyone. I was unaware of the drama for how my father came to know the history of my conception and birth for most of my life.

I found out these details about a week before you and I married. I learned the truth when my grandfather died and left me a letter similar to the one I'm leaving you. He left me his entire estate and a letter explaining why he was writing my father out of his will.

I was enraged with my parents and wanted nothing more to do with them. However, our wedding was imminent. I wasn't ready to share this story with you, so I allowed them to attend our wedding.

They were both against me marrying you. They had planned a society wedding they expected would help them climb the only ladder they agreed to climb together: one of wealth and status. I was so proud of you, standing up to them and having our wedding in your mother's garden.

I never knew how to love but when I saw you, I felt immediately drawn to you. I can't say it was love but I can say you were the only woman for me. I admired everything about you; your beauty, your grace and your incredible mind. I know our marriage was not a happy one nor was it fair to you. For that I am sorry. It is only an excuse, I know, but the only model I had of marriage was my parents; certainly not a good model to follow.

I always said I didn't want children because I didn't know how to *be a father or even if I should be a father. I'm certain I never knew how to love.*

I feel sad about all of it now as I write this, knowing you might have been able to teach me how to be more loving and more kind if only I had allowed for the possibility. It is all water under the bridge now.

I do not know when I shall die or why or how. I only hope you will find it in your heart to forgive me and if possible, think kindly of me.

My deepest desire and dream is it is not too late for you to find the life of love and happiness you always deserved to live. Please use the money I'm leaving you to make your life better than I allowed it to be. I hope happiness, love and peace will abide with you always.

Yours ever,

Edgar

Tears poured down Glory's face. She wept silently and thought *Edgar we could have built a happy and exciting life together. I'm heartbroken you did not understand the possibilities. I'll use the money to make my life better, but I'll also use the money to do good in the world and honor you, the little boy who should have been loved. You deserved much better.*

When she was calmer, Glory motioned to the bartender. When she came to the table Glory said, "Could I have regular Coke on ice, please."

"Certainly," the bartender answered. When she brought the cola over, Glory drank the cola and put the letter back in the envelop. "This doesn't make what you did right, Edgar. I hope you realize now you fucked up big time; even running a red light you fucked up." She put the letter in her tote, took out her wallet and left a five-dollar bill on the table.

The walk home wasn't long, but it was helpful. By the time Glory arrived home she felt calmer and more at ease than she'd been since the terrible day. The day the email and Edgar's death changed her life.

She looked at her house. *It isn't an ugly house, in fact it is kind of cute, but*

I can't live here anymore.

She opened the front door and smelled cinnamon and yeast. She smiled and shouted, "What I smell had damn well better mean cinnamon rolls are baking!"

Rob and Martha walked out of the kitchen. Rob laughed. "I just took them out of the oven."

"Good. I have a lot of shit to get off my chest and cinnamon rolls and coffee will work wonders for my attitude."

Martha hugged Glory. Glory said, "Thanks for leaving me to my own devices."

"You are welcome."

The friends walked to the kitchen. Glory sat down in a chair and sat her tote bag in the chair beside her. She sat quietly while Martha and Rob brought the fresh cinnamon rolls, coffee and cream to the table.

When they all were settled around the table and Glory had added sugar and cream to her coffee she said, "I'm sorry I blew up after we talked to the lawyer. I would never want to hurt either of you, but I needed a little time and space."

Martha said, "You were fine, Glory. It was a lot to take in."

Rob nodded. "I'm glad you are back safe and sound."

Glory laughed. "Sound might be an over statement but I'm back safely. It was a close call. I was so in my head and not paying attention I was nearly run over in a cross walk."

Martha's eyes got big and Rob said, "Wow. How very Shakespearean of you."

She grinned and nodded. "Or, how very Edgar of me. But, I'm here now and ready to share some thoughts with you two."

They sat quietly for a few minutes. Glory took a bite of the cinnamon roll. *Man, that tastes good.* "I wish I could live on nothing but your homemade cinnamon rolls, Rob."

He grinned. "I thought they might be a help to you."

She nodded. "They are. Now, while I eat my cinnamon roll, I have something I want you two to read. After you've read this, I'll answer your questions and share my thoughts."

Glory handed Edgar's letter to Martha and Rob, then ignored them, keeping her head down while she ate her cinnamon roll and drank her coffee.

When Martha handed the letter back to Glory, wiping away her tears, she said, "What an amazing letter, Glory."

Rob nodded and wiped away tears. "Did this letter help you?"

Glory smiled softly. "I'm still pissed at Edgar, but it cleared up a lot. I was shell-shocked when we left Howard Todd's office. I'm not ready to go wild with the money but I have made a few decisions. The money could be a distraction and temptation. If I give into the temptations, it will destroy my life."

Martha nodded. Rob said, "I think that is a distinct possibility. What decisions have you made?"

"Not everything is clear for me, yet, but a few things are. First, I'm taking back my maiden name, Pennington. I have a deep need to live my life with more clarity about what I really want; about who I really am. I think a lot of the travel desires I had might have been me wanting to run away. Running away is a sure way to screw up."

Martha said, "I've never known you to run away from anything."

Glory smiled. "Thanks Martha. I don't want to run away now either, I want to run to. I want to run to the life I really want. The only problem is, I'm not sure what I really want. I have an idea though. Travel, at least for now, might help me to gain clarity about what I want my life to be."

"You certainly have the money to travel now," Rob pointed out.

Glory nodded. "I want to flesh out my ideas a little and then move forward in my life. I feel strongly there is a terrific life ahead for me, but I have to be ready to find it."

Jake and Delbert fed and watered the horses. It surprised Delbert when Jake showed up yesterday and told him he and Liz were getting a divorce. Delbert met her the one time she visited the ranch. Even then he didn't really get to know her.

She had two cameras around her neck the whole time taking pictures of everything. When he asked about it, she had said, "Just working on different shots and composition for a photography class I'm taking."

Delbert was pleased when Jake gave him a framed photograph of himself, brushing a horse. He hung it with pride in his kitchen. *I don't feel as alone with the horse hanging there and I miss my wife a little less. Well, not much less.*

Jake seems emotionally fragile right now. Hope he gets better soon. Sometimes Jake seemed sad, then he'd look angry. Sometimes he sang for no damned good reason. *I know there is nothing better than sweat and the outdoors to heal a heavy heart. It helps me every day.* Delbert asked, "You want to run the fences together or would you like me to do it?"

Jake owned a fair bit of land now. Most of the pasture land he leased out to various cattlemen in the area. He and Delbert ran the fences weekly to be sure there were no problem areas or danger which could hurt or lose any of the cattle. As they grazed down one pasture, they would ride together and move the cattle to greener pastures. Jake loved the work but not as much as Delbert did.

Delbert had said once, "If you give me shelter and a little grub I'd work for free." Jake would never let him work for free, of course.

He had said, "Delbert you do good work and make the ranch a better place. You are worth every penny I pay you."

Today, he said to Delbert, "If you don't mind running the fences on your own, I'd like to spend time working on Sally Mae. She's a fine horse but I want to put her through her paces and see how she does with the riding."

Delbert said, "You got it, boss. It's a fine day. I will take me a lunch on the ride and spend a little time fishing in the creek between running fences. I'll bring you some catfish for dinner."

"Sounds great. Nothing like some grilled catfish to make a man happy to be alive," Jake said and headed for the barn.

Delbert smiled as he watched Jake walk toward the barn. *Whatever went on in Jake's marriage he will be better off without a wife who doesn't love what he loves. She'll be better off too, I'm sure. I'm thinkin' when he finds the right woman everything will click into place. Fine one I am to talk. I found the right woman but ran her off and now I don't know how to get her back.*

Jake walked into the horse barn and went to Sally Mae's stall. He wasn't sure how many horses he would eventually have but he wanted to be ready for anyone who wanted to learn to ride. He had put an advertisement in the McAlester and Wilburton newspapers for horse riding lessons.

He hoped someday it would evolve into therapy for kids with emotional or psychological problems. He'd seen a show on PBS about how effective it was. Some folks had similar therapy for vets returning from war with PTSD. *Hells, bells. I need a little PTSD therapy myself. Working the horses will be a big step toward my own healing.*

Chapter 8

Glory said, "I want to talk with you two about some ideas and dreams I've been having for a few weeks. Before all of this happened, I was feeling a need to move on."

Rob asked, "I wonder if that's what Edgar was feeling too?"

Glory nodded. "I'm sure it is."

"The letter explained a lot," Martha said. "Where the grandfather's estate fits in and why probably Edgar held back emotionally."

"I think so too," Glory agreed. "Even though the way he handled the divorce was shitty, I think he did it because he didn't know what else to do. I'd like to think, after I got over being pissed, we could have had long, honest talks like we did when we first got married."

"But as Edgar said," Rob pointed out, "It is water under the bridge."

"Exactly. The question is what to do about the bridge," Glory said.

Martha laughed. "I never thought about the bridge before; only the water."

"Sticking with the metaphor, Martha," Glory said, "What the hell is the bridge doing there in the first place?"

Martha grinned. "To get you over the water."

Rob laughed. "Exactly right. Where are you going with this Glory?"

"I can't do anything about the abusive past Edgar, or I had. I can't do anything about our wounded marriage. I can't do anything about Edgar's terrible death. I can only do something about the shape of the future. I want my future to be good. I will cross over the bridge, keep the bridge strong, and not worry about the water. Let it go where it will."

"Hear! Hear!" Martha said.

Glory smiled at Martha. "I've turned in my notice at work. I see no point financially in staying in a job I don't need or want right now. I want to create a new way of being for myself. So, Martha, how would you feel about being my executive manager for all of this money and some projects I have in mind?"

Martha started to speak, but Glory held up her hand. "Listen and hear me out. You have the business acumen and accounting training. You are also a great educator. You have the skills I need; I want to take advantage of your skills. I want real freedom, at least for now, from anxiety and worry while I travel and work out what the rest of my life will be. If you'll help me and work for me, I'd not only pay you what you are making at your job now but set up the same benefits you have. What do you think?"

"Yes!" Martha clapped her hands together. "I've been meditating and journaling for weeks now how I could change my work environment. I wanted to work on something, or for someone, to accomplish something meaningful with my life other than just existing. Working with you sounds marvelous and fits into my thoughts for moving forward in my life. I was about to offer to do exactly what you describe. I'm ready for a big change in my life. I've been meditating and visualizing about using my skills in a way to help others, while letting me have the freedom to work how I want to. If my ideas fit with your vision, I'd love to work for and with you."

Glory nodded. "Your ideas and vision are exactly what I want. Us working together being good stewards but not obsessed with holding tight to money."

"When do I start?"

"Is today too soon?"

"Nope. Today it is," Martha answered.

Glory nodded and grinned. "Can you leave your job this soon?"

"A few days ago, I decided to have faith in myself and my ability manifest what I truly want in life. I turned in my notice before Edgar's funeral. I had the strong feeling the Universe would make it possible for my vision to be a reality. I have a few details I need to finish up for my job and then I'm taking terminal leave."

Rob shook his head. "You two move fast when you move. I'm impressed but you have left me a little breathless!"

Martha laughed. "I've been thinking of doing this for a long time. It was a relief to resign. I knew I could find another mundane job if I had to. I wanted the opportunity for something more than a job. I have about four weeks of paid leave I planned to use to give me the flexibility to get started on my new life or find other employment without dipping into my savings. I had not expected to come to work for you, Glory. Now I have a little extra money to play with."

Glory laughed. "Good. I'm glad."

She turned to Rob. "Rob, I'm not leaving you out of this. I know you and Hugh are saving up to build a clinic for low-income and homeless people in Norman. I'd like to be a part of funding Hugh's clinic if you'll let me. My idea is to help Hugh get it started but then soon it would be self-sustaining. Will Hugh let me help?"

"Let you? Holy Moly Batgirl! We'll let you help with startup funding of the clinic. Hugh will be delighted about this," Rob answered. "We were about three years away from being able to get started on it. We have been saving every penny possible."

"Great," Glory turned to Martha. "Martha you have your first big assignment. Get a clinic going in Norman, Oklahoma for the low-income and homeless people of the area. My vision there is to get it up and running with the goal it will be self-sustaining in a few years. I know it has been a dream of Hugh's for a long time."

"Yes, it has, and I get chills thinking about how happy this will make Hugh. However, what about you? What are you going to be doing?" Rob asked.

"I wanted to take a sabbatical," Glory answered. "I feel a little bad about quitting so soon, but they have cleared me for up to six weeks of paid leave. I'm sure it will be easier for my company for me to quit now rather than come back in six weeks only to give a two weeks' notice. There are a lot of good copywriters looking for a job or advancement. It won't be hard to replace me."

"Great idea," Rob said. "What are you going to do?"

"I will fulfill a few of my dreams. First, I want to travel on the open road at least a little, but maybe all across the United States."

Rob and Martha looked at each other but before they could say anything Glory held up both hands and said, "Stop. Say nothing right now. Just hear me out."

She opened her computer and pulled up a website then turned the computer so both could see the screen. "I found a custom wood working place in Seattle, but they also create conversion vans for camping. I've been going to their website for months and dreaming of buying one of those vans but knew Edgar would say no. I couldn't afford to buy one without financing and Edgar would have gone through the roof. Now I can afford to buy one of the vans. They have one ready to go. It is used, so less expensive than a brand new one. It has low miles. I can buy it now that I have money without dipping into anything more than Edgar's checking account."

"Okay, but why buy a conversion van for camping?" Rob asked.

"I'm telling you about what and how I want to spend time on the road. I want to travel around, camping and seeing more of the country. The van is like a tiny home on wheels. I want to write and blog. I want to meet new people. I want to see the landscapes of our country without having to settle with a movie of landscapes. I want to learn new things in new places. I want to get to know me as I am, warts and all. The van will be my home. I have this strong feeling if I take myself out of my old way of living and being, I have a chance, of moving my life forward despite all that has happened. I also feel, although I want and will need support from you both, I must do this discovery, learning and growing myself."

Martha grinned. "I have always liked the Dolly Parton quote, 'No matter where you go, there you are.'"

Glory smiled. "I know and agree with her. The issue is I want space to get to know me and understand who I am. I'm not looking to go anywhere to run away. I want to run to me."

Rob nodded. "I wonder if you could do a few weeks or months camping around Washington and maybe Oregon before heading out across country."

"You're right, Rob. I will since I haven't ever camped. First, I need a change of scene. I don't see me doing anything other than panicking about life and all this money if I don't try making changes."

"It all makes sense," Martha said.

"If I hang around here, I'll be feeling blue and second guessing every decision I make. I've always wanted to travel on the open road. I really want to see the country without hotels and restaurants getting in the way. Edgar hated the idea. I want to be clear; I want to do this for me. Alone."

Rob looked up at Glory. "Wait. Alone? Why alone?"

"I need to do this on my own with no one telling me what I should do instead. I need to prove to myself even if I am alone, I can handle my life."

Rob and Martha sat staring at Glory.

She smiled at them. "I've made an appointment to see a van this afternoon. I was hoping you guys would go with me. Besides, from what I can see online this van is perfect for my needs. I am planning to buy it and I'll need someone to drive my car home."

Rob looked at Martha, shrugged his shoulders and said, "Sure, but you have a minivan in the garage; isn't it good enough?"

"No. It isn't good enough," Glory said. "I'm through with good enough. I want to fulfill some of my dreams. I'm hoping as I fulfill my dreams a little and learn more about myself, I'll know how to proceed with the rest my life. I see a little of the money as being a way to fund this leaving my old life behind while I create my new life. I'm ready for all my adventures to start right now and in all the glorious ways I can make happen."

"What are you going to do with your minivan?" Martha asked.

"Good question," Glory answered. "I thought about leaving it here in the garage but then I thought why? Even if I change the colors on every wall in this house, this would still be Edgar's house."

Rob smiled. "I understand exactly what you mean."

Glory nodded. "What has happened in the last few days, the water under the bridge, I don't think I have the stomach for making this house my home. I'm ready for it to be someone else's house. I've already contacted a realtor and have an appointment with her here tomorrow morning. I will sell the house, sell the furniture, sell my minivan, buy a travel van to be my tiny movable home and hit the road."

She watched her two friends and their stunned reactions.

Glory smiled at Rob and Martha. "The bridge standing over the water?"

Her friends nodded. "The bridge needs to be strong. It needs to be reinforced and tended and cared for. The strong bridge is what I'm working on for my life. If I can keep the bridge of my life strong, the water can continue to flow. If I can't, I risk the bridge collapsing and me drowning, swept away by the water."

Rob smiled. "I love your vision, Glory. I love everything about you staying strong. But, I'm nervous about you traveling alone."

Glory held up her hand like a traffic cop.

"Stop. Just to be clear. I want your support but I'm not asking for your approval or permission. I'm a 25-year-old, fucking grown assed woman, in my mostly right mind. I have an opportunity for adventure and I'm taking it."

Martha grinned. "You are not worried about traveling alone?"

"No, I'm not worried. I'm a little scared and a little nervous but I want to conquer my fears and live my dreams," Glory said. "This is my Mt. Rainier. I want to prove I am my mother's daughter. I want to do what is calling me. I have the same freedom now my mom did when my father died but even better. She had to keep working and I do not. I want to live the life I feel begging me to be lived."

She took a deep breath and grinned. "I've researched and found blogs and videos about women traveling on their own. There is a lot of good information about how to be safe while adventuring. I've been living with and around too many people. Yet I don't feel like I belong anywhere or with anyone except for a few friends like you two."

She smiled and continued. "I want to change the paradigms I've been living in and create new ones. I want to know myself well enough I don't isolate myself. I want to quit being small and insignificant. Although it sounds contradictory, I need to do this alone. I'm fairly sure I'll be just fine. If I'm not, I'll turn around and come back to Issaquah and start over. I have enough money to use a little of it to give my dream a try."

"I'm all in," Martha replied. "Just don't ask me to not fret and worry."

"I won't," Glory laughed. "In fact, I'm counting on your fretting and worrying to free me up to go. I'll leave fretting and worrying up to you two while I have an adventure. When the time is right and I'm settled from the inside out, I'll do whatever comes. I won't do anything if it doesn't feel right. I'm doing good things for and with good people—you two for starters. I have a strong feeling, following my gut in all regards is exactly what I should do right now. I'm leaving the details and safety net up to you, Martha."

"We will have to call you Gutsy Glory from now on," Rob said.

Glory grinned. "Yep. As Joseph Campbell suggested, I will say a hearty yes to my life and my adventures."

Glory drove her new camper van home feeling joyful and powerful. The smell of waxed wood and leather permeated the interior of the vehicle. She thought,

My tiny home is not merely a vehicle. Maybe I should feel sad but for the first time in what feels like a long time I am not sad, depressed or anxious. I feel at home, content and I'm driving on I-90 back to Issaquah.

She thought about her life and how she had been a scared little girl at risk all the time from her father's anger. His anger often seemed to spring out of nowhere for no reason. Her mother tried to protect her, but it wasn't always possible to avoid some physical abuse. The mental abuse, too, was a big part of what haunted her all her life. Being told repeatedly how stupid she was, how ugly she was, how fat she was, made it impossible for Glory to have confidence in herself.

All of my childhood drama and trauma is probably part of why I married Edgar. He was nice, told me how smart I was and how beautiful I was. We talked about every except our future together; we jumped in with both feet and got married. We were so compatible intellectually we didn't consider any other compatibility issue. I'm sorry Edgar, I'm at least as much to blame as you were for the state of our relationship. I hope what I'm doing is something to help you be proud of me and give you some peace. You deserve it at least as much as I do.

She took the exit to her house on Sunset Way. Rob and Martha had gone ahead of her while she was finishing paper work and details with the van dealer. She pulled into the driveway and saw Rob and Martha grinning and waving her into the drive. She lowered the driver's side window down and asked, "Can you believe how beautiful she is?" Martha and Rob both laughed.

Rob grinned. "She is beautiful and so are you. I love the happiness on your face."

"I am happy," Glory answered. "I feel a little weird being this happy so soon after Edgar died."

"Happiness is good. I think Edgar would approve of your happiness" Martha said. "I'm more than a little jealous of your van. It had so much more storage and space than I had imagined. It is beautiful inside and out. I can totally see you driving around the country, writing and blogging and enjoying the hell out of yourself."

Glory got out of the van and hugged Martha. "Thank you. It feels great. Come on, let's go inside the van and take a real look around with no sales people; just us snooping."

After they had looked in every cubbyhole and shelf and touched every surface many times, Glory said, "Enough snooping! I'm starving. I feel like I've been holding my breath for years and afraid of so many things. Now I feel I need to fuel up and get moving."

Martha laughed. "Then let's have lunch."

They worked together making sandwiches and soup. Robert put more of the cookies on the table while Martha made nachos to go with their soup and sandwiches. Glory took bottles of hard cider out of the fridge and said, "Let's celebrate!"

"You know," Rob said, "Every minute passing, I see you blossoming back into the girl I so admired in high school."

Glory turned to Robert and leaning into him she kissed him on the cheek. "Thank you, Rob. That's the sweetest thing I've heard lately. I've spent more time at this table with you two in the past few days, than in all the years of my marriage to Edgar. Thanks for being here with me and helping me move forward."

Glory really felt like she was already moving forward. *Edgar I'm not pissed at you anymore. You loved me enough to be sure I was taken care of. I'm sorry you died. I'd rather you be alive, loving me and here to enjoy this love of friends.*

Martha reached over and touched Glory's hand. "You know we love you and would do anything to help you."

"Yes, I do," Glory said. "I'm counting on you to manage the money side of my life, at least for a while, so I can stay on the road for as long as I need and at the same time help others. I need time and space to figure out what I want to do with the big part of the money."

"Don't worry. I understand. For now, we will hang loose and give you the time and space to adjust. You'll know what to do when the time is right. Then, we'll make it happen," Martha said.

Rob continued to hold Glory's hand. He said, "I know you want to do this road trip and I think it is a good idea but, do you have to do it alone?"

Glory grinned. "Well, I won't be entirely alone. Tomorrow morning PUP, a dog and cat rescue organization here in Issaquah are having an adoption event. I've filled out my application on-line for a little black puppy that is part cocker spaniel."

Rob laughed. "Good for you! A dog is exactly the right companion for you and will help keep you safe."

"I've always wanted to have a dog, but Mom would not let me have one because she was allergic to dogs and she worried that Dad would hurt any dog I had. Then Edgar didn't want me to have a dog. Now I can fill another of my dreams."

Martha grinned. "You will love having a dog to travel with and it relieves some of my anxiety about you traveling alone."

Glory sat in Rob's car holding the fluffy little black dog snuggled in her arms. "I hope I'm doing the right thing. She is just too cute." The dog licked her nose in response and snuggled close into her neck.

"You are taking home your next best friend. Of course, you are doing the right thing," Martha replied from the back seat. "She is totally in love with you already. She has paid no attention to either Rob or I."

"She's so tiny! The folks at PUP said she was about three months old and weighs eight pounds. She probably won't weigh over twenty pounds when she is grown. I don't see how any dog this small will be able to be much support or protection."

"It seems she is already doing just fine with the support," Rob said as he glanced over to the little black ball of fur licking Glory's hand. Glory petted the dog's head. When she stopped petting her, the puppy stood up and placed her front paws on Glory's chest and sounded a quick, sharp little bark.

Glory giggled a little. "What?" The puppy immediately nuzzled under Glory's chin. Glory let out a quiet sigh. "OK, you're mine. Or I'm yours."

Martha said, "She is exactly what a puppy is like. She will love you no matter what. A puppy can help you when you need her the most. What's her name?"

"I have no clue. What am I going to name her?"

"Whatever feels right," Rob said.

"I had names picked out for baby girls and baby boys, but I have no clue what to name a dog," Glory said. She swallowed and thought *I had such plans. I had so many wonderful names I never got to use them. The names were important and meant to be used.*

"You'll come up with the right name," Rob said. "You know it is fine to use a name you had picked out for a baby. After all this little dog is your family now, and she will depend on you to take care of her. Think of it as you are practicing; a mommy-in-training."

Glory smiled but felt sadness creeping in. She would never be a mommy other than to this little furry bundle. She had difficulty getting pregnant and when she had been pregnant, it didn't end well. She miscarried and was afraid to risk ever being pregnant again. She wasn't sure she could bear to lose another baby. Glory said, "She is so small, but one name keeps ringing in my head. Freya."

"Then, Freya's exactly the right name for her," Rob said. "I've never heard the name before."

"She is the Norse Goddess of love, beauty and fertility," Glory answered. "It seems to fit her despite how tiny she is."

"Freya. Sounds great," Martha said, "besides Goddesses do not have to be big to be powerful."

Glory turned around and looked at Martha sitting in the back seat. "My mother used to say, great things come in small packages."

With a grin, Rob asked, "Did she tell you that when you were whining about be so short?"

Martha laughed from the back seat. "She still whines about being short!"

"Inside I don't feel short or small. I feel tall and I'm feeling stronger. On the outside however, when I can't reach things in my kitchen, I still wish I were tall, graceful and had skinny legs."

"Being tall, graceful and skinny are just on the outside," Martha said. "You are short, petite and beautiful."

Glory felt tears coming. She reached back and held on to Martha's hand. She wanted to get home and settle in her new friend Freya.

Martha said, "She is the perfect goddess for you to hang out with."

Jake sat on the balcony of his bedroom and watched the moon rise. The moon was nearing to waning. It always made Jake a little sad to see the waning moon. *I like seeing a full bright moon. It has magic when it is full.* He smiled to himself at his thoughts.

It had been over a week since he returned to the ranch. *I'm glad Liz is going a different direction than spas and shopping. I'm sad the marriage ended but day by day I'm feeling she was right about us. We loved each other, but we weren't a good match.*

He felt he had treated her well but deep inside he had doubts. *Maybe I should have sold the ranch and tried harder to be the man she wanted.* He let those thoughts sit with him awhile. Finally, he realized he would have been a fool to try to make the marriage work by sacrificing himself. *Man makes plans and gods laughs,* he smiled remembering his Daddy saying.

I feel like the waning moon. Little by little the old me is fading away. I have a hole in my heart right now. It's not any more use than a hole in a boat. I can

keep bailing and still I'll have a hole in my heart. Maybe it'll get better in
time. I hope so.

Jake and Delbert were riding the fences together. Delbert said, "Boss, it's none of my business, but you are lookin' mighty tight around the eyes."

Jake laughed. "I'm an Okie bred and born but I've never heard that saying before."

Delbert grinned. "My momma used to say it to my daddy when he had been working too hard and not having much fun doing it. She'd say, 'Bart, grab your fishin' pole and go get me some perch. You're looking a little tight around the eyes'. Then daddy would give her a big kiss and say 'Thanks, Bella' and he'd go fishing for a few days. When he came home, he was all relaxed and mellow and momma was happier too."

"I feel a little lost, Delbert. The divorce was quick and easy, maybe too quick and too easy. Something I committed to for life turned out to be a short-term thing."

"Not everything we plan in our lives comes out the way we want it to. Cora and I are an example of how things don't always go as planned."

"I know, but I'm still hoping for you and Cora. I love the ranch but hate it doesn't feel like a refuge anymore."

"Why would you need a refuge?" Delbert asked.

Jake grinned. "And there you have my problem. Liz and I worked things out as nicely as we could but I'm still feeling the pain. I'm here on my ranch. It is my dream life. Between the horses, running the fences and vetting for a few of our neighbors I'm doing great. But something's just not right."

"Why don't you go walkabout?"

Jake looked at Delbert. "What do you mean?"

"Well, I can remember times when you were a little boy and you and your Daddy would go on a trip fishing, hiking and camping. He called it 'going walkabout'. 'Course Hugh never wanted to go but you two would head off and whatever had been botherin' your daddy was better by the time you got back."

"I never realized 'going walkabout' was anything but me and Daddy going camping by ourselves."

"Everyone needs time and space to let the world go by and the earth take over," Delbert said, thinking again that the three years of Cora being gone might be too much time gone by.

Jake nodded. *Maybe a walk about is just what I need. Rob told Hugh and me about the Middle Fork Trail up where he grew up in Washington. I might give Washington State a try.*

Jake double checked he had everything he needed for his trip. He had fitted out the camper on his truck with a bed, a place for his clothes, water, food and camp stove. He was feeling excited to be going on a cross-country trip to the Pacific Northwest. Rob had talked so much about how beautiful it was, Jake felt the mountains and forests of the Cascades were beckoning him to come see them.

Delbert walked up to Jake and clapped him on the shoulder. "Well, looks like you're all set to go walkabout in fine fashion."

Jake grinned. "Yeah this is fancier than anything Daddy and I did but it will work fine for the long trip I'm takin'."

"You'll do fine and may hap' you'll get your innards straightened out and come back home to the ranch; you'll be better for having gone walkabout."

Jake looked wistfully at his log house. *Damn! I love my house. I will miss my big old bed, too.* He turned to Delbert and said, "That's the plan Delbert. Thanks for taking care of the place while I'm gone."

"It's what I'm here for."

Jake took off his hat and laid it on the passenger seat as he got in his pickup truck. Delbert asked, "You checked everything in this wagon of yo

"Yep, I even changed the oil. She's only got a couple hundred

her. She's good to go for a long time yet."

Delbert grinned. "You take care of her and she'll take care of you."

Jake laughed and then said, "And there you have a metaphor for life."

Delbert shook his head. "I'm a fine one to talk. You have a good trip and come back home in one piece."

"I plan on it."

Chapter 9

Never did the world make a queen of
A girl who hides in houses
And dreams without traveling.
—Roman Payne

It had been only nine days since Edgar's death. Glory felt contented, happy and alive. *Edgar thank you for making my new life possible. I'd rather be doing this with you but because of your generosity I am starting my life over today.*

She took Freya out to the backyard through her bedroom deck and watched her run out and do her bathroom business. On the way back to Glory she got distracted by a butterfly and jumped to catch it but missed. She flopped on the ground then stood up and shook off her failure. *There,* Glory thought, *is a good role model to follow. If I fail anytime along the way, I'll try to remember to stand up and shake it off.* She picked up the little bundle of fur and said, "I've got to get dressed and go help with breakfast."

Breakfast was fun as always with Rob and Martha but a little sad too. Rob was going home to Oklahoma today. Glory said to Rob, "I will miss you, buddy."

"I'll miss you too, but I'm counting on you heading to Oklahoma soon. We can hang out there and show off your fabulous van."

Martha said, "I'll be in touch with you so we can work out a few details. I want to get busy with you and Hugh on getting started with the clinic."

"It will be great to get started. I've got to go, girls! I'm TSA pre-check but it's the middle of the day. The airport will be wild. No telling how long the lines will be, and I have to turn in my rental car."

"Okay," Glory said, "But we will miss you a lot. It has been great being together again."

"It really has," Martha agreed.

"First, I have small gifts for the two of you."

"Rob," Glory said, "you didn't need to buy presents. You coming here, is gift enough for me."

Rob smiled. "Yes, but these gifts are to help my two favorite women get their new lives off to a great start."

He reached into a sack he was carrying and handed a rectangular box to Martha. "This is what every executive goddess needs," He said.

Martha opened the package and pulled out a desk plate on a mahogany stand. It read 'Goddess In Charge'. She held it up for Glory to see. They laughed and Martha said, "This is perfect. I can't wait to have a desk to put this on."

He hugged Martha. "Hugh will be delighted when I tell him all the details of what we are planning."

Then he turned to Glory and handed her a small, soft package. She opened it to reveal a t-shirt. Holding it up she read, 'Never Camp Alone,' with a dog on the front of the shirt.

"It is from the Dog Is Good website," Rob said. "They have a lot of great t-shirts. Check them out online."

Glory hugged Rob. "You always know the right t-shirt to give me. Thank you so much for this and for everything you have done for me."

"You are welcome. You will be fine. Get out there and go on adventures and share with the rest of us living in our mundane worlds."

"Hey, there is nothing mundane in your life or Martha's or mine anymore. We have to stick together and follow our dreams."

After a few more hugs, kisses and tears, Robert left with Glory and Martha waving goodbye as he drove away.

Glory stood inside her new traveling home, touching each inlaid, wooden surface, marveling this beautiful home was all hers. She laid a rag rug her mother had given her from her grandmother. She had made it of many colors with bright floral patterns and dark solids mixing and matching around and around. Glory loved this old rug and was happy to have it. It would be the first personal touch of her tiny home. She thought of her mother. "Welcome home Momma." She could feel her mother's love around her.

She picked up her pen and tablet and made lists of things she would need to get done. She loved how the passenger seat rotated around to become a large comfy chair in the living area of the van. It even had a footrest and reclined. Glory thought, *it's much like a fancy, first class airplane seat it also had a table she could lift from within the arm of the chair. She glanced at the matching chair behind the driver's seat. It almost looks like a living room in here. I love everything in this home and love it is all mine.*

"I don't know about you, Momma, but I'm ready to hit the road."

Martha stuck her head inside the door of the van. "The realtor is here, and do I ever have a surprise for you."

"Hooray! What surprise?"

Martha grinned. "You'll see."

Glory picked up Freya who immediately licked her face. Glory snuggled the puppy and followed Martha from the garage into the house. Martha led her into the living room, grinned and said, "Glory meet Emily Harris. You may remember her from high school."

Glory went over to Emily and hugged her. "Emily! I didn't expect the realtor I called to be my Emily from high school. I thought about you when I called but wasn't at all sure it was you."

Emily grinned and said, "I didn't recognize it was you with the last name of

Shaw. I thought of you and how intriguing it was I would know two women in the area named Glory."

"Thank you so much for coming by so quickly," Glory said.

Emily said, "You are welcome. What an adorable dog you have."

"Thanks! I still can't believe it is you. I loved taking literature classes with you. You always loved the poets. You understood Browning, Keats, Dickinson, and Whitman better than any of the rest of us. I remember feeling like an idiot when it came to Shakespeare."

"You were never an idiot," Emily said.

"When you read Shakespeare aloud, I would suddenly understand what he was saying."

"That's the trick about all poets and poetry," Emily said. "They are written to be living, breathing words you hear with your ears first and then your soul recognizes the words as part of the eternal."

Glory grinned and looked at Martha. "See! Even her explanation is poetry."

Glory and Martha laughed. Glory said, "I kind of expected you to become a literature or creative writing professor. I would never have thought of you as a realtor. If you are half as good at selling houses as understanding poetry you will be terrific."

"Thanks, Glory."

Martha asked, "So, Emily what do you think about the house?"

"Well, I've lived in this area for many years and watched as Glory and her husband changed an eyesore into a beautiful house. It is even lovelier seeing it up close."

"Thank you," Glory answered. She looked around and realized although she didn't like all the white and the bare walls, it was a beautiful house.

"Will your husband be joining us today?" Emily asked.

Glory shook her head. "My husband died a little over a week ago."

"I'm so very sorry!"

"Thank you, Emily. Please don't think this is a grief reaction sale. My husband and I were planning to divorce before he had his automobile accident. I wanted to sell the house before he died; It is what would have happened even if he had not died."

Glory said, "I'll let you guys do all the talking and touring. I will get started on research for planning my first trip."

"Great, Martha can show me around and then maybe we could all sit down and go through the details."

"Perfect." Glory said.

While Martha was giving Emily, the tour of the house Glory went to the kitchen and looked around trying to decide which dishes, pans, flatware and on and on she wanted to have on her journeys. She opened each cupboard door and each drawer and after a few minutes realized she wanted none of it. "It is all plain, mundane and not the least bit what I ever wanted in my kitchen. I'm thinking of bright colors and soft fabrics to create my own cozy tiny home."

She ducked back into the garage and sat down inside her new traveling home taking Freya with her. "Well, Freya, I think we need a shopping trip to find just the kinds of things we'll feel comfortable with." Freya chewed on a toy Glory had bought for her totally ignoring talk of shopping.

Glory picked up the pad of paper and pen she had brought out earlier and made a new list of things to buy for her traveling home. She looked at her grandmother's rug on the floor and said, "Now there are a lot of colors and patterns I can use to help pull things together." She pulled out her phone and took a few photos of the rug and the interior of the van. She began to get ideas of how she wanted this to look. She was thinking of bright colors with soft floral accents. "A modern woman's traveling wagon," she said.

Martha and Emily came into the garage. "Knock, knock," Martha said. Emily was standing beside her looking inside the van and the garage.

"Come in and see my new home," Glory said to Emily and Martha.

"Wow," Emily said entering the van. "This is the most beautiful camping van I've ever seen."

"Thanks. I love it. But I have plans to add a lot of color to complement the beautiful wood. It feels a little masculine and I want it to be all woman!"

"No wonder you want to travel. This is like a palace on wheels but in a cozy way. I love all the wood working details."

Glory nodded. "Me too. I saw the van and knew this was exactly what I wanted."

Glory followed Emily and Martha back inside. When Emily asked how much she wanted to sell the house for Glory said, "I have absolutely no idea. What do homes like this go for?"

"Well," said Emily, "It is a lovely home with lots of potential for someone to put their own stamp on it."

Glory laughed. "All this white was absolutely not my idea."

Emily smiled. "Martha told me about your desire for a different color. Still it is a great house. At 1500 square feet and two bedrooms, each with full bath it will sell quickly. The big fenced yard with the lovely sculpted gardens are a big plus. I'm not sure about the back shrubs and trees, however. They look a little like a jungle. We may want to clean up and prune those."

Glory nodded. "Edgar wanted to keep it as a barrier between us and the rest of the world. I wanted to clear it out and have a gazebo and maybe a vegetable garden."

Emily said, "Those would have been very nice additions to your yard. It won't detract from selling the house but maybe you could get a garden person to come over and tidy it up. The attached two-car garage is also a bonus, especially with our periods of rainy weather. Having the laundry room just off the kitchen without having it in the garage is another great selling point. Few women I know like doing their laundry in the garage."

"It used to be in the garage, but I fought with Edgar until we had it in the house instead. I cannot abide spiders!"

"Great idea. Besides too many spiders would decrease the sale price."

Glory laughed. "Exactly!"

Martha asked, "So what would be the bottom line for this house as far as price?"

"You could easily sell this for four hundred thousand but maybe even as high as five hundred thousand or more, especially if there was a bidding war for it," Emily replied.

"You're kidding!" Glory said.

"No. This is a quiet neighborhood in a great school district and less than thirty minutes to the main Microsoft campus."

Martha smiled. "I think it sounds about right. What do you want to do, Glory?"

"Sell the house as quickly as possible so I can hit the road."

Martha asked, "Would you be willing to take four hundred and fifty for the house if you could sell it today?"

"Absolutely I would!"

Martha turned to Emily and asked, "Have you ever been the real estate agent for both the buyer and seller?"

"Oh, sure," Emily said. "It is not an unusual practice at all. Why do you ask?"

Martha turned back to Glory. "I like this house. Except for the white. To make this a home, it needs changes in color and personality. I would love to live here if you'll sell it to me."

It stunned Glory. She opened her mouth but didn't know what to say.

Martha continued, "I've loved being here with you and I'm ready to get out of apartment living. I've been living in an efficiency apartment for way too long—nearly ten years. I've saved up a significant amount of money for the down payment. I checked with my bank and I'm pre-approved up to four hundred and fifty thousand. With my down payment, the loan won't be anywhere near as high as I'm approved for. If Emily will help us through the legalities will you sell your house to me?"

Glory felt a small thrill of joy. "I will."

"There's only one more requirement," Martha said.

"Name it."

"I get to keep the minivan," Martha said. "I'm thinking of a short weekend trips for myself."

Glory grinned and then said in a very sober voice, "You have to keep all the furniture and dishes and everything in this house."

"Forever?"

"No, only until you want to ditch any of it so I don't have to deal with it."

"Sold," said Martha and stuck out her hand to Glory who firmly shook her hand.

"Well," said Emily. "I'm a little breathless with all of this."

Martha grinned. "I wanted to be sure I wasn't asking Glory to sell her house too cheaply at four hundred and fifty before I made the offer. Will you help us with all the paperwork for your usual fees?"

"Absolutely!" Emily said. "I think four hundred fifty is a very fair price for an instant sell. If we listed it higher, you might get more but you might also get less. We must get an assessment and title search to satisfy the bank, but I'll take care of those things. Please, let me take you two out to dinner."

Over dinner they talked about their desires and dreams. Both Emily and Glory wanted to meet the perfect man and have large families. Martha smiled but felt out-of-place with the conversation. *I'm not looking for the perfect man and although I wouldn't mind being a mother I never, ever want to be pregnant.*

Martha sat in the tub filled with warm water thinking about the conversations with Emily and Glory. She wasn't sure what she wanted in the way of a family or even partners. She had been with one man and the outcome was terrible.

She remembered: *I enjoyed the dating; going out to dinner or movies but nothing else about the relationship was fun or stimulating. The kissing and hugging parts were fine but not exciting nor did any of it turn me on. The physical experience of sex itself was miserable. I remember laying there waiting for him to finish. I felt isolated and used but not loved or desired. I didn't know how to respond. It was a disappointment for him too. We never saw each other again. After the one sexual experience I didn't date anymore. I did not feel attracted to any man.*

Women though intrigued me. During high school I struggled to know if I was lesbian. I had always felt diminished somehow with the idea of being lesbian. Wasn't I supposed to be attracted to men? Surely the right man would come into my life and I would know then I wasn't lesbian.

When she never met a man who attracted her, Martha just put it all out of her mind. It was easier to ignore her sexuality than punish herself endlessly for not being what a man wanted. Worse yet she punished herself for not desiring a man. Every woman she was ever attracted to left her feeling shame at her own desires. Over the years, she continued to think about women and wondering what a physical relationship with another woman would be like. From time to time she would see a photo of a woman or meet a woman and all her anxiety and fears about her physical, sexual self, rose to the surface again. Those longings, however, did not help her feelings of shame.

Martha muttered, "Here you are a grown-ass woman who is twenty-six years old and you don't know about your own sexuality or desires." *What is probably more likely is I feel ashamed of my own sexuality and desires.*

She had experienced orgasms but only by herself and they left her feeling as if something were missing in her life. *It also has only served to increase my shame without creating any sexual gratification or satisfaction.*

She wanted love, desire and belonging in her life. *How can I expect those things from anyone else when I don't experience it myself?* She loved her time with Glory and now Emily but didn't find herself physically attracted to either of them. She loved them both but as Glory would say, "Not in that way."

When she looked at photos of women, she didn't know or when she met someone new, she occasionally had a feeling of attraction, but no one had yet made her feel a committed relationship was for her.

She longed for the close affection of a relationship. She wanted a relationship of friendship and physical stimulation. *More than that, I want passion in my life with another person. To wake in the morning with someone beside her to kiss her, hold her and make her feel alive and wanted was her dream.*

"Maybe I'm just one of those women who are asexual," She muttered. *But then why do I feel this longing inside for someone to be with to create a life together? Why are my sexual dreams only about women and why do I awake filled with shame?*

Glory and Martha were moving forward with the help of Emily. It had been three weeks since they renewed their friendship with Emily. Now they sat around the table at the title company closing on the real estate transaction. All the legal loopholes and title clearances and property assessments were complete.

Martha finished moving in with Glory within a few days of signing to buy Glory's house.

Glory had insisted Martha move into the Master bedroom and she moved into the guest bedroom. She had said, "Really, it feels kind of icky sleeping in the bed where I used to sleep with Edgar. Besides, this will be your house. The bigger bedroom should be yours." So, they had changed bedrooms.

Martha said, "I put down a big enough down payment so my house payments will actually be less than my apartment rent. I should have bought a place sooner!"

"I'm so happy you didn't and could buy this house," Glory said. "I can't wait to see what you do with it."

"I've got a few ideas," Martha said. She loved the master bedroom except it needed different wall colors. She was thinking of getting a red satin down comforter and some yellow and brilliant purple pillow covers too.

Glory felt a burden lifted as she signed the papers selling her house to Martha.

After the last page was signed, Emily asked, "When do you start your adventurous journey, Glory."

"In a day or two," Glory said. "I've taken day trips in the van to various local areas and hiked with Freya. I'm comfortable enough to do real camping now. I hope. First, I will camp here in town a couple of times."

"I think that's a good idea."

"Tomorrow evening I'm camping in Martha's driveway. I'll go to my van and fix dinner for Martha and myself. Freya and I will sleep in the van and have breakfast in the van. Then on Sunday, Freya and I will camp in the Blue-Sky RV Campground here in Issaquah. I've got a reservation already for camping there. I plan to go there after lunch and spend the evening there. In the morning I'll fix breakfast and check out by eleven a.m."

"Sounds like fun," Emily said.

Glory nodded. "I know those first two nights don't seem like real camping but I'm trying to not be reckless in my adventures for Martha and Rob and myself. On Monday I'll take a few days staying with Martha and finish packing for the first out-of-town camping. Doing it this way I can reassess and see if I have adequately prepared myself, Freya and the rig for a real trip."

"I like your plan. I'd probably be too scared to even sleep in the driveway."

"You could do it I'm sure; I doubt you'd be too scared."

Glory smiled at Emily. "I'm looking forward to the what I think of as my first real trip next Wednesday. It's when I'll head to Lake Easton for a four-day trip so I can really try out my rig, try out my courage and get a taste of any adjustments I need to make."

"Did you make reservations?" Emily asked.

Glory nodded and said, "Yes. I took your advice on reservations. I called and they are open. They said it is still cold at night and rainy sometimes but they are open and most of the snow has melted in the campground. I made a reservation for four nights and four days. Afterwards, I'll come back on Sunday afternoon and hang with Martha for a few days to do any shopping or make any needed changes."

Martha nodded. "Glory will be our very own traveling goddess."

Grinning Glory replied, "Goddess on the Road!"

Emily smiled. "I've traveled around the state with friends and family. There is a lot to see in Washington State. There is beauty everywhere and yet each place seems to be unique."

"I have done little traveling," Martha said. "But after seeing Glory's van and her desire to travel, I think I'll give the minivan a makeover and do traveling and camping myself after I get things settled down a little. First, though, I want to spend time nesting in my first ever real home."

Jake had been on the road for nearly a month. He stopped wherever he wanted and saw a lot of amazing things. He had driven north from the ranch. He stopped in the Ozark's a few times enjoying the beauty of the mountains north of where he lived. He went east in Missouri until he got to the Mississippi River. He headed north from there camping at night on the banks of the Mighty Missisip.

He then veered west along the Missouri river to Omaha, Nebraska. From Omaha he went north again camping along the Missouri River. It wasn't as big as Old Miss but still a mighty force to be reckoned with.

He'd been to the badlands in the Dakotas, then west to Mt. Rushmore which was frankly amazing despite the tourist trap it had become. Yellowstone and the Grand Tetons were next. Awe was all he felt in those two places.

As much as Jake loved Oklahoma the sites so far left him feeling the magnificence of this country. *Just think, this trip is only a little of what there is to see in America.*

He'd fished on the Snake River and nearly drowned when a big steelhead salmon fought like the devil trying to get into heaven. Eastern Washington reminded him a lot of home and New Mexico all rolled into one. He'd visited the petrified forest and again felt small by comparison to the eons and magic required to create the petrified trees. *Damn near unbelievable.*

He'd saved western Washington for last part of his journey. The mountains were amazing to him. *Lord love a duck but this is something grand and wonderful!* He stopped every thirty or forty miles to take more photos of their tall peaks covered with big trees; so big it was hard to believe they could stand up on their own. There were pockets of snow still visible at the higher elevations. Crystal clear water ran between the rocks making little waterfalls. *I ain't never seen nothin' like little waterfalls right by the side of the road.* The smell of pine and earth was so strong it felt like a miracle. Jake kept his windows down just to smell the forest. *It's loud travelin' this way but with the CD up loud and me a hollerin' along I'm a happy man.*

Chapter 10

"You can waste your lives drawing lines.
Or you can live your life crossing them."
- Shonda Rhimes

Glory, Martha and Emily sat around the kitchen table eating the delicious dinner Martha had prepared. Zeek's Pizza and red wine.

Glory said, "I love Zeek whoever he is. This hits the spot and I shall miss him on the open road."

"I'm not trying to keep you here," Martha said, "But, hey! If it works, great."

Glory laughed. "I'm not so easy. I am ready to get on the road. I hope I like it as much as I've dreamed of. I am a little worried I won't like it."

"I think you'll love it," Martha replied. "In spite of any reservations I've had you have the perfect RV for you and Freya. You've taken care to create an environment in your van to suit you. You've practiced camping and been careful. You will love camping."

"Thanks, Martha. I'm ready to embark my dreams for real."

Emily smiled. "I'm excited for you Glory and impressed by your bravery."

"Thanks, Emily. I'm glad you are part of our lives now."

Emily nodded. "It makes me happy to be with both of you. It feels like we are renewing our friendships, but even more we are creating together. I am grateful for this opportunity to get to know you both as adults and have a chance at a real life with real friends."

Glory woke before the sun came up. She tried to stay in bed. She reached over for Freya who licked her hand and then climbed on top of her. Freya licked Glory's nose and nudged her under the chin.

The moment the sky was lighter, Glory got up, grabbed Freya and took her out to the backyard.

She sat on the kitchen stoop watching the sun come up through the trees and over the mountains. She thought, *My new life is beginning today. I don't want to waste a precious minute of my life ever again.*

After Freya finished her morning business, Glory took the little fur ball and went out to the garage and into her new van. She sat down in the chair and thought, *Today is the day my adventure starts.* Freya nudged her doggie dish and whined for food. Glory chuckled. "You are one hungry little pup!"

Glory stood up and went to the cupboard where she had stashed the puppy food and put a small scoop in Freya's dish. "Eat up my little hungry mutt!" Freya got busy gobbling up the food. Glory set down a small dish of water and said, "As soon as you finish, we'll go back to the yard and wait for Martha to wake up."

"No need to wait," a voice called from the garage door. "I'm up and have started the coffee."

"Perfect," called Glory. "We'll be in shortly."

While Freya ate, Glory went through her list and checked the cupboards and closets to be sure she had everything. She looked at the red plates, yellow and red flowered mugs and matching yellow bowls. She smiled and said, "Edgar you might have loved these if you had been brave enough."

She loved the curtains she had hung along the windows in bright red and yellow flowers similar to the flowers on the mugs. She had bought a bright red cushion for Freya's bed and one for her chair. She had red towels, yellow cooking utensils and crockery in both yellow and red.

She checked the built-in navigation system to be sure Lake Easton State Park was still in the list of programed places she planned to visit. *After this trip I'll come back and work out any kinks in my packing and my planning then hit the road for an extended trip.* It was only an hour and a half drive east, but it felt like she was going to the moon, or at least China.

Freya finished eating and sniffed on the floor. Glory picked her up before her sniffing led to a floor clean up and carried her back through the kitchen and out the back door. The smell of coffee brewing and muffins baking set her taste buds at attention. After the dog finished, they came back into the kitchen. Martha was at the stove cooking bacon and setting out eggs.

Martha had been absolutely the worst cook ever, but Rob had been teaching her to cook a little and she was getting better. Rob had teased her she could burn water, then one day she did exactly that and nearly set her apartment on fire. At that point Rob stepped in and taught her some basics of cooking.

Martha said, "Rob taught me to make breakfast. Do you want your eggs scrambled or fried?"

"I'm looking forward to your breakfast for me. You are too good to me."

"No such thing. Just answer the question early bird."

Glory laughed. "Scrambled please with cheese. I should cook breakfast for you in the van."

"No. I've actually practiced scrambled eggs until I got them where they taste pretty good," Martha looked in the oven. "The muffins need a few minutes and then I will start the scramble. The coffee however is ready to roll."

"Hooray," Glory said. "I'm glad you are learning to cook. You've always made great coffee though which is good. Without coffee life would grind to a halt, so to speak." She went to the counter, took out a bright yellow mug and her travel mug. She poured a cup of coffee for Martha and filled her travel mug with coffee. They sat down at the table adding cream and sugar to their coffee.

"I can't cook a lot of things yet. But I've learned to fry bacon and scramble eggs. I can reheat muffins from the deli and even make them from a box if needed—I think; I hope. This is my first time to make them from a box. So, fingers crossed. Are you excited?"

Glory nodded and laughed. "I'm sure the muffins will be fine but if not, there is always drive through." She hoped she didn't look too much like a kid on Christmas morning. "But, yes, I'm excited and a little nervous too. Not about the plan but more about me being able to pull it off."

"You will do fine I'm sure. Besides you'll be back here in a few days and we can get any kinks worked out you might have missed. Although, knowing you, the biggest kink will be to take stuff out of the van and leave it here."

Glory nodded. "Oh, I know I over planned. I never over planned when I was younger, but Edgar has trained me well and for once I'm grateful to have learned some of his obsessive tricks to get ready for this change. Mostly I'm amazed I'm getting to do this."

"I am too. I'm happy I'm getting a chance to be a personal executive and personal accountant. I'm looking forward to using my education and training as a CPA and accountant. I'm glad while I'm working for you, I will also be working for me."

"In all of my excitement about my van life and travel plans, I never gave a thought to how much your life is changing too. You've bought a house, quit your job and taken on everything I don't want to deal with. I'm sorry I haven't thought more about your life! I'm most especially sorry I haven't paid attention to your needs and plans. What are your plans?"

Martha shook her head and grinned. "No need to apologize, but thanks anyway. You've had a monumental few weeks with your life upended. I'm not sure about my plans exactly but have ideas about women networking to help each other and maybe setting up funding for startups by women and training and educational scholarships. I also want to help women who need a boost or want to pull themselves up to a new life."

"Sounds great."

"I'm sure I have told you this," Martha continued, "But I've saved up a fair bit of money over the last ten years. Part of it I used for the down payment on the house. I still have money I want to invest in women. My money is not a great amount like what you have, but since you've given me the income and time to work on this, I think I can make a big difference for women with the money I've saved."

"I'm so glad to hear your ideas," Glory said. "When you've got a clearer picture of what you want to do, please share your ideas with me. It might be something I want to be a part of."

"Oh, I will happily share my ideas with you!" Martha said. "We are both setting off on new adventures. Me as a homeowner and executive assistant and you as a travel blogger and intrepid adventurer."

The oven timer went off.

"For now, I want to be a part of muffins and scrambled eggs and bacon. How about you?"

"Perfect."

Freya gave a sharp yike and Glory said, "You can have a nibble of bacon and eggs but no muffins." Freya cocked her head as if considering whether this was an adequate response. She curled up on Glory's feet to wait for her bacon and eggs.

Glory and Martha sat at the table talking about Glory's first trip and enjoying the peace of the morning as the sun's glow filtered into the kitchen. Glory thought the breakfast was one of the best she'd ever eaten and said so to Martha.

"Your taste buds are more alive because you are starting your own life. I'll take the compliment, regardless. As a fledgling cook I'll take any compliments I can get."

After breakfast Martha said, "I'll clean the dishes while you go shower and get ready to go."

Glory hugged Martha. "Thank you for helping make this possible."

"My pleasure. It was always possible you just didn't know it," Martha replied.

After Glory left the kitchen, Martha looked down at Freya and said, "You have to take care of our girl. She hasn't been on her own for a long time." Freya danced on her back legs to be picked up and Martha said, "Okay. Just for a minute though. I have work to do."

Glory hooked Freya's harness onto the passenger seat belt. Glory had bought a great doggie bed. It was elevated so Freya could see out the window while traveling.

Martha said, "Freya is already spoiled rotten. She looks so adorable and so happy and ready to hit the road with you."

Glory smiled and said, "She is more a companion than I ever expected her to be but she is so small I want to cuddle with her all the time. She weighed ten pounds today!"

"I'm sure cuddling is what she wants and food too," Martha answered.

Glory nodded. "Later today after I'm parked at a camping site at Lake Easton I'll write a blog post and let you know I've arrived safely."

"I'm so happy for you and know you will be great at this. Just don't pick up any strange men."

"A man is the last thing I want right now, especially a strange one. Maybe someday but not now."

"Okay," Martha said looking at her watch. "Let's quit gabbing and you get on the road. I've got work to do!"

Glory hugged Martha again, took a deep breath and climbed into the driver's seat of her van. She didn't know what else to say, so she started the van and hollered to Martha, "TTFN!" Martha waved back grinning from ear-to-ear.

Glory backed out of the driveway, grateful for the rear backup camera and said to Freya, "Let's hit the road little doggie." Freya barked in response and Glory drove to the end of the street. She looked in the side mirror and saw

Martha waving a goodbye. She stuck her hand out the driver's window and waved back.

Glory found her way out of the neighborhood on Sunset Way toward Interstate 90. She realized she was leaving town on her own for the first time. She had been talking about doing this for years but now it was real.

Glory didn't see Martha reach into her pocket, pull out her phone and immediately began to talk to someone and scurrying back into the house.

Jake pulled off Interstate 90 at Lake Easton. He wanted to take photos of the lake and surrounding area. *Liz could capture the beauty of all I've seen.* He realized he felt more and more free every day with less and less anger about Liz. "That's a good thing, buddy."

There was a campground that seemed nice, but he wanted a quieter, less developed place to camp. He talked with one of the rangers at the campground who said, "If you want quiet, primitive camping, the best place is up the Middle Fork road." She drew him a map and said, "There's a great place to stop and gas up, fast food and a grocery store too in North Bend. Take Exit 31 and you'll see it off to the right."

"I might just do that in a day or two. I thought I'd try up at Lake Kachess that another fella recommended."

The ranger, Lori was the name on her badge, nodded. "That is a great place too. It's beautiful but more primitive than this campground. I go there a lot when I have a few days off. There is water available but no electricity."

"I don't need electricity," Jake said. "The fella I talked to said there's good hiking there."

"He is right, there is. Both at Kachess and Middle Fork you'll find some of the best hiking anywhere." She looked at his cowboy boots. "Have you been hiking before?"

He laughed. "Oh, yeah. I've hiked all over Oklahoma and a lot of eastern

Texas. I'd never punish my good boots with hiking." He pointed to his cowboy boots. "I've got rugged hiking boots for the trail."

She smiled. "Then you're good to go, Cowboy."

He waved goodbye. *She is a nice woman but not really my style. Don't know why but she didn't trigger a thing for me other than being a good woman ready to help.*

Chapter 11

"If you invest in a girl or a woman,
You're investing in everyone else."
— Melinda Gates

As soon as Glory was out of sight, Martha pulled out her phone and called Jason. "Okay, the coast is clear. I want to do as much as possible in the next four days to surprise Glory when she comes home."

Jason answered. "I'm right around the corner with my crew and we'll be there in a few minutes and get busy working. We've lots to accomplish in a very short time."

Martha went into the kitchen and sat down at the kitchen table to make more lists and searches with her computer. In a few minutes she heard Jason knocking on the kitchen door.

She motioned for him to come in and invited him to sit at the table. He shook his head. "No thanks. If it's all the same to you, I'd like to get the crew working on that sliding door and deck. That is the biggest job we have to finish in only four days. I offered them overtime to work on Saturday."

"That sounds great. It will be a small investment to have things how I want them," Martha said. "While you get going on the guest bedroom, I will do more research on she-sheds."

"Fair warning, it will be very noisy around here."

She grinned. "No pain, no gain!"

Martha had found Jason while looking for a carpenter/contractor through the internet. On his website, *Jason The Carpenter,* his tag-line was "Quality remodels to fit your dreams. Small construction projects at a small price."

When she saw his last name, Walden, she realized he had been one of her trainees at the company where she worked. Jason had taken a sabbatical last year to start a new business as a carpenter. She looked at his website and liked all the woodwork he had on display. Some of his work was beautiful art.

When she clicked on the tab *Garden Sheds*, the array of possibilities stunned her. Many were run-of-the-mill sheds for garden supplies, lawnmowers and tools. However, there were a few that were retreat type sheds. Some were generic appearing, but a few were glamorous sheds and fit the she-shed ideas she had seen. He also had man-caves. They were interesting but not what she was looking for.

Previously, she had thought her she-shed would be her refuge. Now, she felt it was more important for it to become the base of her new work she was planning to build. She needed an office base and didn't want to drive anywhere to work. *Life is too short to spend hours driving to work. A few minutes of walking is more like it. I'm ready to quit using the kitchen table and dinning room table as my office.* She wanted her home to be her refuge. The she-shed would be the office.

The shed had to be beautiful and feminine. It must have covered outdoor space. This would be her office and base of operations. It meant she would need an office and a bigger general room for meetings and planning.

The house was also a priority for her. She made a list of changes she wanted to make to the house itself. She made a note there would need to be a gate and walkway for clients to access the backyard and her office.

First, however, she wanted to remodel the guest bedroom so that both bedrooms had beautiful bathrooms and private decks. Jason and his crew were working on the bedroom project first. She wanted it to be an inviting place for Glory when she was in town. The plan she and Jason came up with was a deck for the guest bedroom as well a small private garden. She wanted a beautiful retreat for guests, including Glory when she was off the road.

There was a lot of work to do in a short period of time. She wanted it to have already been done.

Her phone rang, and she jumped worried Glory was having problems. The caller ID read Emily Harris. She smiled and then said, "Hello! I'm so glad you called."

Emily laughed. "That's the best greeting to any phone call ever."

"No, seriously," Martha said, "You are exactly who I needed right now."

"Oh?" Emily asked.

"I want to pick your brain! I'll tell you what I want to talk with you about but first I want to know why you called."

"Well, after our conversation last night I've done soul searching about getting on with my life."

"Great. Me too."

"I'm thinking of stepping out on my own. I want to have my own real estate agency. I wanted to bounce ideas off you."

"I'm happy to listen and I always have opinions to spare."

Emily laughed. "That will do nicely. Do you have time this morning we could talk?"

"Sure. Come on over. I've got a ton of things I need advice about too. We can coach each other.

Chapter 12

"A Goddess Adventure represents
A combination of heart, head,
And soul work"
— Paula Weisflock

Glory reached up to the front deck of her van and turned the radio to KZOK her favorite rock station. She cranked up the volume and eased her way on to Interstate 90 heading east.

The mountains were a brilliant green touched with the golden sunshine. The light fog was lifting to the sky. The sky was clearing to a brilliant blue and made Glory smile. There was no rain in the forecast for the next few days even though it was only May. By this time every year, Glory longed for dry days and sunshine. Glory felt as if the world had given her a fantastic send off for her first adventure. "Thanks, Mother Nature," she said.

A few miles later, she saw Mount Si in the distance with its rocky, craggy face. As she drove toward North Bend, the mountain got bigger and bigger. It brought memories of her childhood. They weren't all great memories but after her father died, her mom made up for a lot of the pain she had suffered as a child. Living in their house at the end of Tanner Road was loving and peaceful. She still remembered the sound of the river and the smell of the pine in the woods surrounding their home. Her mom had bought the house with the insurance money from her father's death. It was the start of the best years of Glory's childhood.

On her right, she looked up to Rattlesnake Ridge and reminded herself of times in the first few years of marriage when she and Edgar had come to North Bend. She wanted to hike to Rattlesnake Ridge, and he reluctantly

103

agreed to hike to the top. The view of the whole valley enthralled her. She pointed out where she used to live with her mother as the Middle Fork of the Snoqualmie River turned north. Her mother's backyard was where they married. Glory remembered it as a sunny day filled with beauty and love and joy. She had hoped the memory of their wedding would bring Edgar some joy and help them move forward in more loving ways.

She remembered saying to him, "I love it up here. I always loved looking down at the river and seeing where we lived. My mother's home felt like a magical hidden garden; a place where love and peace brightened every day. Don't you feel you are on top of the world up here?"

Edgar had shaken his head. "No. I feel like I'm on a precipice waiting for the world to toss me off this ledge. I would rather sit at home watching the football game and drinking a lager."

Glory remembered how upset and sad she had felt. Now, with the events of the past few weeks changing her reflections on life, she said, "Oh Edgar, I wish we had enjoyed our lives more. I hope you find joy and happiness now. If I haven't said so out loud, thanks for the letter. It helped a lot."

She wiped away a tear and said to Freya, "Okay girly. We will not be sad anymore today. We are going live and love every minute of today."

Glory saw the exit for Easton Lake State Park and drove to the park gate. There, a nice young woman in her park ranger uniform who took her driver's license information and tag information. She gave her directions to the site she had prepaid for saying, "You're a little early but your site wasn't occupied last night so you are good to go there and get set up. The information I have is you are staying for four nights. Is our information correct?"

"Yes."

"Your checkout time will be Sunday morning. Check out time is by 11:00 a.m. It gives us time to clean up and prep the site for the next campers."

Glory nodded. "No problem. This is my maiden voyage in my van and my first time camping more than just in the driveway or local RV campground."

"You will love it. My name is Lori. I'll come by and checkup on you around 5:00 p.m. when I get off work, if you would like. I love traveling alone in my van and camping whenever and wherever I want."

"That's exactly what I want to do," Glory said, "It would be great if you check up on me. I'm a little nervous because I have never done this before. I would appreciate any advice or hints. I have wanted to do this for years and now here I am."

"I'll see you round five then."

"Great. I'll open a bottle of wine and we can sit and talk. In fact, I'll probably have a lot of questions by the time you arrive."

Lori laughed. "Lucky for you I love wine and talking about camping. I'll see you soon. Just follow the signs to your campsite. Relax and enjoy our beautiful day."

Using the backup camera, she backed her van into the parking slot of her campsite. She wanted to have it close to the hookups for electricity and water and the drainage for the gray water tank. She wanted to get settled so she could sit outside her van and enjoy lake. It took a few tries to get the van lined up just right. *I'll get better at this, I hope.* When she got the alignment with the lake and hookups how she wanted it, she got out of the van and went around to the sliding side door.

She opened the door and took out the leash line she had bought for Freya. She attached it to the hook outside the door and then to a nearby tree. When she took Freya out of the van, she clicked her leash to the line. Freya immediately walked around the site, exploring with her nose to the ground. Glory laughed at the little dog investigating the site as far as her leash and the line would allow.

Glory pulled her folding two-person chair out and sat down with a glass of water to read the campground rules and instructions. She had read women camping alone should always have at least two chairs out and a big pair of men's boots sitting by the steps to imply a man was traveling with the woman. "Oops, I forgot the boots." Glory made a note on her smart phone to go to Value Village and pick up a pair of used men's boots before her next trip.

When Freya had finished her investigations, she came over to Glory and jumped up on the chair beside her. "Well, what do you think?" Glory asked the little pup. Freya nuzzled her hand.

Glory sat watching the lake and petting the dog for a long time. She felt at peace and relaxed in ways she had not thought she would. She said to herself and the doggie, "This is what I've always dreamed of doing. I feel relaxed and at peace." She felt a small thrill deep inside. It felt as if her inner self was saying, "Yes!"

The sun rose higher in the sky as midday approached. The air was warming up. "I can take off this heavy jacket now." She stood and stretched, taking off her jacket and put it inside her van.

She pulled out the instruction sheet about how to hook up the water, gray water tank, black water tank and electricity. She plugged in the electric cord, fastened the water hose to her clean water tank and attached the gray water and black water tank hose to the sewage port in the ground. She double checked that everything was hooked up according to her instructions.

She put the instruction sheet back in the pocket of the sliding door. She texted Martha that she had arrived safely and was set up to camp. Martha replied, "Hooray for you!"

I need to ask Lori to check to be sure I've hooked up everything correctly, Glory thought. She closed the van door and locked the vehicle. She looked down at Freya "Let's go take a walk about and see what we can see around the campgrounds. It's time to get a move on."

Glory could tell by the little dog's prancing, it delighted Freya to go on a walk.

Glory put her smart phone in her pocket expecting she would want to take photos for her first blog post. She did not know what she would call the blog, but she didn't have to decide right now. All she needed to do for the time being was to walk and breathe and enjoy. They walked from the campsite and then followed the paved trail towards the lake.

Along the way, Glory spotted the children's play area. She stopped and watched the children on the swings and climbing gym. They laughed, played, chased each other and squealed on the playground equipment. She felt a deep ache and longing for children of her own. "It will come if it is to be," She whispered to herself. Her thoughts helped her to calm back into the peace of the park.

Freya tugged on the leash as she sniffed at everything she found on the ground. Glory pulled her away from other dogs' leavings and bits of dangerous things on the ground. Freya pulled and tugged on the leash with her own ideas about where to walk.

Glory laughed. "Listen, Freya," Freya looked up at Glory. "We will have to get a few things straight."

Freya sat down and looked up at Glory. "You are too cute for your own good, little doggie. I think I need to go on-line and find advice about training a dog."

Freya cocked her head back and forth a few times, then whined and took off walking as fast as the leash would allow. "So much for my expertise with doggie training!"

Glory grinned and realized she hadn't felt this happy in so many years she couldn't think of any time when she had been as happy as this day. She muttered, "I feel a little drunk but only had coffee and water today." She didn't notice the couple that was passing her until the woman spoke up.

"Are you all right, honey?" The woman said.

"Oh!" Glory said, startled and looked at the woman. She was almost as short as Glory's five-foot frame and a little rounder. She had rosy cheeks, white hair, a few wrinkles on her face and the bluest eyes Glory had ever seen.

"I'm sorry; I didn't see you." Then she grinned. "I'm fine just muttering to myself."

The man beside the woman grinned. "I do that a lot and she's always asking if I'm all right. But she rarely calls me honey!" He was taller than the woman and lanky looking with salt and pepper hair and deep dark eyes that were nearly black. He jumped as his wife poked him with her elbow.

The woman rolled her eyes at her husband. "Ignore him. I'm Helen Cunningham and this beast beside me is Ralph."

Glory held out her hand to the woman, and they shook hands. "I'm Glory Shaw. Wait. I'm Glory Pennington and this beast beside me is Freya." At the sound of her name Freya danced on her hind legs in front of Helen.

Helen laughed and bent to pet the dog. "You are just the cutest thing and so is your dog!"

"Thank you."

Ralph asked, "So is your name Shaw or Pennington?"

"Ralph, don't bother the woman. She can be whoever she wants to be."

"Thanks Helen, I really appreciate you saying that. However, Ralph, I'll be happy to tell you. I've been Glory Shaw for four miserable years. My husband was going to divorce me, but he died before he could. My maiden name was Pennington and I forgot I had decided I'm taking back my maiden name."

"Good for you, hon," Helen said. "I say to let the man keep his name. The woman giving up hers is for the birds!"

Ralph grinned. "And now you know why my last name is Richards and hers is Cunningham."

"Wow," Glory said. "I thought only a few rebels ever kept their maiden names when they married."

Ralph nodded. "Oh, we are married all right, and she is a top-drawer rebel. Coming up on fifty years together the end of the month. At first, I thought she didn't really love me because she didn't take my name. Then when she told me how crazy it was for her to have to change her name. She said it amounted to being subjugated to a man by taking his name, I had to decide. Marry a rebel or be miserable. I chose to not be miserable."

Helen grinned. "I've been a rebel since the early 60s. But if he had insisted, I take his name we both would have been miserable."

"Why?" Glory asked.

"Because I wouldn't have married him, and it would have been a tragedy. If I had married him and taken his name, I would have felt diminished all my life."

Ralph reached over and picked up Helen's hand and kissed the back of her hand. "And we've been mostly happy ever since we met and married. I am sorry your husband was leaving you and then he died."

"Me too," Glory nodded. "It's been about six weeks now since he died. I was so angry at first all I could do was swear and shout."

Nodding towards Helen, Ralph said, "Her favorite word is 'fuck'."

"Mine too!" Glory said.

Helen shook her head. "I use the word a lot but really my favorite word is 'love'. I think if we all loved more, we would have less need of words like 'fuck'."

"You are probably right," Glory said. "When I found out Edgar was divorcing me, I kept repeating 'fuck' over and over and over again. As my anger dissipated, I could think more clearly. I have friends who love me and helped me sort through the mess. I haven't said it as much lately."

Helen patted Glory's hand. "That's good to hear." Then she looked up at Ralph. "Let's get a move on, buddy. I've got to go pee."

Glory laughed. "It was nice meeting you. Can I quick take your picture before you go?"

"Sure," Ralph said. "Why?"

"I want to write a blog about my adventures and the people I meet."

"Snap it quick. I'm an old woman with a bathroom calling my name. We can talk more later."

Glory quickly took a photo of their smiling faces. She pointed to her campsite. "I'm in the big black van over there. Please come by and chat anytime. I'll be here for four days assuming my planning was adequate."

Ralph and Helen waved goodbye and Ralph said, "We will come by and check out your rig later."

Glory was grinning ear-to-ear. *I'm probably being silly, but I feel free and happy. I talked with someone I didn't know, and the world kept on spinning.* "Woot!" she said, with a sense of well-being and awe. She tugged on Freya's leash and said, "Let's go walk down by the lake."

Jake loved Kachess Lake. Lake Easton was pretty, but Kachess Lake felt special to him. *I've seen nothing more beautiful than this. I wish I had a rowboat, and I'd be out there on that lake like others are. I wouldn't take my horse on that boat though.* He grinned at the thought.

He spent four nights and four days there. The stars at night were something mighty to behold. Last night, he had hiked up a short trail near the campground but away from the lights. He laid his blanket on a sandy patch of ground and waited for the stars to multiply.

As the stars shining increased, the Milky Way showed up. *It looks different here than at home. There are a lot more stars here.* Jake was glad the moon wasn't up yet but was happy to be high enough and dark enough where he lay to see more and more stars and the Milky Way become clearer the longer he laid there.

I don't know what draws me to the stars. I think I'll buy me a telescope when I get home. At the ranch he had all the lights on a remote control so he could turn them all off. It was when he got the best views of the stars and the Milky Way.

He laid there thinking about his life. *I wish things had turned out different with me and Liz. It's been about six weeks since the divorce and I'm feeling more settled now.*

Jake had gotten an email from her with photographs of the mountains of New Mexico. There were also photos of pueblos and the Native Americans who lived there long before the white man was ever around to steal their land and their religions. The photos made him feel as if something ancient yet still alive was buried deep in the faces of the people in her photographs. *I'm glad you are doing something you love Liz. I wouldn't be surprised to hear in years to come of your fame and fortune as a photographer.*

He had replied to her email with similar thoughts and feelings.

She had written back, "I struggle to believe I haven't been to a spa since our divorce. My nails are broken and often caked with dirt. When I shower the water is muddy for the first few minutes. Yet, I'm happy and content. Every day, I find new miracles through my camera lens. I love every minute of my life dirt and all. I met a fellow photographer. He and I have had dinner a few times. Don't know what will come of it but when I meet a man, I want to hook up with, I'll make it clear about babies before I even let him kiss me. Thanks for everything, Jake."

He smiled remembering that email. What surprised him the most was that he wasn't angry with her anymore. *Better yet, I'm not jealous of the other fella whoever he is. I'm happy she is doing well and moving on although I'd like to see those dirty fingernails just to be sure.*

Jake heard rustling around him. It was a sure sign the night creatures were out too. He wasn't afraid of them but thought *If I don't have to wrestle a bear tonight it would be a good thing.* He stood up, picked up his blanket and reaching in his pocket he took out a small flashlight. He followed the trail back to his campsite and his home in the bed of Little Darlin'.

Chapter 13

"The most difficult thing is the decision to act,
The rest is merely tenacity."
- Amelia Earhart

After returning from their walk, Glory grabbed a quick snack and gave Freya a chewy treat and some water. Glory sat in her chair and pulled up the table from the armrest. She put her laptop on the table and said, "Okay folks, it is time for our first blog." She opened the video camera and said, "Showtime." She turned on the camera and spoke.

"Hello to everyone back home in Issaquah. Freya and I have arrived at Lake Easton State Park. It is beautiful here, and we are camped in a spot right on the lake. I have photos of the lake and the people I met. I'll post photos on the blog in a few minutes. We've already made some new friends. Lori Hughes, an assistant camp ranger, is very nice. She'll be coming by after she gets off work to chat and have a glass of wine. Helen and Ralph are a delightful couple we met while walking down to the lake. Can you believe it? They've been married for fifty years! Amazing. We plan to get together a time or two before I leave Lake Easton to head back to Issaquah. So far, the rig is working great and Freya loves every minute of our trip although she thinks she is the boss. Let me know if you have any ideas about how to convince her to let me be the boss. Goodbye for now and share the blog!"

Glory replayed the video and said to Freya, "Well, I think the video turned out good. What do you think?" Freya looked up from the chew stick for a few seconds and then got busy chewing more. "Must be fine with you too then." Glory took a quick photo of Freya working on her chew stick.

Glory needed to get busy on building her blog website but thought, *I still don't have a name for the blog yet.* She had planned to use a free blogging software and design, but Martha had suggested she buy a domain. *Buying a domain is where the problem is. I want the domain name to reflect the title of my blog.*

"Oh, Freya," She said, "What am I going to call the blog site?" Freya kept chewing. *Obviously, her priorities differ from mine*, Glory thought.

She opened her computer and went to the hosting software company Martha had suggested and created a login for herself. "Now," she said, "Let's look at what to do now." She had to have a name for blog website and there was the rub. She got up and walked to the fridge and pulled out a bottle of water. She sipped the water as she paced around the muttering and mumbling to herself. "Think, think, think Glory! This can't be this hard. Come on, Gloriana, you're on the road and you are ready to post your first video and write the blog." She stopped pacing and looked down at Freya. The dog was merrily chewing on her treat, oblivious that Glory was getting more and more frustrated.

Glory tried out a few ideas for a name for her website. She said, "Glory's Travels? Nope. On the Road with Glory? Nope." Freya perked up and watched Glory as she continued to pace. When Glory said, "On The Gloriana Road" Freya barked. "Is that a yes?" Freya barked in response and then went back to chewing. "OK," Glory said, "On The Gloriana Road it is then."

She sat back down and, on the computer, typed in a search for a domain titled 'Gloriana Road'. *It doesn't like spaces*, she thought. She put in 'glorianaroad.com'. "Bingo!" She clicked on the domain, purchased it and brought up the website dashboard. Glory watched the tutorials on how to build the website and chose a template. It seemed to work for a simple blog with videos.

"For now, I will keep it simple," She said. "Just a photo of the trail we walked today and my first blog post." *I'm talking to myself and a dog!* Glory thought and grinned at how happy she was.

Turning back to her computer she opened the blog editor and typed. When she stopped typing an hour later, she looked up and realized the sun was no longer high in the sky. It wasn't dusk yet, but soon would be. Freya was curled up in a ball, sleeping on her feet. "Wow," she said in a whisper, "Time flies when you're having fun."

She felt exhilarated having written her first blog. She found the media buttons to add her video to her blog post. "This is so much easier than I thought it would be," she said. Freya licked her toes. Glory said, "Just a few more seconds and I'll have published my first blog and video post. Then we can go for a walk."

Freya tugged on the leash wanting to walk much faster than Glory. The scene was beautiful with the sun rays shining low across the water reflecting shades of orange, gold and pink as the sun started the downward path to setting. Glory stopped and took photos of the lake with all the beautiful colors and the reflections from the trees. She heard a whistle and saw the train circling around the far side of the lake. "It could be anytime in the last hundred years," she said as she watched the train.

"Yes, it could," said a voice behind her. Glory turned to see Lori Hughes smiling at her. "I see you two ladies are enjoying the beauty of our lake."

"I'm enjoying the beauty of everything here," Glory said with a chuckle. "Freya is busy smelling every single inch of the park."

Lori bent down and scratched Freya behind the ears. "You are such a cutie. I could just gobble you up."

Freya licked her hand as Glory laughed. "She thinks she is a princess."

"Well, she is adorable," Lori said. "How are things going so far for your first camping trip?"

Glory looked up at the trees and sky and then back across the lake. "I'm pretty much in heaven, I think. Everything is so beautiful, and the campground is much quieter than I thought it would be."

"Give it a month and we'll be full to the brim with families and friends. On the weekends, the campground is usually full but during the week we often have sites available. This early in the season it's easy to find a spot. Middle of the summer is tougher."

"I'm sure that is true," Glory said. "I did not know such a wonderful campground was this close to Issaquah. I've hiked a few trails but not nearly as many as I want. This is my first camping trip of many to come."

Lori held up a bottle of wine. "Are you ready for this?"

"Sure! Let's go back to my campsite and I'll get us two glasses."

They walked back to the campsite talking while Freya continued to sniff at the ground all along the way. Glory was surprised at the ease with which she and Lori seemed to connect. She had other friends with Martha being her closest friend, but Glory realized how much she had limited herself to just a few friends. It was a little scary reaching out to form new relationships, but it somehow seemed like it was exactly the right thing to do. Martha had encouraged her to reach out, but Glory had resisted. *I wonder why I resisted so much?*

As they walked up to Glory's campsite, Lori said, "I have to say your van is beautiful."

"Wait until you see the inside." She attached Freya's leash to the line and then pulled her keys from her pocket. She unlocked the side door and motioned for Lori to go into the van. Once they were both inside Glory saw Lori looking around the van.

"This is beautiful, and the wood working is amazing. Obviously, this is a custom van."

Glory nodded. "I love it."

"Me too! I especially love the brilliant colors and how the feminine is a great juxtaposition for the masculine feeling woodwork."

"I hadn't thought of it that way, but you are right. It feels cozy and loving. Let me get the glasses. The wine opener is in the top drawer there." She pointed to the drawer. She had bought wine glasses without stems so they would be easier and safer to set down while camping.

Lori saw the glasses. "The glasses are beautiful."

"I splurged on hand-painted glasses. I love that each glass has two or three different flowers."

After she opened the wine and they had their filled glasses, Lori motioned to the door. "Let's sit outside and talk."

Glory followed Lori out of the van and set the glasses on the table. "How about I make campfire?" Lori asked.

"That would be great. I've never made a campfire."

Lori said, "I'll build the fire and show you how to use as little wood as possible to have a great fire. You should plan on buying your own firewood since it is against the rules to pick up wood in the forest."

"Thanks for the information," Glory said.

"I'll use wood that someone left here," Lori said. "Lots of people leave what wood they don't use but you can't count on it."

Glory nodded as she added wood to her list on her smart phone.

Lori continued, "A lot of folks just put a bunch of wood in there and throw in a match. It always amazes me that a forest fire can happen with a flick of a cigarette, yet campfires can be hard to light and keep burning. The way I start is with dry kindling or brush and small sticks on the inside the fire and adding a few larger sticks gets things going. Bring fire-starters with you too. You can make them with dryer lint, paraffin and egg cartons or toilet paper cardboard tubes."

"Thanks, I'll remember to make some. Your demonstration was helpful. I thought I would look on the internet for a video of how to build a campfire."

Lori laughed. "I'm sure you would have found a bunch of videos. There are a lot of ways to build a campfire. A lot depends on where you are, what wood sources and kindling are available and what the weather is like. This campfire will only last about an hour but that is what most folks need; a small campfire to sit around and talk. You can always add more wood to make it last longer. My theory is use as little wood as you need for what you need and then more will be available for later."

They sat down in the camp chairs Glory had sat out and quietly watched the fire. Freya curled up on the rug between the chairs and snuggled down for a snooze.

"I think Freya is tired after her explorations."

Glory nodded. "She is a ball of energy but once she has spent her energy she sleeps. I've been amazed by her. It is much easier having a dog than I thought."

"I have a yellow lab named Buttercup. I noticed that Freya has her license tag but no other identifiers. I'm sure you have her chipped since they do that at the pound and most rescue groups. Have you considered a backup ID tag?"

"Should I?"

Lori nodded. "I think so. I have friends in Wenatchee that have built up a startup called PetHub. Their ID tags have QR codes. What it means is anyone with a smart phone can scan the tag and let PetHub and the dog's owner know where their dog is. It is a great backup for your sweet Freya."

"I'll check them out."

"I'll send you the link to their website. It is very inexpensive, and they are great people. Buttercup is my partner in life, and I want her protected."

"You are right, and I want Freya protected too. No fella then?"

Lori shook her head. "Nope. Not interested in men. The right woman hasn't come along yet. But she will or else I'll come along into her life."

Glory said, "I'm impressed with your faith. I am interested in men but chose poorly the first time. Although I'd like to have a life partner, I'm not sure at all I'll ever marry again."

"Why?"

Glory smiled wistfully. "I may not be cut out for marriage. Being a wife is not what it's cracked up to be."

"Marriage is one thing," Lori said, "Having a life partner is something else entirely different and you can have both or none. It seems having a life partner is much more important than marriage. If marriage happens, fine, but I prefer the old ways and I mean the old ways. You stand with your chosen life partner, hold hands and swear fealty to each other. That's it."

"I've never heard of that."

"It's called hand-fasting. Way back then no one accepted hand-fasting with someone of the same gender!"

Glory laughed. She looked down at her hands saw the whiteness where her wedding ring used to be. "I think one of the problems for Edgar and I was that he chose me, we married and then we got busy being a couple. I'm not sure we were ever physically or emotionally a good match. There just wasn't any fire there. Mentally we were a terrific match. We had long conversations about a lot of stuff. We never discussed the things we needed to talk about to make the marriage loving. We weren't a good match emotionally, psychologically, recreationally or socially."

"Then why did you get married?" Lori asked.

Glory thought about this question for a few minutes. "Because it seemed like the right thing to do at the time, I think. Also, perhaps, because we were both lost. Our conversations and long discussions I feel led us to believe we should be together. It wasn't enough."

Lori nodded. "Maybe thinking was the wrong thing to do. For me it is all about feeling. Feeling that something is right is the most important part for me. So, did you get divorced then?"

"Almost," Glory nodded. "Before that could happen, he died."

Lori's mouth dropped open. "Wow. Just wow. I'm so sorry."

Glory smiled softly. "Me too especially since over the last few weeks since his death I realized he was a better man than I gave him credit for. Yes, he was difficult and not in sync with me and my desires. The problems in our marriage were not just because of Edgar's problems. I too have responsibilities for the way things went in our marriage. I've been learning a lot about him and myself. I wish I had been more aware of our inner dynamics years ago. I could have saved both of us a lot of heartache and grief."

"Maybe the Universe has been letting you make your choices and learn from them."

Glory smiled at her. "You sound like my friend Martha. That is totally something she would say."

"Then she is a marvelous woman!"

"She is. You two should meet."

"Matchmaking?"

Glory looked at Lori and shrugged. "Maybe, but I really think it is more like friendship making. Martha is so marvelous and put together. When I grow up, I want to be like her."

"Is she lesbian?"

Glory thought about her answer. "I know she has dated a few men but not over one or two dates. In high-school she said to me one time 'if I met a man like you, I'd fall in love' so maybe she is but I've never known of her dating women. I know that when we talk about men, Martha side-steps discussion of forming a relationship with a man. I wonder," Glory said. "It's crazy I'm her best friend and don't know for sure!"

Lori smiled. "Sometimes when we have close friends, we are afraid to be who we really are around them because we don't want to lose them. Sometimes we don't know ourselves until the right situation presents itself."

"How did you know?"

"I met a guy I really liked a lot. We dated for a few weeks and then one night after a terrific dinner and romantic movie I went back to his home with him. We had sex but not only did I really not enjoy it I knew I never wanted to do that with a man ever again in my life. It was nice when we were kissing and hugging but as soon as the clothes were off it didn't feel right. We decided to be friends instead of lovers." Lori grinned at the memory.

"Maybe because he wasn't the right one for you."

Lori shook her head. "I thought so until I had my first woman to woman encounter. She was so beautiful and the light in her eyes just turned me on. We had a passionate relationship for a few months. Then she asked if I'd like to go to Brazil with her and do nature volunteering."

Glory grinned. "You're here and not in Brazil."

"Exactly. I realized that I enjoyed the sex and her company but wasn't interested in a committed lifelong relationship, at least with her and I didn't want to go to Brazil."

"How did she react?"

"Great. She said she was certain what I would say, but she enjoyed our relationship and thought it might be long-term. When we parted, and she headed off to Brazil she said, 'Hang in there. The right woman will come along. I have faith in you.' Then she kissed me and got in the taxi and headed off. We still write to each other by email and follow each other on-line but we both are happy we didn't join up permanently. She taught me a lot about myself and I'll be forever grateful."

Glory smiled. "That is a beautiful story. I'm hoping that as I get to know myself better and be more of who I really am from the inside out the right man will enter my life. I'd love to have a long and loving relationship filled with children and puppies and joy."

"There you go," Lori said. "Great plan."

Jake had been at Lake Kachess for nearly a week. *That girl at Lake Easton was right. There is really fine hiking around here.* He had hiked a lot and seen the forest up close. There were several small lakes around and each of them different from the others. *I'm feeling relaxed and more at home in my own skin. I haven't thought of Liz much at all the past few days other than wanting her to see the beauty of this place. I want her to be happy.*

Now he thought of her he recognized the pain was still there, but the anger and grief were dissipating.

I'll never be able to forget the death of my child. I know that the signs the marriage was not a good fit were there; I ignored them. I was too full of myself and my own sense of honor and duty to call it quits earlier. Those thoughts helped him let go of his deep anger. He felt lighter and more whole.

If the Middle Fork does me this much good, I'll be able to head home with a lighter heart and ready to pursue my life whatever it brings.

Jake shut the door of his camper. He climbed into his pickup and patted the dashboard said, "Okay Little Darlin' we're finally headed to the Middle Fork Trail. Let's see if it is all Rob cracked it up to be. He drove toward Interstate 90 and then on west to North Bend.

Chapter 14

"No, no! The adventures first,
explanations take such a dreadful time."
— Lewis Carroll

It had been a great four days for Glory. She felt more confident about being on her own and yet she enjoyed the interactions with all the people she met at Lake Easton. She felt an inner peace with her choices recently and had a feeling of being alive she was reveling in.

Glory double checked the campsite to be sure she had cleaned it up and picked up all of her belongings. She appreciated Lori and the park too much to leave even a crumb behind.

She loaded Freya into her seat, buckling her into her safety harness. When she shut the door, Freya stood up with her paws on the window. *She is too cute*, Glory thought. Then she realized *I love my little dog. She is a great companion. I need to remember to tell Rob he was right. It'll go to his head and he will talk about it for years! I will order a t-shirt I saw on the internet: "Go With Dog!" I need that.*

She tossed her jacket into the camper through the back-side door and using her keys to lock that door. She walked around the van making sure all the windows and the top vents were closed. She got into the van and said to Freya, "Okay. Let's go see Auntie Martha." Freya gave a little "yike" in what Glory thought of as her "yes" voice.

When they got to the park exit, Lori came out of her hut and said, "Here's my card. My personal email and cellular number are on the back. Please keep in touch and let me know how things go for you."

Glory smiled at Lori. "I will. We are friends now. I don't have any business cards yet, but I'll send you an email tonight with my details."

"That will work for me."

"Thank you so much for all you've taught me. I feel confident I can keep going on the road and loving every minute of my journeys. Thanks for giving me confidence."

"Hey, it's what friends are for. Tell Martha there is a great gal out this way she might want to meet."

Laughing, Glory said, "Well I might mention it. Can I take a photo of you? It might help to get Martha to come your way."

"Sure. Pull your van up so it doesn't block the exit. I'll come stand by your van next to Freya."

Glory pulled her van up, parked and got out of the van. She went around to the passenger side and Lori stood there petting Freya. Glory took several shots and then said, "Why don't you stand by the ranger hut and let me photograph you there too." She took several more photos of Lori by the ranger hut.

Glory showed Lori the photos on her smart phone. Lori grinned. "Those ought to give Martha a few ideas about me."

"Yes, they should," Glory agreed. They hugged. "Thanks for everything!"

As Glory drove out of the campground, she looked in the side mirror to see Lori waving goodbye. She waved back through the open window.

It had been a fantastic trip and good experience. It surprised her how easily she had met people and made friends. She had several scraps of paper and business cards of folks she had met who wanted her to stay in touch. *I need to get busy writing the first newsletter. I can mail out to those who just gave me addresses and email those who use email.*

Glory had read on-line RV campers were a friendly group of people and from time-to-time they met up with each other; sometimes at planned events and sometimes through sheer serendipity. She now knew many more people and lots of things about their lives. *I can't believe how much more grown up I feel and yet I feel younger at the same time. I wonder what future trips will bring?*

She stopped in North Bend to fill up with gas because it would be an easier in and out than in Issaquah. She was pumping gas into the van when she looked up to see a man in cowboy boots, wearing a cowboy hat walking towards her. As he got closer, she could see his clear blue eyes and curly blond hair poking out from under his hat.

He smiled at her. "I don't know if you meant to have that jacket dragging along with you but thought I'd point it out."

Glory walked around the van and looked where he was pointing and said, "Damn! I thought I'd locked that door, and I'd put away everything."

She pulled her keys out of her pocket and started to unlock the door to put the jacket back in but as soon as she touched it the door opened. "Wow," she said. "I don't understand how that happened."

"I do," the cowboy said. "I had a similar rig once, and it always seemed the lock turned opposite of what I thought it should to engage. I got in the habit of testing it was indeed locked. You are lucky it didn't damage the door. The jacket, on the other hand, looks pretty beat up." He grinned and pointed down at the jacket.

"You're right this jacket is shot." She opened the door and tossed the jacket back in the van. "Thank you so much for pointing this out."

He reached out a hand to shake her hand. "You're welcome. My name is Jake. I'm glad I could help."

Glory shook his hand, felt a little tingle and was aware of how warm and comfortable his hand felt holding hers. "I'm Glory. This is my first trip in this rig but I guess it shows."

The man shook his head, pulled off his hat and ran his fingers through his hair. Glory saw it was a little curly and definitely blonde. "It took me many trips to figure out how to lock the damn door. You're doing fine. Where are you headed?"

"To Issaquah where I used to live and then after a few days of visiting back on the road," Glory answered. "Where are you going?"

"I'm heading up the Middle Fork Road to find a campsite and then do some hiking."

"That sounds great. I love the Middle Fork River. I used to live here in North Bend with my mother. We lived where the Middle Fork turns north. There's lots of good hiking up there. Hope you have a good time." Then she grinned and pointed at his feet.

He grinned. "It has already been pointed out to me that cowboy boots aren't a good choice for hiking. I'm a cowboy but I love the outdoors. And I own more than one kind of footwear."

Glory laughed. "Me too!"

"You don't look like a cowboy or even a cowgirl," He pointed out. "But I'm the sort of person who likes all comers even if they can't ride a horse."

"You are right, I don't know how to ride a horse," Glory smiled up at him. Jake felt a little flip of his heart when she smiled at him.

Glory noted he was tall. Taller than Edgar who had been five feet eleven inches tall. "I might just have to put learning to ride a horse on my list of things to learn to do." It surprised her to realize she was actually flirting with this man and he with her. *Flirting is fine. Besides, we will probably never see each other again.*

He grinned at Glory. She noted the way his smile reached his blue eyes and seemed to light them up. He said, "Let me know when you want to learn, and I'll happily teach you."

She nodded. "I'll think about it. I've got to get going or I'll miss dinner with my friends. It was nice meeting you, your boots and your hat."

He laughed, put his hat back on, touched the rim with his forefinger. "Thank you, ma'am. It was a pleasure talking with you."

"Thanks again," Glory said. As he waved and walked away, she couldn't help noticing his beat up, tight blue jeans and how good they looked on him. She smiled to herself. *Don't get any ideas. You are not looking for a man.*

She double checked to be sure the door was indeed locked. *It was nice to flirt and feel the attraction reciprocated.* For now, though, she needed to drive. Glory was excited to get back to Martha's house and tell her everything that had happened on her first voyage. It felt weird to think of the house as Martha's, but it also felt like freedom.

She got in her van and watched as Jake the Cowboy pulled out ahead of her. He turned right on Bendigo Boulevard toward Mt. Si and the Middle Fork Road. She was turning left toward the interstate. He waved to her, and she waved back. *That was a pleasant little diversion even though I ruined a jacket to meet him. Good thing I didn't care a lot about the jacket.*

She felt happy and free and a little sexy as she entered Interstate 90 and headed west for the short drive to Issaquah. She was smiling, and it felt good. Fantastic. *I wonder what Martha has been doing for these few days? Whatever it is, I'm sure it is good and helping both herself and me move forward.*

Jake smiled to himself as he waved goodbye to Glory at the stop-light on Bendigo Boulevard. He whistled. "What a mighty fine-looking woman, Jake."

He drove toward the heart of the little town of North Bend. *Maybe I should have asked for her phone number.* "Nope. I'm not ready for another woman in my life." *It is too soon.*

He had only been divorced for nearly two months. He hated that he was divorced. When he married he had thought it was for life. But life turned out differently than he had expected. If life had taught him anything, it was the next time he fell in love he would be clear about what he wanted in life.

He was glad that Liz was moving on. She was doing her internship in photography in New Mexico and doing well with that. Jake did not know what she would do after she finished the program. He hoped she'd find what she was looking for and find the love she needed. Being a mother was probably not going to be in the picture.

Jake was glad he and Liz worked out a peaceful divorce. He had wept for hours the day the divorce was final. It felt like a steel door had slammed his heart shut. He still felt a deep ache about not being able to trust himself as a man a woman would want to have babies with. But he had to admit, so far the traveling and camping had helped a lot and his heart was lighter.

I'm free to do what I want. I bought the ranch down in the Kiamichi Mountains of Oklahoma before I even met Liz. I had big plans for a house full of kids, dogs and a loving wife for the ranch. I've got the ranch but nothing else. Maybe now I'm settling down and Liz is doing something new and different to build back her life, things will change for me too. He loved his ranch, small though it was, and he loved his life there. *I wish Liz had liked it more.* "If wishes were horses," he said aloud.

He would never get rich being a rancher and part-time big animal veterinarian, but he was happy with his life there. He had a few horses, boarded and trained several horses. His hopes for a riding school, special events for kids when school was out, possibly helping vets were still just hopes. The pasture rentals helped the money issues a lot. He took care of his animals and was vet for some of the surrounding ranches. All together it made a good living. He made enough to pay all the bills and save some. That was enough. Almost. *All I need is the right woman and my life would be perfect.* Then shook his head. "I'm better off alone, at least for now" he muttered. "Flirting is as far as I'm going."

He knew deep down he couldn't be happy and fulfilled without a loving woman in his life. But he worried he couldn't be happy with one either. *I know no woman will change my life suddenly.*

He thought of Glory and wondered again if he had made a mistake not getting her phone number. "No. You need to pull yourself together and think about how you really want your life to be. Once you know that you can build the life you want." He smiled. *Build it and they will come. If that worked in*

Field of Dreams maybe it will work for me too.

Chapter 15

Glory pulled into the driveway a little surprised the house didn't look different. *Don't be silly. It's only been four days.* Before she could put the van in park Martha was on the front porch waving. Glory smiled and waved back. She let Freya out of her harness, picked her up and walked up to the porch and Martha. "I don't know why," Glory said, "But I thought the house would look different."

Martha smiled. "Just wait. There is more to this house than the front porch."

They walked inside. Martha swept her arm to show Glory the living room. "Now what do you think? I painted the living room walls a light peach and the trim that had been white is now a soft ivory color," Martha said.
"I love the color!" Glory said. Looking around the room she saw that Martha had moved in her own furniture and taken out the old white furniture. "Wow," Glory said "Your furniture looks great in here too. The deep reds and burnished golds look great with the walls. I love that it feels so warm and inviting yet feminine just walking in here."

"Wait until you see the guest bedroom." Martha walked across the living room and to the bedroom hallway. Glory followed Martha. When they reached the guest bedroom Martha stepped aside and let Glory go in first. As Glory walked into the guest bedroom, tears immediately came into her eyes. "My mother's rocking chair is here. I love the red, green and yellow floral bedspread; it matches my chair perfectly. The walls look like butter!"

Martha laughed. "Yes, they do, and the color is actually named butter. I'm so glad you like it."

"I love it." Glory walked over to the bed and touched the bedspread. "This is so beautiful and floor to ceiling curtains to match! Look Freya, there's your bed!" Glory put Freya in the dog bed and Freya immediately rolled around in the bed and then begged to have her belly scratched. Glory obliged. "Thank you so much Martha. This is a great surprise."

"You are welcome. I started working on this room as soon as you were out of sight on Wednesday. It was important for you to have a landing place where you are loved and safe anytime you want to be here. I want you to always think of this as home base where you can come anytime and hang here as often and as long as you want. I might use it occasionally as a guest bedroom when you aren't here but mostly this room is for you."

"Anyone would love to be in this room." Glory hugged Martha. "I knew you loved me but this is a very special room. This room feels like home. I don't know what else to say other than thank you."

"Say nothing more. Your delight is my reward. Did you see the photos on the walls?" Martha asked.

"I didn't notice them, but they are beautiful too. There are photos from my trip to Lake Easton too! And you, me and Rob at high school graduation. You even hung the wedding photos of Edgar and I and the whole party. I love everything about this room."

Martha opened the closet doors. "I didn't have to do much with your things since we had already traded rooms. Are you ready for the next surprise?"

"Yes! Surprise me again."

She walked over to the bathroom and opened the door. "Take a peek in here," Martha said. The walls were the same soft, buttery yellow, but the towels matched the red of her rocking chair. There were photos and paintings of various flowers on the walls. "It's perfect."

"Now," Martha said, "Follow me. The best is yet to come." She walked across the room and pulled back the side window floor to ceiling curtains. There instead of a window was a sliding glass door that had not been there before. Martha said, "Come see what is here." She opened the door and Glory followed her to a small deck and a portion of the yard fenced off to enclose a small, private garden space. There were two chairs and a bistro table with Moroccan tile top, a dog food dish and water dish with a dog bed between the two chairs.

Glory looked up and saw that there was even a bright red awning with yellow trim over the deck which was not only beautiful but would keep the deck dry and cozy. There were some potted plants in multiple shades and patterns of yellow and red. A few were on the deck and others scattered around the garden. A hummingbird feeder hung on the outside corner of the awning.

"This is like a secret garden," Glory said. "It feels feminine and magical. How did you get this done in such a short time?"

"I have great contacts!" Martha answered. "Really. One of my former coworkers struck out on his own about a year ago as a contractor and cabinet builder. Jason has been struggling financially and had nothing going on for the next few weeks. He gladly came and built this garden for you. Jason and I had to sneak around so he could come over and measure and plan things. He special ordered the door and the awning and bought the planters. The prep work he did made it possible while you were gone, he could jump in and get it done in the four days, you were away."

"Amazing. This is sneaking around I do not mind!"

Martha beamed. "I hope you will use this space when you are here to feel you have privacy when you need and want it. I also hope it is a place to comfort you and help you with moving forward in life."

"It is perfect. I'm sure it will be everything you hoped it would be."

Martha nodded. "I think Jason did a great job and so does Emily. I gave her his information, and she is sure she can help him find more projects to increase his income."

"You are already reaching out and helping others! I love it and I'm glad Emily is hanging around. I like her and love what you've done with the house."

"Good. There's more to come in every department." Martha put her arm around Glory's shoulder and said, "I loved the very first morning after you went on your trip, waking up and sitting on the deck off the master bedroom. In fact, I loved it so much, I moved a small coffee pot and a small fridge in there so I can make my coffee and cream as I sit going through emails and online stuff while I wake up. It's heavenly!"

"I always liked sitting out there. Edgar did not," Glory said, leaning her head on Martha's shoulder. "He didn't even want to build the deck, but I convinced him it would increase the resale value, so he built it. It always felt like I had a special connection on the deck I never felt inside the house. I'm over my anger at Edgar but when I think of what he missed out on in life, I realize I'm mostly sad for him and for me."

Martha squeezed her closer and kissed her cheek. "You still have a lot to grieve over and a lot to work out."

Glory nodded. "Yes, I do. Part of me feels I have moved on too quickly and it makes me feel guilty, but I don't want to feel guilty. Part of me misses Edgar at the strangest times and I find myself talking to him."

"I'm sure he hears you."

Glory asked, "Do you believe in heaven, hell, afterlife and all of that?"

"Not really. What I believe has nothing to do with any gods or religious thought. I know for sure the Big Bang or something like that happened and our Universe was born. From those primal forces our planet was formed and eventually pulled itself together enough for life to evolve. Over time, humans came into being and there is a spiritual force in being alive and on this Earth. When we die, it is only our bodies that die. I think we probably continue on but I'm not sure there is a human form. Maybe just energy and possibly thought."

"Your explanation feels about right. It also makes me feel not so silly for talking to Edgar."

"Talking to Edgar is probably the most natural thing in the world for you to do. I also feel talking to him now, understanding his pain, you will heal faster through your conversations. After all you have a history together even though it didn't turn out exactly how you thought it would."

Glory nodded and sighed.

Martha asked, "Are you hungry?"

"Ravenous, but first the bathroom and a wash up," Glory answered.

"You get settled in and I'll do a few things in the kitchen. I've been watching videos on-line about cooking. You are in for a treat! And Emily is coming over. We can all talk, catch up and share our plans."

"Martha, this is the best spaghetti I've had in a long time," Glory said. "I'm amazed you learned how to make something that tastes so good in such a short time."

"Well, it was easy to master bacon, scrambled eggs, muffins and pancakes because Rob taught me those. I decided now I'm living in a real house with real appliances I needed to learn to cook more things. I got on the internet and watched a lot of videos. Some were by famous chefs and some were by ordinary people."

"Well, this is great," Emily said. "Is the recipe complex?"

Martha grinned. "Now I'll tell you the secret I learned to being a good cook. Everything doesn't have to be from scratch. This is actually a jar of spaghetti sauce added to sautéed onions, celery, garlic and mushrooms. The big secret ingredient is Italian sausage. It took a few times to get the spaghetti cooked just right and not sticking together though. I've turned store-bought basics into something that seems from scratch."

Glory took a bite of the garlic bread. "It is yummy and the garlic bread is perfect."

"That's just a loaf of French Bread from the grocery store cut into slices, buttered and seasoned with parsley, garlic salt and grated parmesan. Then I toasted it in the oven. The salad is straight out of the box with a few tomatoes and olives added topped with vinaigrette." Martha sat back looking very pleased.

"I'm impressed," Glory said. "You'll make me fat if you keep cooking like this!"

"No way with you larking all over the country!"

Emily asked, "So how was your first trip alone?"

"It was superb, but I couldn't have done it without Lori."

Martha raised her eyebrows. "Who is Lori?"

"She is a park ranger at Lake Easton. We became friends while I was there. She taught me how to empty the gray water tank and the black water tank— yuck! She also taught me how to build a small campfire," Glory said, "She is great and beautiful too. Her eyes are a brighter green than yours Martha."

"Oh, really. I suppose she also has long, red, curly hair."

"Nope," Glory said and then continued with her mouth a little full, "Her hair is dark, nearly black is curly but short and cute."

"And my hair isn't cute?"

"Nope, your hair is wild and wonderful." Glory reached in her pocket and pulled out her cell phone. "Hang on. Here is a photo of her."

Emily and Martha looked together at the photo of Lori. Emily said, "She is beautiful. She almost looks like something out of a woodland fairy story."

Glory watched Martha and waited for her to say something. Martha licked her lips. "I feel as if I know her."

"In a good way?" Glory asked.

"Oh, yes. Indeed, yes." Martha continued to look at the photo.

"Good," Glory said, "She wants to meet you."

Martha quickly looked up. "Oh?"

"She thinks you are beautiful too. In fact, she said 'Martha looks like a warrior goddess' or something to that effect."

Glory grinned at Martha and watched the blush crawl up her face.

Emily looked at Martha and her mouth opened in a silent "Oh" then she turned to Glory and raised her eyebrows. Glory shrugged and smiled. "So, maybe you could take the minivan for a trip to Lake Easton sometime."

Martha nodded. "Yes, that would be nice." She sighed again and smiled softly. "Thanks for sharing that Glory."

"You are most welcome. Anyway, she loves red wine especially the blended ones. She hikes and fishes and camps as much as she can year round. She is a real adventurous woman."

Martha asked, "Does she have a boyfriend?"

Glory grinned and ducked her head down twirling more spaghetti onto her fork. Then she raised her head and before quickly shoving her spaghetti into her mouth. "She's Lesbian."

Emily laughed and Martha's blush deepened. Martha looked at Emily with raised eyebrows and said, "I might just like to meet her."

Emily tried, unsuccessfully to control her giggles.

Glory grinned. "I think meeting her sounds like the only option. She is lovely and you two might just hit it off."

Martha's blush deepened. She felt embarrassed but also curious. *I've never been with a woman, but I'm definitely not interested in men. Maybe this is a sign.* She had been trying very hard to pay attention to what the Universe put in front of her. Maybe this was something she should explore.

Martha took a drink of the wine in her glass and said, "Let's change the subject." She looked at Glory, smiled and asked, "Would you like to hear some of our plans?"

Glory looked at Emily and back to Martha. "Of course. I didn't know the two of you were working on plans together."

Emily nodded. "We got together the day you left and talked about how we both wanted to move forward in our lives. I've wanted to move forward but have been afraid of failing and afraid of not being satisfied with the results." *Stop Emily. No negative thoughts.* She took a deep breath. "I've decided to quit thinking negatively and concentrate on the positive and see what happens."

"Good for you," Glory said. "So, are you going to give up being a realtor?"

Emily shook her head. "Oh, no. I love being a realtor and I'm really good at it. I would rather be in my own firm so I could pick and choose the houses I sell. More importantly, I could pick and choose who I sell houses to. I want to help people, especially women, find a place to live that helps them to move forward."

"So," Martha said, "Emily called me to ask me to a sounding board for her ideas; a friend who listens and shares and encourages."

"You are an excellent sounding board," Glory said.

Martha smiled her thanks at Glory. "After Emily and I talked I realized I wanted to help women by facilitating the steps they need to take to create the lives they want to have." She grinned. "I think that fits with how you wanted to do with some of the estate."

Glory nodded and Emily took over. "And Martha's ideas fit with my desire to sell to the people I want to help and encourage while making a living."

"So we will work together improving our lives by helping women in need create the life they want to live. We will help with education and employment. With Emily's real estate expertise and knowledge, we will also help women with housing and building their lives."

"How are you going to decide which women to help?" Glory asked.

"We are working on that part," Emily said. "In the meantime, we plan to keep Jason busy. I will have him take a look at my house and discuss the possibilities of a home office there for my real estate business."

"The she-shed will be a reality for me in the backyard," Martha said. "My she-shed will be big enough for an office for me and a meeting room too. It will be the base of operations for our plans."

"Can you do that here?"

"Emily says we can because this street is a multipurpose zoned street. She will work out the legal stuff with the help of Mr. Todd."

"So, have you shared with him your plans?" Asked Glory.

Emily shook her head. "Not completely, but in principle. I have an appointment with him tomorrow to go over our ideas and he will help us navigate the legalities and funding of our endeavors. With your approval. I'm hoping you'll write a letter today letting him know my role in the work with you and Martha. I've already lined up the building permits for the she-shed."

"I'll write the letter," Glory said. "I want to talk more about the work you two are planning. I'm amazed at how much the two of you have done in four days. I approve of all your plans so far and think this is exactly what I want to do with some of Edgar's grandfather's estate. However, I think we may need more structure to do the most good for the most people. Are you thinking to make this endeavor a foundation or company?"

Emily nodded. "Probably a non-profit foundation. Maybe. We both think a foundation may be best for tax reasons and working capital reasons. It is part of what I want to talk with Mr. Todd about. It may lead to other endeavors and include the clinic in Oklahoma."

Martha said, "However, we both think you need to approve of our ideas before we move forward. We each have money to contribute to the cause but neither of us can do it alone or without raising more funds. We want to be sure that everyone we come in contact with and everything we do is because of your vision before you put much more money into the process."

"Thanks for that," Glory said. "I had not thought about exactly what would happen, but I want to do good things with the money. I want to set aside Edgar's grandfather's money as the main fund for anything we do moving forward, including the monthly income from the properties. I'm glad you are in touch with Mr. Todd and I'm sure he'll be able to give us all good guidance. After that we can talk more about specifics."

Glory smiled at her two friends. "So, what is next around here Martha?"

Martha said, "Tomorrow construction begins on the shed. Lots of noise, bright and early! Besides you'll get to meet Jason. I think you'll like him."

Glory smiled. "You know I'm not looking for a man, right?"

"I do. I know it is way too early to think about another man in your life, but Jason will be around a lot so you will meet him."

"Thanks for understanding. I might meet Mr. Right not expecting to. But I expect that to happen when it is the right thing for both me and him. Even if he is a cowboy, I'm not looking for a man right now."

Emily looked puzzled. "Cowboy? I don't think we said anything about Jason being a cowboy."

Glory looked alarmed. "I know. Just saying."

Martha chuckled. "Maybe the man of your dreams will come along on a horse, wearing cowboy boots and a cowboy hat."

"Maybe he'll be driving a pickup with a camper." Glory smiled remembering Jake, his truck and his fine tight blue jeans. "I've been thinking about my travel plans. Maybe I should do local or close to local drives and even one-night trips to get more confident about my abilities. Who knows who I might meet, even a cowboy at a cowboy bar? I hear they have lots of cowboys on the dry side."

Emily held up her hand. "Hang on a minute. I feel like I am missing something here, Glory. What's up with the cowboy stuff and pickup trucks and campers. Did you meet someone?"

"Not really."

Martha laughed. "If 'not really', why do you have that dreamy look in your eyes?"

Glory blinked. "I do not have a dreamy look in my eyes, I'm just tired."

Emily and Martha sat still looking at Glory waiting for her to open up. Glory tried not to think about Jake and how good he looked in those tight blue jeans or how his curly hair kept falling over his forehead or the dimples on his cheeks when he smiled and how his blue eyes lit up with the smile. *I'm not looking for a man and not ready to think about working on a relationship with anyone except myself. I've been through too much pain and trauma in the last few weeks to consider anything but getting myself oriented to what I want and need in my life. I've been a widow for less than six weeks. It's too soon to go all gaga!*

She smiled at the thought of her black van and the luxury of the beautiful interior. She brushed away thoughts of the Middle Fork Road and an old beat-up pickup truck with a camper that was parked there. *He probably lives somewhere like Wenatchee.*

She looked up at her two friends and shook her head. "Okay. First, I am not dreamy eyed. Second, he was just a guy who helped me out."

"What did you need help with?" Martha asked.

"My jacket. Well, not really my jacket. It was really the back-side door to the van. I thought I had it locked, but I didn't, and it was partially open, and my jacket was dragging on I-90 while I was barreling down the road. I stopped at North Bend to fill up before heading back here. He saw my jacket and told me about his experience with a similar door and showed me how to be sure the door was locked. That was all that happened."

"But he was a cowboy?" Martha asked. "Don't see too many cowboys this side of the mountains."

Glory nodded. "I didn't think about that."

"How do you know he was a cowboy?" Emily asked.

"Well, he had on cowboy boots and a cowboy hat and drove an old pickup truck," Glory said. "Those are good signs. He was also wearing old tight blue jeans and took off his hat while he was talking."

Martha asked, "What was his hair like?"

"Curly blonde," Glory reached up to her forehead and said, "His hair fell down over his forehead when he took off his hat." She smiled a little at the memory of how he brushed it back.

Martha and Emily smiled.

Emily asked, "And his eyes?"

"Blue and glittering when he smiled."

Emily asked, "Did he have dimples too?"

Glory nodded. "When he smiled."

Both Emily and Martha laughed.

"What?" She asked.

Martha grinned. "But you didn't really notice him."

"Well," Glory admitted, "I guess I noticed him. I couldn't help noticing him. He was standing right in front of me. He's taller than Edgar was by a lot. He's camping for a few days up off the Middle Fork Road east of North Bend."

Emily said, "And you haven't wondered exactly where up there."

Glory grinned and said, "Okay. Just a little. BUT I'm not looking for a man. It's way too soon to think about any man in my life. He was a pleasant distraction. He was nice and helped me. We chatted and then waved goodby as we left the service station. I'll admit we both flirted a little. I haven't done that since my college days. It felt good to be a woman a man wanted to flirt with and that was all there was to it. There's nothing more to it."

"What's his last name?" Martha asked, "And where does he live?"

Glory tilted her head, "Huh. He didn't say, and I didn't think to ask. I guess that's that and I'll probably never see him again."

After dinner Martha and Glory walked Emily out and waved goodby as she drove away. Turning to Martha, Glory said, "I need a little time with you."

Martha nodded. "Me too. Things have been such a whirlwind and I don't know where to begin."

Glory laughed. "I have an idea. Let's get the last two glasses of wine and go sit on my deck. I have some questions for you."

They sat on the deck enjoying the cool stillness of the night. Glory looked up. "I wish, we could turn off all the city lights at midnight and we could see more stars. It was amazing at Lake Easton to go sit by the lake and look up at the stars. There are many stars we never see. It left me a little melancholy though."

"Why?"

"I'm not sure but I feel maybe it's just that we miss out on so much that is right there in front of us. Like the stars. They are there whether or not we can see them. What a feeling of surprise and awe I had at Lake Easton when I saw them. It felt like a metaphor for life. Life is all around us happening whether or not we notice it. I didn't know I was disconnected from the Universe until I saw the stars. I felt a knowing, somehow, we are all connected to each other and the stars."

"Deep thoughts," Martha said.

Glory smiled and looked at Martha. "Speaking of deep thoughts, I've been thinking about the money. The enormous amount of money from Edgar's grandfather."

"What are your thoughts now?" Martha asked. "I hope you are more comfortable being a wealthy woman."

Glory shook her head. "Not so much but I don't feel a lot of angst about it anymore. Until we have a more formal idea of how we will help others, I want to leave the principal portion of the estate from Edgar's grandfather the way it has been being handled for the past four years."

"I think that is a great idea," Martha said. "The best way to handle this much money is to plan first and spend last."

"Yes. I have no problem keeping the five hundred thousand from the life insurance, the car insurance, Edgar's checking and saving accounts, his retirement and investment funds. As his wife, I am comfortable having that money. The other money doesn't feel like I should spend it unless it has a specific purpose. Money has never been a driver for me. All our marriage I thought it was for Edgar."

"So, have you changed your mind about Edgar and money?"

"I think so. I think he never planned to spend his grandfather's money. Maybe because he felt misery and greed tainted it and perhaps was why he was tight with money. I'm not sure why he was so driven around money, but he spent none of the money from his grandfather's estate."

"I've been thinking about that too," Martha said. "I think you are right about how Edgar handled the money. Between what you earned from the sale of the house and Edgar's personal money it is still a lot of money."

Glory nodded. "Exactly! With your help, I can conserve my money and live it on for many years to come. I know can make a living as a freelance copywriter or maybe even as a blogger. If my dream of being a mystery writer works, I may add money into the coffers instead of taking it out."

Martha laughed. "Please model your protagonist after me. I'd love solving murder and mayhem!"

Glory laughed. "That's actually a superb idea. You could have a soft-spoken and smart partner like Emily."

They both laughed and teased about Martha and Emily as a sleuthing team.

Then Glory said, "Back to the dreaded money conundrum. As you and Mr. Todd work through the settlement of the estate, see if you can set up the accounts so that Edgar's money, other than the checking and savings accounts, is set up to earn money with a monthly disbursement for me at the same rate I've been making as a copywriter. I'd like the money deposited directly to my checking and debit card account. The checking and savings accounts of Edgar's I'll keep for my big expenses and will probably add some to the portfolio from time to time. I want a little cushion since I don't know what will happen in the next few months."

"I'm sure we can work out how you want it to be and let the rest of the money be quietly making money." Martha grinned. "You don't need a pay raise?"

Glory laughed. "Nope. I got a bonus with the van. I have a security blanket in the savings account and checking account. I've put the proceeds of the house sale and life insurance money into a cash account earning higher interest rather than a regular savings account. I don't need the money right now. For now, just the same amount each month I can access with my debit card. I want to travel, write and get to know me more fully from the inside out and build a life I can live with no guilt, anxiety or worry about money."

Martha nodded. "I think you are doing the right thing. You need to allow yourself the luxury the space and time to come to grips with all of this. Mr. Todd and I will take care of conserving the rest of the money."

Glory nodded. "Thanks, Martha. Now we don't have to talk about money again anytime soon!"

Martha reached out to Glory and took her hand. "I have faith in you; it will all be good."

They sat quietly for a few minutes. Then Glory grinned. "So, I noticed when I showed you Lori's photo you were very interested."

"Ah well," Martha answered, "She seems a lovely woman and if she's a friend of yours, then maybe I should meet her."

"Is that all it is?"

"I'm not sure. There was a feeling, almost a tingling under my skin, looking at her face. And those eyes, so beautiful and also a little like she is from some place filled with magic."

Glory reminded her, "And she thought you looked like a warrior goddess."

Martha smiled. "I love how in a photo on your smart phone she would get that impression. I feel happy at her response."

"Good."

"Why good?" Martha asked.

"Because when I met her I thought of you immediately. Then I realized you have no one in your life that is a close and intimate love."

Martha smiled. "Now I know where this is going. I'm ready for this conversation and have not known how to broach the subject. You striking out on your own made me think about whether I am satisfied with being alone and whether you would be satisfied with being alone."

Glory said, "My answer is no I will not be satisfied with being alone. I'm definitely in the loving men intimately category."

Martha was quiet for a few minutes and Glory said nothing. She let the quiet wrap around them hoping Martha would feel it as love and acceptance.

Finally, Martha said, "It has been hard to accept for myself I am not a heterosexual. I've experienced a lot of shame in my life feeling I should be attracted to men and I'm not. I have been going to a life coach and we've been discussing the issues of sexuality. I've never been with a woman intimately but when I saw Lori, I had this wild thought: I can't live my life without her in it. Then I thought: Don't be silly you haven't even met her yet."

"Maybe you should meet her and see what happens."

Martha nodded. "You are right, but I'm nervous. I don't know what to say or how to go about it. I'm not physically a virgin but I feel like I am in this situation and I don't know how to get started."

"I know when the time is right, and the right woman is with you everything will be clear to you. I even asked myself if I wanted a woman to woman physical relationship and after a few seconds I knew the lesbian path is not for me. However, I thought it might be for you. I hope you'll give yourself a chance to know for sure."

Martha squeezed her hand. "I will. I have to work up the courage and faith in myself and her. I have to be able to let go of the shame too. I have a feeling there is something important for me with Lori."

"Good," Glory said. "Besides, she has a beautiful, big, yellow lab named Buttercup."

"Perfect!" Martha laughed. "I love The Princess Bride. What's your favorite line?"

"It's corny and romantic."

"Come on, spill it," Martha said.

"Okay, here it is: 'Do I love you? If your love were a grain of sand, mine would be a universe of beaches'. That's the love I want in my life," Glory said.

Martha looked up at the stars. "Me too. Compared to that, money is meaningless drivel."

Glory grinned but said nothing. *Money is meaningless drivel. You hear that Edgar? It's time to let go of the drivel.*

In her dream, Jake and Glory were hiking along a trail next to the Middle Fork Camp ground. It was a sunny day but not too warm. They crossed creeks of clear bubbling water. They walked up and down trails in deep woods and the occasional meadow. Then they were walking up and up and up. She was getting hot because of the climb and watching his ass in his tight blue jeans. They came to a creek that was crystal clear with water tumbling over the rocks. There was a downed tree across the creek that was wide enough for them to use as a bridge across. Halfway across, Jake bent down with his red and white bandana handkerchief in his hand and got it wet. He wrung out most of the water and handed it to her. "Here, you look a little hot and red in the face."

Glory laughed. "You don't look so bad yourself, Cowboy."

A loud banging startled her. She turned over and was wide awake.

Damn, it was just getting good. I need to do something about this cowboy. Maybe I'll hit a few cowboy bars and she if he hangs out at them. Then she said, "I don't know who he is or anything about him."

Freya jumped on her licking her face and begging to go outside.

"Okay," she said, "Dogs first, cowboys later."

Glory went to the deck door and opened it for Freya to go outside. The banging noise was even louder. *I guess the she-shed is in progress.* Freya came back inside and went running into the bedroom and was scratching on the door.

Glory laughed, "I bet you are hungry, little dog." She opened the door and Freya streaked out of the bedroom and through the hallway.

Glory followed Freya into the kitchen where Martha was dishing up kibble for Freya. "Thanks. You didn't have to feed her," Glory said.

"My pleasure," Martha said. "Help yourself to coffee. I have your favorite lime yogurt in the fridge and there's delicious raisin bread I bought at the bakery down the street in the bread box. It is super yummy. I'm sure it goes straight to the hips. I beg you to help me eat it up!"

"I live to serve you, my goddess," Glory said.

Martha laughed. "Now that is a relationship I like; worshiped and obeyed."

Glory laughed. "Don't get used to it or get too high on your pedestal. Falling off hurts like the blazes."

Martha laughed while Glory fixed her breakfast. She put the dog dish on the floor Freya ate with vigor. She was wagging her tail so hard she had trouble staying standing and the bowl scooted around the floor.

Glory fixed her coffee in a bright yellow mug sitting on the counter, toasted raisin bread and put butter and raw honey on the warm bread. "I love these bright red and yellow mugs," Glory said. "They make me feel alive and loved."

She sat down at the table and Martha joined her. "I'm glad. I saw them and thought they belonged here. I bought the mugs and dishes to match. They fit right in with the mugs Rob had bought too."

Martha asked, "Were your dreams of Jake good."

"Oh, yes," Glory said before she stopped to think. "At least until the banging started."

Martha smiled. "You can't dig more than a few inches around here without running into rocks. Some of them are big enough they have to be broken up before the men can move them. Then they have to be moved somewhere else. Jason will use the rocks for walling spaces in the yard and for decoration."

"Why are they digging?" Glory asked.

"To set a foundation and run water lines and electricity to the shed. It's so I can have heat in the winter and air-conditioning in the summer. Number one on my list was a bathroom with a flush toilet and a kitchenette area for making coffee or tea."

Glory smiled. "This sounds like more than a shed."

Martha nodded. "It is big but not as big as you'd think. I have an office which is about ten feet by twelve feet and then there is a meeting room that is a little more than twice that big. The kitchenette and bathroom will be between with a small entry and reception area. We also plan to have a brick patio along the front of the building so we can have gatherings there and can sit outside when we want."

"Is the yard big enough for all of that?"

"Oh, yes. You know the jungle at the back of the yard."

Glory nodded.

"Well, that goes on for about 15 feet to the back of the lot," Martha said. "I also discovered an old vegetable garden and an old sitting area back there. We are leaving room to keep the vegetable garden and incorporating the sitting area with the private entrance into my office at that end of the building. I love the idea of a gazebo too. Maybe we can incorporate it in the sitting area. There is a lovely marble bench there already."

Glory smiled. "You are amazing."

"Thanks, so is Jason. I told him what I was thinking about and he surveyed the property, drew up plans and got the permits. When he showed me his idea, it blew me away. It will be so much better than the glam girly shed I was thinking of."

Glory reached over and touched Martha's arm. "I feel as if one miracle after another just keeps raining down on us. I also feel a little anxious it will all suddenly go away. Being so close to our dreams and having them slide away from us, would forever shatter us."

Martha stood up and went to Glory. She hugged her. "We will keep thinking ONLY about what we want and what good we can do. We will have to work hard but I'm sure our future is there for us to make the most of. Please have faith in us and faith in your dreams, my dreams, Emily's dreams, Jason's dreams and even the dreams of the cowboy of yours."

Glory smiled and nodded. "I'm trying to keep positive and not worry or feel guilty. It gets a little easier each day. I wish Edgar had not died. Sometimes I feel without his death these miracles would not have happened. Other time, I feel if he had trusted me and shared his conflicts with me, we could have done all of this together. It creates confusion in my mind sometimes. So many great things have already happened. I'll try very hard to have faith this will all be fine."

Martha hugged her close again and whispered, "Faith and love are all we need. Who knows? Maybe someday you will believe it could have all happened without Edgar's death."

"That would truly be a miracle," Glory said.

The doorbell rang and Martha said, "That will be Emily. Dry your tears, we have work to do."

Chapter 16

"Ours is a circle of friends united by ideals."
—Juliet Gordon Low

Emily and Martha walked into the kitchen as Glory finished clearing the table. Looking up Glory said, "Hi, Emily. It's good to see you again."

"Good to see you too," Emily said. Emily turned to Martha. "I heard the noise as I got out of the car. I take it Jason and his crew are hard at work."

Martha nodded. "I was just going to go outside with Glory so she could meet Jason and show her they have already done a lot."

Emily smiled. "I think it will surprise you at all the clearing out of the shrubs and vines at the back of the yard. The yard looks a lot bigger now than before."

They walked out the back kitchen door and onto the kitchen deck. "Wow," Glory said, "I had no idea the yard went that far back."

Emily nodded. "Well, it wasn't an eyesore, but I think both you and Martha will like the result. Martha and Jason have planned for the area to be beautiful both as a yard and a place for women in need."

Jason waved as Martha walked out into the yard with Emily and Glory following. "Hi, Jason. I want you to meet Glory."

He put out a hand to Glory. "It's nice to meet you. I've heard about many ideas for this building. It's great to work helping projects like this get up and running."

"Thank you, Jason. I'm really excited by all the work you have done so far including the guest bedroom."

"Thanks. It was my pleasure." Jason turned to Emily, took off his hat and ran his fingers over his short blonde hair and said, "Hi Emily."

Emily smiled, blushing a little. "Hi Jason. It is good to see you again."

Glory looked at Martha and raised her eyebrows. Martha said, "Hey Jason, I think Emily has things she needs to talk with you about if you have time."

"Always. Just let me give these guys a few instructions and I'll be right with you Emily."

"I'll wait on the deck. Would you like some iced tea?"

"Iced tea would be great."

Martha smiled. "Glory and I are going inside to chat and leave you two to talk."

Emily nodded although she was a little nervous to be left alone to talk with Jason. *I will not be afraid! That's easier said than done. If Glory and Martha can jump into life, then so can I.* She took a deep breath to steady her nerves. *I know they will be there for me if I need them.*

She looked at Jason talking with his crew. *He is such a kind, gentle man. I'd be lucky to have him in my life.* It didn't hurt she thought he was amazingly handsome. His short, dark blonde hair and quiet demeanor put her at ease. She usually felt uncomfortable around men but it seemed different with Jason.

Martha quickly pulled Glory into the house and toward the bedrooms. She said in a loud voice, "Let's sit on your deck and chat." Glory followed with Freya racing on her heels. Freya thought this was a fun game of chase. When they got to Glory's bedroom Martha shut the door. "Did you catch the goo-goo eyes they made at each other?"

Glory chuckled. "I saw them both blushing and feeling uncomfortable and I noticed he didn't take off his hat for me."

Martha said, "He only takes it off for Emily. It's like no one else in the world matters to him when she is around."

"It's a good sign. Emily is shy and quiet. At first, I couldn't believe she was a real estate agent. But she is very successful so maybe this is another step forward for her confidence."

Glory got a chew toy for Freya and walked out to the deck with Martha. She tossed the chew toy onto the lawn. Freya jumped off the deck flew out to play with it. "I still cannot get over how much progress you've made."

"I've only made progress on the structural parts so far," Martha answered. "I wanted to talk with you about the details of your ideas. I have thoughts of my own, but I do not want to neglect your original intentions or even have them warped into something that might not accomplish what you want."

Glory nodded. "I've been thinking about all of this. I want to do what is best for myself and help my friends and help others. When I thought more about it, I found that I really don't have specific ideas and I'm not sure really how to plan any of it."

"I understand."

"Part of my issue is I've been holding my inner self in reserve for so long I now feel a little like a deer in the headlights. My anxiety about the money has decreased. Bottom line is, I want Edgar's grandfather's estate to be the core of all of these projects rather than funding my life."

"I agree," Martha nodded. "Your thought perhaps Edgar spent none of his grandfather's estate because he felt family angst tainted it rings true. If I were Edgar, I would have felt that the money was a part of the misery of his life."

"Yes. It's exactly how I feel about it too," Glory said. "I think it became a prison for his life. It shackled him."

Martha agreed. "I thought maybe you and I could do brain storming and make lists of ideas. From there we can work out where and how we need to work going forward."

"That sounds fantastic. I want us to have a simple basic structure because I have a feeling this could careen out of control quickly. It would be a devastating waste."

"I agree."

"I also want us to work on the name for the foundation as the umbrella for everything we hope to do. Are you ready to write the ideas?" Glory asked.

"Let me go get my tablet pc and we'll write it all down. I had to scoot in here so I could laugh about Jason and Emily and their obvious attraction," Martha said. "I didn't want to embarrass her at all."

"You did the right thing and I'm glad you did."

Glory smiled as her friend left the deck. *I am glad I don't have to do all the follow through of building my dreams by myself. How lucky, I am to have such incredible friends and connections.* It felt great to relax and let Martha take over the burden of the details and management while she spent time re-creating herself into the woman she always wanted to be. *I'm getting there, I think.*

Glory and Martha sat on her bedroom deck going over their list of ideas for helping others.

"I think we have a good start," Martha said. "For the women, we aren't looking to solve all their problems for them but give them an opportunity to create the life they want."

Glory nodded. "We are stepping out into new territory for both of us. I feel powerful just doing it for myself. I feel sometimes that we have separated ourselves from our inner knowing. I'm seeing to have a better balance in my life I need to be really me."

Martha agreed. "I held off quitting my job for years. Not because I worried about money but because I didn't know what to do next. This, working with you, is my next thing to do. Quitting my job was a relief and my inner voice was singing hallelujahs."

Glory laughed. "I'm so happy you quit and joined with me and my dreams."

"They are my dreams too, Glory."

"Good. I don't resent Edgar anymore nor am I furious with him anymore. It is just his last name doesn't fit my new being or my recognition of my being."

"I'm glad your feelings about Edgar have found a peaceful place in your heart. I always loved your maiden name, Pennington. It suited you."

Glory reached out and squeezed Martha's hand. "We are on the right path. Now, I'd like to talk about the name of the foundation. I feel a lot of what happened in our marriage was because of the burden Edgar felt from his grandfather's estate. Additionally, I am sure his biological heritage added to his pain. Having parents be cold to him did nothing to help his emotional and psychological growth. I can't do anything about his parents or their choices. I can do something about his grandfather's money. I wonder about naming the foundation The Pennington-Shaw Foundation. What do you think?"

Martha thought for a few seconds. "I like it. It gives honor to you both."

Glory said, "Perfect. The foundation is about the money and helping others. Edgar's money and my efforts with you will create a lot. Now, I feel it is time to go on the road. At first, I had such clarity about my travels but now I'm not exactly sure of the direction I need to go. I'd like to take a few more short trips before I head out on a longer journey. I have a desire to spend time here with you and Emily and be on the road too. A few short trips would give me that flexibility."

"Maybe you can do cowboy hunting?"

Glory laughed. "Maybe." *It's like Martha is reading my mind.*

Emily and Jason sat on the kitchen deck looking across the backyard toward the construction of Martha's shed. Emily said, "I'm thinking the she-shed maybe needs to be called something else. It is much bigger than a shed."

Jason nodded. "I understand your feeling, but I like the name She-Shed. I was thinking earlier how all three of you women have shed the lives you were leading. Each of you in your own way were ready to bloom. You each are re-creating your new lives out of the old lives you had. The power I feel around the three of you is incredible. The courage to begin a new, big project helping other women and others is amazing. I'm happy to be a partner with all of you.

Shedding. Like a caterpillar resting inside a cocoon until it can shed the shell and become a butterfly. She-Shed. It feels right somehow to call it She-Shed. A place where women can come, leave the past behind, shed the old way of being, and build a new life."

Emily looked at Jason with her mouth open. When she felt his smile as he looked at her she shut her mouth. "Your explanation is amazing, Jason."

"I think this building needs a big pink and gold and silver sign 'She-Shed'." He raised his hands wide to show the size of the sign. "What was it you needed to talk with me about?" He asked.

"You know I want to build my real estate business. I want to not only sell houses for a living I want to help in the endeavors Glory dreamed of."

Jason nodded and she continued, "I had thought I would work from home but really don't want to have my home and my business all combined. I need some separate space for the business. With the She-Shed you are building I thought perhaps having my own She-Shed would be a good idea. The problem is my house is much bigger than this house but my backyard is tiny."

"Would you like me to come look?" Jason asked.

"That would be terrific. When?"

"I can come over after I finish here."

Emily nodded, bit her lip and then before she could chicken out, she said, "That would be great. May I cook dinner for you?"

Jason cocked his head, smiled and asked, "Are you a good cook?"

Emily laughed. "Well, I suppose you should come for dinner and judge for yourself. I can promise it won't be your last meal."

He laughed. "Then it's a date. After I finish here for the day, I'll go home and clean up. What time should I come for dinner?"

She felt herself blushing. "How does seven sound?"

"Perfect."

Emily went home and when she entered her craftsman style two-story house, she felt a little breathless. *What have I done? Have I really asked a man I hardly know to come to my home for dinner? What was I thinking? You weren't thinking. You were letting your hormones run away with you.* She smiled and decided it was high time she had let her hormones give her a nudge. Besides, she trusted Jason and liked his way of interacting with her.

Although they had only met a few days ago, she felt she had known him forever. *Not possible. There is only now, and you just met him.* She felt comfortable and safe in his presence and that was perfect for now. *You felt more than safety and perfection in his presence.* She let that thought settle at the back of her mind.

She went to the kitchen and took out a salmon filet she had planned to bake and save the leftovers for another meal or two. She seasoned the salmon with some ginger, salt and pepper, and then covered it with plastic wrap and set it back in the refrigerator. She got out a brownie mix, added walnuts and raisins to the mix and put it in the oven.

"What if he doesn't like walnuts and raisins?" She asked the kitchen. Then she shook her head. "If he doesn't like walnuts and raisins in his brownies, then he is not the man for me." She set the oven timer and went upstairs to her bedroom to change her clothes and get ready for her company.

Emily opened the door for Jason. "Welcome to my home."

He looked around. "This is a huge house. You live here all by yourself?"

Emily nodded. "It was my grandparents' house. They had seven children, so it was a full house in their day. They left it to me in their will and now all I have to do is take care of the house, pay the taxes and live here. I thought about selling it but I love this house even though it echos a lot with just me living here."

"It's impressive and I love you have changed nothing drastically. Are these the original wood floors?"

"Yes, they are," Emily said. "I've also left the woodwork as it always was, stained and polished, but I changed the wall colors to soft colors instead of the white they always were. I also added Art Déco light fixtures and switch plates. I like them better than the plain ones that were here before."

"I like your choices," Jason said. "How many bedrooms?"

"There are six bedrooms including a large master bedroom with private full bath," Emily said. "Would you like to see the house?"

"Sure if dinner can wait," He answered.

She led him into the kitchen. "Let me put the salmon in the oven and then we can do a quick tour of the house and talk about plans for the future over dinner." She blushed. *I hope he knew I was talking about the house and not our relationship.* A little voice in the back of her head was saying, "Don't worry. It will all come in the time it is meant to. Accept and keep moving forward."

Jason saw her blush and knew she was feeling self-conscious. "Perfect," He said. "I smell chocolate. What is that?"

"Brownies. I hope you like walnuts and raisins," Emily said.

Jason smiled and nodded. "That's how my mom makes brownies. A lot of my friends in high school loved her brownies until they found out they had raisins in them. Left more for me."

Emily was relieved and smiled. "I knew you couldn't be a close friend if you didn't like walnuts and raisins in your brownies."

Jason laughed. "You are a woman of fine tastes and discernment." He watched her blush deepen. It surprised him to find himself delighted at being able to make her blush. But he worried that she was embarrassed and said, "I hope I didn't embarrass you."

Emily shook her head. "No, I liked what you said." She put the salmon in the oven and set the timer. "We have twenty minutes to see the house."

She took him on a tour of the downstairs with the small breakfast nook, large dinning room, the piano room, the study, the family room and the living room. Then upstairs she showed him the bedrooms with two bathrooms plus the master bathroom and bedroom. "This is a beautiful home, Emily," He said. "Anyone would be proud to live here."

They went back downstairs to the kitchen. She said, "I thought we'd eat in the breakfast nook. The dining room feels too big for just two people."

He looked over at the breakfast nook where she had set the dinnerware and flatware for two on a round oak table. There was a small flower arrangement in the center with flowers cut from the yard. "It's perfect," He said. "I like the layout of the house and how well you've adapted the modern conveniences to appear they belong here."

They sat at the table and ate the dinner she had prepared. He said, "I don't know which I liked the best: the salmon, the wild rice or the sautéed mushrooms and green beans but it was all delicious."

"Thank you. Shall we have dessert first or talk and plan first?"

"Let's talk and plan first," he said. "I want to go home with the taste of brownies in my mouth."

She laughed and said, "Sounds like a plan" but in her heart of hearts she hoped he would go home with the taste of their first kiss on his lips. She blushed at the thought as she cleared the table. *You are thinking too far ahead, Emily. Tonight we are working on ideas and getting to know each other.*

Jason stood up and brought his briefcase to the table and set out his pencil, a ruler and a pad of paper. He sketched while she loaded the dishwasher and put away the leftover food. She loved the feeling of him being there doing his own thing while she tided the surrounding kitchen. It felt natural and whole. It felt exactly how she felt being married to the right man would feel. *Whoa,* she told herself. *Don't get the cart before the horse!*

She sat down in the chair beside Jason rather than across. He smiled at her. "I think there are a lot of ways we can do this, but this would be my favorite. It keeps your living room, family room, dining room and kitchen private but uses the large study and smaller piano room as your offices for your business. Since the piano room is behind the study, you could have that as your room for your copier, fax, computer server, filing cabinets and such with the study as the main room and office."

She looked at the drawing. "But then people would have to come through the living room to get into the agency office."

He shook his head. "No. I'd keep the doors that open into the living room just as they are but locked. On the office side I'd have floor to ceiling curtains which would also add to sound-deadening for privacy in your office."

He pointed to the wall by the porch and said, "Then off the front porch, which is spectacular by the way, I'd add another outside door for your clients to enter your office. It looks like, that the long window in the study facing the porch, used to be a door. The other front windows are wider and shorter. So, if I'm right it is easy to do but either way not a big deal. For the piano room I'd add another door that would lead into the pantry room. You'd lose a little shelving in the pantry but still have access to your office directly from the house for your ease of use."

She looked at the design. "I think it looks perfect. I worried that if we built a shed in the backyard like we are at Martha's house it would dominate the yard and make it less fun for a family to gather out there."

He nodded. "I understand and agree. Do you have a lot of family around here?"

She smiled. "I have a brother and a sister in the area. My sister and her husband live over on Bainbridge Island. They are expecting their first baby in a few months. My brother lives in Maple Valley with his wife. They have twin boys. Our parents live down near Olympia but come to visit us often. They live in a manufactured home village for people over 55."

"I have a big family too," Jason said. "I have three brothers and two sisters. Two brothers are older than me. Then there is Billy. He is two years younger than me. The sisters are twins and still in middle school. They were born about seven years after the last Billy. Mom and Dad thought they were through but apparently their bodies had other ideas."

"Do they all live close?"

He nodded. "They live here in Issaquah, North Bend and Sammamish, so we're all close." He smiled at the thought of his family. "I love being part of a large family. I want to have at least two children of my own but would love to have a larger family."

"Me too," Emily said.

Jason looked up at her. Her sweet face and beautiful eyes seemed to draw him in. "Perfect."

They looked at each other for a few more moments. Emily nodded, smiled and said, "How about dessert?"

He smiled. "Great idea."

She got up to serve the brownies and ice cream. He came into the kitchen. "I'd like to help. I don't want you spending a lot of time waiting on me hand and foot."

"Thanks. You can scoop up the ice cream while I cut the brownies. And, don't get used to me waiting on you hand and foot. Tonight you are company."

"What about after tonight?" He asked.

She shrugged. "We'll see." She smiled at the thought of building a relationship with Jason. He seemed so comfortable here and she felt as if she had known him forever.

The drive back home to Oklahoma was not as much fun as the drive to Washington had been. There were beautiful sights to see but Jake felt a longing he had not expected. Driving through Utah he thought, *These incredible rocks and mountain and streams are beautiful but not as beautiful as Glory.*

He laughed and patted the pickup truck dashboard. "Darlin' we'd best keep driving on to home. We are not in the market for a woman."

He turned the CD up louder. "Willie's just the thing to settle me down."

When he arrived back at the ranch, Delbert was working in the barn. Jake walked into the barn and Delbert looked up and waved.

"How are things here?" Jake asked.

"Finer than frog fur," Delbert answered.

Jake laughed. "Then that's pretty darned good I'd say."

"You're looking better. Not nearly so tight around the eyes," Delbert said. "Glad to have you back home."

"I'm glad to be back." Jake checked out the horses and then said, "I will unload my stuff and get things put back in order in the house. Thanks for taking care of things while I was gone."

"My pleasure. Glad you're home." *He does look better, and I am glad he is home. I wish Cora were here, too.*

Jake unloaded his pickup and put his camping gear away in the garage. He carried his clothes and bedding into the house and got the washing machine busy cleaning his clothes and bedding. After he had lunch, he went upstairs. Walking past the four bedrooms he had built for children he stopped and walked into one. "I'm praying someday there will be kids in these rooms. I long to hear the racket of kids and dogs racin' up and down the halls with their momma yellin' for them to quiet down." He couldn't stop the vision of Glory as the mother and her little black dog.

In his own room, he took off his dirty clothes and headed for the shower. Standing in the shower he couldn't seem to get a certain little blonde-haired woman with blue eyes and a beautiful smile out of his mind. He started singing, "I'm gonna wash that girl right out of my hair!" at full volume. After his shower, looking in the mirror he said, "You messed up buddy. You should have gotten her address and phone number or at the very least her last name."

Later that night sitting on his balcony, he pulled the remote lighting control out of his pocket and turned off all the lights around his house. He sat back in his chair and looked up to the sky. As his eyes adjusted to the dark, stars appeared. As more and more appeared, the Milky Way made an appearance. *Let me play among the stars.* Jake smiled wistfully thinking of Glory. He felt the Oklahoma night was welcoming him home.

Chapter 17

"If you don't like the road you're walking,
Start paving another one."
- Dolly Parton

Glory sat on the guest bedroom deck, trying to decide where to go next. She had been on several small overnight trips both on the wet side and the dry side. She had been traveling for a few months off and on. She enjoyed all the trips and meeting lots of nice people who signed up for her blog posts and newsletter.

Her forays into cowboy bars had been disappointing. She didn't see Jake at any of them and felt that perhaps that wasn't the kind of place he would have been. It had amused her at one bar to see several men with ZZ Tops sort of beards, but again they weren't Jake. She had fun learning how to do the country western two step. She smiled thinking of how fun it had been. *I wonder if Jake likes to dance and ride horses?*

Now she was back in Issaquah for a few days break, she was getting restless again. She dreamed of Jake frequently and always awoke wanting to know who he really was and where she could find him. *I loved dancing with him last night. I feel deeply he is out there thinking of me too. Or at least I hope so. I feel we will find each other but worry we will find each other too late.*

She had thought California was next on her list but somehow it didn't feel right. She was eager to be back on the road and her next adventure. She was also eager to trust her gut feelings. She would go where it felt right to go.

Things were moving along here. When Emily had told her and Martha about what Jason had thought about the name She-Shed for the women's project both agreed instantly. It fit perfectly with their goals and purposes. Glory kept She-Shed women's project as a separate entity from the clinic with the general umbrella of The Pennington-Shaw Foundation for both projects. Later on, there might be other projects too. Glory liked the clarity this brought. She would talk with Hugh and Rob about the naming of that part of the clinic project.

She and Martha had talked about the division of labor for the foundation. Glory told Martha, "I probably need to be more involved with the clinic project and let you concentrate on She-Shed projects."

"Thank you! That will be a relief for me," Martha said.

Martha had everything under control with She-Shed project. She was reaching out to community organizations for ideas to frame how She-Shed could work and how to choose which women to help.

Glory was free to go wherever and whenever she wanted. She had only The Pennington-Shaw Foundation at the Norman clinic. *Besides, I am in contact by phone or email anywhere in the country.*

Howard Todd had also recommended separate funding for the various projects with all the money under The Pennington-Shaw Foundation being the source for project funding. His rationale had been that although there were two main projects now there might be others. Glory hoped there would be other projects.

I need to be back on the road and back to writing. Sitting here, restless I could let it all overwhelm me. She had been working on meditation to help maintain balance. *It seems to work. Most of the time.* Her phone rang interrupting her thoughts, and she saw it was Rob calling.

"Serendipity strikes, thankfully," She muttered. "Hi Rob, what's up?"

Rob said, "Hugh, and I wanted to ask if you had planned on coming to Oklahoma soon."

"No, but I can. Why?" she asked.

"Well, this is all feeling overwhelming," he said. "Hugh wants to run a few things by you in person and really wants your input on the clinic location. We have several options in that regard since the new hospital has left a lot of open medical offices available on the east side of Norman. There are also some good available sites on the west side too."

"I totally get the overwhelming feeling," she said. "Your call saved me from a panic attack over everything. I was thinking about where to go next. My original plan had been to go south through Oregon and California but it didn't feel right somehow. I guess I don't have to think about that anymore. Thanks to you, Oklahoma is my next destination."

She felt relieved and eager to go check on things with the clinic. She wanted to travel, and she wanted to write but at this moment she felt adrift, not sure what to do or where to go next. Everything here in Issaquah seemed to have moved on just like she wanted and even better than she had imagined. However, it left her feeling a little like a third wheel on a bicycle.

Rob interrupted her thoughts, "Your coming down will relieve Hugh. He said he had wanted to do this from the start of his medical career but had thought it would be a few years before he would have the money saved to embark on the clinic. Now, I think it overwhelms him at having the possibility for the clinic to happen soon."

"I understand his feelings. Everything here seems to have blossomed into the dreams I'd had for my role in the community, but I still feel like I'm on the outside looking in."

"I thought traveling was what you wanted to do?"

"It was, is. I realized traveling without a purpose was another way to avoid my life. I want to embrace my life, not avoid it."

"Do you regret selling your house and having Martha start the foundation for you?" Rob asked.

"No. I'm clear on that. I'm sure it is not what's bothering me. I have this feeling that traveling for the sake of traveling isn't what I really want. I need to have meaning too."

Rob laughed. "So, do you have a clue what you really want?"

Glory sighed. "I'm clear about the general direction but not sure how to proceed. I'm afraid to verbalize what I want. I'm even a little anxious when I think of all of it."

"Why?"

"I feel like I already verbalized that I wanted to travel and be alone and write and see the country. I could never do that because I was married and didn't have enough money to strike out on my own. Now, money is no object, so I struck out on my own and yet I don't feel how I thought I'd feel."

"How did you think you would feel?"

"Enlightened. Fulfilled. Meaningful," Glory said. "I know it sounds lofty and goofy but those are the thoughts that come to mind. Somehow it feels like the Universe said, 'Okay, here you are' and granted my wishes. It's like Dolly Parton said, 'No matter where you go, there you are.' Now, I feel there is a nugget missing."

"Any clues?"

"A few, but I'm not sure I'm ready for a relationship. I think the alone bit I'd dreamed of was a reaction to the turbulent relationship with Edgar. I'm pretty sure being alone isn't what I wanted deep down."

"Hmmm. Sounds like you have confused being independent with being alone."

"Maybe. In fact, probably. What you are saying is close to the heart of the matter. I still don't want to live in this house although Martha has made it much more welcoming. This house isn't me and never has been. I love She-Shed and how Martha has taken my nugget of an idea and moved forward in ways so profound it makes my head spin."

"Are you jealous of what she's accomplished?"

Glory chuckled. "Me? Jealous?" She shook her head knowing he couldn't see her but feeling the need to do so anyway. He said nothing and Glory took that as a sign he was waiting for her.

"I do not feel jealous of what Martha and Emily have accomplished nor do I wish I'd had a more direct hand in those accomplishments. I think I am longing to have something in my life for me. I also want closeness in my life without being held back or confined. Previously, I defined that as being me traveling alone. I have Freya. She is marvelous and accepts me warts and all. However, she is not enough. I want that in a human relationship too."

"With a man?"

"Absolutely, but I'm not sure a cowboy is what I need."

"What cowboy? Where did 'cowboy' come from?"

"It's crazy. I know. But I can't get him out of my mind. On the way home from Lake Easton I stopped at North Bend for fuel. I met a cowboy. Now I dream about him every night. He was hot but also kind and gentle."

"That can be true of a lot of men, not just cowboys. In fact, I've met cowboys who looked great on the surface with their hats and boots and tight blue jeans, but they were not good people. Those guys weren't men I would want you to hook up with."

Glory nodded. "Exactly. It really wasn't that he was a cowboy or that he was a hottie although he was both of those things. It was that in the brief encounter he triggered a desire in me and not just physical desire. It was almost like a knowing or meant-to-be situation. I've never ever felt anything like that before."

"Did you get his phone number?" Rob asked.

"No! And it is so silly, frustrating, and in a way heart-breaking. I did not even ask his last name. It is making me a little nuts thinking about him, dreaming about him and knowing I will probably never see him again."

"Well," Rob said, "All the more reason to come to Oklahoma. We have oodles of cowboys here that are hotties. I might even introduce you to a few I know that are really good men."

Glory smiled. "Whoa. Not so fast. Thanks for talking and most especially listening. I'll come to Oklahoma right away but only if you promise to do no

match making. I'll let you know if I want you to do that. I want to think about
me a little more and get clarity about me and what I really want. Maybe after
I'm clear about my desires, I'll be ready for a man, cowboy or not. I'll hit the
road tomorrow after I map out my ride there."

"Great. It will relieve Hugh. I promise no matchmaking. Besides, if you
and your cowboy are meant to be, you'll be together. Just have faith," Rob
said.

"Martha says that too, 'have faith'."

"She is a smart woman. Now about driving to Oklahoma. You can drive
from Washington to Oklahoma in two days, but it is a brutal drive. Three or
four days is a much nicer pace."

"Great. I'll probably make it in three since I specifically need to go to
Oklahoma and not just a need to hang out and travel," Glory said. "I'm
planning on listening to audible books while traveling long distances but
stopping a lot along the way for photos or for whatever interests me. Any
suggestions?"

"On books, anything written by Nicolas Sparks is a good choice. On books
and cowboys listen to THE LONGEST RIDE. Other than which book to listen
to, this time of year you might make reservations at RV parks so you aren't
left parking on the side of the road," he said. "A lot of folks are out
vacationing now especially with the Fourth of July so close. When we have
driven, it is to get where we are going. Not to look about. I know there are
several great routes to travel although all of them are long and a lot of it will
be boring."

"Good ideas," Glory said. "I'd thought to only camp in forest or state parks
as I've mostly been doing but this kind of trip maybe I should stick to
commercial RV parks. I went to one here in Issaquah and it was very nice, just
not rustic enough to feel like real camping."

"When you get here," Rob said, "You can park your van beside our house.
We have loads of room for you in the house, but you can use your van if

you'd rather. The previous owners had a concrete pad with electric and water hook up for their RV. They used it as a guest cabin for visitors."

"What about Freya? Is it okay to bring her?" Glory asked.

"Of course! We've already told Ralph about her and the big lug wants to meet her."

Glory laughed promised to let him know her route. She decided he was right and she should probably reserve RV space since summer was in full swing. She was sure they were busy most of the time. It was Monday July second. She could leave in the morning bright and early. She went on-line and mapped out what looked like the fastest route using interstate highways.

First stop would be Boise, ID. It was the second stop she wasn't sure about. Whether to stop in Wyoming or Colorado was the big decision.

Glory arrived in Boise, Idaho late in the afternoon. The sun was lowering in the sky. From Interstate 84 she looked across the city with its verdant trees in full bloom and leaf. The sun painted the distant mountains gold and pink. The mountains reminded her of Eastern Washington which differed from the Western side. The mountains seemed to be more a part of everything, yet there was a desert feel to them.

Verdant is great, but this is beautiful too. There are so many more colors here than in Issaquah where everything is in shades of blue and green.

She continued on the highway to the Meridian KOA. When she pulled into the KOA, she was surprised at how clean it was and how pretty it was. She had chosen a full-hookup site to take advantage of the electricity and the water and be able to use her own shower and bathroom. Having water for making coffee and cooking dinner was important to her. Besides, she liked being able to have lights, refrigerator and microwave to make her life easy.

After she stopped in the office and registered, she followed the camp map to her site. She was pleased to see it was close to one of the dog runs for Freya and yet seemed to be in a fairly quiet part of the campgrounds. She loved there was a big tree that would shade her van. Glory backed her van into the site then got out and checked her alignment with the water and electricity. She got back in the van and realigned her parking for better access to the electricity and water. She looked at Freya and said, "Don't look at me. I don't see you backing up this rig in one try." Freya cocked her head and then whined.

"I bet you are ready for a break."

Freya yiked in her 'yes' voice. Glory went around to the passenger side of the van, hooked Freya's leash onto her collar and then released her from her safety harness. They walked down the road to the nearby dog run. Freya busily sniffed and finally chose the perfect spot for her business. When she finished, she took off running back to the road with Glory jogging behind her. Glory used her key fob to lock the van as they passed by their spot. It was clear Freya needed a walk and Glory wanted to look around.

At the campground office she saw a bulletin board with a poster saying, "Join us every Tuesday evening for the Boise Blue Grass Band jam session." A voice behind her asked, "Have you ever been to a blue grass jam?" Glory turned to see an elderly man and a woman standing behind her. "No. In fact, I don't think I've ever heard bluegrass music."

The woman grinned. "Then you are in for a treat. It is the best kind of music."

Glory smiled and held out her hand. "My name is Glory and my dog is Freya."

"I'm Grace and this is my husband Paul." Glory shook hands with both.

Grace continued, "They are a local band, but they are great. You should come to the session."

"Do they allow dogs?" Glory asked.

"I don't think so," Paul said, "But you should still come to listen."

"I'll think about it but she is still a puppy and I don't want to come back to have things torn up."

Grace asked, "Do you have one of those crate things."

Glory nodded. "I do but I've never used it with her while traveling. Maybe I'll do that for a little while but not stay for the whole thing."

Paul said, "You won't regret it."

"Unless you get hooked," Grace said, "Then you must buy one of their CDs."

Glory laughed. "I can do that too."

After their walk, Glory fed Freya and took her out for another short walk. Glory heated up her left over salmon and wild rice that Emily had brought her this morning before she left Issaquah.

As she sat eating her dinner and watching the evening news on her computer, she thought about her conversation with Rob. She had been to Oklahoma one time for a short one-night visit with Rob and Hugh. This way she had an opportunity to see the states between Washington and Oklahoma and spend a little time in Oklahoma.

Rob had grown to love the state, especially the eastern half where he said if you were in the right parts of the various mountain ranges it felt a lot like being in Washington, except the trees weren't as tall. He had said, "Right up until someone starts talking. When you hear the Okie accent, you know you are not in Washington anymore." Glory smiled at the memory and was looking forward to her trip.

After she finished eating and cleaning up the kitchen area which took about 5 minutes, she opened her computer. She told Freya, "It's time to video the gang back home and post it on the blog." Freya ignored her and kept working on her after dinner chewy treat.

"Hello everyone," she said. "I'm here in beautiful Boise, Idaho. This time I'm camping in a KOA because I'm only staying one night and wanted to have a few modern conveniences. It isn't as lovely as Lake Easton, Wenatchee, Kachess or the Middle Fork but it has a startling beauty all its own. It feels like being in the mountains and the desert all at the same time. The pink, orange and purple sunset was beautiful. I'll post pictures on the blog so you can have a hint of how beautiful this area is. This is a very large campground with lots of spaces. It is almost like a small town inside the city. I met a nice couple, Grace and Paul, who suggested I go to the Bluegrass jam tonight. I've never heard bluegrass music, but I'll give it a try. Send kind thoughts to Freya who will be in her kennel crate while I walk across the campground to the jam session. Love to you all."

She watched the video and decided although she was still a little shy about posting videos of herself it wasn't half bad. She wrote a few paragraphs about the trip to Boise and added in photos to match the paragraphs. At the bottom of the post she put the video she'd just made. Then below she wrote: "One night in Boise and then we are off to Strasburg, Colorado east of Denver. Gloriana on the Road, over and out!"

Paul and Grace were right. She loved the bluegrass music and bought 4 CDs. Grace walked back to her van with her and said, "I thought you'd love it. I have a few CDs of bluegrass and a few I wanted to give to you."

"That's so kind," Glory said.

"Well, Paul and I agreed you are a very nice woman but much in need of musical education. Paul and I picked these out for you to listen to on your journeys. We have duplicates of these at home, so it is not like we are making any kind of sacrifice."

Glory took the CDs and was reading each label. Grace tapped on one and said, "This is my all-time favorite."

Glory read the title, "Trio. Emmylou Harris, Linda Ronstadt and Dolly Parton. I know their names but don't know if I've ever heard their music."

Grace shook her head, "Then it's high time you did! Everything anyone wants to know about women is on that CD. Listen to it as you drive. You might learn a lot about yourself. Then listen to a little Lyle Lovett or Willie Nelson and you'll learn about cowboys and love."

Glory looked up and grinned. "Just what I needed to know." She reached out for Grace and hugged her. "Thanks for the music. I'll listen and take what I hear to heart."

Grace patted her hand. "That's the ticket. Listen to the music. It may help keep life from being too hard. At least that's what it has done for me." She smiled and walked a few steps then turned and waved at Glory. "You take care of yourself and your little dog too!"

Glory waved back and turned to the van. She unlocked the door surprised Freya wasn't barking. She looked in the crate and saw Freya laying curled in a ball asleep. When she opened the door, Freya looked up, yawned and stretched before coming out of the crate. Glory picked her up and hugged her close. Freya licked her chin giving Glory exactly the welcome home she needed.

"Well, I guess you're fine to be alone for a short period of time," Glory said. She loved her little dog and was glad Rob had talked her into getting a puppy pal. Holding Freya made Glory feel relief from her grief and longing. The mere act of cuddling and holding Freya felt like love enveloping Glory.

Glory woke early and was on the road before sunrise. It was 900-mile ride, but she wanted to get to Colorado today. There was an RV park in Strasbourg, Colorado. That would leave only 650 miles to go to be in Norman, Oklahoma.

The drive across Wyoming was more beautiful than she had expected. When she finished listening to The Longest Ride, she put on the Trio album Paul and Grace had given her. She listened to the women singing and felt her heart lift in joy and love.

Grace was right about this album. It embodied everything about love and women. After she had listened to the album three times she said to Freya, "I'd better learn something about cowboys if I'm going to Oklahoma." Freya yiked her 'yes' and Glory switched to Lyle Lovett.

She loved the album. Song after song hooked her and made her feel like the cowboy singing was singing to her although she laughed at the image of a cowboy riding his horse on his boat.

The miles flew by for Glory. She stopped for fuel and to let Freya walk and piddle. She ate in her van. It amazed her at how long it was taking to get across Wyoming. It felt like the road was getting longer and longer and she wasn't getting any closer to Cheyenne. About then Lyle Lovett started singing about 'you can't get the hell out of Texas' and she said, "Buddy, you meant Wyoming, didn't you?"

The scenery of mountains and rocks and an incredible big blue sky helped a lot, but the journey was wearing on her. When she finally reached Cheyenne, put gas in the van and fed Freya and herself, the sun was setting. She was exhausted but had reservations in Strasbourg and didn't want to have a long drive tomorrow.

She got in the van, put on some Willie Nelson and kept driving. She loved his mellow voice and the mix of a cowboy singing jazz and love songs. The drive through Denver was awful even though rush hour was long over. Still the traffic was more than Glory had ever driven in other than rush hour in Seattle which she always tried to avoid. By the time she was heading east toward Strasbourg she had a headache and her fatigue threatened to overwhelm her.

Finally, around ten in the evening she pulled into the Strasbourg campground. After checking in and finding her slot, she parked the van, fed Freya and took her out for her last walk. She didn't notice the clear sky or brilliant stars. She went through the motions as quick as possible to get in bed and sleep. When she was back in the van, she closed the curtains, locked the doors and collapsed on the bed. She was unaware of any dreams she might have had. Sleep was her only need.

Freya barked loud and insistent waking Glory. "Okay, princess," Glory muttered. "Let's get you outside to pee."

Glory climbed out of bed, slipped on her sandals and took Freya to the dog walk area. Freya was quick about getting her job done and then begged to be back in Glory's arms. "You are a spoiled little doggie." She picked up Freya and let her nuzzle under her chin.

Gloriana felt exhausted but was awake now with Freya. She fed the pup and dressed while the dog finished her breakfast. She quickly made herself some coffee but decided to stop for breakfast along the way. A drive through sandwich sounded great.

The sun was welcoming the brilliant day as Glory left the campground heading for the first fast food place she could find. She got her sandwich, orange juice and a coffee refill then was back on the interstate heading east. "Only 650 miles left," she said to Freya. The response was a hearty yike. Glory was numb with exhaustion and wanted to go back to bed. "Remind yourself to never do long road trips without time out for rest and recreation," She said aloud.

Jake was sitting on the back patio of Helen and Tom's house. He had been in Norman for a few days now. He had come at the insistence of his nieces and nephews to celebrate the Fourth of July. He smiled. *Not that it is ever a burden being around family. I should head back to the ranch but feel a little isolated down there now. I must have gotten used to living in both places—the ranch and Norman.* "I'm not buying a place up here."

Helen walked out and sat beside him. "How are you doing little brother?"

"I'm okay, sis. I feel a little lost but I'm at peace about me and Liz."

"That's good. I love the photographs she sent me of the kids racing around the backyard. She really has a talent there."

Jake nodded. "I'm glad she is doing well. It takes a lot of pressure off her and me too."

"Do you know what she will do next?"

Laughing Jake nodded. "She met a fella in the wilds of New Mexico. She is hooking up with him and they are headed to the badlands to do photography and watch archeology friends of his dig in the dirt."

Helen shook her head. "I'd never in a million years picture her as a woman in hot desert climes taking photographs."

"She swears her fingernails remain broken and dirty all the time. I can't imagine but I'm glad she is happy." Jake grinned.

"What about babies?"

"Not happening ever, she says. She had some kind of IUD thingy placed that keeps her from getting pregnant or having periods. She said on our last phone call, 'It's perfect. I can have sex and not worry about babies and not have periods. Some genius must have thought this up!' I'm happy for her."

Helen reached out and touched his arm. "Maybe, but you seem sad."

"No, not sad exactly but I'm kicking myself a lot over not getting a particular beautiful woman's phone number."

Helen smiled. "Who is she?"

He shrugged. "I have no idea."

"I'm confused."

"I met her at a gas station in Washington. We flirted for a few minutes and each went our separate ways. I keep having dreams about her and thinking about her so much I can hardly think of anything else."

"Maybe you should go back to Washington."

"I thought of that. They have more than just one woman there though."

Helen laughed. "Hang out here a few more days. I'm having a dinner party in two nights for Hugh's clinic project. He'd love for you to be here for that."

Jake nodded. "He mentioned that. He said a rich woman up in Washington is a friend of Rob's and she is coming down to approve his plans and choices for the clinic."

"She seems very nice, but I haven't met her. I've heard Hugh and Rob talking about her though."

"Was she at Rob's wedding?" Jake asked.

"I don't think so," Helen answered. "But still they are friends so it would be nice to have you here to support Hugh and Rob."

"You got it, sis."

Chapter 18

"Life is hard;
You may have noticed."
— David Clemens

Thirteen hours had passed on the highways for Glory's trip to Oklahoma. There had been a lot of construction along the way between Colorado and Oklahoma which slowed down the trip. The trip had required two hours longer than she had expected with the construction and extra stops to keep herself alert and awake. *There is only so much bluegrass and country music can do to make up for physical fatigue.* She tried to smile at the thought but was just too tired. She was feeling a little disoriented with her fatigue and was glad to see a sign saying only eleven miles left to reach Norman.

Glory called Rob. "Hey Rob," she said, "I know it's late but I'm nearly to Norman. Have you guys eaten yet?"

"No, Hugh just got home, and we were thinking to order in some pizza. How long until you will be here?"

"I'm south of Moore so only 10 or 15 minutes."

"Great then, I'll order the pizza."

Glory exited on Robinson street going west. At the corner of Crossroads Boulevard and Robinson street she saw to her left the ubiquitous Waffle House a mainstay in the south and to the right was the 7-11 packed with cars getting fuel, cigarettes, beer and snacks. *You are in the south,* Glory thought and then smiled.

She turned right and drove north on Crossroads Boulevard to Woodsboro Drive. Turning left, Glory drove west toward Hugh and Rob's house. She loved this neighborhood. All the houses were a little different from the one next door but all had lush lawns and beautiful gardens and shrubs. This street felt exactly right for Rob.

Glory pulled up in their driveway on Woodsboro Drive. She felt totally depleted of energy. Rob was out the door before she could turn the van off. He opened the driver's door. "Hurry! Shut that thing off and get out and hug me before I explode!"

She turned off the ignition on the van, unbuckled her seat belt laughing, "Give me a second or two!"

Then she stepped out of the van into Rob's arms. It felt so warm and safe in his arms. Although she had seen him a few weeks ago, his welcome stirred her deeply. She was so grateful for this man who loved her and treated her as his sister. He enveloped her in a big hug and said, "I'm so glad you are here, and I love the 'Love The Mutt You're With' t-shirt."

"Me too," Glory said and then choking a little she cried and before she knew what was happening, she was sobbing. *What is going on with me?* She thought. *I'm a total basket case. I'm crying for no damn good reason. Here I am safe and sound and ready to help people and all I do is cry.*

Rob pushed her back a little. "Hey sweetie. It's all going to be okay. Let me get the cutest dog in the world out of the van and we'll go inside where you can have a proper cry."

Glory nodded and while Rob was getting Freya, she continued to cry as she stumbled toward the house. Rob followed with Freya in his arms.

Hugh opened the door and reached out for Glory, enveloping her in his arms while helping her walk up the one low step and into the house. "Oh, girl," he said, "Get in this house and I'll get the tissues."

Glory tried to stop crying but trying to stop it only made her tears and sobbing worse. Once Hugh walked her into the living room, she collapsed on the nearest sofa in a pile of tears and weeping. Freya jumped up beside her. The little dog licked her tears away, whining with worry. Glory choked out a small laugh. "I'm all right Freya."

Hugh walked over to her with a box of tissues. Handing them to her he said, "There you go. Laughing and crying is just exactly what you need."

Rob then handed her a glass of ice water. "Have a few sips of this. You're getting dehydrated with all this crying."

Glory took the glass and sipped a little of the water. It tasted good, and she hadn't known she needed it. She could finally stop crying. She smiled at the dog and the two men. "My goodness! I'm sorry. I had no idea that would happen."

Rob sat down beside her hugging her gently to him. "You're just exhausted and overwhelmed. No apologies needed. You've been through a lot and have been busy traveling and taking care of everyone except you."

Glory nodded. "Maybe I'm just tired. The drive was much longer than I expected and to be honest it was boring as hell in parts and other times I was too tired to enjoy the beauty."

"I'm sure you are tired. A lot has happened to you in the past few months."

Glory nodded. "Maybe. All I felt at first was anger and then freedom. It seems like the better things get overall, the sadder I am which makes absolutely no sense at all. I'm not even mad at Edgar anymore. I do not understand why I suddenly needed to cry other than fatigue. I've done a lot of camping and driving and feel like I'm looking for something or someone and not finding it."

Hugh sat beside her with Freya on his lap. He rubbed her shoulder. "I think it is all finally catching up with you. You and Edgar were together a long time and although the marriage was in trouble, you had no idea he would die so suddenly."

"Yes, but I've learned he was a much better person than I gave him credit for being."

Hugh nodded. "Good. Added to all the grief and upset over the divorce you also now have to deal with a fortune you never expected to have. The shock of your inheritance alone puts a lot of pressure on you."

"I agree. I'm doing better with the money considering how much it is. I'm getting to do what I said I wanted. I'm helping my friends and a lot of other people too."

"You are doing so much for others I worry you are not doing for you," Rob said.

"I bought the van and brought this little black beauty into my life and I'm finally traveling and love the traveling," Glory responded. "So, it makes no sense I have broken down weeping before I even entered the house."

"Honey, maybe it is just all too fast to process. Besides a two-thousand-mile drive in three days is a lot to do by yourself."

Glory blew her nose. "You both are probably right but I really thought these fucking episodes of tears and monumental weeping had stopped."

Hugh laughed and Rob said, "She's doing better now she has said her favorite word. That's a good sign."

Freya yiked and Glory said, "We'd better get her outside before she wears out her welcome on your lovely bamboo floor."

"If she does, we know how to clean it up." Hugh picked up Freya and said, "Come see the backyard I have in store for you little bits."

Freya licked his chin and when he put her down, she ran out on the lawn and piddled and then went loping around the yard with her ears flying. Hugh let her run around for a few minutes then picked her up to bring her in to meet Ralph.

Glory laughed watching the dog's joy. "Wow! I've never seen her do that before. I guess she's been cooped up in the van a little too long. Two thousand miles is a lot for a little pup."

Rob nodded. "Sometimes a girl just has to let her ears fly." Hugh handed Freya to Rob and left the patio door open. Hugh brought Ralph into the living room on a leash.

Hugh said, "I think they will be fine together, but she is so small he could hurt her not knowing she was a friend for him." Rob held Freya out to Ralph and let him sniff her.

Ralph whined and sat down in front of Rob, his tail beating an excited rhythm. "Okay," he said, "I'll put her down, but you be gentle." Rob put Freya on the floor in front of Ralph. He sniffed her again, and she promptly reached up and licked his nose.

He licked her back and then smiled his doggie smile with his tongue hanging out. Hugh took the leash off. Ralph pushed Freya a little with his nose, turned and ran outside. Freya raced after him, nothing but a little black blur. She barked and chased him and then suddenly she ran back in the house and he followed barking and chasing after her. In a few seconds Ralph turned around and Freya was barking and chasing Ralph. They played this big dog, little dog game of chase and for several minutes.

Glory said, "Well, the game of chase might get old quickly, at least for us." She laughed watching them chase each other back and forth barking with glee.

Hugh said, "One of them will tire in a few minutes. Just watch."

Before long the two dogs stopped racing and chasing and settled down and curled up together on Ralph's big bed in the living room.

Rob said, "And there you have it. Friends playing and resting together."

Glory's heart swelled at how peaceful and sweet the dogs looked together. The big dog, Ralph, was laying on his side while Freya snuggled in close to Ralph with one of his legs laying across her and she with her head tucked under his chin.

The next morning, they went to view several office spaces. When they pulled up in front of the last building Glory said, "I like the architecture of the exterior of this building. It has an elegant old and yet modern look. It reminds me of mid-twentieth-century buildings and yet seems more modern."

Hugh said, "I love the exterior of this building, too. The red brick with white concrete trim is really beautiful against the blue sky. I've been inside and it is a mess; rather like a rabbit warren. The exterior and interior was built out and finished at different times. It used to be an obstetrician's office. There's a ton of space and we can remodel the inside however we want. We could also just put a sign out and see patients."

Glory said, "Show me the inside and let's talk about it. I have a good gut feeling that this might be the one."

There were lots of exam rooms on two floors with several office spaces, reception areas and waiting rooms. There was even a lab space already built. Hugh said, "We could put X-ray in here, but it would be very expensive, take a lot of room and require certified and trained technicians. The new hospital north of here about two miles has great out-patient diagnostic facilities. I think having on-site lab is great because it is a lot cheaper for patients and us."

"There are lots of medical spaces on the east side of Norman, many of which we showed you this morning," Rob said, "But none were as perfect as this one on the west side. It is so close to home it is hard to resist."

Hugh said, "I love I'd be able to walk or ride my bike to work every day."

Glory nodded. "In the Seattle area it is common for folks to drive for hours to and from home every day just to work a job. I've always thought driving a long time every day was a waste of personal and family time."

"I don't have to drive an hour each way but during our 20-minute rush hour it can take as long as twenty to thirty minutes to get to work and back," Hugh said. "I listen to music or books, but I'd much rather be at home than driving. I really want it to work out with this building."

Rob said, "This was my first choice, but I was worried about the number of parking spaces."

"What did you decide on the parking?"

"First, we'd like to put a bicycle rack close to the building on the south side for anyone who rides a bike to and from the building," Rob said. "Then, as far as parking cars, we came up with several ideas but finally decided once we have the clinic open all the employees including the health care providers will park in the shopping center across the street."

"What did the shopping center say about parking?" Glory asked.

"They will lease all the spaces facing our clinic for a very low price. We would put signs on each space with each employee's name. There will be a few left over for overflow patients," Hugh said. "There are fifteen spaces total we can lease."

Rob said, "The building is not perfect, but the owners will give us a contract for leasing the building for a year. We have to pay for any renovations. At the end of the year we would have an option to buy the building at a set price for today's market. We have signed nothing, yet, which is why we wanted you to come down and look at it."

"I like the building and with your renovations feel it can be a very nice and welcoming clinic," Glory said. "You've thought of everything including the parking."

"Not quite," Hugh said.

Rob nodded. "We have no idea what to call this clinic."

Glory nodded. "This was an unexpected problem when we started this project. The umbrella for all the projects within the funding for them is The Pennington-Shaw Foundation." Glory said. "Does that help?"

"Wow," Hugh said. "Are you aware that Pennington is a common name here in Oklahoma?"

"No but please use the Pennington name if you want. It might make the whole endeavor here more appealing to the public too if the name is one that historically has meaning for Oklahoma. Did Martha tell you what they are calling the programs to help women get on their feet and become productive?"

Hugh nodded, "Yes and I love the whole concept of She-Shed. For the women to come out of their old ways of living life, shedding that which was holding them back makes great sense. I think we need to think on this more because the name needs to invite people to come to the clinic. I'd also like to mimic our desires for the clinic in the first place, but with honor and nobility not with the poverty and lack many of our patients experience every day."

"Keep thinking," Glory said. "I have faith you will come up with the perfect name. Next, I need you to make a formal plan for the building and clinic operations and submit it to Martha. My attorney suggested we have a board of directors but until that happens let's go with make a plan, submit it to Martha and then you can get started. It's time to be making a difference on a real level."

Hugh looked at Rob. "You tell her."

Rob grinned. "You are right about needing a plan. I was already working on the plan. I'll send Martha what we have as a preliminary plan but as we get a better idea of what we need, we can be more specific."

"Also," Hugh said, "When I talked about what I planned to do with this clinic and put in my notice at the hospital, many healthcare providers and others voiced interest in helping with the project. People in the community want to get involved with the work of refurbishing the property here and getting donations for equipment and furniture for the offices, exam rooms and other rooms. Some local health care providers have signed on to donate four to eight hours a week working in the clinic."

Glory smiled. "There, those are exactly the things I want to happen. I feel if we plant the seed for each project, they can become self-sustaining endeavors in a few years. Then each endeavor encompasses more and more people. The community of people involved and supporting the project grows like ripples in a pond. I love the concept of a whole community getting involved with helping each other and bringing kindness and love to the forefront."

Glory felt relaxed and at home when they were back in the van heading for lunch. "We have a real treat for you at the Service Station. It's our favorite lunch place," Rob said. "Their green chili burgers are the best I've ever eaten."

"I've never had one but I'm game to try it. I am happy with all the work you've done so far with the clinic. But I'm even more delighted, money Edgar didn't feel free to spend, is creating loving and kind projects."

Hugh nodded. "It is sad his childhood tormented him. I'm sure it made things worse for him with his grandfather's estate coming to him the way it did. Keeping his father from inheriting must have been a big burden. I wonder if it kept him from being able to deal with his emotional and psychological self."

"It's the saddest part of this whole ordeal," Glory agreed. "I did not understand all the things Edgar went through in his childhood. It tainted his whole life."

Rob said, "I wish his parents had loved him enough to shelter him from the sadness and grief of his conception."

Glory looked out the window thinking of all Edgar had missed in life because of three other people. The brother who betrayed his brother, was out of the picture too soon to affect how Edgar was raised. "I wish they had loved him more than their pride and greed. Love would have solved so many problems for Edgar moving forward in his life and maybe for our marriage. It is easy to see now why he was afraid of having children."

She took a deep breath. "Now my goal is to give as much love to all around me as I can and help people with his money so that Edgar's life and death will not have happened in vain."

Rob nodded. "I know Hugh feels as I do that this bounty came to us through sacrifice. We want to honor Edgar's sacrifice, not only for you, but for Edgar. Maybe it will help bring peace to Edgar if we all work to do good things with the money."

They all sat quietly in the van, driving the short distance to the restaurant. Glory felt peace and love surround her. *Edgar, I hope you were listening. I'm heading up these projects and spending your money to honor you and the life I wish you had loved.* "It's hard to believe he died only three months ago. It feels like a lifetime ago."

They ordered their lunch and got busy munching on the fried okra and fried mushrooms. Glory said, "This is probably the best thing I've ever eaten in my life! I've had fried mushrooms before, but I've never eaten okra in any form."

Hugh laughed. "Wait until you taste the burger and hand-cut real french fries from real potatoes. They are a little slice of heaven."

"We must be sure and ask for mustard for the fries," Rob said.

Hugh looked puzzled. "Not catsup?"

Glory shook her head. "I absolutely love mustard on fries, and they don't get as soggy as catsup makes them."

Hugh shook his head. When the burgers and fries arrived, he asked for the mustard for Glory's fries. The waitress said, "A woman after my heart. It is absolutely the only way to eat fried potatoes."

Hugh grinned. "All right. I'll try it." After the first bite he looked at Glory. "You are right. This is delicious."

After they finished eating their lunch and were back in Hugh's minivan, Hugh asked, "Are you free this evening?"

"Sure. Why?"

"My sister is having a cookout to welcome you to the community of Norman. This time it will just be family and we really want to make you part of our family. At some later date she wants to have a get-together to include community leaders who want to be a part of this project."

Glory felt the tears threaten again but choked them back. "I'd love to come and feel honored you want me to be part of the family. Shall I bring the van with me?"

"No need. Hugh and I will be happy to be your chauffeurs. We want to bring Ralph and Freya too. My sister has a golden doodle named Lucy. She is totally sweet, and Ralph adores her. Since he loves Freya it will be a doggie love fest."

Glory smiled. "I'm off the walls excited by all you two and Norman are doing. It feels like I had an idea and it is exploding into incredible projects I never would have imagined all by myself. Being welcomed as part of the family is like the cherry on top."

Hugh said, "As my grandmother used to say and I believe: when you do the right things, in the right way, at the right time, everything will come out right."

"That's perfect." Glory smiled to herself feeling safe and secure and included. *Edgar we are making a difference in people's lives including mine. Thank you.* Her circle of friends was growing so fast it was hard to keep up. *But I'd rather have to work to keep up than left behind.*

After they arrived back at Rob and Hugh's house Glory said, "If it's okay with you two, I'd love to have a nap. Lunch has left me mellow and sleepy."

"Perfect," said Rob. "You will want to rest enough to enjoy the evening. We'll be leaving here for dinner in about three or four hours. You've plenty of time for a nap. We'll watch Freya for you."

Glory went back to the guest bedroom off the kitchen and closed the door. She sat in the rocking chair in front of a small television and took off her shoes. She rocked for a few minutes letting her toes wiggle and scrunch in the thick shag carpeting. "I'd better get up and get in bed before I fall asleep sitting up."

She pulled the covers of the bed back and lay down between the coolness of the sheets. She tucked the pillow under her head and before she could think of anything, she was asleep.

Two hours later she had to get up to go to the bathroom. Getting up awakened her more so she took a shower. Glory changed into a summer dress that was a soft yellow and white plaid with bold red hibiscus flowers patterned over the dress. She brushed her silky blond hair and left it loose flowing down her back. She looked in the mirror and saw she was getting a tan even in the short time she had been in Oklahoma.

When she walked through the kitchen to the family room, Rob looked up at her and grinned. "Now there is the beautiful woman I love."

"Thanks. I feel much better after a nap."

"Great, Hugh is getting changed and will be out in a few minutes and then we will head over to Helen's house."

"I'm a little nervous to meet his family," Glory said. "I'm already confused with all the new faces and names of people I've met. I think I've met as many new people in the past few days as I've ever known in my life."

"Well, if you keep traveling and meeting folks and writing about your experiences meeting people is bound to happen."

Glory nodded. "Yes, it is. So far, I've written something every day on the blog, except for yesterday when I was too tired. I've added lots of photos and a few videos."

"I know," Rob said. "I've read every one of your posts. They get better each day."

"It's a little daunting to write and even more frightening to hit the 'publish' button. Every time I do, I quake a little inside. Maybe everything I'm writing is unmitigated crap and people will just shrug off what I have to say."

"Not a chance," Rob said. "Your sense of humor and whimsy combined with the obvious deep realities you are sharing hooked me right away."

"Yes, but you are my friend."

Hugh walked into the room. "No more 'yes, buts'. Your writing is good and working its way toward being great. I'm enjoying your blog and not just because we are friends. I love how you are sharing your experiences in ways I haven't seen even if I've been to the same or similar places."

"Thanks," Glory said. "Your response is the best thing I've heard about my writing."

Rob grinned. "Enough jibber-jabber. I'm ready to get in the van and go to dinner. Helen's dinners are not ones to be late for. All the food will vanish before we get there if we don't get going."

Chapter 19

"New love is grand.

Savor all the crazy,

Muddled might of it."

— Eli Easton

.

Rob buckled the dogs in their security harnesses in the very back seat. Glory had worried that Freya would be a problem in a different car, but she snuggled close to Ralph and went to sleep for the whole ride.

Rob said, "I can't wait until you see Helen's house. It is an old farmhouse on Pickard Avenue that she and her husband Tom bought when they got married. They have refurbished and remodeled the house. It is beautiful."

"I'm looking forward to meeting her and the rest of your family."

"She has five kids. Three girls and two boys. They are a rowdy but loving family."

Glory looked out the window. *Do not cry.* She was thinking of the children she would never have and seemed unable to put aside the longing to hold her own baby in her arms. "I am very excited to meet them and hope they don't mind lots of hugs and kisses."

Hugh looked at her in the rear-view mirror. "The oldest girl, Lisa, is thirteen and thinks she is all grown up and sophisticated. The youngest girl, Julie, is a little bossy and a real tomboy but loads of fun. Anna the middle girl is so sweet and will want you to hug her and kiss her."

Glory smiled. "Then I'll seek her out! What about the boys?"

Rob answered, "The oldest boy George is a quiet boy, but he is sweet and kind. Ricky the youngest is a great kid but one bundle of energy bursting through the seams all the time. He is my favorite."

Hugh said, "George is my favorite. He loves science, reading and geography. He and I can spend hours together looking at the stars, digging up rocks, talking about books—especially Harry Potter books, or just sitting around quietly together. He always wins when we play chess. I need to work on my game."

Rob laughed, reached over and patted Hugh's arm. "George is the mini-Hugh of the family."

They pulled into the driveway and children poured out of the house, waving and squealing their greetings. Hugh and Rob bundled up children with hugs and then turned to introduce Glory to them. George asked, "Where's Ralph?"

Hugh grinned. "I'll get him, and he has a new friend Freya."

"What's a Freya?" Anna asked.

Bending down to talk to Anna, Glory said, "She is my new puppy. You will love her. She is tiny and sweet and cuddly."

"Yes, she is," a soft, man's voice said. Glory recognized the voice. A frisson of happiness mixed with anxiety tickled the back of her neck. She stood up and looked to see Jake walking toward her. He didn't have his hat on. His curly blond hair was hanging over his forehead. He had on his tight blue jeans, a blue plaid cowboy shirt and his old scuffed up cowboy boots.

She grabbed Rob's hand and whispered, "My cowboy."

Jake grinned and Rob stood beside her with his mouth hanging open. Jake nodded. "I hoped we'd see each other again. Just didn't expect it to be at my sister's house and you with these two fellas."

Glory could only nod her head in reply.

Rob looked from Glory to Jake understanding dawning on him. He grinned. "I think it is high time you two properly met. Glory, this is Jake Casey. He is Hugh's younger brother. Jake this is Gloriana Pennington, one of my best friends from high school in North Bend, Washington."

Jake stepped forward, took Glory's hand. "I'm delighted to see you again and thrilled to know your full name."

Glory nodded. "Me too. No wait. I already knew my full name. I'm glad to know your full name too."

Ricky tugged on Glory's dress. "Jake Casey is not his full name. His full name is Jacob Samuel Casey. We call him Uncle Jake."

Glory looked down at Ricky. "Thank you so much for telling me. Is it okay if I call him Jake?"

"Yeah, sure. Everyone else does."

Glory look back up at Jake. His blue eyes sparkled, and his dimples were deep as he smiled and looked down at Ricky. "Thanks, buddy, for helping me out."

Then Jake lifted Glory's hand, kissed the back of her hand and tucked it into his arm. "Let me walk with you inside and introduce you to our sister Helen and her husband Tom."

Glory sat beside Jake at the dinner table. She felt near trembling with the excitement of him being so close. He occasionally reached over and held her hand for a few seconds. It felt perfect to her. A tiny voice nagged in the back of her head, '*Calm down. He is just a man you met, and he is handsome and charming. Don't get too excited by his presence.*' She was trying to be calm, but it was hard.

After dinner, Jake said, "If it is okay with everyone here, I'd like to take a walk with Glory so we can chat and get reacquainted."

"Sure," Helen said, "If that is what Glory wants to do."

Jake looked questioning at Glory and smiled. She felt her insides soften a little at his smile. *He's a guy you just met. Well, just met two times now. Settle down. You are going for a walk, nothing more.* "That would be nice," Glory answered. "It is all overwhelming to know the Jake I met in North Bend at a service station is actually Hugh's brother."

"I'm sure it is," Helen said. "It's a big surprise for me too. You two have a good walk and talk." She pointed at Jake. "You behave like a gentleman, Jake. It's what I expect of my brothers. When you get back baby brother, I expect you to help with the cleanup."

"Yes ma'am. Your wish is my command."

Hugh laughed and shook his head. "No need to hurry back, baby brother. I'll help with the cleanup. Just let me know when you are ready to head back to our house, Glory."

"If it is okay with Glory," Jake said. "I'll be happy to drive her over to your house. I have a feeling we need a really long talk without pressure."

Glory looked at Jake and was pleased to see that his face was sincere. He was smiling but not in a teasing way. *What is it about him that feels so right?* Then she asked, "What about Freya?"

"We can take care of her for you," Rob said, "As long as you are comfortable with Jake driving you home."

She smiled softly. "I think he will do fine."

Jake and Glory turned walking out of the dining room as the rest of the family looked at each other in a mixture of joy, awe and confusion.

Rob said, "I have a feeling about this."

Helen nodded. "So, do I. I hope it isn't too soon for either of them. Life hasn't been easy for them lately."

Jake took Glory's hand walking north to Boyd Avenue. They turned and walked toward the University of Oklahoma campus. Neither of them felt a need to talk yet but Glory felt the warmth of his hand as safety and security. It felt more intimate to her than anything she had ever experienced with a man. He squeezed her hand. "You doing okay?"

She nodded. "I'm a little stunned by all of this." She decided to be honest with him so she could be honest with herself. "I didn't think I'd ever see you again. I thought about you a lot. I thought about seeing you again but didn't have the least idea how to find you. Seeing you suddenly appear at Hugh's sister's house is a shock. To not only find you here but find out you are the brother to my best friend's husband is just wild. It's almost unbelievable."

He stopped and turned toward her. He wanted to be honest with her. He had a feeling tonight would be one of the most important nights of his life. "You are important to me. For me to do or say anything to hurt you or make your life harder than it surely already is, would be horrible. The thing is though, I could not get you out of my mind. Even when I'm sleeping you are in my mind. I dream of you every night and wake thinking of you every morning. I have kicked myself daily for not getting your last name or a phone number."

"Me too. I wake up having dreamed of you and sad you aren't there."

He looked in her eyes to see if she was being truthful. "Really?" he asked, hoping the answer was true. "It would be more pain than I could bear if you are saying anything other than what is deeply true."

She nodded. "I'm being honest with you Jake. I decided when we started this walk, I must be honest with you and with myself. I couldn't bear the pain of seeing you tonight and not at least be honest with you."

"Thank you. It is good to hear."

Glory knew she had crossed over into wanting to form a relationship with this man. He was so different from anything she had ever thought of in a man and yet seemed so right for her. She wanted to trust her gut but was still a little shell-shocked at his reappearance in her life.

He turned to walk beside her and tucked her arm across his placing his hand on top of hers.

She felt the warmth of his body on her hand. *This feels so right. Please let it be right.*

After a few more minutes he asked, "How about we go across to the North Oval and sit for a bit and talk?"

"That would be great." As they approached the oval, she looked around at the old buildings, landscaping and little places of intimacy. The sun was lowering in the sky casting a pink and gold glow over the world around them. "This is a beautiful campus with all the red brick and white trim. I never thought the campus would be this big."

He smiled. "I love this campus. It is a part of my life. It is much bigger than you can see here. It goes for about three or four miles south and a few blocks east of where we are now."

He pointed to a bench under a tree looking across the street. "Here we are. This is the North Oval. Over there," he pointed east, "Is where the original campus was built. Then over there," he pointed north, "across Boyd Street is Campus Corner where lots of the students and some folks in town hang out."

She looked around. "It is beautiful. The old buildings and the small-town feel of Campus Corner are perfect. The flowers are perfect too." She looked at Jake. "Did you go to school here?"

He nodded. "For the first couple of years. Then I went to Oklahoma State University. Boy, did I feel like a fish out of water at first. I'm totally an OU fan. Sooner born and bred. I'd never thought I would go to the Aggie school."

"Why did you?"

"I wanted to be a veterinarian. That's the only place in the state where I could get the degree I wanted, and I didn't want to move away from my family."

"So, you are a veterinarian?"

"Yep. I don't have a formal practice but take care of my animals and those of a few of my neighbors down by my ranch. I can take care of dogs and cats, but I mostly do big animals especially horses. They are my life."

She heard a wistful tone in his voice and looked up at him. He was looking across the oval but didn't seem to look at anything in particular. "You okay?"

He looked down at her and smiled. He seemed a little sad. "Yeah, I'm okay. I think I need to tell you some things about me. Just in case."

She wrinkled her forehead. "Just in case what?"

"Just in case there is something starting between us."

Glory nodded but said nothing. *She also felt there was something starting between them but didn't know if she was ready yet for any relationship with a man. Somehow, she felt drawn to Jake and felt deep comfort sitting beside him on this park bench. For the first time she could remember she felt safe and at ease with a man. She was glad he was thinking there might be something important between them. Okay, Martha, I will trust my gut.*

"You should know I've been married before."

"Me too," Glory answered.

Jake didn't seem to hear her and continued. "My wife and I divorced a few months ago."

"Why?" Glory asked. Feeling a chill of fear in her chest from the memory of the pain of her own divorce came flooding back. *You didn't get divorced,* she reminded herself. *But if Jake divorced his wife and was mean, I could not stand to be around him. Am I wrong about Jake? The pain of Edgar's dismissal of me and our marriage is fresh in my heart.* She sat still and silent waiting to hear what had happened with Jake and his wife.

Jake continued. "It was a very painful thing; it still is. I'm trying to move on but it is harder than I thought it would be. I thought she loved me enough to have a family with me. Instead, when she got pregnant she didn't even tell me. She was waiting to decide whether to have an abortion when she miscarried."

"Oh, Jake, I'm so sorry." She could feel his pain and disappointment. Her grief of losing her babies rose to the surface and brought tears to her eyes. She worked to hold them back and listen intently to Jake. She wanted to hear his story not become the story.

Jake nodded. "Thanks. I wanted to work it out, but she refused to discuss having children. I couldn't stay in a marriage knowing I would never have children and she had not wanted the child I had created with her. I never even knew she was pregnant until after the miscarriage."

Glory reached out and touched his arm. "I'm so sorry. Did the divorce go smoothly?"

He nodded. "Yes. In many ways, it was just too easy to get out of what I thought would be a lifelong relationship. When I settled down and let go of the anger at her, we could talk about it all. It was as loving as a divorce can be. It's been about three months, but it is still hard to take and still hurts. We are in contact by email and phone occasionally. She's creating a new life that fits her better. I've been at loose ends dreaming of you," He looked at her and asked, "What about you? You said you were married before."

Glory smiled and was pleased to know although he had continued with his story, he had heard her. Just being heard and acknowledged was a new sensation for her. Knowing he had been dreaming of her, as she had him, thrilled her deep inside.

"My story is heart breaking too but in different ways. Edgar, my husband, sent me divorce papers by email at my workplace."

"Damn! That's harsh. I'm sorry he did that to you. Divorce is hard enough without adding insult to the pain."

"I know. It was terrible. The divorce was only the beginning though. I think of it as The Terrible Day. Things just kept getting worse that day. I left work after I read the email and went home. A few minutes after I got home, really upset about the impending divorce and not knowing what to do, the police came to the door."

"Why?"

She held up her hand. "Just wait. You won't believe it. I still can hardly believe it and it happened to me." Taking a deep breath, she continued. "The police told me that my husband Edgar ran a red light and was killed by an oncoming cement truck." She snorted a laugh. "Can you imagine getting divorced by email and widowed by a cement truck in just a few hours of the same day?"

"No," Jake said, shaking his head and smiling. "I cannot. That is nearly an unbelievable story."

She quickly looked at him. "Do you believe the story?"

He nodded. "Yes, I do, but it is a stunning story. I have no reason to believe you would lie even if the story is wild and crazy. I have a gut feeling you would never lie to me."

She searched his eyes and saw the truth in Jake's eyes. "The one thing you can count on with me Jake is that I will never lie to you. Life is too important to live it with even little falsehoods. Right now, I feel like we are an unlucky couple, unsure of what we are doing and what comes next."

He smiled. "I think we should change at least taking out the 'unlucky' bit."

Glory felt a small thrill of hope deep inside but shook her head. "Jake, I like you. Maybe even a lot. But I've been a widow for about as long as you've been divorced. I'm willing to drop the word 'unlucky'. It seems the Universe wanted us to meet again. We have both been dreaming about each other. But I'm not sure I'm ready to be a 'couple' with anyone yet."

He tucked her arm close to him and took her hand in his. They sat quietly for a few minutes. Jake was so quiet and still that Glory worried that she had said something wrong. He finally said, "I feel the same way too but I'm also really attracted to you. You mentioned trusting your gut level feelings. I usually do, but in North Bend at the service station I didn't follow my gut and ask for your phone number. I feel like us meeting again and having close ties within my family and your friendship with Rob, is important."

"Me too."

Jake smiled at her. "It is a miracle and I don't take miracles lightly. It feels like it is a message from somewhere telling us we need to at least consider having a relationship. I don't want to lose the opportunity to find the right woman. I think you may be her, but we have a lot to talk about and work out before going further with this. At the same time, going further with this feels right."

Glory took a breath, looked into his eyes. She felt nothing but honest and kind regard coming from his eyes and from him. "I feel the same way, Jake.

Can we start with being friends for now?"

"Can I have your phone number?" Jake asked.

Glory pretended to think it over but then smiled. "Only if I can have yours."

Jake and Glory walked around the campus for a little longer. He pointed out various buildings and their functions. After about an hour he asked, "What's next?"

"Next you drive me back to Hugh and Rob's place. Tomorrow I'll be heading back to Washington."

"No hanging around to get to know each other better?" Jake asked.

Glory leaned a little closer. "Can we get to know each other better over the phone and email? We can even do video calls."

Jake smiled and touched her cheek lightly. "We can do all of that. I can't imagine wanting to talk with another woman the way we have talked this evening. It has never happened for me. I think I'm falling for you but like you I don't want to rush things."

"I think I'm falling for you too," Glory said. "I love the way we talked tonight. I need time to be sure my emotions and my gut instincts are in sync before I dive into a relationship."

"You sound like my mom. She used to say if your gut says 'no' and you do it anyway, then woe betide you. If you gut says 'yes' then get your butt in gear."

Glory laughed. "My gut isn't saying no. It is saying yes, but my emotions are all over the place and I want to be sure on a deeper level. I want to get to know the real me a lot better before I make any commitments to anyone. I have a strong feeling me knowing me better, especially with you, is important."

Jake kissed her gently on the forehead. "I totally agree. I can be a patient man and will wait for us to know ourselves and each other better. Then we can talk about what's next for us. I hope the 'us' will be a couple sometime soon." Jake leaned into her to rest his forehead against hers. Glory felt the warmth of his breath creating a bond between them.

Glory smiled. "Let's wait and see at least for a little while. I can promise right now there is no other man in my life." She took the risk and kissed him lightly on the lips and then raised her head from his and watched his eyes glistening a little.

Jake nodded. "Thank you Glory. Hearing that makes a big difference. I can promise you right now there is no other woman in my life." He grinned. "Or man either."

She laughed and poked his ribs. "Good to know! Now it is time for you to take me home in that beat-up pickup truck of yours."

"Hey! Be careful there. Little Darlin' is my first and only vehicle I've ever owned. Well, except for my tractor and four-wheeler." He grinned at the look on her face.

"Little Darlin' is it?" Glory asked.

"Yep, she's my number one gal until another one comes along and pushes her into the number two spot."

"How hard will that be?"

"For you, easy."

Glory woke in her room at Hugh and Rob's house. She rolled over in bed remembering last night. Jake was gentle and kind. *I think I'm falling in love for the first time ever.* Remembering the way, he kissed her good night on the front porch made her feel warm and cherished. She could still feel his gentle touch of his left hand on her waist, just above her hip. *What a small but significant feeling. It felt like he was letting me know I was his and he was mine. The tenderness of that kiss was nearly my undoing.* The kiss was sweet and definitely one making Glory want more.

She sat up in bed, stretched and looked for Freya. She wasn't in the room but the door was cracked open. *Rob or Hugh must have let her out. Time to get up and about.*

She went to the bathroom, brushed her teeth and pulled on an old, soft pair of blue jeans and a t-shirt. This one was black with lots of 'hippy' style flowers and a cute dog saying, 'Let That Shit Go!'. When she walked barefooted from the guest bedroom into the kitchen, she could smell coffee and something hot and yeasty.

"Good morning, Glory!" Rob said from across the room in the den area. He was smiling and holding Freya on his lap with Ralph beside him. Freya jumped, nearly flew, off Rob's lap and raced to Glory.

Glory laughed. "Good morning everyone especially you little girl." She picked up the dancing dog who snuggled and wiggled all at the same time. Glory felt the joy of the puppy in the greeting and it made her feel even happier than she already did. Joy was in high spirits today.

Rob stood and walked toward Glory. "Hugh has already headed to the hospital, but he asked me to ask you if you could stay around for a few more days. We would like to share a few details with you and get a better handle on things before you head back to Issaquah."

"Sure. I can stay a few days. I had planned to leave today but I feel like I need to rest here if that is okay with you guys."

"Mi Casa es su casa," Rob said. "I think I said it right. I'm trying to learn Spanish and so is Hugh. We will need it in the clinic. Hugh estimates that at least half the patients will be."

Glory smiled. "Don't ask me if it is right. I think however that was a yes I can stay for a little longer visit."

"Our home welcomes you to visit and stay anytime you want as long as you want."

"I love your house, but it is so big compared to what I had in Issaquah," Glory said. "Everything here seems big and spread out."

Rob nodded. "In Oklahoma, there is a lot of room to spread out."

"There would be at least four houses on your one lot if this were Issaquah. I love your house and yard. The openness feels great and yet with the way you have decorated it all feels loving and cozy."

Rob came over and gave Glory a hug. "Now is the time for coffee and homemade cinnamon rolls. I'm working on some modifications. These have pecans and dried cranberries with some cardamom."

"Smells yummy and I'm starving this morning."

Rob poured them both cups of coffee and set them on the breakfast table. He opened the oven door and after checking the rolls he took them out of the oven. He put a cream cheese and whipping cream frosting on them. "We'll let that cool a few minutes then we can have a taste test. Let's sit and talk." He brought cream and sugar to the table and motioned for Glory to sit down.

"So how was it?"

Glory smiled. "I'm assuming you mean my walk with Jake."

"I am and you know it. Spill the beans."

Glory put her chin in her hand. "It was wonderful."

Rob raised his eyebrows, and she tapped him on the arm. "I know that sounds goofy or too high-school girly but really, it was wonderful. Jake showed me the campus which is more beautiful than I expected. Then campus corner with all the small shops and eclectic people and stores. It is really a very intriguing place."

Rob nodded. "Yes. And…"

"We talked a lot and I think there is something there. Maybe something wonderful but also a little frightening."

"Hugh and I had talked about this long before you made your trip here. We were worried about Jake. He seemed so isolated and lonely but also calm and peaceful. He was spending all his time at the ranch and seldom came up to visit. When he came back from his Washington hiking journey, he seemed different but anxious in a way we couldn't define. Sometimes he would sit, and smile and it seemed like he was thinking of someone or something special. We wondered if he'd met someone but when we asked, he would just say 'maybe', smile and walk away. Hugh thought perhaps the time in the woods in a different place had given him some peace."

Glory smiled. "Well, the Middle Fork is the place to find peace. You remember the house I grew up in?"

Rob nodded.

"The Middle Fork ran right by our addition. I always thought it was a beautiful river. It always brought me peace just to walk down to the river's edge and watch the water flow over the rocks."

"I remember that feeling too," Rob said. "Until last night we thought the trip was all there was to the peaceful and nearly contented change in Jake. But the faraway looks and soft smiles were something new and different for him. He has never been that way."

Glory blushed. "We talked about that last night. We both were kicking ourselves for not getting each other's phone numbers. I've dreamed about him every night since our first meeting. He said he had too."

Rob patted her hand. "Well, this needs more talk and discovery I'm certain. For now, let's have those cinnamon rolls."

Chapter 20

"Drama is very important in life:
You have to come on with a bang.
You never want to go out with a whimper."
— Julia Child

Martha debated about whether she was doing the right thing. Glory was in Oklahoma and Jason and Emily were busy doing things on the building and housing end. She had a few days to herself and decided to go to Lake Easton to meet Lori. "Am I crazy?" she asked herself. "Maybe," she answered.

From the moment Martha saw the photo of Lori she could not stop thinking about her. Maybe because Lori had said Martha looked like a warrior goddess was part of the attraction. Martha smiled to herself. *Maybe. But maybe it was Lori's dark green eyes or her black curly hair that is attractive. I'm still uncertain about the sexuality issue. I hate the feeling of shame coming with those thoughts. Being lesbian is nothing to be ashamed of. I wonder if my shame comes from my religious upbringing? I've never been with a woman physically. I've never even kissed a woman. Hell's bells, I've never even held hands with a woman! I know nothing from just a photo.*

Martha turned her minivan into the Lake Easton park and pulled up to the ranger station. She was disappointed to see a man there. "Where's Lori?"

"She doesn't come on today until later. I can ask her to come to your site if you'd like."

Martha nodded, a little disappointed. *But this will give me a chance to get set up and play with my self-conversion minivan.*

She paid her fees and went to her assigned camp site. She parked the van so that the sliding door faced the campsite table and the lake. She wanted to see the lake even when in the van. She opened the sliding side door. Looking inside at her make-shift conversion she had done mostly by herself in her garage, she was very pleased. It wasn't as posh as Glory's van, but she thought the results would work fine. For now.

The back seat had folded down flat, and Martha had put a 4-inch foam pad on top for her mattress. Jason had helped her take out the captain's chairs on the second row. He used a scrap piece of plywood to make a temporary floor so she would not stumble or fall because of the tracks where the seats had been. He had told her if she really liked van camping, he could do a lot more to help her. He said he could fix the front passenger and driver's seats so they could turn around into the van living area.

Everything fabric was in shades of red, pink and purple. She had a folding double camp chair that sat nicely behind the front seats. She pulled the heavy, light-blocking curtain closed blocking out the front seat area and front windows. She laid a deep purple, shaggy rug on the floor and looked around the space. *I like it a lot. It's cozy and comfortable.*

When she was sure everything was ready for her camping adventure in a minivan, she went outside. Locking the van, she went for a walk around the lake. She was nervous about meeting Lori and needed to work off her anxious energy.

She had not told Lori she was coming here to meet her. In fact, she had never even talked with Lori. She was a little nervous about just showing up here, *but I couldn't help myself. I hope it all works out. Hell, I'm a little nervous it might work out. I don't know what to do with any of it. If I don't do it now, I never will. Lori told Glory she wanted to meet me. I hope she meant it."*

Walking around the campground, she had to agree with everything Glory had said about the place. It was all beautiful. The lake was shining blue in the sunlight. The light breeze made the surface of the lake ripple a little and it looked like a sheet of blue satin with glittering beads sewn on. A few birds swooped down to the surface of the lake and then up again into the air. There were rowboats and kayaks out on the lake with people enjoying the water. The trees towered over everything. Their scent was a heavenly mixture of pine, spruce and hemlock. She walked around the full circle of the campground back to her site. Her nerves had not settled even though she tried very hard to tamp them down.

As she was entering her site, she saw Lori walking towards her dressed in her green ranger uniform. *She looks stunning in her uniform.* The closer she got she could see her short, curly black hair and deep green eyes. Lori waved cheerily to Martha, and she waved back. She felt nervous and her mouth was suddenly dry. *Settle down, girl.* When they were close, Lori said, "Hi Martha! I'd know you anywhere."

"Hi," Martha responded, still nervous.

Lori reached out her hand Martha. Martha took her hand and felt the calluses on Lori's hand but also the pleasure of touching her hand. "How are you doing with your site?" Lori asked.

"I'm not sure." Martha looked around. "I've never camped before. I'm just following Glory's lead without jumping in to buying a fancy van."

"That's cool," Lori nodded. "I can help you learn what you need to know about camping. Why don't you show me the inside of your van?"

Martha pulled her keys out of her pocket and promptly dropped them. Lori bent over and picked them up. "Butter fingers," Martha said. Lori smiled back. Martha thought her smile was the most beautiful thing she had seen today. She turned and unlocked the van sliding door. She motioned to Lori, "Enter my abode on wheels."

Lori stepped up to the van and climbed inside. "You've done a great job on this in a very short time."

Martha joined her aware of Lori's closeness and the smell of lilac in her hair. "Thanks. I was worried I wouldn't be able to stand up in here but obviously that is not a problem."

"It's a little close," Lori said, "But it feels just right in here. Cozy and inviting."

"I'm glad you like it. Jason is a friend who helped me knock this together quickly so I could come out here and meet you."

"I'm glad you did." Lori turned to face Martha. "I have to work for a few hours but get off at 6. Would you like to have dinner with me?"

"Sure. What did you have in mind?"

"I'd like to show you my camper van too. It is a little bigger than yours but still a mini-van. I have things a little different in the layout. My van is my home. I live in it 24/7. I'll drive over here about 6:30. I'll bring steaks if you can provide something to go with it."

Martha nodded. "I'd love that."

"Good. Can I bring Buttercup?"

"Glory told me about Buttercup."

"She is my yellow lab and for now my only partner. She is a good dog and loves everyone."

Martha grinned. "I love dogs but couldn't have one in an efficiency apartment. Now I have a home I was thinking about getting a dog but haven't done so. I'd love to meet Buttercup."

"She will love you." Lori quickly kissed Martha on the cheek and waved goodbye. "See you soon."

Martha was too stunned to say anything and just waved. She reached up to touch her cheek where Lori's kiss lingered like warm sunshine.

Later that evening Lori came back driving her red minivan. It was much like Martha's as far as model but a little bigger. Buttercup was hanging her head out the window with a big grin and her tongue lolling out. Martha chuckled at the sheer joy on the dog's face.

After introducing Martha to Buttercup, Lori showed Martha the inside of the van. She could see what Jason was talking about for her van. Not only were there a lot more shelves, the back seat had been taken out completely, and a bed built up on a platform. There were drawers underneath the platform supporting the bed. Buttercup promptly jumped on the bed and pulled a pillow out of the pile of pillows and laid her head on it. Lori said, "It's her favorite pillow. She sometimes drags it outside to lie on."

Martha smiled. "She is adorable. I love her."

Under the bed were six drawers where Lori put all of her clothes. On the wall above the bed was a shelf with a lattice front on each shelf, holding things in. On the shelf were books and CDs. Beside the bed, were smaller shelves with drawers. Lori opened them one by one to show Martha that this was where she stored her toiletries, scarves, and jewelry. At the foot of the bed was a television mounted on the wall. There was a shelf that folded down so Lori could use her computer there or use it as a table when on the road. The walls were oiled, natural pine boards.

Lori said, "It is fully insulated with a solar panel on the top so I can have electricity even on the road."

"Does it get cold in here during the winter?"

"Sure, but I have a small ceramic cube heater I sit on the kitchen counter during the winter. The space is well insulated and small enough it keeps the place cozy."

Then Lori showed Martha the kitchen area complete with running water using a similar jug system as Martha's, but she also had a cooler that could run on electricity or propane. "I have a propane tank on the back of the vehicle for cooking and the cooler."

Then Lori said, "You mentioned that Jason could fix your front seats to turn around into the living area. I did that and I love it." She showed turning the seats around and Martha could see how much difference it would make in her van. The seats were comfortable and helped the living space to feel more open. Lori said, "And this is the best part of the chairs." She rolled over two upholstered cubes putting one in front of each seat. "Now we can sit down and put our feet up," She said as she sat down and put her feet up.

"I love it. Having the seats turned around with foot rests makes it feel like a home."

Lori nodded. She stood up and opened the top of one cube. "And they are more than foot rests they are storage. I have an extra blanket and sweaters in this one. In the other is rain gear and boots. Over on the side opposite my kitchen I have one skinny hang up closet."

"What's the other door?" Martha asked.

Lori grinned and opened the door. "This is my biggest luxury. Here's my throne." Martha looked inside to see a toilet, a tiny sink and a shower hanging on the wall above the toilet. "Lots of folks don't bother with this but I'm fairly shy about personal hygiene and prefer to have my own shower and toilet. Besides, this is where I live and I can't always count on having a shower or toilet available."

Martha grinned. "I like your throne."

"Yeah. I don't sit there often. It's hard to rule anything with your pants down."

Martha laughed. "I'm glad to see you have my kind of humor. I think too much thought over being proper is a waste of time."

"Life is too short to waste it on bullshit," Lori said. "Let's get cooking so we can have a real talk."

Lori and Martha pooled their resources and cooked dinner. Lori grilled the steaks over a wood fire she built in the campfire ring while Martha tossed a salad together with olives, shredded parmesan and oranges. She carried the salad out to the picnic table along with some garlic bread she heated in a skillet. Buttercup was lying beside the table on a rug Martha had put down for her. She had her head on her favorite pillow snoozing. When Martha walked up to the table, Buttercup reached up a paw. Martha sat the salad and bread down and then knelt beside Buttercup, scratching her behind the ear.

Lori grinned. "You keep doing that and she'll be your devoted companion for life."

"There could be worse outcomes in this life but few better," Martha said. She loved the silky feel of her ears and the adoring look in her eyes. She felt her heart soften at the look from the dog. She had heard the adoring look was a survival technique innate in some animals and human babies. She thought it was love and friendship.

Lori brought the steaks to the table. "I can see she loves you. That's important because I love Buttercup."

Martha smiled. "Anyone who doesn't love Buttercup has a chunk of coal for a heart." She stood up and sat across the table from Lori.

"I like to save the bits of fat and meat that I don't eat so Buttercup has a little treat, but I don't feed her from the table."

"Good to know."

While they ate, they talked and got to know each other a little better. Finally, Martha jumped in with both feet. "Glory told me you are lesbian."

Lori smiled. "Yes, I am."

"I'm not sure whether I am or what to do next."

"You are doing fine. It confuses you because you would know exactly what to do if I were a man sitting here."

Martha laughed. "You're right. We women are raised to know how to do this with a man. I did not want to leave you sitting at home to find another woman. So, I came to meet you."

Lori laughed with her and then shook her head. "I have no plans to find another woman. I saw your photo and wanted to know you too. I'm glad and thankful you came out to meet me. I was trying to figure out an excuse to come meet you."

"Thanks. I was a little nervous but couldn't resist meeting you after I saw your photo. That doesn't change that I feel like a fish out of water. I've never been with a woman before. I've been with a man one time and never, ever want to do that again."

"If I were a man, and you were a woman, or the other way around, the first thing we would do is get to know each other, maybe over dinner. That's what we are doing now," Lori said. "The next thing we would do is spend time with each other doing mundane things like movies, dinner, coffee, walking. Just like we would do if we were a heterosexual couple."

"What if I don't know for sure?" Martha asked.

"You don't have to know for sure. Just follow where your heart leads you." Lori shook her head. "It isn't always easy. I had a partner for a few months. When we separated, although we enjoyed each other's bodies, there was no real long-term spark there. It's not different from relationships between men and women. Sometimes it is just physical and sometimes it is much more."

Martha nodded. "That makes sense. Thank you for being so kind and forthright with me and explaining these things. At my age you would think I would already know this stuff."

"Age is never a predictor of our level of understanding of life. I've known children who have a good understanding of life and old folks who still are lost on their path. From the time I first saw your photo, I was attracted to you."

Martha laughed. "Glory told me you said I looked like a warrior goddess."

"You still do. I'm sitting here looking at you and I'm totally smitten in a way I have never been before. I feel I'm in the presence of something magical." She reached out and touched Martha's hand.

Martha responded with her hand, twining her fingers with Lori's. "I've never felt like this with anyone before."

They walked around the lake together, hand-in-hand with Buttercup following along and sometimes leading them. When they were back at the campsite, Martha was unsure about what would happen next or even what she wanted to happen. Lori turned to Martha. "I have to work early tomorrow and for the next several days."

Martha said, "I had planned to be here only tonight. I've got a lot of things back in Issaquah needing my attention tomorrow."

"How about I come for a visit next weekend? Would that work for you?"

"Only if you'll bring Buttercup. I have a large fenced yard dogs love. But you'll be sleeping in a house unless you'd prefer to sleep in your van in the driveway."

"The house sounds fine."

"Great," Martha said. "I bought it a few weeks ago and have been busy dolling it up to my tastes. I'll get a doggie bed for Buttercup too. I want her to feel loved and at home."

"I can't wait to see it. I'll bring Buttercup, her food and a few toys. She will love the yard I'm sure. I'm excited to see your place." Then Lori leaned into Martha and kissed her softly at first. Then Martha, unable to resist, pulled Lori close and deepened the kiss. When they finished the kiss Lori said, "I'll try to wait until the weekend." She turned, waved, got in her van and left.

Martha went inside her own van. She felt more breathless and alive than she had ever felt. It surprised her to think of not only Lori but of Buttercup too. *I'm on the road to discovery. I loved the kiss.* She smiled at the thought. *Now I understand what I've been missing. Tonight, was much better than any date I've ever had with a man.* She undressed and went to bed. She dreamed of Lori and all that she wanted to do at home to prepare for Lori's visit. The next morning, she drove through the gate of the park to check out. Lori was there but so was another ranger. Lori smiled. "I hope you had a pleasant night."

Martha grinned. "The best night I've had in a long time. I dreamed of you."

"That's wonderful to hear. I dreamed of you too." Lori smiled and reached out to touch Martha's hand. "I'll see you this weekend."

"With Buttercup," Martha said.

Lori laughed. "We are buddies. We come as a team anywhere we go."

"That's a team I'd like to spend a lot more time with," Martha said. She waved goodbye and as she drove out of the campground, she looked in the rear-view mirror to see Lori with her hand raised in farewell. Just the site of her left Martha a breathless and longing for her presence.

Martha and Emily sat on the backyard deck and talked about Martha's experiences with Lori.

"I'm so impressed with your courage," Emily said. "Just getting up the courage to set up the van nearly over night and head out to Easton to meet her was amazing."

"Thanks, Lori is amazing too. I love her dog, Buttercup. She is sweet and mellow but filled with joy. She is the color of butter, so her name fits her perfectly. Her silky ears are seducing in themselves. I'm both excited and nervous that she and Buttercup are coming for a visit next weekend."

She looked at Emily and saw her watching as Jason worked on the finishing touches of Martha's She-Shed. Martha said, "He has done a great job in a short time."

Emily nodded. "Yes, he has. I can't wait for him to start at my house."

"So, are you two going to be an item?"

"I think so. We had dinner together a few nights ago, and I felt the attraction was mutual. I've never dated so I'm not sure how all this goes but we seem to be moving forward."

"Don't worry about how this goes, just let your gut and your feelings guide you. If it feels right, it probably is."

Emily nodded and turned back to Martha. "Thanks for that. It is a new way of being for me, but I want to be honest and open too."

Martha smiled. "We are all having new experiences and learning new things. Being honest and open with each other, but most especially ourselves, is the only way to go. Now let's get down to business with our foundation planning."

Emily picked up the stack of papers she had laid in front of her. "All the details are in these papers. However, I can give you the summary of the meetings from yesterday." She laid out the details of her discussion with Mr. Todd including he would donate his time as legal advisor for the foundation.

"That is great. Who would be the President of the board?"

"He recommended it be Glory and she should have veto power. This is after all her money and her plan. But she should also be able to get lots of sound advice and creative input. Being able to say no if it didn't feel right to her is the final say on any project. She would be the CEO and the President of the foundation board."

Martha nodded, "That sounds good. What about the financial advice? I can do the accounting bits and take care of the day-to-day workings of the foundation, but I can't do much more than that."

"I had the same thought and so did Mr. Todd," Emily said. "He advised that I talk with Mr. Edwards at the bank. I dropped into the bank could talk with Michael Edwards who managed all of Edgar's money. I asked if he would join the board as financial advisor and he will help us find a CPA who will serve on the board."

"Great."

"He also recommended that we have someone from the community who was involved with volunteer organizations, especially those that were for women. I agreed that was probably a good idea too but wanted to talk with you and Glory about it first."

"I wonder about the community member though. I don't really know many people in the community at least at that level. I wonder if Sara Merriweather would be a good choice for that?"

"What a great idea! She already knows both you and Glory. Plus, she knows the community well and is a social worker to boot."

Martha nodded. "I'll call her and see if she will help. We have Glory as President, Emily as what?"

"I was thinking Vice-President of Housing Resources."

Martha smiled. "Perfect. I'm the CFO, chief financial officer until we have a CPA on the board and probably COO as well since I oversee operations. Mr. Todd is Legal advisor and Mr. Edwards is the financial adviser. Then we have as yet not known Community Liaison but hopefully Sara. So, seven board members. Do we need more?"

"I asked Mr. Todd that question, and he said we were probably fine with what we have now as a beginning but might expand it as time goes by. He also advised that we run this all past Glory before we go any further on the board settings. If Glory approves Mr. Todd will draw up all the legal papers, we need for The Pennington-Shaw Foundation. Although he does not wish to be paid as a board member, the board will pay his legal fees but at a reduced rate for the foundation."

"Cool," Martha said. "What did he think about The Pennington-Shaw Foundation as the umbrella for all the different projects?"

"He said we were exactly right to do it that way. What we have so far is She-Shed branch and the clinic in Oklahoma. For now, he'll get the ball rolling on the umbrella foundation and She-Shed program."

"Whew! You've been very busy for the past few days. It all sounds great. I'll call Glory and run it by her."

"Good. We need to schedule a board meeting to go over where we are now and what are plans are advancing. There is more than enough to keep us busy."

Martha laughed. "I should say so."

Jason walked up to the deck. "Well, I'm finished for now. The landscapers will be here later this afternoon Martha to go over the plans for that part. The folks with the awnings that are being special made for the shed will be here on Thursday the twelfth of July, day after tomorrow. Do you need me to be here for that?"

Martha answered, "If you think you should that would be great. Otherwise I think we are fine. Be sure to get me your final invoice for the work you did here."

"I'll have it to you by tomorrow morning," Jason looked at Emily, took off his hat and said, "First I'd like to show you ladies around the interior and exterior of She-Shed."

Emily stood up and Martha followed suit. Jason took Emily's hand and led the way while Martha followed behind smiling at the two in front of her. It made her happy to see them like this. It also made her think of Lori and their time together at Lake Easton.

Chapter 21

"Life has a way of changing the path
you are on when you least expect it."
— Deborah Blake

After touring She-Shed, Martha said, "I've got things to do inside."

"I need to get home too," Emily said. She turned to Jason, "Would you like to come to dinner this evening and go over our plans for my house."

He shook his head no. "I need to go home and clean up but then I would like to take you out for dinner if that's okay with you."

"Sounds great," Emily answered and blushed a little.

Martha said, "Now you have settled dinner plans, I'll see you two soon. Enjoy." She smiled, waved and walked back into the house.

After Martha went inside, Jason turned to Emily. "I want you to know, I'm falling for you. Tonight, is a date but I don't want to talk about plans until we talk about us."

"That sounds good." It surprised her at how calm she was about all of this. When she was with Jason, she was calm, yet she became anxious when she was on her own. *I need to be around Jason more.*

They sat at a table JaK's Grill. Emily said, "I've driven past this restaurant a lot, but I've never eaten here."

"They make great steaks and incredible desserts," Jason said. "I like the filet the best but please order whatever you want."

When the waiter came and took their orders Jason said, "If you don't mind,

I'd like to start our conversation about our relationship."

Emily nodded. "Me too. I'll be less nervous about it as soon as we talk about it."

"I want to get conversations like this over and done with so I can move on to the next thing. It's not that I want to rush things, but I don't like to leave things so long it gets messed up."

Emily smiled. "I'm the opposite. I stew over things forever and make all kinds of excuses for why I should not do what I want to do. I miss out on a lot overthinking things. Since I've been working with Glory and Martha, I'm actively trying to let myself have what I want."

"Good. That's actually a relief for me to hear you say so. I don't know where this is all going but I know I've never met a woman like you who made me feel so good just being with her."

"I feel the same."

Jason smiled. "We've only known each other for a few weeks. I've fallen in love with you and I'd like for us to be exclusive to each other. I have dated little since high school but the few times I have I've been uncomfortable and eager to get home, by myself. With you I hate going home by myself."

"You are the first man I've dated since college. I have been so shy and nervous, even when I felt the need to date, I've backed off into a corner and done nothing. I'm not sure I even know how to date."

Jason grinned. "Then we'll do it our own way without regard to society rules."

Their food came and as they ate Emily realized she wasn't paying attention to the food but felt great joy being with Jason.

Finally, with her meal half eaten, she blurted out, "I love every minute I'm with you. I know that sounds bold coming from a shy woman but since I've known Glory and Martha, I want to do what they are doing. I want to live my life being true to myself."

Jason reached across the table, took her hand in his. "I love every minute with you too. I also love you are being true to yourself. It is what attracted me to you from the first."

Emily nodded and smiled. "Thank you. I'm glad we are together and with you in my life I can't imagine being with anyone else. If it's okay with you, I'd rather call dinner finished and not have dessert."

"Do you have any brownies left over?" Jason asked.

"I do and ice cream too," Emily answered and grinned.

Emily and Jason went back to her house. Before they had time to get to brownies and ice cream, they were in each other's arms. The kissing led them upstairs and her bedroom. Jason looked around. "This your grandparents master bedroom."

Emily nodded. "I've changed nothing in here other than the bed. I've got a generic frame holding up the queen-size mattress and box foundation but really want to incorporate it more into the footboard and headboard which are too small. Maybe you can help me with that. Other than that, this is how I've always remembered this bedroom."

Jason leaned down and kissed her. "Can we talk carpentry later? Right now, I want you in my arms in bed."

She smiled up at him and took off her dress and then the rest of her clothes. She took his hand and walked to the bed. "You might want to at least kick off your shoes first."

He grinned, chuckled and kicked off his shoes. "As you wish." He pulled his shirt out of his jeans.

Emily unfastened her bra and reached out and touched his chest and moved closer to be in his arms. Jason lifted her up in his arms and gently laid her back on the bed. He kissed her neck and moved down to her breasts. She pulled him up to kiss her on the mouth. "I've waited all my life for you."

After their lovemaking, Emily revealed, "I've never made love before and that was so much better than I imagined."

Jason rolled over, shocked and looked at her. "I did not realize you were a virgin. I wish I had known before. Did I hurt you?"

She smiled. "I wasn't a virgin. I had sex with some boy in high school and though I wanted it to be good it wasn't. I didn't like him very much, but I wanted to have sex and be done with the virgin thing. This was making love; entirely different from just sex."

Jason laughed. "Well, that's one way to go about it. I'm glad you didn't stick with him."

"Me too. Let's go have brownies and ice cream. I'm hungry now."

She jumped out of bed and put on her robe. He pulled on his pants and t-shirt and followed her barefoot lead down stairs. They sat at the breakfast table eating their brownies and ice cream.

Jason asked, "Now we are both a little more settled and less anxious, do you want to talk about the plans you want to do?"

Emily nodded. "Yes, I do. And I want you to be my partner."

Jason looked up startled.

"I'm not proposing marriage. Yet," She said with a grin on her face. "What I'm suggesting is you and I work together refurbishing old houses. We can buy them as is and make them available to women from She-Shed to live in or sell them for profit."

"Sounds great. I have a little money saved up to add to the coffers. You can do the paperwork as a real estate agent. I can tell you if it is a house worth saving. Any work I can do myself saves us on investing more money."

"My thoughts exactly. I have money saved too and I think we can get The Foundation to give us some money if we apply for a grant, but I don't think we will need it right away. I want what we do together to pay us our work. The idea is to not go into debt but use our resources for good."

"Great idea," Jason said. "Then after the women get their lives back in order, they can rent their houses from us at reduced rates depending on their income. We can even sell them the home at the lowest rate possible."

"Yes!" Emily said. "You understand what I want."

"You are what I want." Leaning over, Jason touched the edge of her mouth where a small piece of brownie dangled. He put the crumb in his mouth and then kissed her. "You are all I need or want."

"That works out well for me," Emily said and kissed him back.

Chapter 22

"Those of us who embrace the
Feminine know its strength."
— Betsy Cornwell

Martha was a bundle of nerves.

It was Friday afternoon, and the landscapers had been here all day putting in the new plants in the sculpted garden beside She-Shed headquarters. They had created walkways through the yard with stepping stones and dark red mulch. The awnings were up and to Martha they seemed to be the perfect finish for the building. They were plaid maroon and pink with sliver trim. It was a perfect setting for the beginnings of helping women find stability and purpose for their lives.

What had her nerves twitching was Lori. She was coming here to visit for the weekend and would be here in an hour with Buttercup. Lori called Martha and asked if she could come today instead of tomorrow. Martha was nearly breathless and yet delighted Lori had called and was coming for a visit. *She wants to see my home. I'm so glad I don't live in an apartment anymore. I hope she wants to be with me more than just a friend.*

Martha went through the house, now her home, double checking everything was clean and tidy. She checked the guest bedroom and deck for the umpteenth time to be sure it would be perfect for Lori. She stood in the bathroom and looked in the mirror. What she saw was a woman with a light blush on her face, soft freckles and wild, curly red hair. Her eyes seemed a deeper darker green than she had remembered. She told her reflection, "All right warrior goddess it is time for you to settle down and accept whatever comes from this weekend."

She smiled at herself. *I'm hoping for more than just touches and innocent kisses. Maybe this bedroom won't be used this weekend.* She looked up and saw that her blush had deepened. She chastised herself but then decided instead to accept her own desire and smiled deeply. She continued to pace and walk through the house touching everything to be sure it was placed exactly right including the bed for Buttercup.

When the doorbell rang, Martha had to restrain herself to keep from running across the room and jerking the door open. When she opened the door to see Lori standing there with Buttercup beside her, she took in a short, quick breath and whispered, "Hi."

Lori leaned in and kissed her softly on the lips. "Hi. Can we come in?"

Martha laughed. "Oh, yes. Please do." She opened the door wider, stepping aside to let Lori and Buttercup come in.

"Wow," Lori said, "I love this room." Buttercup licked Martha's hand and Martha bent to pet the dog receiving a big licking kiss on her cheek.

Laughing at the dog Martha stood up. She looked at Lori. "I'm glad you like it. Come in and let me show you everything." She led Lori to the guest bedroom. She pointed to the bed. "You can leave your things here," and thought, for *now.* She showed Lori the deck and bathroom.

Lori said, "This is a perfect retreat for your guests. I don't think I've ever seen anything more perfectly welcoming before."

Martha smiled and reached out her hand. Lori took her hand. "What's next?"

"I'll show you." She led Lori and Buttercup back to the living room and through the dining room and on to the kitchen. She opened the back door and let Buttercup out. Buttercup took off running and racing around the yard. Both women laughed at the dog's antics.

"Buttercup loves your beautiful yard. Your house is lovely," Lori said and turned to Martha. "Where is your bedroom?"

Martha knew she was blushing, but she took Lori's hand. "Come with me."

Lori smiled and followed.

Martha led her back to the bedroom hallway and back to her room. When they walked in the room with its deep rose walls, lots of silver and gold trimmed frames and trinkets Lori gasped. "Wow, I've never seen a bedroom like this."

There were also small clay sculptures of women and replicas of ancient goddesses on a small gold or silver shelves hanging on the walls. Crystals adorned several surfaces including one small table with a wand and a fat smiling goddess. Above the table was a painting of chakras and a woman giving birth through each level of the chakras. Lori touched the painting's frame. "This is marvelous and powerful."

The ceiling was painted a dark purple that was almost black. Martha looked forward to Lori seeing the invisible stars on the ceiling when the room was dark. On the bed was a red silk down comforter with red and purple and bright yellow pillows tossed on top. The room had a soft glow of electric candle lights, even from a chandelier over the bed. Lori stood looking around the room with her mouth open. "This is the room of a warrior goddess."

Martha breathed a sigh of relief. "You like it?"

Lori nodded. "Yes. It is perfect. I'm in awe of everything in here. I would never have thought of these combinations of soft and bold colors. Or of the modern and antique art. But it leaves me feeling as if I've walked into a room that always was and always will be. There is a lot of rich and ancient magic living here."

"Yes." Martha nodded. "I'm so happy you feel that too. Most of the crystals and many of the statues and figurines are gifts. Magic in this room, my private space, is what I wanted to express." She pulled her fingers through her long red hair and said, "I wanted something that Magdalene would think was both comforting and powerful. A retreat and a source of power if you will."

Lori looked at Martha. "You've read Elizabeth Cunningham's Magdalene series, haven't you? This might be the cave in Magdala."

Martha nodded, smiled softy. "I've read all the books several times. The cave is exactly what I was thinking for this room."

"I read those books over and over," Lori said. She pulled Martha close, held Martha's face in her hands and kissed her passionately and yet softly. When she stopped, Martha stood transfixed and returned the kiss in the same way.

Before her thoughts could form, Martha said, "Welcome home."

Lori smiled and whispered, "It is good to be home. Finally."

After an hour in each other's arms Lori asked, "Do I have to sleep in the guest bedroom?"

Martha touched Lori's lips. She laughed. "No. I didn't leave you to unpack in there until I knew for sure this was where you wanted to be."

Buttercup jumped on the bed nuzzling both women who laughed at her antics. Martha grinned. "Welcome home, Buttercup."

Lori laughed. "Thank you, Martha. I didn't know this was where I wanted to be until I came into this room. Now it will be difficult for me to be anywhere else."

"Good. I want both you and Buttercup to think of my home as your home. I decided this week to make this room every deep feeling and thought I had about me as a woman. If this had not been right for you, we could be friends but nothing more. I'm glad we will not be just friends."

She got out of the bed and pulled on a gold and red silk robe. "Go get your things and unpack in here. Half of the dresser, chest and closet are empty waiting for you and your things. The same is true in the bathroom."

Lori stood up. Naked she walked over to Martha and kissed her again. "Thank you."

Martha returned the kiss. "You must put on something because I'm starving, and I can't think while you are standing naked before me."

Lori smiled. "You have a robe, but I don't have a robe."

"I've thought of that too." Martha turned away, went to the closet and on the empty side of the closet was one hanger with a purple and silver silk robe hanging on the rod. "I bought this for you. I hope you like it."

Lori went to the closet and carefully took the robe from the hanger. "It matches yours except for the colors. Did you buy this specially for me?"

Martha nodded. She went to Lori and helped her put on the robe. "I did and you look so beautiful and strong in this robe." Martha turned Lori to look at herself in the mirror. Lori reached up and squeezed Martha's hand on her shoulder. "I will always cherish this robe."

Chapter 23

Saturday morning Emily awoke to see Jason sleeping beside her with his hand on her hip. She loved the soft, gentle warmth of his hand. She reached up and touched his face gently.

He opened his eyes and kissed her. "I hope I am not dreaming the woman I love is here in bed beside me."

"It feels a little like a dream," Emily said. "I'm sorry I woke you but needed to touch you to be sure you were really here."

He pulled her closer. "I'm here." He kissed her again and then held her close in his arms. "I feel like I'm drowning in your love and yet I've only scratched the surface."

She ran her fingers through the fine, soft hair on his chest. "Me too. I never want you to leave my bed or my home."

"We have to get up and out of bed sometime. I never want to spend any time or be any place but at your side."

She nodded. "I know. Me too."

Jason looked down at her and lifting her chin up so he could see her eyes asked, "Emily Harris will you marry me?"

"I thought you'd never ask." She smiled. "Yes, I'll marry you and the sooner the better."

"Really?"

"Absolutely. I knew the first time I met you a few weeks ago that I loved you and wanted to marry you."

"If we could get married today, would you do it?"

Emily looked up at Jason. "In a heartbeat."

He sat up in bed and looking down at her said, "Then get up, get dressed and be ready to leave in an hour or two."

She laughed and sitting up asked, "Are you serious?"

Reaching out to her he brushed his fingertips across the top of her breasts. "I wish we were already married."

She leaned forward and kissed him. "I'd prefer to marry clothes on."

He laughed. "Then get busy getting ready."

"What are you going to be doing?" Emily asked.

"I need to pick up something special for you at my house and pack a bag. Then I'll come pick you up and we will head to Las Vegas, find a chintzy chapel and get married."

"Sounds perfect. Are we flying or driving?"

"Oh, we are flying. Last night while you were sleeping, I booked a flight on a 24 hour hold to fly to Vegas later today. I had planned to work up the courage to ask you over breakfast, but this works even better."

"Sure of yourself, were you?"

He got out of bed and pulled on his pants and shirt. "I was pretty sure of you and that you are the woman for me. I was prepared to get down on my knees and beg. This was better and easier on my knees."

Jason bent down and kissed her again. "Get dressed and I'll be back in an hour. I want to spend the rest of my life, from this day forward, married to you."

Emily quickly got out of bed, showered and fixed her hair and makeup. She looked in the mirror. "You are one crazy woman Emily Harris." Then she laughed and went back into the bedroom.

She looked through her closet for the right clothes to wear. She had never wanted a big, fancy wedding so had never thought of what she would wear to her wedding. *You are one strange woman. What girl doesn't dream of her wedding? Me, I guess.* She knew she was smiling and was happy to know her face reflected her joy.

She took several dresses from her closet and finally settled on an ivory suit with a pale green silk shirt. She got out her gold and ivory sandals and looked in the mirror. *Well, it isn't really a wedding dress, but it is okay.* Then she took it off and said, "Okay is not good enough." Standing in her slip she continued to go through her closet tossing the rejects on the bed. The doorbell chimed interrupting her frantic searching for the right dress.

She went downstairs and saw Jason holding a large white plastic bag. She opened the door. "I'm glad you are here. I need help to find the right dress to wear to our wedding."

Jason smiled. "Let's go upstairs and look."

He started up the stairs leaving Emily no choice but to follow him up the stairs. When he went into the bedroom, he laughed out loud. "Are there any clothes left in your closet?"

"Other than sweaters and ski gear, not much," Emily replied.

He pushed aside some clothes on the bed, laid the garment bag he was carrying on the bed and unzipped the bag. "Look at this and see what you think."

Emily walked over to the bed and opened the bag. Inside was a white silk and lace sheath dress. She touched it and felt the light beading on the bodice. "It is beautiful. Where did you get this?"

"My sister. It was my mother's wedding dress and then my sister's wedding dress."

"Your sister just gave it to you?"

"Well, yeah, after I asked if I could borrow it. I had to beg a little." He grinned.

"When did you ask her for the dress?"

"Early last week," Jason answered.

Emily stood in front of him with her mouth open and her hands on her hips. He held up his hand. "Please don't be angry. I told her about you and how I love you and wanted to marry you but hadn't asked you yet. I told her I wanted us to be as happy as she and her husband always were. Since you are about her height and size, I asked if I could borrow it."

Emily worked hard to not laugh. "What did she say?"

"She said I was crazy, and you would probably want to buy your own dress. I told her I thought you would want to marry right away because you weren't a woman to wait to get what you wanted."

Emily nodded. "Good answer. You were so sure I'd fly off to Vegas with you the moment you asked me to marry you, you had a dress for me?"

Jason shrugged. "Not sure, exactly. I hoped."

She walked over to him and kissed him soundly. "Hope is a great force in the world," she said. "Will you help me try on this dress?"

On the plane to Vegas they sat holding hands and ignoring everyone and everything around them.

Jason said, "I called my sister on the way back to your house and asked about wedding chapels that would take last-minute people wanting to get married. She sent me a text with two possibilities. Then she demanded I take you to a jeweler before heading to any 'damn chapel on the strip'. Those were her exact words."

Emily laughed. "I love your sister already."

They went to a jeweler on the strip and Emily saw a replica of an antique engagement ring and wedding band. There was a modest round diamond in the middle with rubies surrounding the diamond. The band was gold with swirls similar to the band of the engagement ring and tiny rubies between the swirls. She loved it at first sight. Jason tried to talk her into one with a bigger diamond and she said, "No. These rings are exactly what I want to wear for the rest of my life."

While Jason was paying for her rings, she went to the men's counter looking at the bands for Jason. There was a dark gold band similar to the wedding ring he was buying her but without the rubies. She bought it and when she gave it to him tears glistened in his eyes. He kissed her. "We don't know if it fits."

"I think it will. I tried it on my thumb."

Lifting the ring out of the box Jason put it on his left ring finger. "You are a marvelous woman to have guessed my ring size."

"Just remember how marvelous I am," she said and kissed him.

"Always. I could never forget that."

After they married in a sweet but short ceremony, they went to the Bellagio Hotel where Jason had reserved the honeymoon suite. On the elevator up, with the bell hop leading the way she asked, "How and when did you get all this arranged?"

"I have an inside secret weapon," Jason answered.

"Oh."

He grinned and kissed her. "My sister took care of the details so we could get here and get married."

"I must thank her when I finally get to meet her. First the wedding dress, then the rings and now this." Emily looked up at Jason. "I'm impressed with both you and your sister."

"I had to beg. She said, mom would kill her when she found out. I said mom would give her a reprieve when she met you."

"I hope so." Emily laughed. "I'm eager to meet your family but after the wedding night."

By the end of the weekend, Martha and Lori were both deeply in love. Being apart, even for a few hours was heart-rending for them. Sitting on the deck, with Buttercup between them they watched the sun go down. Holding Lori's hand in hers, Martha said, "I wish you could stay here forever."

"Me too. I have to go back to Easton tonight. I start work at six in the morning."

"I know," Martha said. "I will miss you and Buttercup so much. I wish that it wasn't such a long drive to Easton."

"I have to work to keep living. It's not just the money. I need to be in the forests and working to stay sane."

Martha nodded. "I understand; I wish you were closer."

Lori looked at Martha and thought she was the most beautiful woman she had ever seen. What she loved most about Martha was her wild combination of strength, courage and innocence. It left Lori amazed and thrilled just being with her.

"You have your work here," Lori said. "It is so needed by so many women. I cannot imagine you in any other home than this. Your She-Shed is marvelous, and any woman would love coming to this bit of paradise and being blessed by your presence and your gifts."

Martha squeezed Lori's hand. "I feel as if my life will somehow dim when you leave today."

"Not possible. The light here is more than just you or me. It feels as if some universal force or power of love feeds the surrounding energy of you, this house and the whole foundation."

"I feel that too, but selfishly don't want you or Buttercup to leave."

Lori stood up and went to stand beside Martha. She reached down, pulled her up into her arms and hugged her. "I don't want to leave either. Can we talk about the possibilities of a future together or is it too soon?"

Martha took Lori's hand and walked out to the garden in the backyard. Buttercup pranced beside them. When they were in the garden Martha sat on the bench and motioned for Lori to sit beside her. Buttercup curled up at their feet. They sat hand-in-hand and talked about the possibilities of a future.

After they had talked for nearly an hour, Lori said, "If it is okay with you, I'd like to live here with you."

"Absolutely! I require that Buttercup live here too. You and Buttercup would fulfill the dreams I've been having all weekend. But what about your work?"

Lori shook her head. "I don't know for sure but I have a strong feeling destiny wants us to be together. I love this place so much and want to live with you for a long time. We might even get married."

Martha laughed. "Perfect."

"For now, I'm willing to accept that we are in love and want to be together. Is that enough?"

Martha nodded. "Yes and is exactly what I want."

"I'll come home every time I have over one day off. It won't always be on the weekend. I have two weekends off every month though and that will be wonderful for me."

"Sounds like the beginning of something marvelous," Martha said.

"But, fair warning. I want this to continue on for a long, long time. I'll see what transfer and job possibilities are out there for me."

Martha brought Lori's hand up and kissed the back of her hand. "It would please me down to the ground and back."

Lori laughed. "I've never heard that saying before, but it will please me too."

Buttercup yiked. Martha smiled at the dog. "I've learned a little doggie language between Buttercup and Freya. That sounded like agreement."

Chapter 24

"Choose blindly with your eyes open.
Walk and whistle in the dark.
You're not the whole story, only a part.
Even the teller is changed in the telling."
—Elizabeth Cunningham

Jake and Glory talked on the phone several times since their re-meeting and even had a video call too. He called Glory on Saturday morning and asked, "Do you have plans for the next few days?"

"Nothing in particular. What did you have in mind?"

"I'd like to show you and Freya where I live. But it means a road trip for a few days. Are you up for a road trip?"

"Sounds great to me and I'm sure Freya will love it." It had been nearly fifteen weeks since Edgar's death. Glory was feeling more and more sure that moving on was what she needed to do. "If we get to know each other better maybe, we can make rational decisions about our relationship."

Jake laughed. "I don't know how much 'rational' fits into my idea of a relationship. I want to get to know you better though."

"Great. I want to bring my van with me so I can leave from your place to go wherever I'm heading next."

Jake had hoped she would ride with him but he would take what he could get. "I've got a few things to do here at my sister's house. Would two hours from now work for you or do you need more time to pack?"

"I'm all packed," Glory said. "Remember, I live in a van now. I was planning to go back to Washington tomorrow. I'll let Martha know I will spend a little more time here in Oklahoma."

He smiled into the phone knowing she couldn't see him. "I've fallen for an independent woman."

Glory laughed. "Exactly what I am working to be. Maybe you'll be able to prove yourself worthy."

"Exactly what I am working to be," he answered.

After they hung up Glory went into the kitchen to have breakfast with Hugh and Rob. She hugged them both. "Jake has invited me to go see where he lives. I took him up on the invitation, so I'll be leaving in two hours to follow him to his place."

Rob grinned. "You will love it. It is nestled in the Kiamichi mountains of southeast Oklahoma. It is beautiful and reminds me a little of North Bend but warmer and lots more sunshine. He bought it before he married Liz and has worked on building it up. Liz went there only one weekend and hated it. It was another blow to his heart."

"Thanks for telling me, Rob. I knew the ranch was important to him and it was important to him for her to love it too."

"Yep. It's a small ranch for now. He's working on building it up. He has a few horses, rents out some pasture land to other folks in the area. He does training and teaching riding horses. He does veterinarian work when he is there for friends and neighbors. The rents pay the mortgage, so he is happy and has a lot of freedom."

Hugh added, "He plans to have a riding school and wants to do therapy work with kids with mental issues. He teaches a few kids and adults how to ride already."

"I've never ridden a horse," Glory said. "He must teach me."

"He will. He is a great teacher." Hugh looked up to Glory. "I hope you are both ready for this relationship. You have both gone through a lot of pain in the past few months."

Glory nodded. "I agree Hugh and we have decided to take it easy before we get in too deep."

"Can you do that? It seems like you are fairly deep already," Rob said.

"I don't know." Glory shook her head. "If I were a few more months post Edgar's death, I am sure I wouldn't be able to hold back. I can barely hold back now. I would love to dive in deeper and deeper. Right now, I need a loving companion so much I don't trust my instincts. My gut is telling me Jake is the man for me."

"He is a good man," Hugh said, "even if he is my brother. I don't want to see either of you hurt over this relationship. I'd love nothing more than to see you two live your lives together in love and honor. You both deserve nothing less."

"I promise I will do my best to not hurt him. And I trust him to not hurt me."

"Then I'll trust you both to take care of each other. Now would you like to hear our idea for a name for the clinic?"

"Yes!"

Rob said, "We wanted your name to be in it but worried about religious connotations and then Helen told us to quit being so dense and just use your name."

Hugh grinned sardonically. "My sister set us straight in that regard; she's good at that. Then you mentioned you had taken back your maiden name, and that seemed to fit not only to give you honor but for being in Oklahoma too. We thought maybe call it the Pennington Community Health Center."

Glory smiled. "I love it. It has my name, and it is a community effort too. Have you worked out the plan for the funding from the foundation?"

Rob nodded. "Yes, we've finished the proposal. I faxed the papers to Martha today. She will go over it and get back to us if there are questions. Then she will run it by each of the board members. She hopes to get back to us in a few days."

"That's perfect." Glory hugged Rob. "The board will approve it I'm sure. Besides, I have the power of thumbs up or down. We want Mr. Todd and Mr. Edwards to go over the proposal and get a contract ready for us all to sign. I'm so excited for you two and for Norman."

Hugh said, "We are too. Thank you for reaching out and doing this for Norman."

"You are most welcome. Any community that Rob wants to help, I want to help. He's always been there to support me and now I can support him, you and Norman."

Glory followed Jake east to Oklahoma Highway 9 then at a small city called Seminole they turned on to US Highway 270 driving southeast. They drove through some beautiful places and small towns with names she had never seen. They went through Wewoka, Holdenville, McAlester and Hartshorne. As they traveled the mountains gradually appeared and everything was a lot greener. Eventually they left the highways behind and traveled deeper into the mountains.

They crossed a cattle guard and followed a dirt road until they came to a gate with a sign above it "Jake's Ranch". Glory followed Jake through the gate and waited while he closed it again. He stopped beside her van and asked, "What do you think so far?"

"It is beautiful. Are there any towns nearby?"

"Not much to speak of but we can go over to Wilburton if we need. It's big enough it has a college, grocery stores and a hardware store," He answered. "Then there's McAlester that is bigger with a different college. It even has a Wal-Mart and a medical center."

"How far is Wilburton?"

"About thirty minutes away."

Glory nodded and smiled. "Lead on, Cowboy."

Jake grinned and walked back to his pickup to lead them to his ranch house. *I'm happy Glory agreed to come see my ranch. I bought it and built the frame of the house and barns before I married Liz. I poured my heart into the house. I filled my home with my desires and love of my family, life and dreams to come.*

Liz had been here only one time. She like the scenery, took a lot of photos and even rode with him one day. She didn't feel the way he did about the ranch, including the stars. Her photos of him with the horses though was a true gift from her to him. He realized she needed to take pictures as a life calling.

I think it is exactly what she is doing now. I am glad we became friends after the divorce. If we had started there, we would have known we weren't right for each other as mates.

The day after the divorce was final, he moved to the ranch as his home base. It had been a beginning of a healing time for him. His trip to the Pacific Northwest was the real turn around other than he couldn't settle down at the ranch after meeting Glory in North Bend. Liz's reactions about the ranch had heightened his delight that Glory had said yes, without hesitation, and she followed him all the way here.

Please, Glory, fill my life with joy and love me and my ranch. He would never say those words to her out loud he knew. It would be unfair to them both. *If I'm disappointed in this endeavor I do not want her to suffer for it.*

When they arrived, Glory saw a very large two-story log house with a porch all along the front of the house and sides. There were four dormers on the front of the second story. She followed Jake around to the back of the house and she could see the porch extended all along the back of the house as well. It sheltered the porch all around by the second story of the house. On the second floor there was a balcony at one end looking out across the meadows and mountains. Jake drove into a large garage and parked his truck. He motioned for her to park next to him.

When she parked, he opened her door. "Welcome to Jake's Ranch."

Glory smiled. "It is beautiful, Jake. It is much bigger than I thought it would be. Rob said it was a small ranch."

He laughed. "Around here this is a small ranch. I've only got about three hundred acres so far."

"Wow. It seems like a lot."

Freya barked and Jake said, "Let me get the princess out so she can have a sniff, squat and piddle."

Glory watched as he took care of her dog but didn't let her off the leash.

"We'll want to keep her on leash when she is out and about for now. It isn't safe up here for any dog to be out on the loose really, but one this small would be lunch for some critters that naturally live around here."

"Like what kind of critters?" Glory asked aware this was the first time she had used the word critters.

Jake smiled. "We have foxes, bobcats, cougars, coyotes and the occasional black bear. They are mostly out at night but if she wandered off into their territory, they would not hesitate to eat her for lunch. The other risks are the snakes. Copperheads and rattlesnakes, you have to watch out for."

Glory looked down around her feet. "Oh, my. We don't have snakes that are poisonous around where I live. We have bears and cougars though. I didn't know it was so dangerous here."

"It's dangerous everywhere but since I don't have a small fenced area yet for our little girl here, we will have to take care to walk her outside on the leash until I get a fenced-in yard built."

Glory nodded not sure she would be comfortable in the out-of-doors here. But it delighted her that he referred to Freya as 'our little girl' and the building of a fenced-in yard.

Jake led the way into the house which Glory immediately loved. The kitchen had an old wood-burning cookstove in the corner and a new gas stovetop. There were three ovens one of which was a microwave. She pointed to the wood stove and asked, "Does that still work?"

Jake shrugged. "Maybe. I've never tried it. I like how it looks like it belongs in here. I found it in one of the old barns when I bought the ranch. Come on, let me show you the rest of the house."

"I love the kitchen. If the rest of this house looks like this, it will be hard for me to leave."

Jake smiled. "That's the plan." He took her hand leading her through the house, room by room. Glory stood in awe of the main room on the first floor. It was the biggest room she had ever seen in a home. The ceiling was vaulted with pine beams. At the end was a red and yellow sandstone fireplace that covered most of the end wall. Jake said, "All those stones are native to this area. I love their soft colors."

Glory nodded. "It is a beautiful fireplace."

There were pine bookcases on each side of the fireplace and a large painting of the ranch over the fireplace. There was a dining area in front of the fireplace with twelve chairs surrounding a beautiful rustic table.

There were photos on the wall to the side the fireplace of Jake working with horses. Glory pointed to the photos. "These are marvelous. I think they are good enough to be in a museum."

Jake walked up to Glory and embraced her from behind. "I glad you like them. Those are examples of the work Liz is doing now."

Glory reached up and touched his arm. She loved the feel of his embrace. "She does magnificent work. I'm glad you two are at peace. It makes this feel all the more loving."

Jake kissed the top of her head but couldn't speak. He didn't want to cry in front of Glory right now. After a few moments he could speak, he took her hand and said, "Let me show you the other end of the room."

On the opposite end of the fireplace, in a corner, was a small seating area meant for quieter conversation. In the opposite corner was a big screen television with a huge circular couch with foot rests and small tables. Jake pointed it out. "I did not plan to have a television here, but Hugh and Rob said they wouldn't come down here if they couldn't watch OU football. So, I got a television service with a round space ship looking thingy on the back roof."

Glory laughed. "I know nothing about OU football."

"You need to learn that right away." She laughed but saw he was serious. She bit her lip and nodded. Jake nodded curtly back and continued the tour, grinning as he turned his face from her view.

Jake led her into what looked like a game room with a pool table, foosball table and a large round table with cup holders built in and a green felt top. Jake saw her looking at the table. "That's for our monthly poker game. Over yonder under that little window is where Hugh and George play chess. Now that's a game I've got no patience for."

"Good to know," she said and watched Jake grin in response.

"Now for the upstairs," He said.

"How many bedrooms?"

He led Glory upstairs with Freya tagging along behind. "There are four with two Jack and Jill bathrooms for guests and I hope later children. Then there is the big bedroom with a big private bath and deck for me," Jake said.

He showed her the guest bedrooms and bathrooms first. Then at the end of the hall there were double pine doors with leaded stained-glass panes. He opened them and led her into his bedroom. On one end that would be the front of the house was a smaller fire place than downstairs tucked in between two of the dormer windows. Each window had a cushioned window seat with doors beneath for storage. In front of the fireplace were two rocking chairs with a table and lamp between them. Glory walked over and sat in one of the chairs and rocked a little. She felt herself relax and settle. She imagined sitting here with a baby in her arms. It was the same vision she had every time she sat in her mother's rocking chair.

She looked up to see Jake smiling at her. "What?" she asked.

"I've longed to see a woman sitting there, quiet and loving the space."

"It is a wonderful spot and I could sit here forever."

"That's my dream," Jake said. Before Glory could say more, he sat down in the other chair. "I sit in this chair in the evenings where I read before going to bed. I love this corner."

"I can see why," Glory said.

Jake reached out a hand to her. They sat quietly for a few minutes. Freya curled up in front of the fireplace and went to sleep. He stood, reached out his hands to help her up from the chair. As he did so he bent and kissed her softly on the lips. "Thank you, Glory."

He turned toward the rest of the room. He made a sweeping gesture to the rest of the room. "That four-poster bed belonged to my Granddaddy and Grandmomma." Jake walked over to the bed and caressed one of the posts. "I inherited it but it was too big for our house in Norman, so it sat in a storage shed until I built this house."

"It is perfect. It is beautiful. Is it oak?"

Jake nodded. "Yep, and my Granddaddy built it himself."

Glory walked over to the bed and felt of the wood. It was smooth as silk under her hand. She loved the scrollwork on the footboard and headboard. The posts were topped with what looked like an acorn design. "I love this bed," she said. "It is beautiful, rustic and yet feels like love lives in every grain of the wood."

Jake walked over to her and turned her toward him. "I'm going to kiss you now just so you know."

When the kiss finished, Glory put her hands on his chest. "Thank you," she said. "That is the sweetest kiss I've ever had."

Jake leaned in and put his forehead to hers. "We should keep moving unless you'd like to crawl in that bed with me."

She smiled. "Not just yet. Show me the rest of this marvelous room."

Jake took her hand and led her outside on the deck. It looked west over meadows, fields and the paddock and barns. In one corner next to the house was a hot tub, covered and waiting. There was a small cast iron table between two Adirondack chairs that were handmade and beautiful. He took her to the chairs and offered her one. They sat there in companionable silence for a few minutes until Glory said, "I've never seen a more beautiful view than this." She reached for his hand and he took it in his.

"I cannot explain to you how thrilled I am," Jake said.

Glory smiled at Jake. "I'm glad you are happy. I am happy too. I feel like for the first time in months I can relax and just enjoy where I am."

He squeezed her hand as they sat and watched the sunset begin. The sky filled with orange and pink and purple in an ever-changing array of stunning beauty. When dusk settled in, Jake looked over to see that Glory was asleep. He gently removed his hand from hers, covered her with a light blanket and headed downstairs with Freya in his arms.

Chapter 25

"Ecstatic Love is an ocean,
And the Milky Way is a
Flake of foam floating on it."

~ Rumi

Glory awoke an hour later. She was a little disoriented until she saw the soft blanket that covered her. She looked to her right and saw the note on the table with her name on it. She opened the note and read:

I thought I'd let you sleep and rest. I'm downstairs in the kitchen prepping for dinner. Take your time waking. The bathroom is to the left of my bed. There are clean towels and extra toothbrushes if you feel the need. Come down when you are ready, and I'll fix dinner for you. Love, Jake

Glory smiled at the note and got up from the chair. She tucked the note in her bra. She didn't know what would become of this relationship, but she wanted to cherish every moment of every event.

She went into his bathroom which was another delight. The floor was covered with Mexican terra-cotta tiles. The cabinets were pine and the walls a soft peach echoing the lighter shades of the tile. *The color reminds me of Martha's living room.*

On one end was a jetted double sized bathtub beside a large open glass shower. In the middle was a double his and hers sink with a beautiful polished wood top. There were drawers on both sides of the sinks with drawers in the middle. She walked to the end of the room where there was a double walk-in closet. One side was empty, and the other had Jakes few clothes and hats and extra boots. She smiled at the boots and went back to the sinks.

She used the sink that had only a toothbrush and toothpaste there. She got a washcloth from the rack behind her and washed her face and brushed her teeth. She opened the drawer to see a clean, new brush. She ran the brush through her hair and looked in the mirror. She talked to herself, "You may be in too deep already Gloriana." She double checked that her hair and face looked clean and presentable and turned to go downstairs to Jake.

She entered the kitchen to find him at the old butcher-block table chopping vegetables for a salad. He looked perfect, chopping precisely yet with ease. She loved the way his long fingers held the blade he was working with and seemed to glide with each stroke of the knife downward along to the next section of the onion he was chopping. She smiled watching his intent gaze on his hands while his hair had fallen on his forehead. When he finished chopping the onion she said, "You look like an expert chef."

He looked up and smiled. His smile made her heart trip a little. "My momma would not let a single one of us kids get our driving license until we could cook proper meals from scratch."

"Maybe more moms should insist on that," Glory said.

He laid down the knife, rinsed off his hands and came to her enveloping her in his arms. He said, "My Momma and Daddy had strict rules but by the time we graduated high school we could all cook, do our own laundry, clean up the house and take care of the yard. Daddy made sure we could each change the oil in our cars and knew how to maintain a car whether through the summer or winter. They used to joke when all the kids moved out, they would have to hire help around the house."

Glory chuckled. "Well, I learned to do a lot of after it was just my mother and me. She worked long hours to keep up with everything we needed."

Jake took her hand and led her to a stool beside the table. "You sit right here while I finish fixing dinner."

Glory asked, "Do I need to help you?"

"Not tonight but maybe later on it would be fun to cook together."

"You like to cook," she said, and he nodded.

"Yep, I do. One time one of my friends showed me a poster about living Zen. I'm not religious but all the points on the poster made sense. One of them was to make cooking and cleaning a meditation of love and service. I did that and my cooking got better."

Glory looked at Jake. "There is so much depth to you I feel I'll never live long enough to learn what you know."

"What I know," Jake said, "Would probably fill a nice teacup but I'm happy to drag sharing my wisdom out for about 70 years or so to keep you around."

Glory laughed. "Hold up there, Cowboy. I haven't committed to lifelong. Yet."

He grinned. "Why don't you tell me a little about your childhood?"

"First tell me what culinary feast you have for me."

"Okay. I'll let you off the hook for the moment. How does fried catfish, buttered corn on the cob, coleslaw and corn bread sound to you?"

"I've never had catfish but I'm ready to try it," she answered.

"Good. Now it is time for you to spill the beans and tell me about your childhood."

"Well, my mom and I lived together in North Bend. Before my Dad died in a horrible accident, it was a miserable life. He was a drunk and a mean drunk. When he came home, he would beat me and my mom. If we were quick enough to be in bed before he got home, he would sometimes just throw things around and yell and scream," Glory said.

Jake stopped what he was doing and looked up at Glory. "I'm so sorry. I did not know you had such a miserable childhood."

Glory nodded. "Thanks, but it wasn't all miserable. When he was sober, he was kind and gentle. My mom thought about divorce, but she loved him despite everything. When I was eight years old, he got in a bar fight in the local bar. He got beat up pretty bad but could walk. They said he stumbled out of the bar and took off walking from the bar, headed for home but got turned around. No one saw him walk across the interstate overpass. He tripped and fell and went over the side of the barricade and landed on the interstate. He didn't get run over because he fell onto the shoulder. However, he landed on his head. The coroner thought he probably died shortly after he fell from a fractured skull and a broken neck."

"Oh, Glory, I'm so very sorry," Jake said and came to her and held her hands in his.

Glory nodded. "Mom was upset and sad for a few days but within a day after the funeral she sat me down and said 'You need to know this was entirely your father's fault he died. Neither you nor I could save him. His life insurance will pay for us a house of our own and I'll put the rest in savings for when you go to college. I'll take care of you but I will also live the life I've wanted to live. I hope when you grow up you will too.' So, she got busy living. I helped her around the house, studied hard and got a scholarship to the University of Washington. She joined a hiking and mountain climbing group, Outdoor Women's Alliance, and spent every time off she could with either them or me. They have a motto, 'She believed she could, so she did.' My childhood started out bad but ended well."

Jake hugged her. "Now I understand where you get your strength from. I wish I had met your mother so I could hug her too."

"I do too," Glory said, swallowing back the tears. "Next time you're in Washington we'll drive up to Mount Rainier and you can say hello to her."

Jake looked down at Glory. "I thought your mom died?"

Glory smiled. "She did. She wanted to climb Mount Rainier. Remember, 'she believed she could, so she did'? She worked hard on her climbing skills and finally made it. She hiked up to the peak of the mountain but on the way down, she slipped and fell in a deep crevice. The crew she was hiking with could not retrieve her body. In a strange way, her staying there, where she accomplished her life's dream, was a relief for me. She gets to spend eternity exactly where she loved to be."

Jake held Glory close, and they were quiet for a few minutes. Finally, Glory said, "I'm hungry you know."

Jake chuckled. "You are a demanding woman."

"You have seen nothing yet, Cowboy," Glory answered.

After dinner they walked outside with Freya on a leash beside them. She sniffed and found a perfect spot to do her business. Jake held Glory's hand in his and they strolled through the back garden and over to the barn.

Jake showed Glory his horses and talked with them. "This here is Thunder," Jake said as they walked up to a stall. "He likes to pretend he is mean but if you have an apple in your pocket, he'll be sweet as pie." Jake reached in his pocket and held out a small apple to the horse. Thunder nibbled delicately on the apple while Jake petted his nose and neck.

"On down here is Sally Mae," she is an older horse but still spry enough to love a good ride in the fields. "She is gentle as they come and loves if you scratch her behind the ears." He showed Glory and then gently guided her hand up to scratch behind Sally's ear. Glory smiled at the way the horse leaned her head into her hand. She loved the warm silky feel of the horse's ear.

"And the last one I have," Jake said leading Glory to the next stall, "Is Bogart. I bought him a week ago. Haven't worked with him very much but he is getting the hang of being ridden and following orders. Don't pet him yet though. He bit the hell out of me the first time I came up to him. He still has a few skitters about him." Glory smiled at Jake and how much thicker his accent became while talking to and about the horses.

He saw her smile and asked, "What are you smiling about?"

She looked up at him. "I was just thinking about how much I like being with a cowboy."

He smiled back. "That's good to hear. I like being with you. How about we go back to the house, turn out all the lights and sit on my bedroom deck? There is something I want to show you."

"Is that a pickup line?"

He shook his head. "I hadn't thought of that, really. There is something special I want to show you before the moon comes up. But, let me know if it works as a pickup line. I might use it."

Glory laughed. Jake grinned to himself delighted in her laughter and that she didn't shy away from petting the horses.

They walked back to the house, hand-in-hand, with Freya tagging along at a little dog trot on her leash. They went up the stairs to Jake's bedroom. He folded a blanket and laid it in front of the fireplace for Freya. She climbed on the blanket and went to sleep almost immediately.

"That's one tired little doggie," Jake said. He took Glory's hand, turning off lights as he went. They walked onto the deck and sat in the chairs. Jake pulled a remote control out of his pocket and turned off all the outdoor lights. He reached for her hand and said, "Just lay your head back and wait for the show to begin."

Glory didn't know what to expect, so she said nothing. She laid her head back against the chair waiting for the show to begin. Gradually, as her eyes adjusted to the darkness, she started see stars; lots of stars. In about five or ten minutes she saw a meteor flash across the sky. She gasped in delight. Jake just squeezed her hand in acknowledgment but said nothing. *This is better than Lake Easton.*

The darker the sky became the more stars came out and soon she could make out the Milky Way. The longer they watched the more stars popped out until it seemed to Glory, she could reach up and touch the Milky Way itself. They sat holding hands, but Glory felt a powerful urge, a need really, to be naked and in his arms.

She stayed still for a few more minutes but the bolder the stars became and the clearer the Milky Way became the more she knew she had to be naked. Glory followed the urge of the stars, stood up quietly and tugged her shirt over her head. She stepped out of her shoes. She removed Jake's note from her bra and tucked it inside her jeans pocket. She let her jeans drop to the floor of the balcony and stepped away from her jeans. Finally, she removed her bra and her underwear tossing them on her chair. She looked to Jake and saw he was watching her in awe. He started to say something, but she put a finger to her lips to quiet him.

She walked around her chair and then to his. Taking his hands in hers she pulled him up to standing in front of her. She unbuttoned his shirt and pulled it off his shoulders and tossed it into the chair. She unbuckled his belt and unbuttoned his jeans. She let him help her pull them down. She had forgotten his boots, but he pushed them off his feet. One toppled over the edge of the balcony and quietly he said, "Oops." But nothing more. She reached for him and he wrapped her in his arms.

She felt the warmth of his chest against her breasts and his arms soothing her. It felt like a blessing she had been waiting her whole life for. He kissed her neck, and she arched it up just in time to see another flash of falling stars. She moaned as he continued to kiss her neck and then down to her breasts. She pushed his underwear down with her hand and he moaned in return. He whispered, "I think it would be safer to be off the balcony."

"I agree."

He led her into his bedroom and over to the bed. He had removed his underwear on the way in. He pulled back the comforter and sat on the edge of the bed. She saw he was erect and longing for her. He reached his arms out to her, and she came to him.

They kissed passionately and then Jake asked, "Are you sure Glory? This is a big step."

"I know," She whispered. "But I really want you and want you inside me now."

They climbed further into the bed and were quickly entwined in each other's arms and legs. Glory felt more alive and more right with herself, and the Universe, in this moment than any she had ever felt. She smiled at her thoughts.

So, this is how it feels to ride the Milky Way.

Chapter 26

"I didn't get there by wishing for it
Or hoping for it,
But by working for it."
- Estée Lauder

Jake and Glory sat at the kitchen table the next morning eating scrambled eggs and left-over catfish. She said, "I'd never have thought to have catfish, or any fish for breakfast but this is superb."

"I'm glad you like it," Jake said. "Catfish is a food group all its own in Oklahoma. I need to take a ride around the ranch and check the fences to be sure they are all still standing and sound. Then I'd like to take you on a short camping trip to a place I think will be special to you."

"Special how?"

Jake grinned. "It's a secret, at least for now. Would you like to ride the fences with me?"

"I've never ridden a horse that doesn't require quarters."

He laughed. "Well, Darlin', these are quarter horses, but I don't think they are anywhere near what you're talking about. I'm a great teacher if you'd like to learn."

"What about Freya?"

"We'll take her with us. I have a special harness I can put on my saddle and she can ride with me."

Glory smiled and nodded her head. "Okay. I'm game if you will be patient with me. I have no boots either."

"You don't need boots, at least not to learn. Your sneakers will be fine.

You will want to wear jeans and long-sleeved shirt, however. You go get ready and I'll clear the dishes away."

Glory stood up, leaned over the table and kissed Jake. He smiled up at her and she smiled back. She said, "I hate doing dishes, so I won't argue."

She went up to their bedroom and realized she had not thought of it as his bedroom. She smiled and said, "Girl you are in big time." She went into the bathroom and turned on the shower. She quickly rinsed off and then dried off. She had just finished dressing when he walked into the room. She was sitting on the rocking chair and was tying her shoelaces. She stood up, but he motioned her to stay where she was.

He walked over and bent down to her and kissed her gently on the lips. "I love seeing you sitting there with the morning sun shining on your hair."

She smiled up at him and pulled his face down to her and kissed him again.

He placed his hands on the arms of the rocking chair. "I want more than anything to stay here and play in the bed over there with you. But if we don't get the fence riding done, we can't go camping this evening and I really, really want to show you this special place."

She grinned. "Your loss, Cowboy."

He grabbed her hands and pulled her up to stand in front of him. "Darlin', I'll cash in my chips later. It's time to teach you how to be a cowgirl."

"I'm ready," she said.

He gave her a quick kiss. "Okay, Freya let's head on out."

Freya jumped from her bed and followed as Glory and Jake went downstairs. She sat and waited at the back door for her leash.

"That's amazing," Glory said. "She has already learned that she has to be on leash here."

Jake bent down and put the leash on Freya. "She is a smart little doggie."

He took them out to the stables and Glory saw that Thunder and Sally Mae had been saddled but there was also another man standing there with them. As they got close Jake said, "Hey, Delbert, thanks for coming over."

"No problem," Delbert said.

Jake pointed to Glory. "Delbert, this is my friend Glory Pennington."

Delbert extended a hand to her. "Nice to meet you Glory. I've kin that live south of here that are Pennington's. You related to them?"

"I don't know. I've never looked at the family tree."

He shook his head. "Most folks don't. All the same if you figure it out you are, they are good people."

"That's good to know."

Jake said, "Delbert here has become a great friend for me like he was with my Daddy. Not only does he help out around here he makes it possible for me to go away for a few days at a time."

"It's purely my pleasure," Delbert said. "There ain't many jobs in these parts a man who just wants to work on a ranch can find. This is perfect for me. I get to work on the ranch, help out and live here too. I get to have my personal space which means a lot."

Glory looked around. "Where do you live? I don't see another house around here."

"Oh, no ma'am. I like my privacy too much to live close to here. There's an old hunting cabin about half a mile away. Jake lets me live there for free."

Glory looked at Jake and smiled. Jake held up his hands. "Hey, it isn't charity. Delbert is refurbishing the cabin, putting in plumbing and electricity while he also helps around here and lets me be free to work with the horses or go on trips like I want to. It's actually the original old homestead cabin for the property."

Delbert nodded. "It's a fine arrangement and suits us both. I've plowed up about a half-acre back there and planted me a garden with okra, corn, watermelon, cantaloupes, cucumbers and tomatoes."

"Sounds great," Glory said.

"We'll see. I'm hoping for a great crop, especially the okra and cantaloupes. Some okra's already coming on and the cantaloupes are looking mighty promising. I don't know how folks can live without them."

Jake walked over to Sally Mae and brought her up close to Glory. He said, "We'll go slow and easy today and get you, so you have nothing to fear being on top a horse. Then after a few days of riding, I'll teach you more. Today is just walking around looking at fences and walking back home. Only difference really is that the horse does the walking."

Delbert smiled. "She is as gentle as a kitten. You'll do fine."

Delbert held the reins of the horse while Jake helped Glory into the saddle. Jake guided the horse around the paddock teaching Glory a few things about riding and guiding the horse. Glory said, "This feels wonderful up here, but I feel like she is in full control of everything."

"It only seems that way. When I quit guiding her around, she'll stand there like a stone until you let her know you want her to move and where you want her to move."

"How do I do that?"

"First relax. Then take the reins in your right hand. Hold on to the saddle horn with your left hand." He helped her place her hands as they should be. Then he said, "Now if you lean forward a little and up and gently touch your heels to her belly she will walk forward."

Glory did as Jake instructed. After Sally Mae walked, she asked, "How do I stop her?"

"Just pull back a little gentle on the reins while you sit back in the saddle," Jake said.

Glory did as he told her, and the horse stopped. Jake walked over and said, "Good. You did great for stop and go. Now for right and left and backup."

He went through the instructions and within about thirty minutes Glory could start, stop, backup and turn right or left with the horse.

Delbert watched the way Jake worked with Glory and Sally Mae. *I'd say the love bug has bitten those two in a big way. I wish Cora were here to see Jake in love. It feels real and deep this time.*

As Glory was more and more comfortable with being on Sally Mae, Jake saw her grinning from ear to ear. "How do you feel now, Glory?"

"I feel powerful and thrilled."

He patted her leg and said, "That's my Darlin'."

It excited her to be able to sit on a horse and do the rudimentary things of riding but his calling her 'my Darlin' made her even more delighted.

"Let me get Freya's harness on and then we can go for a short ride to run the fences."

Delbert smiled and walked back into the barn. *Nothing quite like seeing a cowboy in love and a woman loving him.*

Freya was happy riding on the horse. Glory thought she would be afraid of the big animal but Freya, so far, liked every animal she came across. Her grinning face was evidence of pure joy in the adventure. As they rode Jake gave Glory more and more hints and instructions about riding. She loved that she was learning something new and alien to her. She had never even considered riding a horse. They rode a little faster but did not go into a full gallop. Jake wanted to be sure they took no risks today.

They went from pasture to pasture. Glory got to see the expanse of the ranch Jake owned. She saw herds of cows munching on the grass. There was even a small herd of white-tailed deer at the edge of the forest. The deer didn't seem to mind that Glory and Jake and Freya were riding by. They saw no dangerous animals.

When they arrived back at the ranch in a few hours, Glory was tired but felt vibrantly alive. At least until she climbed out of the saddle. "Holy Moly!" she said. "My thighs do not understand what I've done to them."

Jake laughed. "You'll get used to it. After you work those muscles out, you'll be fine. For now, head on into the house, take a shower and then we'll head out to go camping."

"You want to take my van?" She asked. "It is a little nicer than your Little Darlin'."

Jake grinned. "Are you going to be jealous of my pickup?"

"No, I decidedly am not," Glory answered. "However, I love the comfort of my van. You haven't camped until you sleep in my van."

"I'm not sure I agree but I'd be happy to take your van. But, where we are going is a secret, Darlin'."

"Not to worry," Glory said. "I'm happy to let you drive, Cowboy."

"Yeehaw," Jake said. "I get to drive."

Glory shook her head, grinned and headed for the house as quickly as her sore legs would carry her.

The hot shower felt tremendous. "I could stay in here forever," Glory said.

"No, you can't," Jake's voice said. "I need a shower too."

"You can join me if you'd like because I'm nowhere near ready to get out."

Jake grinned. "I thought you'd never ask."

She turned to him. "I've never had sex in the shower. Is it as good as everyone says?"

He took her in his arms. "I don't know for sure; I've never done it either. Shall we find out?"

She nodded. He kissed her loving the feel of her wet body and the smell of her hair.

After their lovemaking in the shower, they rinsed off and stood together in the bathroom drying

off.

Glory said, "My thighs feel better."

Jake grinned. "I thought so too."

She laughed. "We are daring young things, but I loved every minute of that."

He walked over and kissed her lightly. "I love every minute I am with you. I think the bottom line for me is I am falling in love with you."

She felt tears coming but choked them back. "I'm falling in love with you too, Jake. I have to be honest though. I love every minute I am with you but I'm scared as hell of making a mistake and fucking up."

"I understand, really I do," He said. He caressed her cheek. "I'm yours and you can count on me."

She nodded. Then Jake grinned. "Besides, if you are worried about fucking up, I'll let you be on top all the time."

She laughed and as he turned to run away. "Don't think I won't remember that, Cowboy."

She heard his laughter in the bedroom. She could not stop smiling as she finished drying off.

They both dressed and gathered a few things for the night. She tossed him the keys and said, "Here you go, Cowboy. Take me to your special hideout in the woods."

"Your wish is my command, Darlin'," he said, taking her hand and heading downstairs with Freya at their heels.

Chapter 27

"Love is a friendship set to music."
— Joseph Campbell

They loaded up the van, waved goodbye to Delbert and headed down the dirt roads until they got to the highway. Glory asked, "Why did you bring fishing poles?"

"Because without them we won't have dinner."

"You're sure you can catch a fish?"

"Yes, ma'am," Jake answered. "I'm not just some beautiful woman's play thing you know."

She laughed. "Well, if you don't catch a fish, I'll make you some mac and cheese with tuna."

"From a can?"

"Oh, yes, and it will taste great. I'm not just some handsome cowboy's play thing you know?"

He grinned and looked at her. "So, you think I'm handsome then?"

"I never said I was talking about you, Cowboy."

He laughed and shook his head. "You are getting bold for your britches, Darlin'. Don't worry. Where I'm taking you, I always catch fish. Might be a bass, might be catfish. You can never tell until you pull 'em in."

They continued to laugh and banter as they drove. Glory, of course, was totally lost and said so. He tapped her GPS. "You don't have to worry about being lost with this. It's so flat where I'm taking you any old GPS could find you."

"Why are you keeping this such a secret?" She asked.

"Because I think it might be important to you, even if just a little bit."

Jake smiled at her discomfort about not knowing where they were going. He relented and said, "I will tell you this though: it is a place a friend of mine owns. We used to go camping out here all the time. We still go from time to time but not as often as we used to. He's married with two kids now and another on the way. He spends most of his time with his wife and kids."

"Does he have a house where we're going?"

Jake shook his head. "No, not where we're camping. He has a house along the way but where we're going is a special place. He wants to keep it natural as it is as long as he can. Back when we both first graduated high school, we talked about what we wanted to do with our lives. He was and still is adamant: every extra penny he has he buys a few acres of land. I've done the same thing around my property for several years. He wants to leave it to his children hoping they might by then have better ways of using the land than destroying all of nature around them."

"I can understand that," Glory said. "Out in Washington there are stricter laws about land use but there is still a lot of building up that threatens our natural resources. The land is beautiful but sometimes the average person really can't do much about the political and money-grubbing schemes of others."

Jake nodded. "I used to vote only when it was convenient but now, I vote every election. It is the only possible way that the average Joe gets to say his peace."

Glory hesitated but finally said, "You know before we go much further in this relationship, I think we should talk about our feelings on politics and religion."

Jake nodded. "I agree we should do that but I'm nervous about it."

"I think it is at least as important as whether to have children," Glory said. "My mom said when she was young a lot of women had decided not to have children because the world seemed to be in such disarray, they hesitated to bring their children into the World."

Jake said, "I've heard similar things from my parents and their friends. It seems the world is always in disarray. The final decision for me, about children, is if good people don't raise more good people, then we are signing our planet's death certificate."

"I agree. But for the sake of my children, or maybe even our children, I think we should be on the same page about these things before we consider a long-term relationship or marriage."

"This terrifies me Glory."

"Why?"

"What if I believe or want differently than you do? Will we walk away? I don't think I could handle that now. I'm in too deep."

Glory looked out the window. She felt the same way. She sat quietly and said nothing for the moment. She didn't want to destroy what they had started together, but she didn't want to give up on herself ever again to please anyone or to make anyone else happy with her. Jake reached over and held her hand. She finally said, "I'll go first but only if you say nothing until I finish."

Jake said, "Thank you and I'll be quiet and listen."

Glory began, "I don't know for sure about anything I believe except that I believe these things to be true. I am good enough for people to love and admire me and want to be with me. I have as many brains as the next person even if I don't have a penis." Jake laughed and Glory said, "I know it sounds funny but I'm serious."

"Yes ma'am," He answered but couldn't wipe the smile off his face.

She continued, "I don't believe there is only one god or maybe even any god. I believe the Universe is filled with mighty power including that we humans, on this planet feel a need to connect with each other on a spiritual plane. If some call that religion, I suppose that's fine for them but only if they do not use it as a cudgel against anyone else or any other belief systems. I believe in science when it is not corrupted by big money interests. I feel the energy of those around me and want them to feel my energy. If others need to call that God that's fine but religion is just totally out for me."

Jake nodded but remained quiet. Glory took that as a good sign and continued. "I believe our founding fathers lived within a framework of have and have not. I don't believe they intended women, black people, native or first nation people, or people who were not wealthy landowners should ever be allowed to vote. We women and the people I've mentioned have had to fight tooth and toenail for every right we have and I sure as hell will not give up my rights to be with a man. Even you, Cowboy."

He grinned and said quietly, "I think you are a little fired up, Darlin'."

"Do you disagree with me, Cowboy?"

He chuckled. "Not so far but I'm glad you don't have a penis."

She laughed and punched his shoulder which made him only grin more.

"That's about it. Now it's your turn."

"Okay but don't expect me to be as fired up or eloquent as you were, Darlin'."

"Continue on, Cowboy."

He reached over and took her hand in his. He said, "There is nothing you said I do not agree with you on 100%. The only things I will add is I think we each have a limited amount of time on this earth and we are beholden to live the best life we can and do as little damage to ourselves, each other and our planet as possible."

He looked around including through the rear mirrors and then said, "I want to be clear about this next part but want to be careful too. I believe love, kindness and hope are the forces keeping humanity and perhaps even the evolution of our species advancing. I don't know what power directs it all or even if there is a power directing it. But I believe the forces of good over evil must be constantly active. For me, family and children express those forces. I'd love to have a houseful of children we give birth to Glory. If that can't happen, I still want a houseful of children no matter where they come from. It is through children we create the world anew for the future."

Glory looked at him and saw a tear travel down his face. She reached over and gently touched the tear. She asked, "Are we clear on everything now, Cowboy?"

Jake nodded but didn't say anymore.

As they drove, she watched the rolling hills, fields of hay, beautiful trees that seemed to belong to this land although they were nothing as big as she was used to seeing. They crossed many small waterways that were creeks or small rivers but no big bodies of water she saw in Washington. The sky took her breath away. It seemed to be much bigger here than in Washington. She felt as if some mighty hands had pulled back mountains and forests to open the windows to the heavens. The sky here was bluer than she ever remembered skies being in Washington.

She was torn about the two states. She didn't want to leave Washington but was falling in love with Oklahoma as much as she was with Jake.

He reached over and touched her arm. "You might want to start paying attention to the signs along the road right about now, Darlin'."

"Why?"

"You'll see."

She pulled herself out of her deep thoughts. She saw lots of signs with names she was not familiar with. Some were names of towns, some names of forests or state parks but most were names of creeks.

Jake looked over at her and smiled. *She is the woman for me. I hope she sees how right we are for each other. She is so brilliant and beautiful but I don't think she fully realizes it. I hope that will change over our lives together.*

Glory said, "Oh!"

Jake grinned and asked innocently, "What?"

"That sign said the creek we crossed over was Pennington Creek. I've never seen my family name on anything."

She looked at him and saw the grin. She smiled. "You are taking me to Pennington Creek."

"Yes, Ma'am. I thought you should see it before you head back to the Pacific Northwest."

She leaned over and kissed him on the cheek. "Thank you, Cowboy."

He nodded. "My pleasure, Darlin'."

"Is that where we will camp?"

"Yes, but not exactly here. That creek meanders and wanders all over the place for about 25 miles. My friend's land includes a section of the creek. It is our secret camping place."

Glory smiled. "I will camp on a creek with the same name as I have. Damn. It is a great surprise Jake. I won't be able to top that."

"Give it time. I'm sure you'll think of something."

In another few miles Jake turned the van off the highway and onto a gravel road. They passed a farmhouse that was two stories tall and white with a red shingle roof and black shutters. There was a rope swing hanging from a large sycamore tree and bicycles and tricycles scattered through the yard. Kids were playing chasing each other around the yard. Jake said, "There's my friend's house."

"Aren't we going to stop?" Glory asked.

"No. I talked with him yesterday while you were napping and asked if I could bring you camping. He said sure and invited us to visit. I told him the next time, assuming there is a next time, I'll bring you here to meet him and his family. This trip I wanted to be just the two of us with no one else around."

Freya yiked from the back where she was in her travel kennel. Glory laughed, "Freya doesn't want to be left out."

Jake said, "I'll never leave you out Freya." The dog settled back down on her bed and went right back to sleep.

They took a dirt road that was little more than a trail and, in a few minutes, Glory could see the creek. Jake stopped the van on a sandy verge. They got out and he let Freya out on her leash. They walked down to the creek's edge and Glory said, "This is beautiful Jake. The trees are bigger than I expected."

"Well, here they have more water, so they grow taller. The aquifer is not very far down at this point in the state so there is always water in this creek. Hundreds of springs feed this creek and a few other creeks. That's why it is so green in this part of the state."

She turned and put her arm through his and said, "Thank you so much for bringing me here. How did the creek get its name?"

"That's less clear. There have been Pennington's in Oklahoma for over a hundred years. There is an old tale, may or may not be true, about a fella named Alonzo Pennington. He was part of a gang when this was Indian Territory. The gang rode between here and South Carolina robbing banks and killing folks. When they wound up here, they would hide with relatives in the area. One time they road too far into Texas and the rangers chased them all the way up into Southeast Oklahoma where they caught him hiding with family. The rangers didn't bother with a court. They threw a rope over a tree and hung him and his gang right beside this creek. Some say they call it Pennington Creek because a Pennington was hanged by this creek. My guess is that it is just as likely because there were lots of Pennington's living in the area but it makes for a good story."

Glory laughed. "Well, unless you are a Pennington."

"I reckon that is right," Jake said. "Shall we go fishing, Darlin'?"

"Sure, but you need to teach me how. I've never been fishing."

Jake shook his head. "How sad you have never done some of the best things in life. I'll help you catch up, Darlin'."

She grinned. "That would be nice, Cowboy."

Jake carried two lawn chairs closer to the creek while Glory got two beers and the leash line for Freya. When Glory walked down to the creek where Jake was she saw he had a small Styrofoam box with dirt in it. "What's the dirt for?"

Jake ducked his head. "The worms."

"What worms?"

"The ones we will use for bait." He looked up at Glory and when he saw the look of horror on her face, he laughed out loud.

"No really," she said. "We aren't going to kill worms just to catch fish, are we?"

Jake nodded. "Yes, we are. And then after we catch the fish, we will kill them to eat for our dinner."

Glory's eyes were big, but Jake did not relent. "Listen, Darlin', there was some lion or another that sang about this in some cartoon movie I saw with Helen's kids. It is the circle of life. When we die, we are food for worms, so they get a piece of us back. It is the way of nature. We don't kill unnecessarily but we have to eat, or we die. For generations this has always been the way."

"I know and I love meat and fish," Glory said, "But I've never been directly involved in the blood-letting."

"And that is part of the problem with our world. We don't own responsibility even for the food we eat. All life is precious because it sustains life. When negligence, meanness and greed enter the chain then life becomes less and less precious."

Glory nodded. "You are right. I just think I can't put a worm on a hook."

"That's fine. Your Cowboy will help you with that part. I'll even take care of the fish for you too, but you will help catch them."

"Deal," Glory said.

It surprised her when in less than ten minutes she had caught her first catfish. It was really fun, but Jake said anything less than ten inches was too small to keep, and he tossed it back into the creek. "That fish needs to grow up some and make more babies," He said.

They kept fishing, drinking beer and talking. When they had three good-sized fish Jake said, "You can go up to the van and get corn ready to roast. I'll clean the fish and be up to show you how to cook them over a campfire."

Within a few minutes she was back at the van with Freya. She pulled out the small picnic table she had bought and set it up beside the van. She got the coleslaw out of the cooler and set it on the table. Then she pulled the husks of the corn back, removed the silk like Jake had shown her then pulled the husks back up. She put the corn in a bowl of salt water to soak the husks and keep them from burning too much as well as flavor the corn at the same time. She sat out butter for the corn and pulled a bottle of Riesling out of the cooler chest. She wasn't sure what wine went with catfish, but this was what she had.

By the time she had those things out on the table at the campsite, Jake was walking up to the camp with fish filets in his hands. "I'll wash these inside the van and then make the fire," he said. Glory went in the van and helped him clean up the fish and get the grille grate they would use to cook the fish on.

She went back outside and played with Freya while Jake built up the fire in a large metal fire pit. Before long he had the grill propped up on a few sticks over the fire. He laid the corn on the edges of the grill and then the fish. He put butter and seasoning salt on the fish. When it had cooked a few minutes, he turned the fish over and cooked the other side. By that time the corn was roasted. They sat side by side at the table enjoying their dinner.

Glory said, "This fish tastes even better than what we had last night, Cowboy."

Jake nodded. "It always tastes best straight out of the water and grilled on an open wood fire. I've never had wine with catfish, but this is great, Darlin'."

Glory chuckled. "Yep, nothing like a good German wine with Oklahoma catfish."

They carefully picked out some catfish being sure there were no bones in it. Glory got out a little shredded cheese to mix with the fish and Freya's kibble.

The little dog was so excited by her food for the evening she could hardly stay standing in one spot long enough to finish her dinner.

While it was still light, they took the dog for a walk and when they returned to the van Freya begged to go inside. They took her in, and she immediately crawled into her travel box and went to sleep.

As the evening progressed, and the sun went down, Glory and Jake sat side by side in their lawn chairs holding hands. She said, "I've never seen sunsets like these in Washington. It seems like Oklahoma has cornered the market on sunsets."

Jake grinned. "I could give you all the scientific reasons explaining why they are so stunning if you'd like."

"No. I like the magic part best."

He lifted her hand and kissed the back of her hand. "Me too."

When the sun was finally down, she said, "I'm ready for bed if you are, Cowboy."

He stood up and smiled at Glory. "That is exactly what I'm ready for, Darlin'."

They went inside the van and let the queen-sized bed down from the back wall. Glory opened the shade covering the moon roof before settling in beside Jake on the bed. "I thought we might like looking up to see the stars from bed."

"That is the second-best thing left for the night, Darlin'."

She smiled at Jake and curled up close to him with his arms wrapped around her. "Yes, it is, Cowboy." She felt loved, alive and blessed as they turned to each other in a bed they had never made love in.

Chapter 28

The next morning Glory awoke to the smell of burning wood. Jake wasn't in the bed beside her and Freya wasn't in her box. Glory dressed quickly and when she opened the door, she saw another small campfire and Jake sitting in a chair by the fire drinking coffee. He looked up at Glory. "Good morning, Darlin'."

She smiled. "Good morning, Cowboy."

Jake stood up, walked to her and enveloped her in a hug. "Glory, I love you. Will you marry me?"

Glory laughed. "Let me have coffee first and then we can talk."

Blushing, Jake said, "I'm sorry. I was sitting here thinking of how to ask you to marry me and when you walked out, I blurted it out. The sight of you with the sun on your hair simply makes me glad to be alive."

She kissed him and smiled. "That's probably the best explanation of a marriage proposal in the world but I still need coffee first."

He poured her a cup of coffee and carried it to the small table between their chairs. "You sit down, and I'll bring over the cream and sugar." She sat down and let him bring the cream and sugar. When she had her coffee ready, she took a sip and smiled up at Jake.

"That's perfect, Cowboy." Wrapping her hands around the coffee mug she said, "I love you too and I know you love me. I thought I loved Edgar, so I married him and look how that turned out."

Jake nodded. "I'm not sure you know how it would have turned out if he hadn't died."

"You are right."

Jake continued, "The only thing I know for sure is that I love you."

Glory looked up at Jake. "I know. I believe in that love and I love you too."

"Good then. We have at least one point of agreement." Glory smiled as Jake sat down in the chair next to her. She reached out for his hand.

Holding his hand, she said, "I love you more than I ever thought I'd love anyone. I know the physical part is perfect."

"See," Jake grinned. "Another point of agreement."

She laughed. "Now just hear me out, Cowboy. I'm not saying no but I'm not saying yes either. At least not yet."

"I can see you will make me work for this, Darlin'," Jake said. "I intend to work on our relationship. I've worked hard for everything good in my life and I don't expect it to be easy to win you over."

"You have mostly won me over already. I'm really not trying to make things hard for you."

"I know, but I also know you aren't as ready as I am to run off and get married."

Glory laughed and squeezed his hand. "I am nowhere near ready for that." Glory stood up and walked to stand beside him. She bent over and kissed him gently. "I love you, Cowboy."

Jake tugged on her hands and pulled her over to sit on his lap. She loved the smell of him, of his rough smell, a little dirt, a little sweat and a lot of campfire smoke. She loved so much about him. *Why can't I just say yes?* She laid her head on his shoulder. He kissed her forehead.

"So," Jake said, his voice a little hoarse and subdued, "As I recall I got a 'maybe' from you on marriage." Glory nodded and Jake continued, "I really want to seal the 'maybe' part of the deal."

"How?"

Jake grinned. "I'm so glad you asked, Darlin'. I want to give you the world, but I am not a rich man. I have a small gift for you to seal the deal."

"What gift, Cowboy?"

He dug in his jeans pocket and pulled out a small box.

She sat up. "Oh, no. No engagement ring until I'm ready."

Jake laughed. "I'd be ashamed to give this bauble to you as an engagement ring. It is too damned cheap for an engagement ring."

Glory blushed. *You jumped to conclusions about what he was asking. Maybe he just wanted to have a woman to hang around him.* She started to push away, but he held her tight.

"Please," he said, "I know you don't trust a lot of things in this world, but you can always trust me to never hurt you and hopefully never make you sad, at least not on purpose. This is not an engagement ring. I was pretty sure you'd say no to getting married yet, and I didn't have time to buy a great engagement ring. But you said you loved me, and you said maybe." He opened the box to reveal a ring that was silver leaves joined creating a ring. There were small garnets looking like berries between the leaves. "I want you to think of this as a joining ring, a maybe ring. You and I joined as maybe."

She looked at him. "If you keep on, you'll make me cry. You make me cry, the deal is off, Cowboy."

He smiled, put the ring on her left hand. "I don't want you to cry but I want you to know as long as you will wear this maybe ring, I'll wait for your yes, Darlin'. When you say yes, there will be a real engagement ring, one worthy of your beauty and our love. If you change your mind about us, you take off this ring and give it back. I'll work hard to understand."

Glory leaned forward and kissed him gently on the lips. "I'll work hard to get to yes because I really love you." They leaned their foreheads together. "Besides the way you smell is nearly irresistible, Cowboy."

He laughed a little. "That's probably the best thing I've ever heard a woman say, Darlin'."

She smiled softly. "My biggest fear is that I will marry again and again my dreams for my life will be pushed aside by a man."

"I can see how that would be a horrible path for you. I want only your happiness including your dreams."

Glory nodded. "I want to do things I've never done before. I want to see things I've never seen. I want to be wild and free just like I feel when we are out riding horses. Getting married feels like the only wildness left would be stolen moments of experience like riding a horse. I want my life to be more than stolen moments."

Jake pulled Glory closer and wrapped his arms around her. "I'd give up everything I own to have you in my arms every day for the rest of my life. Now I've found you and had a taste of what might be for us I can't imagine living without you."

Glory gave him a squeeze. "Me either but I'm scared."

"I want to protect you from everything in the world, but I have a feeling some of these fears are ones you have to conquer yourself. I can be here for you, support you and love you but I can't conquer all of your doubts. I promise to be here to help however I can."

She nodded. "Thank you. I believe all of that is true and will always be true, no matter what. I want to be with you forever, but I can't say yes right now. Your ass is fine in tight blue jeans and that would be hard to walk away from, Cowboy."

He leaned back and laughed. "Woman! I hope you get to yes soon. I'll hold out for maybe for now, Darlin'."

It had been a week since Glory had followed Jake to his ranch. They made love every night and sometimes in the middle of the day. She smiled softly remembering the first time they made love. The room was filled with the glow of the fireplace. The big oak bed felt as if it were imbued with the magic of deep longings and delight, an extension of the Milky Way. The whole experience had felt warm and true and magical. He had been gentle and yet their coming together had felt natural and filled with abandon. Glory had never had such strong feelings during sex. She felt both beautiful and desired; things she had never felt with Edgar. It was all better than she had ever thought it could be. The depth of those feelings was a little unnerving.

He taught her more about horses and put her to work helping to keep them healthy and sound from feeding to brushing to riding to training to cleaning out the stable. *Who knew shoveling and raking horse shit could feel so good?* She felt as comfortable on a horse as driving a car. Freya was learning too and loved riding with Jake on his horse. She followed Jake around with something close to hero worship listening to everything he said and following his directions. Glory smiled. *Freya is in love with him too.*

She stood on the balcony of Jake's bedroom looking across the meadows to mountains. They were not as big or striking as many of the mountains in Washington. However, they reminded her of Mount Si and how at her mother's house she could see the mountain from her bedroom window and from the backyard patio.

She looked down at the beautiful ring she now wore on her hand. She rubbed the ring between her fingers and found herself reassured by the treasure of their promise to each other. She felt conflicted about not saying yes to Jake's marriage proposal. If she were honest with herself, even saying yes to maybe left her feeling conflicted. She loved him with no doubt but worried if they married, they would both end up hurt and alone again. She couldn't face such a possibility.

What if she couldn't get pregnant or miscarried again? Jake wanted a big family as much as she did. Losing a baby was a heartache they had both endured. She wanted to never feel such deep loss again. She also knew she had no control over the grief life brings. She wiped away the tears that began as she thought of her own two babies who had died before she was very far along in the pregnancy. Knowing Edgar never wanted children, her babies, made it even harder to bear. She was sure the grief was similar for Jake. Liz never wanted children and had doubts about keeping the one child Jake had made with her. The miscarriage guaranteed the pregnancy would not be the child Jake longed for.

Glory looked around the ranch and felt a deep love not just for the house but the ranch itself. Off in the distance she could see Jake training Bogart, a new horse he had bought a few days before she came to the ranch. She loved the look of him on the back of a horse. Taking off his hat he wiped his brow with a kerchief and then looked up to see Glory standing on the deck. He waved to her with a silly, boyish grin on his face. Glory smiled and waved back. Freya trotted alongside of Jake and Bogart fully enchanted with the big animal and Jake. Sadness washed over her. If Jake ever had to give up his ranch and his life on the back of a horse, it would be a shame. She would not let herself cause such an event.

Jake had offered to sell his ranch if she would marry him. Glory did not want to be the cause of him losing what he loved. He had said, "As much as I love this place and built it with my mind set, I would marry and have lots children living inside my home, I'd give it up in a heartbeat to have you by my side. This house and everything in it is just stuff." Glory felt deeply that this was not true or at least not completely true. This house was a part of him and now of her and even of Freya. This bedroom was a treasured retreat for her. It was where they first made love. She loved everything about the ranch, well, except for the snakes and spiders. Jake had even promised to kill every spider and snake in Oklahoma if that was what it would take to get her to say yes. She smiled at the memory.

"Oh, Cowboy," she whispered. "What am I going to do with you?"

Chapter 29

"Home isn't where you're from,
It's where you find light
When all grows dark."
— Pierce Brown

Glory stood in Jake's arms on the front porch of his house. She didn't know what else to say except goodbye for now. Jake had asked her to stay, but she had said, "Give me a few weeks back in Washington and maybe I'll have a clearer path forward with you, me and everything."

"Okay, but this is me saying I don't like it one little bit. I don't know how I can go on without having you here in my home and my bed and my arms."

She reached up and touched his face. "I think I'll be right back where you want me but for now, I have to know for sure it is what I want without hesitation. I never considered living anywhere else but Washington. I love Washington and now I love Oklahoma and everything you've shown me even the worms. But I need to go back to where I came from and be sure."

He nodded and held her close. "I understand and I agree but please don't ask me to like it, Darlin'."

"You know your truck will get jealous if you keep calling me that, Cowboy," she said.

She felt his grin against her head. He said, "She is just Little Darlin'. She doesn't hold a candle to you. You are the real full deal, Darlin'."

She smiled, held back tears and reached up to kiss him. She looked at her van. "Freya is all strapped in and waiting for me."

Jake nodded. "But she isn't happy either. Look at that sad little face."

"No tricks with guilt about puppies allowed," Glory said.

"It was my last best shot," Jake said, "For now at least."

He walked her to the van. She got in, rolled the window down and fastened her seat belt. Jake kissed her again. "I'll never get enough of that."

She kissed him again. "Neither will I. Have faith and hope, Cowboy."

"And love, Darlin', always love," He answered.

She drove away with tears rolling down her cheeks. "Oh, Freya," she said, "We got in too deep."

Glory drove a different route home this time. She had intended to go south and get on I-10 and head to Huntington Beach, California where her Aunt Mary, her mother's sister, lived. That would have added at least two more days to her trip back to Washington. She needed to get home and talk with Martha and Emily. She drove west on I-40 until she got to Albuquerque, New Mexico. She stopped for the night there, exhausted and slept until morning light. Back on I-40 she drove until she got to Bakersfield and worked her way over to I-5 and headed north, for home and again drove until she was exhausted.

She got up early the next morning and drove all day until she found a KOA just south of Portland, Oregon. She had stopped a few times for bathroom breaks for herself and Freya. The poor little doggie seemed subdued and depressed. *That pretty much mirrors my feelings.* She had written no blogs nor taken any photos. Martha had called her twice just to check up on her and be sure she was okay. Glory knew she was not okay but didn't know what else to do but drive.

"Maybe I made a mistake, Freya," Glory said. "Maybe I should have just said yes and stayed." Freya looked at her and sighed.

Now I'm miserable, Jake is miserable and so is Freya. But I will not second guess myself. I need to come home and gain a little clarity even if it is just a glimmer.

Glory put kibble in Freya's bowl, but the dog ignored the kibble and stayed in her crate and bed. Glory opened a can of tuna and got out some crackers and a fork. She ate from the can and then said, "Think of it as dinner." She tossed the can in the trash. "Nope, not even close to dinner. It's just food." She showered and went to bed. But couldn't sleep. She couldn't read either. It was after midnight in Oklahoma, but she needed to talk with Jake.

She took a chance, opened her computer and made a video call to him. He answered on the first ring and said, "Hang on a second, I need to situate the camera."

She smiled and waited for him to come on screen. When he did, his appearance shocked her. He looked terrible with bags under his eyes and his face a little gray. She asked, "Jake are you okay? You look terrible."

He smiled which helped his face a lot. "I'm fine, just not sleeping well."

"Did I wake you?"

"No, I tried to go to bed but just couldn't sleep so I got up and tried reading a book but couldn't remember anything enough to turn the page."

"Same scenario here," She said. Freya yiked and begged to be up on the bed. "Hang on, Freya wants to talk to you too."

Jake grinned. "Of course, she does."

Glory pulled the little dog onto the bed and immediately the dog went to the laptop and licked the screen. Jake laughed and said, "I can feel those doggie kisses all the way here in Oklahoma."

Glory pulled the dog back and cleaned the screen with the tail of her gown she had tried to sleep in. Jake said, "You look pretty tired yourself. Are you okay to drive?"

Glory nodded. "I've been a little blue without you around and so has Freya. She didn't eat today at all."

Jake leaned close to the camera. "I miss you both so much I can't think straight."

"I know. Me too. I keep listening to the Trio album, but all the songs are sad and remind me of you."

Jake nodded. "I keep listening to Lyle Lovett and Willie Nelson with the same results."

Glory laughed. "Aren't we a pair?"

"A couple. We're living on maybe-time. I must admit, I don't care for it very much," Jake said.

Glory touched the screen with her left hand. "Me either. I'm still wearing the ring to prove I'm devoted to you on maybe-time."

"Thank you for that. It really helps a lot. I've been thinking," Jake said. "You've been down here in Oklahoma and spent time with me. I haven't seen where you live."

"I live in my van so yes you have seen where I live and even made love in my bed, Cowboy."

Jake grinned. "I loved every moment, Darlin'. Still, I'd like to come to Washington. I've only really seen the service station in North Bend and the hiking trails along the Middle Fork Road. While those are nice, it's not where you live. Can I invite myself to come see you?"

Glory could not stop the tears streaming down her face. "Oh, yes, please. Please come if you can."

"Good," Jake said. "I can't leave for two days because I have a new horse coming in day after tomorrow. As soon as I get the horses settled Delbert can take care of things while I come see you."

"That's perfect," Glory said. "Are you going to drive or fly?"

"I think I'll fly this time. It takes three days of driving to get there which is about how long it would be from now until I arrive."

"Thank you, Jake. I'm a mess right now and debating what I should do next but can only think of you, Cowboy."

"Hooray for me! I can only think of you, Darlin'. I'll send you my flight information. I guess I'll be flying into SeaTac."

"Yep. I think there are some direct flights from Oklahoma City to Seattle. Let me know when and I'll come pick you up."

"You don't have to do that, Darlin'."

"Yes, I do. If I don't, I have to wait another hour to see you. I'll go bat shit crazy, Cowboy."

He laughed. "I love it when you curse and swear. By all means please meet me at the airport."

They talked for a few more minutes and then Glory yawned and so did Freya. Jake said, "Now we have a plan I think we all can get much needed sleep."

Glory smiled and nodded. "I think I can sleep now."

The next morning Glory got up bright and early. She fed and walked Freya and then got in the van and headed north to home. Breakfast was drive through sandwich, coffee and orange juice. She wanted to be home already so she could talk with Martha. "I'm not wasting time cooking or cleaning. I'm going home."

Freya yiked a strong and loud "Yes!"

When she reached the Washington border, she felt a weight lifting from her shoulders. She drove north through Portland and Vancouver. Next was Woodland. Before she got to Longview, she saw signs for Mt St. Helens. She did not remember when the volcano blew in 1980. She was born several years later. What she had learned of the eruption was awful.

Then there was Edgar and the horrible accident that killed him. She knew he must have been distracted to have run the red light. She also knew his troubled soul had worked hard to tamp down the pain and lack of love in his life. He died young and suddenly. He did not expect that to happen.

As she thought about the eruption of the volcano and Edgar's accident, her mother's and father's deaths, she realized that anything could happen at any time. "No one guaranteed any of us to have any time other than this moment, Freya." The little dog cocked her head and yiked her 'yes' yike as if saying, "Well, Duh." Glory smiled. Even Freya felt better today after talking with

Jake last night and so did she.

"It's time for the three of us to quit dilly dallying around, Freya and get on with living." The little dog yiked and grinned. Glory was sure she agreed.

Chapter 30

"As we travel through life,
Life will not only take us to unexpected places,
But it will also take us to places that we already know."
— Anthony T. Hincks

Glory drove through Tacoma on Interstate 5 at the tail end of the morning rush hour traffic. She made great time and pulled into Martha's driveway in Issaquah about 10:30 in the morning. She was pleased to see Emily's car in the driveway and Jason's truck parked at the curb.

She went up to the door with Freya in her arms and rang the doorbell. To her surprise, Jason answered the door.

"Hey you. We didn't expect you to be here until later this afternoon. Come on in." He called out, "Hey girls, Glory is here with Freya in her arms."

There were squeals followed quickly by Emily and Martha running to Glory and hugging her. Glory finally said, "Enough. I need to pee!"

She thrust Freya into Jason's hands. "So does she." Glory went to the guest bathroom and relived her bladder. When she was washing her hands, she looked in the mirror and said, "You look a little better than last night. That's what sleep can do for you." *And love,* she thought.

She went out to the kitchen where she found her three friends sitting at the kitchen table. She looked down to see Emily and Jason holding hands. She smiled and said, "I see someone is in love in this room."

Emily held up her left hand. "Not just someone and not just love. Two people in this room are in love and married."

"What?"

"I know!" Martha said. "They ran off and got married nearly two weeks ago. Can you believe it?"

Glory was stunned. She didn't know what to say. Emily stood up and so did Jason. He said, "I hope you are not angry with us. We decided we wanted to be married right now and if people didn't like it, they could just throw us a big assed party." He was grinning from ear to ear.

Glory laughed. "Then a big assed party you shall have." She hugged them both and said to Martha. "You look smug too."

Emily said, "She is in love with Lori and her dog Buttercup. They are a real thing now."

"Is Lori here?" Glory asked.

"No," Martha said, "Just on her days off."

"I've got to sit down," Glory said. "This is almost too much. I need something to drink."

Emily said, "Wine coming right up."

"I'd rather have real coffee with cream and sugar," Glory said. "Drive through coffee is a bitter dose worthy only for the caffeine."

Emily smiled. "Then coffee you shall have."

Martha reached across the table and took Glory's left hand and picked it up. "What's this I see on your finger?"

Glory said, "It is a maybe ring."

"What's a maybe ring?" Jason asked.

"It's a I-wasn't-ready-to-say-yes ring."

Emily laughed. "I've never heard of a maybe ring. Jason and I race to get married while you and Jake take your own sweet time."

Martha looked at Glory. "I understand but do you love him?"

"Yes, I love him and really a lot more than even I can put my arms around. Cowboy, just said to hold still, and he'd be here in a few days."

Martha grinned. "So, he's coming here."

Glory nodded. "Last night he said he'd be here in three days. So this is the beginning of one day down. I'm still not sure about getting married so soon but I miss him so much it hurts. He is in worse shape than I am. None of us are sleeping well including Freya. She hasn't been eating because she is so sad."

"He's coming here to live?" Martha asked.

Glory shook her head. "No, just for a visit. We have made no commitments other than maybe and that we are in love. I do not want to leave the Pacific Northwest entirely and he doesn't want to leave his ranch in Oklahoma. I don't know where or what we will do other than be together as much as possible. He's coming here for a visit and I'll accept that as enough for now."

"Where's he going to stay?" Jason asked.

"I guess where I will stay," Glory said. "In my van."

Martha grinned. "We have more news up our sleeves. You should hear it before we go any further. I'll be right back."

Martha stood up and went out back kitchen door to She-Shed office. She came back with a folder filled with papers. "Yesterday the property manager at the Management company called and asked if you'd like to have documents for all the properties you own. I said yes."

Glory raised her hand. "I don't want to live in some apartment or condo."

"Just hold on and listen for a few minutes," Martha said and pushed the folder across to Glory. "You are right there are apartments and condos. They are part of the monthly income from properties. There are also some business building with several tenants. But the best part is there are houses too."

Glory smiled, nodded and waited for Martha to continue.

Emily took over, "We were just sitting here talking about how you need a landing place to live and not just a van. Everyone needs a home, a retreat where they can refuel their energies. There are several possible houses. There is one that isn't leased out right now."

Martha nodded. "When Edgar bought this particular house, he told the management company to take care of the house and watch after it but under no circumstances offer it for lease or sale. I think I know why but you open that folder and see for yourself."

Glory opened the folder and picked up the house keys inside. She looked down at the papers and saw a photo of the house she had grown up in just off Tanner Road in North Bend. Tears welled up in her eyes. "I can't believe it. My mother's house. How did Edgar get it?"

Jason said, "He had the management company monitoring the house and if it ever came up for sale, they were to buy it no matter what the cost of the purchase. They bought it for him two years ago. It has been sitting empty for the past two years."

Glory sat silent, crying and wishing Edgar had told her about the house. *Oh, Edgar. We could have had lots of children in that house.* It had four bedrooms and nearly a half-acre of wooded yard, some of it old growth forest. She shook her head, wiped her eyes with the tissue Emily handed her. *Edgar you missed so much life and love you could have had.*

Martha stood and came to kneel by Glory. "It is your house now. You can do whatever you want with it. We were about to go out there and look and see what we need to fix make it livable. Would you like to go out there now with us?"

Glory nodded. "I want to take my van with me, and I can at least sleep in the driveway. But someone else needs to drive. I can't. I'm too tired and too shell-shocked."

Emily fixed them each a go-mug of coffee and a little baggie of peanut butter cookies. "No point in going on an adventure without fuel," She said handing them each their coffee and cookies.

Glory kissed her on the cheek. "Thanks, Mom."

Martha drove Glory's van and Glory sat in the passenger seat holding Freya. Glory could hardly believe she was going to her old home in North Bend with Jason and Emily following. She had not been back since clearing out all of her mother's things and selling the furniture. She held Freya close, happy Rob had talked her into a dog. Freya was quiet and loving for the 15-mile drive east on I-90. Glory said, "Don't worry Freya. We won't be on the road long."

When they exited the interstate and drove on North Bend Way, Glory felt a burden lifting from her. She said, "I know where I will live, at least for now."

Martha reached over and patted her hand. "I thought you might."

They turned north on Tanner Road where the Middle Fork of the Snoqualmie River turned north. It felt like coming home to Glory and in a real way it was. She hoped Jake would feel it was home. She didn't want him to sell the ranch; not only because he loved it but because she loved it too. She had loved growing up in this house, in North Bend, with her mother and could see herself, Jake and children in this home she loved.

They pulled into the driveway and Glory said, "I can tell you right now it needs pruning, gravel on the driveway and paint. Lots of paint."

Martha smiled. "Yes, but it is still a beautiful house. You will love living here much more than in Issaquah."

Glory nodded and knew Martha was right. "It reminds me of Jake's house. It's not a huge log house, but it is a part of the nature surrounding it and it feels like home," Glory said.

Jason and Emily had pulled up behind them. They all got out and Jason said, "Well it looks sound from here. No sagging or buckling of the structure. The roof is intact but needs cleaning. The yard's a wild mess but a few days of work will set that right."

Glory pointed to a large rhododendron that had hundreds of buds on it. "That is the whore bush."

Martha laughed. "I remember your mother called it that."

"Why?" Emily asked.

Glory grinned. "When it blooms in spring the blooms are large, as big as your hand, brilliant scarlet flowers. It is the boldest plant I've ever seen. Mom bought this house after dad died because of the flowers on that bush. She had said, 'This is obviously a home for women since there is a whore bush out front.' Just the two of us in that big house but I was loved and so was she."

Jason said, "That's a great story. I can totally see you loving a whore bush in your front yard. Let's see what we have inside."

Glory handed him the keys and said, "I'll follow you in. I want to really see the house and feel it. I'll leave the details of what needs to be done up to you."

When they walked in the house memories and love flooded Glory. "I remember standing and looking out each window thinking whoever built this house put the windows so that whoever lived here only saw beauty."

Emily said, "The windows remind me of a book, The Constant Princess by Phyllis Whitney. In the beginning story when queen Isabella conquered Granada, they learned from the Muslim slaves that every window in any building must glorify God. The quote I remember the best is: 'Every window is like a frame for a picture: they make you stop, look, and marvel' and then 'at every turn of every corner we know that we are living inside beauty'."

Glory felt tears on her face. She whispered, "Exactly."

They stood quietly together in the hallway until Jason reached out and asked, "Would you like to be alone?"

Glory shook her head. "No, but I don't want you to move a single window in the house. I have ideas about adding windows though."

He smiled and said, "And so it shall be."

Glory pointed to a wall and said, "I want that wall taken out. This front room is too small for any good use. Mom used to use it as a boot room but I really don't want a boot room by the front door."

Jason walked over to the wall and looked up at the ceiling. "I agree this wall should come out but let's go around the house and look at everything. You tell me as we go along changes you'd like to make and I'll take notes." He smiled. *So much for me taking the lead and telling her what I think. This is the better and right way.*

"Let's go look at the bedrooms first," Glory said. She led them to the master bedroom and said, "I don't know how you will do it but I'd like to put another double window in the wall facing Mt. Si. Then I'd like to open this room up to the smaller bedroom next door and use that entrance opening into a sitting area for Jake and I and then into our bedroom."

Jason smiled and nodded. He went out of the bedroom and into the next bedroom. He came back in and said, "I like that idea a lot Glory. It is a small bedroom. We could also make the closet area and master bathroom bigger by shutting off this doorway and building the closet out to here. Then it would be a walk-in closet accessed from the bathroom."

Glory nodded, "Yes. I love that idea. I want a big jetted tub in the bathroom and an open clear glass shower."

"You read my mind," Jason said. "Let's keep looking."

They looked at the other two bedrooms and Jason said, "I think I can build the front out a little and put a Jack and Jill bathroom between these two bedrooms. Then we can change the guest bathroom in the front hall into a small washroom for visitors use and then some of the space can work for the master bathroom. We'll need the room for the jetted bathtub."

Glory hugged Jason. "I love every bit of what you describe. I'll let you work out the details of construction and we can talk later about colors and stuff like that."

They went back through the hallway and into the living room. Emily said, "Oh my. I love that window and your backyard. More of the Alhambra love of the surrounding world right in your living room."

Glory said, "I must read that book immediately to understand what you are talking about, but it really is my favorite view. And with the front wall down, I'll be able to see the whore bush too."

Martha laughed. "I love that bush and always have. I think I'll put one in my front yard too."

"That would be so cool," Glory said. "It is an honor to have a whore bush in the front yard. Magdalen rising."

Jason laughed. "I don't understand all of that but it is obviously important. Let's head on into the kitchen."

As they entered the kitchen Glory said, "I don't know what happened in here, but it is all wrong."

Everyone looked around the kitchen with ceramic tile counter tops that were uneven, and many tiles broken and some missing. There was a carpet on part of the floor with burn marks from the fireplace and the cabinets were dark and sticky to touch. The rest of the floor was stained carpet and two different patterns of linoleum. The only saving grace in the kitchen were once again the windows and patio doors with the perfect view to the outdoor gardens.

Glory walked over to the stove, opened the oven door and out wafted the smell of grease, rot and mildew. She took a quick look inside. She found a large porterhouse steak rotting on a grilling pan. The inside of the oven was caked with grease and dripping with slimy rot. She slammed the door shut and standing with her back to the stove said, "I'll pay anyone of you a thousand dollars to clean that stove. I'm not cooking on that stove until it is clean."

Jason asked, "Can't you buy a new stove for that kind of money?"

"Great idea!" Glory grinned. "Let's buy all new appliances, cabinets, countertops. And for all that is holy let's get rid of these nasty floors!"

Martha laughed and walked over to the refrigerator. She opened the door. "Really? You want to give up a cracked refrigerator complete with mildew, mold and a gallon of clotted, rotted milk?"

Glory stood behind Martha and looking over her shoulder into the refrigerator she saw mold and mildew with a crack down the back of the refrigerator. Indeed, inside the refrigerator was a gallon of clotted, rotted milk. "It will be a sacrifice but one I'm willing to make. I want everything new and fresh and exactly how I dream it to be for this house."

Martha smiled. "I think you can afford to do exactly that."

Glory nodded. "But I don't want to use any of the foundation money. I want it to be out of the sale of our house in Issaquah. I have used none of that money yet. This is a good way to use that money to build my life."

"That's perfect," Martha said.

"I will also use a little of that money to buy a used small car or SUV for driving around town. The van is big and cumbersome to drive around town every day. I want something that gets great gas mileage too. The van isn't bad but I don't want to waste the miles or gas driving it around town."

Jason said, "I think that is a sound idea."

"Thanks Jason. Now back to the house. I want all hardwood floors throughout the house. I want real wood not fake and not cheap snap together. I also want those baseboard heaters gone. I want central heat and air-conditioning installed. We don't need it often out here, but we also rarely get much of a breeze either."

Jason agreed. "What I plan to do is gut the interior and start over. I'll leave the basic floor plan but make the adjustments we talked about for the main. We'll put in new wall board and ceilings. I also smell that a lot of cats and dogs have been in here and left lots of smell and stains behind. We will clean the subfloor and seal it after we take up the old linoleum and carpets. Having all the interior building new will solve a lot of that problem."

"I'll live in the van until this house is livable," Glory said. "I'll use the shower a time or two before the gutting is in full swing."

"I want to make it easier for you to live in the van," Jason added. "I'll be sure that the first thing we do is find a spot in the yard on either side where we can build a pad for your van to be parked and plugged in. You can't depend on the solar panel around here with all the shade and trees so you will need the electricity. I probably can work out a hook up for sewer and water too."

"That would be great." Glory said. "I could use the van for guest quarters."

Jason nodded. "I'd like to get a landscape architecture specialist out here give us some suggestions for the yard. There is a lot of potential for real beauty here. Is there any place in the yard special for you?"

Glory smiled. "Other than the whore bush there is a place back in the yard's corner I love. I want to have a meditation garden and quiet taking place. That space feels ideal. There's the opposite corner of the backyard straight out from the house that is a swamp much of the year. Maybe a deck or something like that would be great over there."

"Let's see where you want the meditation garden and go from there," Jason said.

The four friends walked along a rock path back to the corner forested area. They pushed a few overhanging limbs and bushes aside. When they got to the middle of the area, Jason said, "I know right where you want it," and he pointed to a depression in the ground where ages ago a tree had fallen. "The whole area is green with ferns and trees and huckleberry bushes for accents."

Glory smiled. "Yes. And I want a goddess statue in the middle of the depression."

Martha stood beside her. "I love this idea. How about a statue of Guanyin? She is known as The Goddess of Mercy and The One Who Perceives The Sounds Of The World."

"That would be perfect."

"I'll take care of finding the statue, Jason," Martha said. "It will be my gift to Glory and her home."

Glory hugged Martha. "Thank you. I can't wait to show Jake my home."

"You know it won't be ready before he arrives on Friday, right? This will take a few weeks," Jason said.

She smiled. "I know but he will love this place. At least I hope he will. As soon as you have gotten a place ready for my van will you do this garden next?"

"Sure," Jason said. "I can even have it ready before Friday if we can find the right statue locally. I'll get my crew out here to gut the interior tomorrow so shower tonight but after that you must use the van."

Martha nodded. "I'll see that we have the statue here before Jake arrives. It will be a blessing for you, Glory, but also for the land and your home."

"I can feel that already."

"You and Jake, in your relationship, will feel you are in balance between the feminine and masculine. With the feminine energy at the ranch and the masculine energy here would be perfect."

Glory nodded. She thought Martha had it exactly right. She also felt that although Jake was masculine, and she was feminine that somehow, they were in harmony on a deep level. "You are right. That is exactly how it feels for me too. It also feels as if, were we not together, both our lives would remain in chaos and isolated misery. We need to figure out how to be independent and complimentary and interconnected."

"There," Martha said, "You have the conflict and miracle of being a couple."

Glory stood with her friends loving the smell of the forest, the sound of the river and the feel of the breeze in which she had grown up. The love and honor she and her friends had for each other seemed amplified here in this spot. She wanted Jake here so the group could bring him in to their circle of friends. *They will love each other, I'm sure. I wonder what he can bring to The Pennington-Shaw Foundation?*

Glory waved goodbye to her friends and then clipped a leash on Freya. "Let's go for a walk and talk to the neighbors. We'll see how many still live here."

As they left the driveway, Glory saw Glen who was the neighbor across the street. He and his wife Celia had raised their children here in this neighborhood. Glory waved as she was walking toward Glen. He waved back. She said, "Hi, Glen. You probably don't remember me."

"I do," He said. "You're Debbie's daughter."

"You're right, I am. I'm moving back into our old house."

"Great. I was sorry to hear about your mother's death, but I suppose dying doing something you love is as good a way to leave Earth as any."

Glory smiled. "I grieved when she died but eventually, I came to love she died after climbing to the top of Mt. Rainier. Knowing she is up there always with the mountain brings me a lot of peace."

"I'm glad," Glen said. "Are you moving in today?"

"No, the house is a real mess," Glory said. "I will live in my van for a few weeks, while we gut and remodel the house."

"It probably needs the remodel. The people who bought the house from your mother didn't do much except create mess and chaos in the house and yard and in the neighborhood."

"I'm sorry to hear that."

Glen nodded. "It still is a pretty house but I'm looking forward to seeing a different color than pea-soup green. Mostly I'm looking forward to having you back in the neighborhood. We missed you."

Glory looked around the neighborhood. "I've missed living here."

"What does your husband think about the house?"

"I don't know. I didn't even know he had bought it. He died nearly five months ago, and I found out today I own my mother's house."

"I'm sorry to hear about his death. I'm glad he bought your house and left it for you."

"Me too. Say hi to Celia for me. I want to walk around the neighborhood and see who else is still here."

"There have been a few changes in the neighborhood. But a lot of folks who lived here during your time are still here."

"Great," Glory said. "I'll visit with you later."

Glen waved watching her walk with her little dog. He was glad she was back but wondered at the sadness in her eyes and what all she had been going through. *Oh, well. She is home and we can all help her establish her life here.* He knew Celia would want to talk with her.

After her walk with friends and neighbors from long ago, Glory and Freya walked back to her home and her van. She said to Freya, "We need to go shopping for a car. I can't be driving that van all the time. It's for travel and living in while traveling. I need a regular car or SUV for daily life."

I know I could buy any car I wanted in Bellevue, but I'd like to buy locally. I'd rather buy a used late model and conserve my money for other more important things.

She packed Freya into the van and they headed to the only local new car dealer in town. She talked with the dealer about her needs. She finally said, "I want a small, fuel efficient SUV or car with all wheel drive. I'd rather buy something used with low miles if you have something that would meet my needs."

The dealer, Hank Walters, said, "We have two on the lot that fit that bill, and both are loaded with similar features. They are small SUVs that seat four comfortably and five in a pinch. The mileage is good on both vehicles. They are very flexible, multi-use and reliable. I have one myself and love it."

"What is the difference between the two," Glory asked.

He answered, "One is white, and one is red."

"Let's go drive the red one. Can we bring Freya along?"

"Sure. She will be riding in it too."

They got Freya's harness set up from the van and walked over to the car. Glory said, "I like how it looks from the outside."

"Open the doors and hatch and look it over," Hank said. "Also, this car is one owner. The first owner bought it here and about a year later decided he wanted a big pickup truck to haul his travel trailer."

Glory opened the doors and hatch. "I like the black leather upholstery. It's all wheel drive, right?"

"Yep. I personally wouldn't have anything that isn't all wheel drive. Around here winter can be mild or a beast; you never know."

"That's how I remember winters here. Will you take a check if I like it?"

"Sure, so long as we can confirm it with your bank."

"I bank at Umpqua although I haven't been into the local one here, yet."

"They are a good bank and good community partners too," Hank said.

Glory smiled. "Let's take her for a spin." She hooked Freya in her harness in the back seat.

Hank said, "The back seats fold down flat creating a large cargo area for hauling things or big shopping trips."

Glory grinned. "That might come in useful!"

They went for a drive along North Bend Way and then across to the Interstate. When they headed back toward North Bend, Glory said, "I like this car a lot. But you saw the van I drove onto your lot."

"Are you looking to trade that in?"

Glory laughed. "No way. I've only had it a few weeks. I'm buying a car because I want better gas mileage for around town and locally but mostly it is big to be driving around for every day. I can't figure out how to drive both vehicles home."

Hank smiled. "That's no problem. I'll be happy to drive this car home for you. It will take about an hour or two for the service department to do the detail check. We always do that before we drive a car, we have sold off the lot. We want your ownership to be worry free from the start. If you give me your address, I can bring it home for you."

"That would be great."

She drove her soon-to-be-car back to the dealership, wrote the check and signed a pile of papers. The dealer called her bank and verified the check was good. On the way back to her van the dealer said, "I think I knew your mom, Deborah Pennington."

"You may have. I am moving into our old place off Tanner Road. You knew my mom died on Mount Rainier?"

"Yes. I didn't know her well, but I liked her and thought she got a rough deal in her marriage. I knew your father too. When he was sober, he was a nice man. Sober just wasn't a regular status for him."

"Yes, it is exactly how he was. But my mom was a strong woman and a great mother. I've learned that sometimes hardship makes us stronger and when we are true to ourselves and others great miracles come along."

"Obviously the apple didn't fall far from your mother's tree."

They shook hands when the purchase was complete. Glory drove back toward her house stopping at the grocery store along the way. She picked up some already prepared food for her dinner tonight. She bought yogurt and bacon for breakfast. She also treated herself to a half dozen bakery fresh cinnamon rolls and hoped they tasted as good as they looked. *They won't be as good as Rob's.* She told Freya, "I can't eat like this all the time or I'll be a pudgy woman! I've got to keep walking and working every day to work off the calories."

Freya barked assent.

Glory stored all the groceries in her van and drove back to her house. She smiled as she pulled in the drive. "I'm home momma." *The house is a right mess but I'm so happy to be here at home. I can hardly wait for Jake to be here. He will love it here I know.* She felt a twinge of sadness knowing Jake would love it but knowing it would also complicate things. His ranch was beautiful, and they both loved it.

Glory walked through the house for the first time by herself. Each room brought memories of her mom and their life living in this house. She went out to the backyard and walked around. Freya followed on her heels every step of the way. When they were in the backyard, Freya sniffed every corner. Glory laughed watching Freya and the squirrels. When a squirrel crossed Freya's path, she raced chasing the squirrel barking and making sure the squirrel knew there was a new boss in the backyard.

Back in the house, she laughed at the kitchen and dining room. "I don't know what you folks were thinking with the mess that is here but we will dump the whole thing."

She opened the garage door and walked into the garage. She checked to be sure the washer and dryer were hooked up. "At least I can have clean clothes and sheets." She went back in the house and called Freya. The little dog came racing into the house with a silly doggie grin on her face. "You're having a high old time, little girl." Glory picked up Freya. "Let's go to the van and settle for the evening. I want to do another video and blog about this adventure."

Glory was standing on the front step of her house, locking the front door when she saw the dealer driving up in her new SUV and a black car followed him.

She walked down the drive to meet them. A woman of about fifty years of age got out of the black car.

Walking up to Glory Hank said, "This is my wife Beverly."

The woman reached out to shake Glory's hand and said, "Everyone calls me Bev. I love your little dog." She reached out to pet Freya who loved every second of the petting.

Glory smiled. "It's nice to meet you Bev."

"My husband," Bev said motioning to Hank with her thumb, "Asked me to follow him out here to deliver your car and drive him back home. When I heard who you were, I wanted to come and meet you in person."

"Thanks, I'm glad you did," Glory said.

"I knew your Momma in high school. She was a year ahead of me which as you know means I thought she was a lot older than me."

Glory laughed. "Yes, I remember how that worked."

"Your Momma was always kind and one day in particular she helped me out of a tight spot. A bunch of the football boys had me backed up against the wall by the Gym. They were teasing me and wanting to show me 'what a real woman' does with her body."

"Oh, no! That must have been awful."

Bev nodded. "Your mother walked right up to the boys and slapped the one closest to her on the back of the head. He yelped and then your mother said, 'When I walk away from here I'm calling your mother to let her know what a little creep you are. I'm sure she doesn't know how you are behaving.'"

"Wow!" Glory said.

Bev nodded. "It terrified me they would hurt both of us, but her threat sent them running. She followed through and not only called every boy's parents herself she told the principle too. Those were some very unhappy boys for quite a while."

Bev grinned at the memory. "I wanted to meet you and tell you I knew your mother and admired her."

"Thank you so much, Bev. That means a lot."

Bev smiled. "I love telling people that story. It is important to let men and boys know what is acceptable and what is not."

Her husband stepped forward. "If it is okay with you ladies, I'd like to show Glory around her car. I want to be sure you know where everything is and how to use all the features."

Bev winked at Glory. "Sure, hon. Just do a good job and treat this girl right."

"Yes ma'am," he said. He smiled at Glory. "Let me show you a few things about your car."

When Hank and Bev left Glory knew she had made two more friends. Bev had said, "If you need anything at all just call me. Hank give her your card and put my number on it too."

Glory smiled as Hank did exactly what Bev told him to do. He grinned every time he told her to do something. It was obvious their relationship was one of love and good humor. She wanted that for herself and Jake.

Chapter 31

"You could tell she was a free spirit,
A gypsy, just by looking at her.
A smile like that doesn't come from a sad soul."
— Nikki Rowe

True to his word, Jason had built a pad on the east side of the house where an old wood stack had been. He put a new cast iron wood stack frame at the back of the yard so it would be away from the house and the wooden fence. The pad was gravel and level. He drove the van into the backyard and up on the pad. It was perfect in Glory's mind, but Jason wanted to work on it more tomorrow. Jason had even set up a small picnic table with an umbrella on the patio so she could sit outside and eat without being cramped up in the van.

Glory couldn't believe it was already Friday and how much work Jason and his crew had done.

Jason said, "I've got a team finishing up on the gutting and cleaning the slab up. Once it is completed, we will work on putting up the new wallboard."

"Then what's next?"

"We'll do the main bedroom and bath first. I want you and Jake to have a comfortable place to live until we finish the rest of the house."

"That will be great."

"I have a specialized crew joining us tomorrow to work on the plumbing and electricity for the van." Jason grinned, "We won't come knocking until after 10 so you two lovebirds can have a sleep in."

Glory laughed. "Thanks, but I'll be surprised if we aren't up and about earlier. How did you get a crew to work on Saturday?"

"Many construction folks would love working any day for good pay."

Glory chuckled. "Whatever it takes that I can afford, I want it done as soon as possible."

Glory strapped Freya into her harness in the back seat of her new car. She loved the color and the way it drove. It was much easier to get around town than with the van. She went around to the driver's side door, opened the garage door and backed out to the cul-d-sac. It was much easier to back the car up than it was the van. Avoiding the two big trees on each side of the driveway was important. Glen and Celia waved from their driveway and she waved back.

"Well, Freya, we're on our way to bring Jake home."

Freya yiked with her "yes" and Glory smiled. She was a little nervous but also excited. She had cleaned her van, emptied the gray and black water tanks although that was disgusting and harder to do not hooked up to sewer lines. She stocked the refrigerator in the garage with some food, beer and wine. She had done all she could do to make tonight as perfect as possible. His plane would land about 10:30 p.m. and then they would be together and driving back to her home soon. She hoped Jake would fall in love with her place as much as she had fallen in love with his place.

The drive to the airport was quick and easy at this time of night but still took about forty minutes. She parked in the garage and then left the windows cracked open a little so Freya would have plenty of air. She put Freya in her crate so she wouldn't hurt herself jumping around. The puppy whined a little and Glory said, "Don't worry. I'll be back soon with Jake in tow."

She hurried into the airport and found Jake's plane had landed one minute earlier. Glory felt her excitement ratchet up a notch as she went to the baggage claim area where they had agreed to meet. It felt like hours had passed although it had only been fifteen minutes before Glory saw Jake's cowboy hat and him. She called, "Hey, Cowboy."

He turned and walked to her quickly. "Darlin', I need a kiss."

She pulled him close to her and gave him what he needed. He dropped his carry-on bag to the floor. "That was a fine start." He took her in his arms kissed her again. "I'm so happy to be here with you in my arms."

She grinned. "Me too. Let's get your baggage and get home as quick as it is safe to be, Cowboy."

"Your wish is my command, Darlin'." He turned to the luggage carousel. His bag was one of the first on the carousel and he grabbed it and came back to her. She loved his grin and could hardly contain her impatience to be with him. She held his hand and led him to the escalator to take them to the garage.

"Is Freya at home?" he asked.

"Not a chance," Glory answered. "She wanted to come inside, but I left her in the car with the windows cracked. I don't think she understood why she couldn't come inside."

Jake laughed. "I can't wait to see that little girl. I missed her too."

Jake held Freya on his lap for the ride home. "Is this a new car?" he asked.

Glory nodded. "Newish. I bought it three days ago. I couldn't drive that big camping van around town, and this gets better mileage. I sold my mini-van to Martha, so I decided a good compromise would be a small SUV with all-wheel drive."

Jake looked around the car. "For something that's not a pickup I like it fine."

Glory laughed. "Well, some of us have to suffer with make do." She glanced over at Jake. "I'm a little nervous about all of this."

"Why? You know me and love me. I know you and love you and Freya. What's to be nervous about?"

"A lot has happened while I was away and in the past three days, Cowboy," Glory said.

"A lot happens around you all the time. As long as you are in my life, anything that has happened will be just fine with me, Darlin'.'"

"Then I have a story to tell you. Sit back and relax and let me tell you about my home."

The sun was shining brilliantly through the trees. Glory looked up through the sunroof of her van and saw brilliant blue skies with no clouds. She reached over for Jake who was still asleep. He felt her hand and reached to pull her closer to him. She kissed the back of his neck and said, "It's almost eight and the construction crew will be here in about two hours."

He rolled over. "Then we have two hours for lovemaking." Freya barked and Jake said, "Or maybe not."

Glory laughed and got out of bed. She put on her robe and slipped on her slippers. "I'll let her out, but I wanted you to come with me to see my yard and the house in better light."

Getting out of the bed, Jake said, "Let her out and I'll be two steps behind you."

Glory opened the door of the van and let Freya out. She stepped out onto the pad and looked around at the beautiful day. She heard Jake step down out of the van and looked around. "Wow. I had no idea."

Glory turned to him and smiled at the look of wonder on his face. He said, "This is spectacular. It isn't Oklahoma, but it sure is beautiful."

Glory nodded. "This is the yard and house I grew up with."

"I love it but it seems a little wild yet."

Glory nodded. "It hasn't been cared for in the last two years. There's lots of work to do to make it a home again but we've got a good start on it. I want to show you something special though." She took his hand, and they walked back to the meditation garden. She sat down on one of the benches and he sat beside her.

"This feels like a church."

"It sort of is. It is a meditation garden and a quiet place to be. I've always loved it back here. Martha and Jason made this possible. I wanted this place of peace finished before you got here."

He looked down at her and put his arm around her shoulders. "I love it. I can see coming back here to just unwind and sit."

Freya raced up and jumped up on Jake's lap. He laughed. "Your gypsy dog is happy here too."

Glory nodded. "Jason went around the fence and dog-proofed it but the fence is old and rickety, so he wants to replace it with a new fence."

"Show me the house," Jake said.

Glory took him inside and told him the plans for the house. Jake said, "I love all of this. Will Jason let me help finish it out?"

Glory nodded. "I told him you built your own house and that you would want to dive in and help with this house."

He grinned. "Well, I have ulterior motives. I like your van and all but to have a big bed to share with you would be about perfect."

"Then I better feed you and get coffee into you before they get here."

She led him out into the garage where her car was parked. On one wall was a table with an electric camp stove and some cooking gear. Beside it sat a microwave, a coffee maker and a toaster oven. There was a large refrigerator and freezer standing beside the table. There was also a small round picnic table with chairs in the kitchen's center space. Glory's car was parked in the remaining space on the other side of the garage. By the back door was a washing machine and dryer.

Glory said, "Jason set this up for me as a make-do kitchen for now. I asked that he finish the master bedroom and bath first and then the kitchen."

"Good thinking on your part. This is a good setup for make do."

"You go get dressed in your work clothes while I make breakfast," Glory said.

Jake and Glory were finishing their breakfast outside on the patio when Jason and his crew arrived. Freya raced up to Jason who picked her up and rubbed her belly.

Jake stood up and walked toward Jason. "Hi, I'm Jake."

Jason smiled. "I'm glad to meet you. I'm Jason."

"I told Glory I'd like to help you with anything around here on this project if you could use and an extra set of hands. I'm good with a hammer and nails," Jake said.

"I will appreciate your help. Let me introduce you to the crew."

And just like that the men are friends and off to work, Glory thought.

Chapter 32

"Do the work in your unique style."

— Lailah Gifty Akita

Glory's phone rang, and she saw who was calling. "Good morning Martha. How are you today?"

"I'm grand. How are the lovebirds?"

"Jake said we are finer than frog fur which I hope means we are great."

Martha laughed. "I've never heard that expression before. I wanted to ask you if Lori and I could come out and I could show her your place?"

"I'd love that. The men are doing manly things. There's a testosterone cloud over my backyard. I could use estrogen fumes around me."

Martha laughed. "If it is that bad, we'll come right now."

"Be sure to bring Buttercup with you!"

"We will. Freya will be blown away by Buttercup."

Lori and Martha arrived about an hour later. They came around through the side gate holding Buttercup on a leash. Glory brought out more lawn chairs to the patio. After introducing Freya and Buttercup the dogs were chasing and playing in the big yard. The women talked about what the future might hold for all of them. They watched as the men were working digging troughs for the plumbing and electricity from the van pad. Jake was complaining about all the rocks.

Jason said, "Hey without rocks you don't get mountains."

Jake mumbled a reply, and the women laughed.

Martha smiled. "We have news we'd like to share."

"Let me guess. You two are in love and want to get married?"

Lori looked at Martha. "Does she do that often?"

"Not until recently but of late she has been a blooming fortune teller."

"Where are you going to live? Please don't tell me you are abandoning The Pennington-Shaw Foundation. I couldn't handle it all without you, Martha."

Martha smiled. "No, I'm not abandoning you. We will live in Issaquah in my house."

"But Easton is so far away."

"I've wrangled a part-time position at the Lake Sammamish State Park," Lori said. "I'll volunteer with the foundation on my off time. Since I'll be living with Martha, my expenses will go down."

"That sounds perfect," Glory said.

Martha nodded. "I think so too. We want to get married here in your backyard."

"Of course, you can but it's a mess. The men are working on the house first and the landscaping later after the house is finished."

"That's not a problem," Lori said. "I'd love it if you'll let me I'll take care of the landscaping. You won't even have to pay me."

"Of course, I'll let you if Jason hasn't already lined someone else up."

"Perfect. I'm a certified landscape architect, if my credentials help turn the tide in my favor. Doing this yard can be a start of me building a small part-time landscaping business on the side. I need a portfolio of work I've done to build my business. This yard can be the first one."

Glory laughed. "The tide is with you all the way. Let's go ask Jason right now and then I'll show you my meditation garden he and Martha built for me. Besides, I need to introduce you to Jake."

Martha grinned. "I'm more than ready to meet your cowboy."

The women walked over to where the men were working and swearing. Jake looked up. "I'm not so sure about all these rocks, Darlin'."

Glory laughed. "You'll do fine, Cowboy. I want you to meet my best friend, Martha."

Jake stood up, wiped his hands on his jeans and reached out to Martha. "I'm pleased to meet you, Martha. I've heard so much about you I feel like I know you."

Martha smiled. "I feel the same way. This is Lori, the love of my life."

Lori blushed a little and Jake said, "You are both every bit as lovely as Glory said." He reached to shake hands with Lori. "I'm please to meet you Lori."

"Thank you, Jake. I'm happy to meet you as well."

Martha said, "Well, we will let you get back to work Jake. We need to talk with Jason."

Glory motioned to the rocks. "Looks like you have more rocks to move."

Jake shook his head. "I haven't seen this many rocks in one place in my whole life."

Glory grinned. "They should be no problem for a big handsome cowboy like you. Surely you can handle these little old rocks."

Jason laughed and then quickly stopped laughing when Jake looked up with a solemn face.

Jason suppressed a grin. "How can I help you ladies?"

"Lori and I wanted to talk with you about the landscaping," Martha said and discussed letting Lori do the landscaping of the yard.

"Sure," he said. "I haven't called the fella that did the landscaping in Issaquah yet. With you working close and getting to be part of the family it would be great."

"Good," Lori said. She turned to Glory. "Show me around and then we can talk about ideas."

Glory led the way back to the meditation garden. One the way she said, "This walk way needs help and fine tuning. I like it a lot but it is overgrown and the gardens beside it are frankly a sad mess."

Lori nodded, "I can take care of that easily enough. I'll use the rocks they are digging up to outline the bedding areas and then get more slate to add to the walkway unless a better idea comes up."

"There is a ton of pruning that needs to happen too."

When they got to the meditation garden, Lori said, "This is wonderful. I love the concept here."

Glory nodded. "I dreamed about this and Martha and Jason made it happen. I think it still needs pruning work and maybe a few hanging plants or bird feeders. Even wind chimes would be great back here. Overall, it is close to perfect."

They walked back toward the house discussing flowers and colors and native versus invasive plants. When they got to the patio Martha looked at Glory's van and asked, "How are you getting around? This van doesn't look all that mobile right now."

"It's not. When I want to go on a trip, I can take down the table and benches and then drive on out the side gate. For now, though it is where Jake and I are living. Come with me," Glory said. "I'll show you my new car, my make-do kitchen and the skeleton of my house."

Glory toured them through the house and the progress made with the remodeling which at this point looked like an open skeleton of a house. Then she took them out to the garage, turned on the lights and opened the garage door.

"Wow," Martha said, "I love your car."

Lori rubbed her hand on the car. "She is a beauty. I love cars."

"Would you like to take it for a spin?" Glory asked.

"Really?"

Glory smiled. "Stay right there. I'll get the keys and you girls can go for a ride in my car."

She went out to the van and got the car keys. She handed the keys to Lori and off they went with Lori driving the car. When they returned about ten minutes later Martha said, "You chose well. I like it a lot."

Glory nodded. "Thanks. I like it too."

"What did Jake say?"

"He said, it was good for a car that's not a pickup. But, honestly, I think he would have said anything last night to get me into bed."

Lori laughed. "Well, he's right. It is a good for a car that's not a pickup."

"This is some kitchen you've got," Martha said. "Despite the rustic look of things, it seems like a good setup for getting started."

Glory nodded. "I make Jason clear out the spiders regularly, though."

"Are you going to leave the laundry set up out here in the garage?" Martha asked.

"No way. I asked Jason to wall in the laundry area and then have sliding doors in the kitchen, so I don't have to walk out to the garage and fight off spiders to do laundry. I just can't stand spiders."

Lori grinned. "Then it is a good thing you have me to do the landscaping for you."

Glory nodded. "And I thank you for that and for many other things. When did you girls want to get married?"

"We'd love to get married right now but we both agree we want to have the wedding here so we will wait until they finish the house," Martha said. "In the meantime, Lori and Buttercup will move in with me in two weeks. That's when her transfer to Lake Sammamish State Park starts."

"That will be perfect for me," Glory said. "And Lori, I want to be sure you know I appreciate the offer of landscaping for me for free but I really don't want you to do if for free. Your work has value and I want to honor that by paying you for your work."

"I told you so," Martha said.

Lori blushed. "I want to be a part of everything you are working toward."

"And I want you to be a part of it too," Glory said. "But I want no one to be a sacrificing or undervalued member of our team. We will pay you a fair wage for the work you will do for me or the foundation. I personally will pay you for the work you do here at my home. Martha, check up on what certified landscapers are paid in the area and set up Lori as a part-time employee for the foundation. However, for my private landscaping, let's pay her from my money not the foundation's money."

Martha grinned, saluted. "Yes, Ma'am."

Glory watched Jake as he got out of bed and went into their new bathroom to shower. They had christened their bedroom last night. They still needed more furniture and a real bed, but the main bedroom suite was ready for living in.

She got up and went to the garage kitchen to make coffee. She put some buttered toast and yogurt with fruit on a tray and carried it back to their suite and set it on the card table in the sitting area. She heard Jake moving around in the bedroom but went back to the garage for coffee and cream and sugar. She carried the coffee tray into their bedroom suite just as Jake was walking into the sitting area.

"My god, I'm a lucky man, Darlin'."

Glory smiled. "And I'm a lucky woman, Cowboy."

He kissed her then groaned. "I'm sore in places I had no idea existed before working with Jason."

She laughed. "Remember, you volunteered."

He looked around. "I told Jason, today I would ask you to go with me to buy furniture for this bedroom."

She smiled. "Good thing because that is exactly what I had in mind for you today."

He laughed, picked up a piece of toast to munch on while he drank his coffee. "I'm glad you talked Jason talked into replacing this window with patio doors."

"Me too. I hope they finish the deck soon so we can have breakfast outdoors from our own bedroom. I loved the deck of my bedroom in Issaquah and I'm glad Jason agreed with my suggestion built one here."

"Lori will work on the landscape today," Jake said. "I think she and Martha seem well suited to each other."

Glory nodded. "They are. Almost as well-suited as we are."

Jake reached over for her hand. "When are you going to say yes and marry me? I want you to make an honest man out of me."

Glory laughed. "We have just a few things to hammer out before I say yes. Soon, I'm sure, I'll be ready for a real engagement ring, Cowboy."

He smiled. "Darlin', I thought you'd never ask."

Glory's phone rang. She saw it was Hugh and Rob calling and so put them on speaker phone. "Good morning, boys."

"Good morning, Glory!" they said together. Jake laughed and asked, "What about me?"

Hugh said, "I take it my brute of a brother has made himself at home with you, Glory."

"Oh, yes, he has. He even pushed hard to get the master suite finished so we could move in and sleep on a real bed and shower with a real shower."

"I don't think getting clean was his main motivator," Hugh said.

Jake laughed. "How right you are, brother."

Rob asked, "So Glory why are you calling it the master suite?"

Jake said, "I asked about that and suggested we call it the Glory suite, but she smacked me on the head and said, 'absolutely not!' There's just no pleasin' some womenfolk."

Rob and Hugh laughed, and Rob said, "Then I'll say nothing more."

Glory said, "I've called it the Main Suite just FYI. If you menfolk are through gabbing nonsense, did you call just to tease me or is there some other reason you called?"

Hugh said, "I'm a little more sober reasoned than Rob is so I'll ask you."

"What?"

"Could you and Jake come down to Oklahoma for the grand opening of the Pennington Community Clinic?"

Glory said, "We'd love to come. When is the grand opening?"

"Well," Rob said, "That's why we are calling now. Things moved along much faster than we thought with all the help and volunteers who jumped in. We will be ready to open in a week. We've set the party for next Sunday evening and the clinic opening for patients Monday morning. Helen has plans for a fundraiser at the Open House too. We know it is short notice, but we really want you two to come to the clinic opening."

Glory said, "I'm so pleased things are moving along so quickly, and I think Helen's idea about a fundraiser is great too. My goal is to get things like the clinic started but then community involvement keeps it going."

"Exactly," Hugh said. "So, can we count on you guys for the weekend?"

Glory answered, "Yes."

Jake said, "We will get some real furniture and real mattress for this bedroom today. An air mattress isn't all it's cracked up to be." Glory chuckled but Jake continued. "Today is Monday. We could leave here by Wednesday I think and be there by Saturday evening if we drive or we could fly."

"You two decide how you are transporting yourselves and just let us know," Hugh said, "You can plan to stay here with us."

"Thank you, guys," Glory said. "We will talk it over and let you know."

Chapter 33

"I'd like to see you

Dance around a caldron naked."

— Zoe Forward

After they hung up, Glory said, "Ordinarily for a trip this far away I'd want to fly especially after my last two experiences with long-distance traveling. We have talking to do and I'd rather take Freya with us than leave her behind. How about we drive down this time?"

"I like the way you think. Some nice long talks will suit me fine and I'd hate to leave our dog behind for this long."

Glory smiled, pleased he had referred to Freya as 'our dog'. "I'll get dressed so we can go buy us a real bed, Cowboy."

Jake kissed her. "That's a great idea, Darlin'. I will see if I can wrangle up a pickup truck to haul it home in."

When Glory finished dressing, she came out of the suite and walked out to the backyard. Lori was busy moving rocks around and forming designs around the gardening beds. She stood and waved to Glory and came over for a chat. "I'd like you to come over and let me show you something I thought of."

"Sure," Glory said and followed Lori to the spot where she had been moving rocks around.

Lori pointed to the rocks. "We have some big rocks that work well for edging the beds, but we also have a lot of smaller rocks too. I bought a bucketful of these small red rocks to go with the black, gray and white small rocks in your yard. What do you think of the designs I made with them?"

Glory looked down at the swirling patterns and intricate ins and outs of the red rocks. "I like that a lot. Where were you thinking to put these designs?"

"I was thinking to pick up those slate pieces and move them to the meditation garden between the square pavers. Then," she said, walking over to the path from the patio to the back corner, "I could dig this a little deeper, put sand and fine gravel on the bottom, lay in the designs and put sand over the top and work it into the designs. My vision is that the walkway leading to the garden is also a path that has feminine symbols and ancient symbols. It would feel like we are all walking into ourselves back home whether toward the garden or the house."

Glory looked at Lori. "Have you always done mystical things with gardens?"

"No. I've researched ancient feminine symbols and what they mean. When you showed me the meditation garden, I decided to create a feminine experience here in your yard. I feel I'm awakening more to the divine feminine."

Glory nodded. "I like how you are expressing that here in my yard."

"Wow," a voice behind her said. She turned to see both Jason and Jake standing with bemused looks on their faces. Jake said, "I have a lot to learn about women."

Lori laughed. "Good luck with that."

Jake borrowed a pickup truck from one of the construction workers. They drove to Issaquah to a furniture store Martha recommended as having lots of beautiful things that were not the usual run-of-the-mill furnishings.

When they walked inside the store, Jake looked around with his mouth hanging open. He turned to Glory. "I've never seen a place like this. I bet there's not a furniture store within a thousand miles of Oklahoma like this."

Glory nodded. "It feels good to see all these beautiful, but different furnishings. It also feels a little overwhelming."

A woman walked over to them. "Hi, my name is Cynthia Morton. I'm here to help you find what you want for your home."

"I'm Glory and this is Jake. We are remodeling our home from the studs out. We have our bedroom and a bath built and finished but no furniture to put in there. Jake feels an air mattress isn't adequate."

Cynthia smiled. "Jake is right. I can help you with finding the perfect bedroom furniture. What color are your walls and what kind of flooring do you have?"

Glory said, "The walls are a light peach with antique ivory trim. The floors are reclaimed Douglas fir and all the doors in our house are Hemlock."

"That sounds beautiful. Do you think you are looking for something modern, or antique of a specific era?"

Jake said, "At home in Oklahoma we have a hand carved, four-poster oak bed. I don't know about eras, but I think I might know what I like and don't like if I see choices."

Cynthia smiled. "Let's walk around and see what strikes your fancy."

After a few minutes Glory pointed. "I like that bedroom suite over there."

"That's a beautiful suite," Cynthia said. "It is a little pricey, but it is top quality and solid reclaimed Western Red Cedar."

They walked over to the furniture and Jake ran his hands over the wood. He looked at Glory and said, "This is hand worked not machine milled."

"You are right," Cynthia said. "A local woodworker who makes very few pieces of big furniture like this created it. He has made many mirrors and jewelry chests that sell as fast as we get them in. He is in big demand these days because he is doing a lot of remodeling for a charity group and so is turning out fewer big pieces. This set has been here for less than twenty-four hours. I expect it will sell very soon."

Glory felt the hair on the back of her neck rise and looked at Jake. He smiled and turned to Cynthia. "Is his name Jason Walden?"

Cynthia looked stunned. "Yes, it is. How did you know?"

Glory said, "The charity work he is doing is for my foundation. I had no idea he could produce art like this." Glory walked over to the bed and ran her fingers over the intricate filigree scroll work on the footboard. Up the posts at each corner was more of the filigree with various birds perched on branches. On the outward face of the footboard squirrels chased each other. On the headboard a few rabbits studiously ignored the squirrels. "I love this bed. I want to buy the whole set."

Cynthia said, "It is expensive. Perhaps you'd like to know the cost before buying this."

Glory nodded. "Yes, but unless the cost is prohibitive, I want this bed and furniture in my house."

Jake grinned. "She is a woman who knows her own mind."

Cynthia smiled. "I love when anyone knows what they want and ask for it. The big box furniture stores don't sell things like this. In my personal opinion, I think Jason has under-priced this suite. He priced the bed at eight thousand dollars. That price includes the bedside tables. The dresser and chest of drawers would be another seven thousand."

"So fifteen thousand all together?" Glory asked.

"Yes," Cynthia said.

"I agree with you. For this quality of hand-carved furniture, Jason isn't charging nearly enough. This is the bedroom suite we want. How much extra would it cost to have this delivered to my home in North Bend today?"

Cynthia said, "We will gladly deliver it today at no extra charge. Would you like a mattress as well?"

"Definitely," Jake said.

Glory laughed and added, "Make it a great mattress, top of the line. Not only do Jake and I deserve it so does this bed."

Cynthia smiled. "Let's fill out the paperwork and I'll get the fellas working on taking it to your home."

Chapter 34

"The ache for home lives in all of us.
The safe place where we can go
As we are and not be questioned."
— Maya Angelou

On the drive back home Jake said, "We didn't need the pickup truck, but I've enjoyed the driving."

"Do you think I went overboard buying the bedroom furniture?"

"Are you kidding? I'd mortgage the moon to buy Jason's bedroom furniture. You really didn't know Jason could do this kind of work?"

Glory shook her head. "It is a total surprise."

Jake grinned. "I can't wait to see the look on his face when we move that furniture into our bedroom."

Glory felt the warm glow of him knowing the bedroom belonged to them as a couple and the pleasure they bought the bed together and both loved it nearly sealed the deal for her.

Jake pulled the pickup truck into the driveway at home. "I like where you live Glory. In fact, if I didn't have the ranch, I love in Oklahoma I wouldn't bat an eye at hauling all my stuff up here and live here with you forever."

She reached over and took his hand. "That means a lot Jake. Really."

He asked, "Can I borrow your car for a few hours?"

"Sure. Mind if I ask why?"

He shook his head. "No particular reason but I want to drive around and get a good look at the lay of the land and all there is to see here, and the surrounds."

"Surrounds?"

"That's Okie for the surrounding area," he grinned.

"Here are the keys," she said. "Call me when you are on the way home and I'll have dinner ready."

He kissed her. "You are a wonderful woman, Glory."

By the time Jake arrived back home, the bedroom suite had been delivered and Glory had arranged everything how she wanted it. Jason wasn't there when it was delivered but she was hoping he would be back home before Jason saw the bedroom suite.

She heard the garage door open and ran to the kitchen and opened the door leading out to the garage. Jake was closing the big garage door and getting out of the car.

"I'm so glad you are back," Glory said.

"Is something wrong?"

She smiled and shook her head. "Nothing is wrong, but they delivered the furniture and I wanted you back in time to see Jason see it in our room for the first time."

Jake grinned up at her. "When I realized I'd been gone two hours, I came back to be sure and be here before Jason got back."

She kissed him. "You are one hell of a Cowboy."

"And you are my Darlin'," Jake answered. As they shut the door from the garage to the kitchen, Jason came in through the patio door.

"Hi you two," he said. "The work crew told me someone had delivered furniture."

Glory nodded and grabbed his hand. "Come see our bedroom."

She led him through the sitting room and into their bedroom. She stopped and motioned him to come all the way into the room. He walked in and then was still and quiet. He asked, "How did you know?"

Jake grinned. "We didn't. It was another one of those times when everything seemed to come together."

Glory nodded, grinning. "We both fell in love with it. Why didn't you tell me you could create a work of art like this?"

Jason shrugged. "I don't know. I was thinking of giving it up because I had to charge so much for people to buy handmade custom designed furniture."

"Did someone order this bedroom furniture?" Jake asked.

"Well, a lady came in one day and told me about a bed she had seen in Norway with animals playing and chasing each other. The way she described it I knew I wanted to make it. After I finished the bed, I made the dresser, bedside tables and the chest of drawers. I didn't plan on selling it, but when I worked with you Glory, I trusted that someone would want it and pay what it was worth to buy it."

Glory walked over to Jason and took his hands in hers. "This is singularly the most beautiful furniture I've ever seen. Please tell me you did not knock the price down just to sell it."

Jason shook his head. "No. I promise I didn't. I used my usual formula of two times the cost of materials plus my wages per hour at the current minimum wage in King County."

Glory smiled. "You could have charged twice as much for this furniture and I would have bought it."

"Really?"

Jake laughed. "I offered to mortgage the moon to have this bed in our home."

Jason grinned. "Well, maybe I should charge more."

Glory nodded. "I think so. This is not minimum wage workmanship. Thank you so much for this treasure. It will always be in our bedroom in this house."

Jake smiled at Glory standing there hugging the man who created the piece of art that was their bed. *She is more than anything I had thought would be my partner in life. Her kindness, generosity and spirit graces the room with her glow.* It humbled him to watch her talk with people and get things done. All the while she was beautiful and fun to be with. He felt the box in his pocket and hoped that in the next few days Glory would say yes so, he could give her the engagement ring she deserved.

"Well, fuck!" said Glory. She was on her hands and knees looking under the bed and seeing nothing.

Jake chuckled. "Ah, the dulcet tones of my Darlin's favorite word makes the morning complete."

Glory glared at him and he worked to put on a concerned face. "What's up, Darlin'?" He tried but couldn't keep the smile out of his voice or off his face.

"I can't find my nice shoes I want to wear to the grand opening."

"The sandals with the silver straps?" He asked.

"Those are the ones."

Jake walked over to her and held them up for her.

Glory stood up, brushed off her jeans. "Where were they?"

Jake pointed to Freya. "She had dragged them into her carrier box."

Glory took the sandals and laughed. "I wonder why she would do that. They aren't chewed on?"

"Nope. She didn't chew on them at all. I'm no dog whisperer but perhaps she likes having some of your things close when she is in the crate. I know I like having your things close by," he said pulling her close for a hug and light kiss on the forehead.

Glory smiled, kissed him quickly on the nose. "No time for frolicking, Cowboy. I'll be ready soon so we can get on the road. How about you?"

Jake pointed to his suitcase and backpack. "All ready, Darlin'. Of course, I didn't have to search for shoes or exactly the right ten or twelve dresses to wear to one party." He ducked as she took a swipe at him.

"You sir, are a good old Cowboy who needs nothing but jeans, leather and plaid."

He chuckled. "Yeah but you love me anyway so I'm good to go."

She smiled and watched him as he picked up her bags and carried them out. *Damn, he looks good in those tight blue jeans. I am the luckiest woman in the World. A great man who loves me. Another man who cared much more than I thought. Wonderful friends. A woman could hardly want more.* "Except a baby," she whispered to herself.

She and Jake had not been using any form of contraception even condoms. The possibility of pregnancy was there, but she had been disappointed too many times to hope even if she got pregnant, she would not miscarry the pregnancy. Her doctor had told her to give her uterus a rest, get more rest herself and wait and see what happens. It had been two years since her last pregnancy. She understood that miscarriages happened for many reasons and seldom did the reason rise that a woman could not carry a pregnancy to completion. Her last period was June 28. That was about five weeks ago. She had bought pregnancy test strips but had not used one yet. She wanted to give it a few more days before she did anything. *If I'm pregnant, I don't want to jinx it.*

She sighed. "I will not worry about it but I will continue to hope and hold hope close to my heart."

She tidied up their bedroom taking care to dust the tops of the dresser and chest and bed frame. She loved this furniture. It felt wild and free and filled with love. She could hardly believe her good fortune in buying this furniture. Yes, it had been expensive, but she felt was probably underpriced despite the high cost. It was a true work of art. She hoped, she and Jake would spend their lives making the best loving use of the bed.

Jake came back into the bedroom and stood watching her tidy up the room. He could see her loving care in each thing she touched to tidy. He felt the deep ache of tears behind his eyes watching the woman he loved. *I never expected to find this treasure and yet I know she is exactly the woman I longed for all my life.* He touched the small box in his pocket as if it were a lucky talisman. He hoped that their long drive to Oklahoma and their devotion to each other would turn the tide from maybe to yes.

She turned and smiled at Jake and he felt his heart leap. He smiled and walked over to her, took her hands in his and kissed her gently. "You are a goddess," he whispered.

She smiled and returned the kiss. "And you could be a gallant Cowboy if you would carry my last bag out to the van."

He grinned, bowed slightly. "As you wish."

She grinned. "Don't go all Princess Bride on me, at least not yet."

He chuckled and picking up her case. "I'm Cowboy, remember? No way I'm Princess." He turned and carried her bag out to the van.

Glory laughed and looked out the window. She said, "Well, wherever we are, we live in Eden whether here or on the ranch."

Chapter 35

"And then it happens all at once and unexpectedly.

That is how things happen, I suppose.

You pack your bags

And find yourself walking yourself home."

— Shannon L. Alder

Glory drove the van out of the driveway for the first long trip she and Jake would travel together. She was excited, nervous and longing for the trip and the hours they could spend talking. She looked in the rearview mirror to see one painter scraping away the loose paint and adding primer. One was taping plastic over the windows. She smiled and said, "When we come back home our house will be all shiny and new."

Jake took her hand. "I can't wait. I'm ready to feel settled."

"Me too." She quickly glanced at him to see his soft smile as he looked back at the house. *He loves it here. That makes me happy.*

She knew he thought the little square box in his pocket was a secret, but she had seen him touch it too many times to not understand exactly what was in the little box. She smiled at the thought of him slipping an engagement ring on her finger. She was looking forward to their talks so the surety of their love and the confidence in her choice would be firm.

She asked him, "So what is the weather like in August in Oklahoma?"

He grinned. "Wild and volatile. Or maybe just sweet and dreamy. Or sometimes hot and steamy."

"Which one?"

He shrugged. "It's just not predictable any time of year. We could have cool sunny days or blistering hot days. We could have no rain at all or rain all day for several days. The rain can be gentle, soft and sweet like it is here but warmer. Or the rain could be a frog strangler and flood everything for miles."

"What's a frog strangler?" Glory asked.

"Rain that is so intense even the frogs get choked up."

Glory laughed. "Well, I packed sun dresses and long-sleeved dresses so I'm ready for anything."

Jake nodded. "That's the best way. Then you don't have to be uncomfortable or stick down the middle of the road."

When they were near the Indian John Hill rest stop Glory said, "Let's get out here and take a walk and look around. The views are spectacular."

Jake said, "I have seen no views out here that aren't spectacular."

Glory nodded. "That's how I felt about Oklahoma." She pulled off the Interstate and found a parking spot close to the doggie run. She parked the van and turned off the ignition. "I wonder if it is because no matter where you live the spectacular views become familiar and you forget how special they are."

Jake kissed her on the cheek. "Thank you, Darlin'."

She smiled. "Let's get out, walk around and let Freya have a break."

They got out of the van and Jake opened the crate Freya was riding in. "Come on sweetheart, your momma wants to take a walk."

Glory watched the little dog happy to have Jake put her leash on and take a walk. Glory loved them both so much she could hardly believe it. Jake took her hand, and they walked across to the pet area so Freya could have a sniff, squat and piddle as Jake called it. He said, "What you said about the views is I think the hardest thing in life to deal with."

"How so?"

"Well, I look at you right now and ask myself, 'How did I get so damn lucky?' and then I see other couples who have been together for years and wonder why they are even together."

Glory nodded. "I've seen that too. I sometimes think maybe their life together has become a habit and they are just too weary to consider changing things or moving on."

Jake nodded but said nothing.

"However, I've met a few couples who are obviously still deeply in love and enjoy being together. That's what I want. I want a way we can be married, live together in happiness, mostly, and honor each other in every way."

Jake kicked at a dirt clod with the toe of his boot. "That's how Momma and Daddy were. They would have some ball busting fights now and again but mostly they laughed with and at each other and worked hard to build a life together that was solid and loving."

Glory looked at the distant mountains. "I've no personal experience of a relationship like that. I wish I had lived with parents who were like that. My mom turned out to be a great mother and woman. But those first eight years of my life were hell. I used to blame myself for all of that thinking my father wouldn't have been so terrible and cruel if I had been a better child."

Jake caressed her wrist with his thumb. It felt kind and loving to Glory, but he didn't speak which deepened the feelings.

Glory was quiet for a few moments. "I worry that we will get married and that the act of marriage will change us somehow. That we won't be the loving, kind and frankly goofy couple we are now."

Jake grinned. "One of the things that Liz complained about was that I wasn't serious enough and I was too goofy. I couldn't change for her and wouldn't be able to for you either. I am goofy. I love life and living. I love adventure but also love quietly sitting by a fire and doing nothing at all. I love you so much that just touching your hand fills me to the brim, Darlin'."

"What about when I'm old and gray and wrinkled, Cowboy?"

"Well, I'll be in the same condition. I'll be old and gray and wrinkled and still a pain in the ass."

Glory laughed. "That you are sometimes but mostly it is endearing."

Freya finished her squat and piddle and tugged on the leash. Glory and Jake followed her lead holding hands and enjoying the close quietness between them. When Freya slowed down, they headed back to the van. Glory had worried that with only two seats Freya wouldn't be happy in the crate, but she seemed to settle into it without complaint.

Jake took off the leash and Freya went straight into the crate and curled up in a ball. Glory handed him the keys and said, "I need to go to the bathroom, but then will you drive for a while? For some reason, I'm just not interested in driving and I'm feeling a little tired."

He grinned. "I'd love to drive. It feels weird letting a woman drive me around. I know that is sexist, but it is just the way I am."

She grinned and kissed him on the lips. He pulled her closer and deepened the kiss. Freya barked, and they both laughed. "I guess she isn't into PDA," Jake said.

"What's that?"

Jake grinned. "Public Displays of Affection."

"Ah," Glory said. "Well, I'm much more into PDL." She went to the bathroom. She had the pregnancy test strip in her pocket but decided she would wait one more day.

When she finished, she went back outside. Jake stood beside the passenger door of the van. He opened it for her. She climbed into the passenger seat. Jake reached across to her and said, "Darlin', I think we are in for a hell of a ride. PDL sounds like what I want to do every chance I get."

Glory couldn't help her big smile as Jake closed the door. *Oh, man oh, man. I love him.*

Jake got in the driver's seat, adjusted his jeans a little and Glory saw him settle the little square box to a more comfortable spot. He looked over at her to see her grinning. "What's got you all tickled?"

"Oh, just life itself, Cowboy."

"It looks good on you, Darlin'."

They drove for several more hours until they got to Boise, Idaho where Glory had made reservations at the same KOA, she had stopped her first time driving to Oklahoma.

"Wow," Jake said as the sunset painted the mountains in purples and pinks and oranges.

"I know," Glory said. "I didn't think I'd like the dryer side and its mountains, but these are spectacular."

Jake nodded and pulled into the KOA Campground. "This is a nice park. I can see why you stopped here."

Glory smiled. "This is where I first heard bluegrass and country music."

"Then I love this place!" Jake said. "I owe them a debt of gratitude." He got out with Glory to check in. She took out her credit card, but he put his hand over hers.

"This date is on me," he said and handed the clerk his credit card. She smiled and ran the card. She handed him back his card and said, "If you'll just sign here Mr. Casey."

While he was signing the clerk looked on Glory's left hand and said, "Mrs. Casey we have a nice shower and toilet facilities if you want something more than your van provides."

Glory could feel the blush on her face but also could feel the warmth at being called Mrs. Casey. "Thank you," she said. Jake looked at Glory and grinned. He thought, *I think she is hooked.* He handed the receipt back to the clerk and said, "Thank you so much."

"You are welcome so much. I hope you have a great stay with us Mr. and Mrs. Casey."

"We are planning on it. Come on, Darlin'. Let's get parked and take Freya out for a sniff, squat and piddle while we walk and talk."

Glory took his hand and walked out feeling a little light-headed.

Jake backed the van into their assigned camping spot and succeeded on the first try getting perfectly lined up with the utility hook-ups.

"Damn," she said. "You make that look easy. I have to try a few times to get it lined up."

Jake grinned. "After you've backed up a few horse trailers, you'll understand that this is a piece of cake."

"I don't know."

"I do. You will do fine."

They got the van hooked up and the leash line up so Freya could have a little freedom. They took Freya to the doggie area. *Holding Jake's hand is about the best feeling in the world. Except kissing or making love.* Glory smiled to herself.

Jake looked up to see her smiling. *She is so beautiful and so smart. I can't believe I'm so damned lucky.*

They walked back to their campsite, talking of nothing and everything.

Jake brought out the camp stove he had suggested she buy so they could cook on the picnic table rather than in the van. He set it up and said, "There you go, Darlin'. What's for dinner?"

"Well, Cowboy, I thought I'd cook something vegan," She said.

"As a side for the meat we will eat?"

She grinned. "You'll see."

He stood with his mouth open and then seriously he said, "You know I love meat, right?"

She nodded and chopped vegetables. "So, what's really for dinner?"

"Stir fry," Glory answered.

"And?"

"Oh, I might add a little something in that you'll like."

Jake decided to wait and see. But damn! He didn't care all that much for vegetables. A guy like him would eat them, of course, but every bite of vegetables should be followed by a bite or better yet two bites of meat in his book. The only possible exceptions of okra, pinto beans, corn and black-eyed peas. Even then a ham hock or fried chicken didn't go amiss.

Glory watched him stew and try to get his head around eating a vegetable only dinner. She said, "Why don't you build us a little campfire while I go get the rest of the things I need out of the van."

She turned and climbed into the van. She pulled out the foil-wrapped package in the refrigerator. She took out the Italian salad dressing and soy sauce. She had precooked rice and brought that out too. When she came back to the picnic table Jake was building a small campfire similar to the one Lori had taught her how to build.

She opened the foil packet a little and sprinkled in the dressing and soy sauce. As he was standing up and turning toward her, she closed the foil again and picked it up tilting back and forth to spread the liquids over the meat in side. She smiled at him. "Do you trust me Jake to feed you well and safely?"

He nodded but said nothing.

"I'm a great cook, and I prepared something special for this evening."

He smiled hopefully. "What's special about this evening?"

"Well, I'll tell you if you will let me see that box in your pocket you have been fiddling with for a few days."

It delighted Glory to see him blush.

"But," he started.

She held up her hand and smiled. "If I will be your wife and do my best outdoor cooking for you, trust me enough to let me see what's in your pocket."

Jake rubbed the palms of his hands which were suddenly sweaty on his jeans. Glory sat on the picnic table bench and waited with her hands in her lap. Jake stood watching her and couldn't help but look at her in awe. She was a tiny thing but felt big and powerful at the same time. Finally, he came around the table and stood beside her. He rubbed his hands again, took a deep breath and asked, "You know I love you something awful right?"

She nodded her head.

"You know I'd do anything for you too."

She nodded again.

"And I really love living with you in North Bend, but I love my ranch too."

Glory swallowed. "I love you, too Jake. I loved my time with you on your ranch. Your home is beautiful, and I love every inch of it. But I don't want to leave my home in Washington either."

"Does that mean you won't marry me?" He asked.

"No, but I'm asking you to live in Washington with me."

Jake sat down on the picnic table bench. Glory scooted down to sit beside him. He put his elbows on his knees and let his hands dangle between his legs. After a few minutes he said in a very quiet voice, "I can't believe the Universe brought you to me and we are stuck in the middle of our lives without a real solution at hand. I can't go on without you Glory. You are the fulfillment of my dreams. But I love my ranch."

Glory said, quietly, "I know Jake and I love you and my home too. We have special beds in both places where we are at ease and bliss. I don't think we should let that go by. I don't know how to resolve it completely, but I think we must be able to. I want to marry you if we can live in Washington. We could visit Oklahoma and live on your ranch too, couldn't we?"

Jake looked up at her and couldn't bear the pain he saw in her eyes. "Where you are is where my heart is. I can't say no to living in Washington."

Glory reached out and took his left hand in her right hand. "Okay, you're breaking my heart now Jake."

He looked up at her shocked. "I thought you wanted me to live in Washington with you?"

"I do, but surely there is a way to be married, live in Washington and keep the ranch. You have Delbert there to watch over things. You've spent two weeks with me in Washington and the ranch is still in good working order."

He nodded. "What about my horses?"

"I don't think there's room in the backyard for Freya and four horses," Glory answered.

Jake smiled sadly. "But I need them. I miss riding them and smelling them and feeding them and grooming them. I had plans to start a riding academy for children with mental health issues."

"I know," Glory said. "Can't that still happen in both Oklahoma and Washington?"

Jake looked up at her. "I don't know. I seriously had not thought of doing it in two places."

Glory smiled at him. "Cowboy, you know neither of us are idiots, right?"

He grinned but said nothing. "You know I love you more than life itself. I'd live in Oklahoma year-round, but I wouldn't be happy. I worry that if we don't work together to meet each other's needs and desires in a few years, we will be like the sour couples that stay together but not for any reason related to love."

He nodded. "I feel that sometimes folks stay together out of stubborn spite."

"I do not want that marriage," Glory said. "I want to have a vibrant, rowdy, ever-changing marriage filled with love and kids and dogs and horses and whatever else we pick up along the way."

He squeezed her hand. "That sounds perfect."

Glory touched the curl of hair on his forehead. "Good. Everything else is just details unless either one of us puts up stubborn barriers to life."

He nodded. "I love our life in Washington, and I love my life in Oklahoma. Are the winters up there as bad as they say?"

Glory shrugged. "They can be mild, sort of. But they can be brutal. Even as much as I love Washington, I dread the rainy and brutal weather from November to March."

He stood up and pulled her up and into his arms. "Glory Pennington, will you marry me?"

"Only if you show me what's in that box."

He blushed and then reaching into his pants pocket, pulled out a small red leather box. He opened it to reveal an engagement ring with a large diamond in the middle and two smaller yellow diamonds on each side. They were mounted in a platinum and gold braided band ring. "It's perfect," Glory said.

Jake reached for her left hand and saw the maybe ring still there. He asked, "So you are through with that ring?"

She pulled the maybe ring off of her left hand and put it on her right hand. "Not completely. I want to wear it to remember that maybe is always the right answer when I'm not sure. How's that?" she asked.

Jake kissed her. "Thank you for that, Darlin'." He took her left hand and slid the engagement ring on. Then he took both her hands in his and kissed her. "It's perfect now. Or will be when you get that meat you are hiding cooking."

Glory laughed. "I thought I had you fooled, Cowboy."

"Almost, Darlin', but I can smell meat a mile away."

They put the sirloin chunks, onions, peppers, pineapple and shrimp on the skewers. Jake cooked them over the open fire while Glory cooked the rice and vegetable stir-fry. They sat at the picnic table to eat their dinner. They talked of the now and the future letting the past be at peace. Glory watched Jake sneak little bites of steak and shrimp to Freya.

She said, "This is just about perfect."

"What's missing?" Jake asked.

"Oklahoma and Washington working hand-in-hand."

Jake waited, and she continued. "What would you think about keeping both my house and your ranch? We can live in Washington from May or June through September. We would avoid most of the tornadoes and the brutal heat. Then we head to Oklahoma for the winters. Between times we can have short trips back and forth."

Jake smiled. "I can live with that. We can have the Oklahoma ranch as our winter retreat and the Washington home as our summer retreat. That feels right to me."

"Me too," Glory said. "When we have kids, we'll make sure they won't miss school. When they are out for summer break, spring break and Christmas break we can fly to Washington and spend time at our home in North Bend."

Jake put his arm around Glory. Leaning her head against his shoulder, Glory said, "The foundation can help with your dream of a riding academy and helping children with mental health issues and maybe with Vets and PTSD too. We could have it happen in both states."

"That would be grand, nearly as grand as marrying you," Jake said. "But I'm not looking for a handout."

"I know. Whatever we do has to be mostly self-sustaining. The foundation is just to get the ball rolling. However, we will need volunteers, stables, caretakers and wranglers too at both places. I want to do research on this. I'll give Martha a heads up and she can get the ball rolling. Moving forward is the path for all of it; you, me, Oklahoma, Washington, kids, dogs, horses."

"And love," Jake added.

"Absolutely!"

After dinner they took Freya for another long walk. Glory felt not only happy and loved but she knew this evening she had somehow clicked her into her place in the Universe. It almost felt physical. She felt whole for the first time in her life. She had not taken a pregnancy test yet but thought she was probably pregnant. *If I'm pregnant I think the conception happened while riding the Milky Way.* A small part of her was afraid, but she had the distinct feeling it might be different this time.

As if reading her thoughts, Jake asked, "When would you like to start a family."

"Soon," she said. She took a deep breath and said, "I have used no birth control since being with you Jake."

He looked at her and smiled. "That's good," he said. "We've been practicing mixing dough now we'll just have to wait for your body to get busy being an oven."

Glory bent over laughing. When she could control herself, she said, "I have no clue why metaphor is funny, stupid and endearing, but I do."

Jake pulled her closer putting her arm under and around his arm. "That's me all right. Funny, stupid and endearing. I'm built to please and delight you, Darlin'."

She smiled and pulled closer to Jake. The feel of his warm body next to her helped her to settle down and feel the love. "I love you, Cowboy."

He kissed the top of her head. "I love you too, Darlin'."

Chapter 36

"The goal of life is to
Make your heartbeat match
The beat of the universe,
To match your nature with Nature."
— Joseph Campbell

When they crossed the border from Kansas into Oklahoma Jake said, "Yippee we are almost home."

"Are we staying with Rob and Hugh?"

Jake nodded. "I talked with Hugh last night and he said, they were expecting you to stay with them and if I behaved myself, I could stay there too."

Glory chuckled. "I hope you can behave then. I'd hate to sleep alone just because you were a bad boy. Please tell me you didn't tell him about the engagement."

"Nope. I'm saving that bit of news for when we are all together," Jake said. "We should be able to arrive just in time for dinner. I told Hugh we'd meet the family at Legend's. It is a great restaurant in Norman and he has reserved a room so the whole famdamily can be together in one room."

"Sounds perfect," Glory said. "Do I need to change clothes?" Glory felt a little guilty about the pregnancy test she took this morning. It was positive, and she was very excited. She didn't want to tell Jake until they were stopped and dressed and ready for dinner. She wanted it to be a surprise for him just before the party.

"I thought we'd stop at the next rest stop," Jake said. "We can clean up and change into nicer clothes. We don't have to wear fancy dress, just be presentable. You are beautiful just the way you are."

Glory smiled. "Keep sweet talking Cowboy and I might just have to marry you."

"I've never been known to quit talkin', Darlin'."

They held hands and chatted about the scenery. Sometimes Glory thought he seemed to know every fence post, cow and horse in Oklahoma. Every field seemed familiar to him. She smiled. *Oklahoma is in Jake's blood. I'm sure his heartbeat and the heartbeat of Oklahoma are synchronized. To make him leave the place he loves long-term would be unthinkable and cruel. I never want to hurt him as badly as that would hurt him.* It made her happy he did not have to leave his beloved Oklahoma behind.

She thought about Edgar and how sad it was that he never really seemed to love anything passionately. He missed so much of life he could have had but kept it all at arm's length. *Edgar, you've made all this possible and also taught me how not to live my life. I hope you love what you see.*

When they pulled into the parking lot at Legends Restaurant, they could see Rob and Hugh's minivan and Helen and her husband's bigger van.

"With all the kids in your family a lot of vans are needed."

Jake nodded. "And soon, we'll need more than that little SUV you bought or my pickup."

Glory smiled. "Let's take Freya for a quick walk over there at the edge of the parking lot before we go in."

Jake got Freya out of the van and they walked over to the east side of the parking lot to let her do her thing. Glory put her hand in Jake's. "Would you like to know a secret I learned this morning."

He smiled. "I love hearing secrets."

"It may top the Pennington Creek camping site secret," she said

Jake grinned but waited silently.

Glory tip-toed up to his ear and whispered, "I'm pregnant."

He turned with his blue eyes brighter than she'd ever seen them and he asked, "Really?"

"That's what the test strip said, Cowboy," Glory answered nodding.

He wrapped her in his arms and hugged her close. "My life is careening toward perfection, Darlin'."

Glory laughed and hugged him back. Freya yiked to be picked up. He scooped the little dog up and held both her and Glory in his arms. Freya licked first Glory's face then Jake's. They both laughed at the dog's antics and Jake kissed Glory again.

"Are you worried?" He asked.

She shook her head. "No, I'm not. Not this time. This time it feels right."

"When?"

"It's all an estimate based on the first day of my last cycle which was the twenty-eighth of June. According to the calculator I'm due sometime the first week in April."

"Holy cow! I'm gonna be a daddy!" He looked at her, sobered a little and asked, "This isn't an April fool's joke is it?"

Glory laughed. "No! I would never do that to you or me. It is too important."

He kissed her. "I love you, Glory."

"I love you too, Jake. We should go in. We are already a few minutes late and I don't want to keep your family waiting, Cowboy."

He kissed her. "They are your family now too, Darlin'."

"I know and I love it."

Jake put Freya in her crate in the van, tucked Glory's hand around his arm and then they walked into the restaurant. The Maitre'd led them to the private room where the family was gathered. When they entered Rob came up to her and gave her a big hug. "I'm so happy you guys came for this event."

"We wouldn't miss it," Glory said.

"You look great. This cowboy must agree with your system."

Glory held Jake's right hand in her left hand. "Yes, he does."

"You love him."

"Oh, yes, I do."

Jake said, "Hey Rob can you settle everyone down for a few seconds? We want to make a couple of announcements before we sit down to dinner and I'll burst if I don't tell everyone soon."

Rob grinned. "I had an inkling this might happen. I prepared for just this event. I've got the champagne ready for the adults and sparkling cider for the kids."

"I'll take the cider too, please," Glory said.

Rob's grin deepened, he kissed her cheek and squeezed her arm. He said, "Of course."

Glory blushed a little as Rob turned to the room. "All right family. These two crazy and wild kids have announcements to make. Grab your glasses and be ready for a toast or two." He turned and handed Jake a glass of champagne and Glory a glass of cider.

Glory saw that this difference of drink did not go unnoticed by either Hugh or Helen who both gave her knowing smiles. She tried not to smile or acknowledge their knowing looks, but she knew it didn't work. She was too damned happy to fake it or hide it. Jake pulled Glory forward still holding her hand. He said, "Hello family!"

They all shouted hello back.

He smiled and said, "I've been up to Washington state visiting Glory and getting to know her better. I've been begging her to marry me since she was here last in Oklahoma."

Everyone laughed. "Yeah. I know. Why would a gorgeous goddess marry a cowboy like me?"

More laughter ensued.

"Turns out she is partial to cowboys like me. Last night she said yes."

Everyone applauded and cheered, and Helen made a toast, "For the most unlikely but best suited couple in the world we all wish you nothing but love, happiness and a bountiful life."

They all drank to the toast and then Rob raised his hand and said, "It is my very best guess that there is something else they wish to tell us."

Jake blushed a little and then turning to Glory said, "This wonderful woman just told me we will be blessed with our first child sometime around the first of April and no it is not an April Fool's joke. I asked."

Laughing and cheering ensued with everyone gathering around them. Rob kissed Glory on the cheek. "Well done, girly."

"Thanks, Rob."

Helen finally corralled everyone and got them seated at the table. Glory and Jake were seated in the middle seats on one side with Rob and Hugh on the other side. Helen sat at one end of the table and her husband Tom sat at the other end. Children and close friends of the family and a few of Hugh's professional friends filled out the table.

For some strange reason Glory thought about Dickens and The Christmas Carol. She reached for Jake's hand and looking in his eyes she said, "God bless us every one."

He grinned and kissed her, which brought a cheer around the table.

"Ya'll will have to stop that hootin' and hollerin' or you'll make yourselves hoarse," Jake said. "I plan on kissing this woman a lot."

Another cheer went up.

The next morning Glory woke to find both Freya and Jake gone from the bedroom. She had slept well last night and was feeling refreshed. She lay quietly for a moment and touched her abdomen. She didn't really think she would feel anything. Her waist felt a little thicker, maybe. She had thought at first it was from eating too many cinnamon rolls. *That might be the case, but you are pregnant too!* She grinned at the thought. She thought she was about 8-10 weeks pregnant but couldn't be sure. She would have to talk with Hugh about that.

She got out of bed and got dressed in yoga pants and a t-shirt and went out to the kitchen to find breakfast. On the counter was a plate of fresh cinnamon rolls with a note.

Good morning, Darlin',

Here are fresh cinnamon rolls Rob made especially for you. There is fresh coffee on the counter and orange juice in the fridge. I've fed Freya, and she is with me for now. I'll be back around 11 to pick you up for the grand opening party.

I love you, Jake.

Glory smiled as she got a cup of coffee and a glass of orange juice. She sat them on the table and then brought a small plate, fork and the cinnamon rolls over to the table. Using her smart phone she checked for emails and messages. When she finished that she called Martha.

"Good Morning," Glory said.

A groggy voice asked, "Do you know what fucking time it is?"

Glory looked at her watch and said, "It's 8:30 a.m."

"Maybe in the wilds where you are," Martha said. "Here it is still dark thirty."

"Ah, well if it is a problem I'll wait and tell you my secrets later."

Martha sat up in bed and screamed, "No! Don't you dare keep any secrets from me."

Glory laughed and said, "Okay. I said yes to Jake, and he gave me the most beautiful gold and platinum and diamond engagement ring. I'll send you a photo after we hang up."

"Wowser, that is fantastic news. Are you going to live in Oklahoma?"

"Only in the winters. Summers and vacation and school breaks will be in North Bend in our new home."

Martha said, "Good. I wouldn't want to have you stuck in the wilds of Oklahoma all the time. Now can I go back to sleep?"

"Well, sure. Unless you'd rather hear the other secret."

"Spill it, before I explode."

Glory grinned and said, "I'm pregnant."

"Yippie fuck!!" Martha shouted.

"Well, yes. That is generally how it starts."

"When, when, when?"

"I don't know exactly," Glory said. "We've had a lot of intimate times together."

"That's not what I mean, and you know it. When?"

Glory touched her belly again, grinned. "Around the first of April."

"That is so cool," Martha said. "Are you having any morning sickness this time? I know you were puking your guts out last time by this point."

"No," Glory said, "But I think my waist is a little thicker. That could be because I've been craving cinnamon rolls like crazy and eating them like crazy too. I'm about 8-10 weeks pregnant I think."

Martha laughed. "Hey, momma, eat what you want and love every minute of being pregnant. I'm so excited for you both I can hardly stand it."

"Thanks. I am excited too, and it feels right and okay too. Jake is over the moon. He is thrilled both that we will be married soon and having a baby shortly after."

"When's the wedding?"

"We haven't set the exact date but after we get back to Washington and before I'm the size of a baby elephant. Jake says the sooner the better. He even suggested we could get married in the driveway if needs must."

Martha laughed. "Spoken just like a true cowboy. No way are you getting married in the driveway. This will be special and in your glorious back yard. I'll let Lori know and we'll work together to figure out the best date. She doesn't want to get married until you and Jake are married."

"Why?"

"She said you would probably want to get married in your backyard and she thinks you should go first and then we will get married a week or so later."

"Well, it is August 18th now. Can we pull a wedding together and get married before the end of August or first of September?"

"Do pigs fly?" Martha responded.

"Um, well, no."

"They do now. Have you got a calendar handy?" Martha asked.

"Yep, looking at it now."

"Well, the way I see it, by the time you guys get back up here it will be about August 25th. Would two weeks later be too long to wait? Like about September 8th or 9th?"

Glory laughed. "For Jake maybe. But he'll live through that little speed bump. Pulling off a wedding and letting everyone know with only 2-3 weeks' notice is a big push. Can we do that?"

"We are goddesses. We can do any fucking thing we want."

Glory laughed. "Fuck yes!"

"Okay. I'll get rolling on checking things out. Lori will want to help. She'll make sure the yard is perfect. By the time you are on your way back home, we will have ideas ready and a few things taken care of that will need the most time. Let me know ASAP the exact date."

"That's great. Hey Jeff, the fella that lives next door, was talking about selling his house. He and his wife divorced, so he wants out. She has already moved to Idaho near her family. She wants the house sold too so she can use her share of the profit to buy herself a new home. He has ideas about how much he should get but I'd like to buy that house before anyone else gets a crack at it. I want to use it as a guest house for family and friends, especially with a wedding or two coming up. I'd also like to use it as an emergency landing place for women if needed."

"You want me to get Jason to talk with him?"

"Yes, please," Glory said. "I do. Tell Jason to ask what his bottom dollar is if we buy the house if pay him cash and take over immediately. You probably must get Mr. Todd and Emily involved too."

"Will do. I'm writing all of this down now I'm fully awake. What else can you think of?"

"Cinnamon rolls and coffee."

Martha laughed. "Of course. Go eat your cinnamon rolls. Lori, Emily, Jason and I will get busy. I'll keep you updated by text messages, but we should plan to talk at least once a day."

"Thank you so much Martha. You are the best friend any woman ever had."

"Yes, I am. It is what I was meant to be."

Glory smiled as she hung up the phone. She liked getting to have her dreams fulfilled without a lot of fuss and muss. The money helped make that possible. *However, I there isn't anything I've done that I couldn't have pulled off myself with a little scaling back of the luxury bits. What was really required, was for me to believe in me.*

Well, Edgar, your blessings from your grandfather's estate continue to bring hope and happiness for many people. I hope this helps you settle into whatever dimension you are in. Thank you, Edgar for loving me enough to make this easier.

Glory took a sip of coffee and ate her cinnamon roll. "It will be a great day."

Chapter 37

"Every woman wants a cowboy."

— B.J. Daniels

By the time Jake arrived back at Rob's and Hugh's house, Glory was ready for the party. She dressed in a sunny yellow and pink sundress. She put on her silver sandals and was finishing her makeup when Freya came racing back into the guest bedroom. Glory turned laughed at the silly dog trying to jump into her arms. "Here you goofball," she said and picked up the wiggly bundle of black fur and gave her a kiss on the top of her head.

Jake came into the room. "I can't run as fast as she can but would love a kiss too."

Glory smiled. "Your wish is my command, Cowboy."

She walked over to him, put the dog down as he pulled her close. He kissed Glory on the lips. "I love you, Darlin'."

She smiled. "I love you too, Cowboy."

"Are you feeling okay?"

She nodded. "I've been sleepy but otherwise I'm fine."

He smiled. "Momma never had much morning sickness but she could sleep twenty-three hours a day in those first months. Hugh said it was because her body was using a lot of energy growing a baby."

"Well I'm feeding enough cinnamon rolls to my body to grow a baseball team."

Jake laughed. "You ready?"

She nodded. "What about Freya?"

"The doggie door is in so both she and Ralph can come and go as they wish."

"Does she know how to use it."

"Ralph showed her one time, and that was all it took. She's a pro at it now. I took her with me so she wouldn't wake you up."

"I appreciated that."

They walked out to the driveway and got in the van. Jake said, "Folks are already showing up. One of the local doctors who is an obstetrician, Faith Brown, offered to talk with you later today if you want."

"That would be great. With the baby coming in the spring, I guess I'll need an obstetrician here and one in Washington too."

"We could stay in Washington this winter if it would make you more comfortable," Jake offered.

Glory shook her head no. "When we come back for the winter, I'd like to fly down rather than driving the van. I need to check with the airlines about Freya though."

"Good idea. We can winterize the van before we come back here for the winter. Did you call Martha?"

Glory laughed. "She is over the moon about the wedding and the baby."

Jake grinned. "Have you set a date for the wedding?"

"Not yet. I wanted to talk with you first. If we get married on the 8th or 9th of September that would give us about two full weeks after we get home to plan out the wedding. Do you have a preference?"

"I'm so glad you waited to talk with me about this. The 8th was our parents' anniversary. It would feel weird to get married on the same day they did. How's the 9th with you?"

"Perfect. I'll let Martha know so she can get busy."

As they approached the clinic Glory could see the clinic parking lot and bank parking lot were full. Jake parked in the shopping center parking lot. When they got out of the van Glory said, "I didn't expect this many people to show up."

"Neither did Hugh, but Rob knew better. They are both thrilled to the stars with everything," Jake said.

"Then let's go share their shine," Glory said.

After the crowd thinned out Dr. Brown came up to Glory and Jake. "Hugh said we can use one of the OB rooms and we can talk and do an initial exam if you'd like."

Glory said, "That would be terrific. Can Jake come too?"

"Sure he can. We'll see if we can hear a heartbeat yet."

Glory and Jake followed Dr. Brown to an exam room on the north side of the first floor. Dr. Brown said, "Glory if you'll sit on the end of the table and slip your underwear off, I'll give you a sheet for your lap."

After Glory did as Dr. Brown asked, she reached for Jake's hand. Glory thought he looked like a deer in the headlights. She kissed his hand, and he relaxed a little. Dr. Brown logged onto the computer and said, "Some docs like me who will volunteer at the clinic already have log-ins for the system. It is the same system most of our doctors use. It makes it easier for us to keep track of our patients no matter which facility we are physically in."

"Wow," Glory said. "I didn't know that was possible."

"With some systems it is not. I think most systems will be like this one in a few years as every office and hospital shares information. If I lived in Washington, all I would have to do is login with this clinic login and I could access your information."

"That's awesome."

Dr. Brown nodded. "Let's get started with you. I'll take a brief history and put in some data. Then we'll know better where we stand." Glory answered her questions.

Dr. Brown said, "Well I think you have the due date correct but please know babies come when they are ready and not when we think they should."

Glory nodded. "I told you about the two miscarriages, but this pregnancy feels different."

"That's good. Often when miscarriages happen, we don't know why. Seldom is it because of something the mother or father does. Occasionally, but in fact rarely, it is because of a genetic defect that hasn't been diagnosed. Stress can add to the equation. The fact you feel differently with this pregnancy is a great sign."

"Whew," said Jake. "She has suffered over those lost babies. It is a relief to hear what you have to say on the subject."

Dr. Brown smiled. "Now Glory, you have a lot of choices you can make. Your chart is set up now so that anytime you are in Norman I can access it at any of the linked clinics including this one. If your obstetrician in Washington uses the same system, he or she will login and keep your chart updated. I'd be delighted to be your obstetrician when you are here in Oklahoma but will understand if you want to think about it more."

Glory nodded. "Hugh told Jake you are the best. I trust his recommendation. Besides, I like you."

Dr. Brown smiled. "I admire what you are doing for our community. It is an honor to be your obstetrician. Please, though, call me Faith. I love my name and am superstitious. I believe in having faith in ourselves and our bodies. Faith pulls us through a lot of hardship."

Glory smiled. "Thanks Faith. I feel the same way. You said we might hear the heartbeat today?"

"Let's try it. You'll need to lay back and put your feet on the end of the table. We won't need stirrups today."

Glory laid back and Jake pulled up a chair to sit beside her and hold her hand.

Faith open a drawer and pulled out a small ultrasound device. She said, "We have been using equipment like this for many years. They have gotten better and better over the years. Sometimes when a pregnancy is 7-9 weeks along, we can hear the heartbeat. You are at 8 weeks and 6 days, almost 9 weeks. There is a great chance we can hear the heartbeat today. Once I hear the heartbeat, I am relieved."

"Why?" Jake asked

"When I hear the heartbeat and it sounds normal, I have never had a single baby miscarry or have anything else horrible happen to it."

Glory squeezed Jake's hand. "I'm ready to hear her heartbeat."

Jake looked at Glory. "Her?"

Glory shrugged. "I could be wrong."

Faith laughed. "I'll never understand how some mothers know from the beginning that things will be fine and even know the gender of the baby before we can identify it on ultrasound."

She pulled the skirt of Glory's dress up a little, keeping the sheet covering her below except for her lower abdomen. She said, "This will be a little cold" and she squeezed gel onto Glory's lower abdomen. Then she put the ultrasound head on Glory's belly. She said, "Let me find your heartbeat first." In a few seconds Glory could hear her own heartbeat. Then Faith moved the ultrasound lower and along the midline of her abdomen. Suddenly there was faster heartbeat. Faith smiled, turned up the volume and said, "That's your baby."

Jake put his head on Glory's shoulder and cried. When he was calmer, he said, "Thank you Darlin'.

She touched his cheek. "Thank you, Cowboy."

Faith smiled. "Congratulations you two. There is a baby in Momma just growing and getting ready to help spread your love around."

Jake asked, "Do you think she is okay?"

Faith nodded. "Nothing is certain, but right now everything is perfect. Wait here a minute you two."

After she left the room Glory said, "I can't explain how I feel right now but it is marvelous and wonderful."

Jake bent over and kissed her. He said, "This is singularly the best moment

I've had in my life other than when we first made love."

"I think I might have conceived her that night, riding the Milky Way," Glory said.

"That's more magic than I can wrap my head around, but my heart loves your magic."

Faith came back in the room with Hugh. "I needed Hugh to show me how to connect this ultrasound with the computer so I can send you a recording of your baby's heartbeat. It's a little different from the one at my office."

Jake grinned from ear to ear. "You mean we can listen to it again?"

"As many times as you want to, baby brother," Hugh said.

"Thank you," Jake said. "This means the world to me and Glory."

Glory smiled. "Just knowing our little girl is alive now is a treasure I will keep close to my heart."

"A girl?" Hugh asked.

Faith said, "She is probably right. Get over here and show me how it works on your system."

Hugh went to the computer and input a few commands and said, "Now let's hear baby girl and we'll record her heart beat for Momma and Daddy."

On the way back to Hugh and Rob's house Glory said, "I'm so happy right now I can't think of anything other than cinnamon rolls and sleep."

Jake laughed. "I think I can arrange both things for you."

Glory opened her phone and then her email. She clicked on the mp3 link Faith had sent her. She played the heart beat over and over.

"To me, that sounds like a miracle of love Darlin'."

"Me too, Cowboy."

After a good night's rest and waking to another batch of fresh cinnamon rolls baked by Rob, they prepared to leave for Jake's Ranch. They sat at the breakfast table chatting with Rob. He said, "I cannot believe all that is happening and how fast it is happening."

"Me either," Glory said. "It is exciting and thrilling and a little scary sometimes, but it is all grand."

Jake grinned. "I'm so happy right now I feel the need for heavier boots to keep me on the ground."

"Don't worry," Rob said, "There is a lot of work to do. Also, there is much to look forward to. Soon everything will seem to be just like it should be."

"When are you coming up to Washington, Rob?" Glory asked.

"I booked a flight for me to come the week before the wedding. The bowling alley will be fine without me there. Alice can take care of everything at least as well as I can. Then Hugh will come out two days before the wedding. We will both fly back here Tuesday mid-morning."

Jake said, "Thank you so much for coming out for our wedding. I think Helen and Tom may work it out to be there too. Maybe even with the kids."

Rob said, "I'm sure they will be there. Where are you going to put all of us?"

"We have two bedrooms and the van at our house, plus we have two bedrooms and an enormous room we can put sleeping pads or cots in dormitory style next door. We are buying that house too. By the time of the wedding, we will have closed on it and be able to have it available for guests."

"You move fast," Hugh said.

Jake laughed. "I just stay out of the way, brother."

Glory rolled her eyes at the two brothers. "Martha and Lori have a guest bedroom in Issaquah if needed. There will be plenty of room. I hope the kitchen is finished by the time of the wedding. But if needs be, the kitchen in the house next door is up and working fine as far as I know."

"I have dibs on the wedding cake and groom's cake," Rob said.

Glory laughed. "I'm counting on it. Also, I read that you can get an on-line officiant certificate and marry people. How would you feel about doing that too?"

Rob said, "I had already thought about that and looked it up. I was just waiting to see if you two asked."

"You goober," Glory said. "Yes! I really, truly would love for you to marry us."

"What she said," Jake agreed. "It would be great to not have to have anyone we don't love and know at our wedding."

"Consider it done," Rob said. "I'll let Martha know and we will take care of the legal end of things."

They said their goodbyes and loaded up their belongings and Freya in the van. Rob had given Glory a cake box with a dozen homemade cinnamon rolls in it. "That should get you started," he had said when he handed her the box.

Glory had a CD that Faith had given her with the preliminary exam results and heart beat results to give to her doctor in Washington. Glory felt more alive than she had in her whole life.

Chapter 38

"True love is rare,
And it's the only thing
That gives life real meaning."
— Nicholas Sparks

Glory woke feeling refreshed and hungry. She rose from bed, put on her robe and went to the balcony. The blue sky and smell of pine on the cool breeze felt refreshing. Looking across to the stables and paddock Glory saw Jake raking and cleaning the area with Freya jumping and bouncing behind Jake and attacking the rake. She could hear Freya's yikes and Jakes laughter. *I love the sight of them happy to be together and playing even while working.*

She turned and went in search of coffee. To her delight when she entered the kitchen there on the counter next to the coffeemaker were a small handful of wildflowers beside a note. She picked up the note and read:

Good morning, Darlin',

I thought a few Indian Paintbrush and Bluebells would brighten your morning. The box of cinnamon rolls is by the microwave. The two I ate were perfect. I love you. Freya is with me. I'm teaching her to be a ranch dog.

Love you, Jake

Glory laughed. "Good luck with that, Cowboy."

She fixed her coffee, heated two of the cinnamon rolls and carried her breakfast back upstairs to sit on the balcony and watch the morning, Jake and Freya.

After she ate she showered and pulled her favorite blue jeans and t-shirt out of the chest of drawers. She went to the closet to get her sneakers and head out to the barns with Jake and Freya. Sitting on the floor in front of her sneakers were a new pair of boots. The note on the boots said, *These are your first cowboy boots, Darlin'. Give them a try and learn the beauty of a great pair of boots.*

Glory laughed out loud and said, "Okay, Cowboy. I'll try them."

She put on heavy socks and then the boots. She thought they were too small while putting them on but when she stood up, they felt like a perfect fit. She walked around the room for a few minutes and then said, "They feel a lot better than I thought they would." She looked in the long floor mirror and liked the look. "Well, Cowboy let's see how they do walking around the ranch for a few hours."

Glory went out to the paddock where Jake was exercising his new horse. He looked up and saw her watching and tipped his hat but kept working the horse. When Freya saw Glory, she raced across the paddock making a wide swing around the horse. With her little black ears flying when she got to Glory, she skittered to a halt and rolled in the dust under the fence. Glory laughed and picked her up. "So has Cowboy taught you how to be a ranch dog?" In answer Freya yiked and licked Glory's face. The dog was delighted with the day. "I think you are growing little girl. We need to get you a new collar. This one's a little tight." Glory made a note on her smart phone to log-in to PetHub and get one sent to the Washington address.

Freya wiggled and Glory put her back on the ground. Freya immediately raced to where Jake was riding the horse around the paddock. When Freya was close, she changed her gait and mimicked the horse's gait on the right side of Jake and the horse. Jake grinned and said, "Good dog. With me." In a few minutes he halted the horse and dismounted. He walked the horse over to the fence where Glory stood. Freya stayed by his right side matching her pace to his with the horse following.

Jake leaned over the fence and kissed Glory. "Good morning, Darlin'."

"Good morning, Cowboy. I'm amazed at Freya," Glory said.

He smiled again. "You have a fine doggie there. She understood every command I gave her with little prompting and knew to avoid the horse's feet. I've seen a lot of big dogs not understand that."

"It impressed me how she matched not only your gait but the horse's too."

Jake nodded, "That is the sign of a good herding dog. I think she must have border collie in her."

"Well, she is a rescue pup and supposedly part cocker spaniel. No one knows for sure. I'm not seeing curly hair on her yet. It is a little wavy, but that's it, so who knows," Glory said.

"Would you like to go for a ride out to Delbert's house with me?" Jake asked.

"Sure," Glory said. "Does he know we're coming?"

"I texted him and he said that would be fine. I want to talk with him about moving up to a Foreman position and maybe even get him to build a house up closer to our house. I'm sure he'll have ideas about all that."

"Why build another house?" Glory asked.

"I think he will need more help when I'm not here regularly and I'd like for him to work out these details so that when we are back here in the winter, I can move forward with the Oklahoma academy for kids."

"This seems fairly isolated," Glory said, "Do you think you'll get many kids?"

"Not at first but when we get the ball rolling, I think we will have lots of kids coming here at least on the weekends," Jake said. "I'm taking the attitude of if I build it and make it financially possible for families, they will come."

"Paddock of dreams, Cowboy?" Glory asked.

Jake grinned. "You got it, Darlin'. By the way, you look fine in those boots."

"Thank you for the boots," Glory said. "I wasn't sure at first, but they are much more comfortable than I thought they'd be."

"Wait until you are riding, and you'll see that they can be useful. Let me go get Sally Mae saddled and we'll head out. As good as Freya is I want her riding in harness on my saddle again."

"Thanks for that. I worry about her out here in the wilds. Will this horse be upset with her riding?"

"Nope. She's gentle and has already gotten used to having Freya around. I bought her from a fella who has to move into a retirement center but hated that his family thought they should put her down. She's only about seven years old and plenty of time left on Earth."

"What's her name? She is beautiful with that golden coat and brown mane."

"She is a beauty all right," Jake said, "She is part palomino which is where the gold comes from. Her boots and mane are pure quarter horse though. Her name is Betsy."

When the horse heard her name, she looked up and nodded. Glory laughed. "She seems to know who she is."

"That she does. I'll be right back with Sally Mae and we'll head over to Delbert's place."

Jake came out of the barn leading Sally Mae to stand beside Betsy. "Just so you know, I called and asked Faith if it was okay for you to ride horses since you are pregnant. She said it was fine so long as it was a walking pace but that the further along in the pregnancy the greater the risk to you and the baby."

"Jake! I never thought of that. Thank you so much for checking. I'm so confident of this pregnancy, I never thought to ask."

Jake saw she had tears starting down her face and reached out for her. Glory took his hand. "I'm so sorry. How could I not have thought of that? I will be a terrible mother."

"You will be the best mother ever. Well, except maybe for my mom but you'll be damn good."

Glory chuckled. "Thanks, but I had forgotten until now I was pregnant. I will have to get used to this."

"Every time you crave cinnamon rolls or need to take a nap an hour after you have gotten out of bed, that can remind you," Jake said. "Faith said you can ride until about sixteen weeks as long as you are not galloping or trotting with the horse you are fine. We'll just take an easy, peasy little walk on our horses to see Delbert."

Jake helped her up on to Sally Mae and then got Freya situated on his saddle in her special harness. "She looks ecstatic to be going for a horseback ride." Glory had forgotten how good it felt to be riding a horse and how different everything looked from this height. She was more relaxed this time and Sally Mae seemed to remember her or at least felt relaxed with her rider. She was glad Jake had asked Faith about the riding but decided she would not push it too much physically from now on.

When they got to Delbert's house he was outside working on the fence around his house. He waved, put down his hammer and came over to where Jake had tied Betsy and was helping Glory down from Sally Mae.

"Hey Delbert," Jake said. "The place is looking great." He took Freya off the saddle and sat her on the ground.

Freya immediately went to Delbert and begged to be picked up. Delbert smiled and bent down and lifted her up. She immediately gave him lots of kisses which made his smile even bigger. "I've never been much for pets but she is a sweetie. I could get to likin' having a dog around, I think," Delbert said. *Cora always wanted a dog and a big Maine Coon cat too.*

Jake said, "You should have seen her this morning in the paddock. Every command I gave her she followed without me having to teach her. She didn't bother Betsy at all and trotted right beside her during the workout."

Delbert gave Freya some ear rubs and said, "You are one smart little cookie." Freya agreed with a yike.

"Jake thinks she might have some border collie in her."

"That gives me an idea," Delbert said. "Kelly O'Neal has a border collie who is due to deliver a litter any day now. I might just ask him to save one for me. I'm not interested in having any people livin' with me but a pup might just be fine."

Glory smiled and Jake said, "That sounds great. Can we sit down and have a chat about my future plans?"

Delbert look at Glory and grinned. He asked, "Are you really going to keep this fella around?"

Glory held out her hand and Delbert looked at her engagement ring. "Well, I guess he sorta thinks you're serious about him."

"I'm so serious it hurts sometimes," Glory said.

Delbert grinned. "You both have it pretty bad I'd say. Come on in and sit a spell. I put the coffee on so we could relax and talk." Delbert led the way still holding Freya in his arm and said to her, "I think I might have a bone you'd like to chew on little lady."

Once Delbert settled Freya with a bone and they poured their coffee, the three sat around Delbert's kitchen table. Glory looked around the kitchen. "I love your house Delbert. It is cozy and yet totally welcoming."

"Thanks, Glory. I've been working on it for about a year now. I pretty much have it how I want it though I want to add a few more shrubs and maybe a peach tree too." *I'm hoping Cora will come back home and like what I've done around the place, including the music room.*

Jake said, "Well Delbert I wanted to talk to you about some ideas I have. I was wondering if maybe you'd like a little bigger place up by the house. I'd like for you to be my foreman and not just a hired hand."

Delbert scratched his ear. "I'm honored that you want me to be the foreman of your ranch and I'd do a fine job. But if I had my druthers, I'd stay livin' right here in this cabin. I've gotten fair attached to her. I like my peace and quiet here. Besides I've been fixing this place up with hope for the future."

Jake nodded, understanding that Delbert was hoping Cora would come home.

Glory reached over and touched Delbert's hand. "I can tell by the work you've done that you and this cabin are meant for each other."

"I worried that you might feel you deserved more than this if you were the foreman," Jake said. "I also thought it would be a good idea to bring on at least one hired hand to help with running the fences and doing work around the place."

Delbert nodded. "When you aren't here it is hard for me to keep up with all of it. I can ask around if you'd like and find someone reliable and honest to help me out. In fact, my nephew Conrad is looking for work. He's a lot like me. A quiet but an honest, hardworking man. He's been doing over-the-road truck driving and wanting something quieter and less stress. He was in the service in the Middle East. He thought truck drivin' would be good for him but it's not much better than the war. He's saved up money but doesn't really have anything to spend it on. Right now, he is at loose ends and seeking something different for his life. If we hire someone, like Conrad, then he's got to have a place to live."

"That is for sure and certain. I haven't seen Conrad in a long time but I'm sure he'll do fine here," Jake said.

Delbert looked at Glory. "Pennington is his last name. He's the kin I was tellin' you about. He's my sister's son."

Glory smiled. "That is cool. I must talk with him some about relationships. I think I'll get on-line and look stuff up."

"I thought you might."

Jake smiled, glad that Glory and Delbert seemed comfortable with each other. He knew them having a good relationship would help him a lot. He asked Delbert, "You got any ideas about what to do for housing the new hand?"

"If it were me," Delbert said, "I'd build a bunkhouse with a few bedrooms, a common hanging out spot and a kitchen. Then if we have temporary hands, they can live in one of the rooms. We might even want to build a couple of apartments above the carriage house for married hands. Might be that if we get things situated right, we would have more horses to board."

"When the academy is up and running, I'm sure that will be the case," Jake said.

"If you want, I'll happily be the foreman," Delbert said. "I'll get guys I know who build barns and such and we'll get the bunkhouse built. I'm sure Conrad would want to help too. He is a fine boy with a hammer and nails. We'd build a good place for the fellas. Nothing fancy but something sturdy and safe."

"That would be great Delbert," Jake said. "Just let me know the details before you get too deep into commitments. I like the idea of Conrad though. If he wants the job that would be good with me. Someone you know and trust would suit me fine. I trust your judgement just want to know what's happening when I'm not here."

"You got it, boss. I really appreciate your trust in me and love living here in this cabin." He looked over at Freya who was curled up with her paw on her bone. Delbert smiled and said, "I think a pup would suit me fine." *Being here alone without Cora isn't how I want my life to be. A pup won't be a substitute for her but will be a fine companion.*

Chapter 39

"Follow your bliss and the universe will
Open doors for you
Where before there were only walls."
— Joseph Campbell

Glory and Jake left the ranch early on the morning of August 30th. Glory was very sleepy this morning and dozed during much of the ride for the first few hours. When she awoke, they were near Ponca City, Oklahoma. She said, "I have to pee."

Jake grinned. "Me too. According to Helen you will need to pee more frequently than usual."

"She told me that too," Glory said as they pulled off the interstate.

Jake drove to the Dairy Queen. "Let's take a break here."

"Okay but it is not lunch time."

"It's eleven and the only thing really between here and the border are places without nearly as good food as here. I'm wanting a chili cheese dog with lots of onions and mustard," Jake said.

"That sounds good," Glory said. "And a chocolate milk shake too."

Jake grinned. "You go to the bathroom and I'll walk Freya. Then when you get back, I'll go in and order. We can eat out here at the picnic table and let Freya have a little more time out of the box."

Glory went inside to use the restroom. She loved how thoughtful Jake always was. That he cared for both her and Freya warmed her heart. She went back outside and took over Freya from Jake. She had just sat down at the picnic table when her phone rang. It was Martha calling.

"Hello," Glory said.

"Hi, Momma," Martha said. Glory loved the new nickname. "Our lawyers closed on Jeff's house this morning. We sent certified checks to both Jeff's and his wife's accounts about an hour ago."

"Awesome. That happened fast," Glory said, "Did he balk at all?"

"Only a little until we offered him something close to his asking price. Cash sales without banks and financing and all that can happen fast."

"How much did he want?"

"Six fifty," Martha said. "The lawyer pointed out that because of the remodeling Jeff had done it was only a two-bedroom house and did not have a garage. The highest going for that sort of house is around five. Howard Todd did a telephone conference call with Jeff and his ex-wife and her lawyer. We offered five fifty and his wife demanded they accept, or she would sue. His lawyer brought him around to reality and so they took our offer."

Glory said, "What a hassle that must have been. It still seems like a lot of money."

"It is a lot of money, but I let the lawyers take the hassle out of it. I got a nice email from Jeff's ex and I'll send that to you. She sounds like a nice woman who chose poorly."

"Well," Glory said, "It isn't always clear you are choosing poorly until later."

"Yes, she said that in her email. Now on to better news."

"Great. I can always use happy news."

"Jason went through Jeff's house and said other than a few poor design choices it was in good shape. He thinks it can be ready for company well ahead of your wedding. We got the cleaners in there and will update the furniture a little. The furniture they left are really just cast offs. We'll do any big remodeling that's needed after the wedding."

"That sounds perfect. Be sure they set the cable and internet up. I wondered about a pool table for the big room."

"Those are great ideas," Martha said. "I'll get that set up too."

Glory waved at Jake who was coming over with food. She realized that she was starving now. She said, "Jake is bringing over our chili cheese dogs and milk shakes, so I need to hang up unless there is something more we need to talk about right now."

Martha laughed. "No, Momma. I'll send you messages if I need anything."

Jake sat down as Glory hung up with her call to Martha. "I wasn't sure whether to get regulars or foot-longs, so I bought the foot-longs."

Glory grinned. "They look wonderful. What are those?"

"Those, Darlin' are tater tots. You will love them, trust me."

Glory took a bite of the chili dog and moaned a little. "That is marvelous," She said. Picking up a tater tot and dipping it in mustard she popped it into her mouth. "That is perfect."

Jake grinned. "I told you it was great. That milk shake isn't some concoction out of a machine either. It is real ice cream, real chocolate and real milk."

Glory loved it too. "We should dine out like this more often."

Jake laughed. "Occasionally will be fine. Your usual healthy way of eating is better for the baby."

"Yes, but this elevates my mood. Maybe a balance would work. I talked with Martha."

"And how is Auntie Martha doing?"

Glory laughed. "I hope to remember to call her that next time. She'll love it. She is essentially the aunt every child wanted."

"Not a mother?"

"I'm not sure. I guess I've never thought of her as the mother type," Glory said. "We'll see. The good news is that the foundation bought the house next door to our house in North Bend."

Jake grinned. "Did Jeff try to rake in the big bucks?"

Glory nodded. "He wanted more than any house in the neighborhood had gotten in the past few years. We paid him a little above average but not near as much as he wanted."

"So why did you buy it?"

"Lots of reasons really," Glory answered. "Jeff was a good neighbor to mother, and me and helped us a lot from time-to-time. He had been wanting to sell his house for a long time but hadn't really gotten serious about it. With our offer as a take-is proposition he is off the hook and can move on. Also, I think we will need overflow for guests occasionally. Most important, it can be an immediate emergency shelter for some women. I'd like to have three or four different places spread out between North Bend and Issaquah. Maybe as many two women and their children living together for emergency shelter. Then as they transition into other programs and possibilities, we can help get them personal private housing."

"That sounds great to me," Jake said. "How is Martha handling all this?"

"Right now, she is working with other groups and outreach. She is meeting with folks and getting suggestions. She was telling me about a woman who has a social sciences degree in women's issues, and she has bought a large house with several bedrooms. She'd like to live there in a small apartment on the first floor and then turn the rest of the rooms into two-room efficiency apartments for mother and child occupation. She has had no help with financing and right now is living in the house and doing maintenance by herself."

"Sounds like it is right up your alley."

"Yes, it does but I want to be sure her ideas fit with the foundation plans before we get in too deep. Martha suggested background checks on everyone to be sure there are no nasty surprises later on."

"That's a great idea," Jake said.

Glory nodded. "There are shelters around but many of them so far are connected to churches. The biggest problem with that to my way of thinking is they try to get the women into their church and then help them. I want the help to be free of any group insisting on certain religious behaviors."

Jake nodded. "I totally get that. I knew missionaries from a local mega church that went to South America to set up a medical mission. I donated money only to find that they wouldn't give care to people who didn't come to the church and become Christians. I'm just not okay with that."

"That's the whole issue there in a nutshell," Glory said. She wiped her fingers and face. "I've finished all my tater tots, my foot-long and my milk shake. I'll go pee again and then I'll be ready to go."

Jake laughed. "I don't know how you can eat and talk at the same time. I'll finish my lunch while you go take care of business."

She grinned and stood up. "Don't take too long, Cowboy. I'm thinking of a nap."

Glory woke from her nap and asked, "Where are we? It looks pretty damned flat out here."

Jake laughed. "It is. We are in the plains of Kansas and almost to Colorado."

"Good. When will we be stopping again?"

"In about five minutes. There is a rest stop ahead."

"Hooray, from me and my bladder. I can't believe I'm peeing so often."

Jake grinned. "I'm told that will get better in a few weeks until the last couple of months. Then it all starts again."

"Well, I'm not impressed," Glory said. Jake laughed. "But other than that I feel great. The nap helped a lot."

"I'm eager to get home," Jake said. Glory smiled thinking how wonderful it was that he thought of North Bend as his home.

"What are you going to do first when you get home?" Glory asked.

"Research about horse facilities nearby. There is no reason to not work on setting up the academy as soon as possible. I've got Delbert working on this down at the ranch and I'll work in North Bend too. I think you are right about setting it up with good people doing the day-to-day and me coming in to teach lessons and train volunteers."

"I'm so glad you are settled with that. Maybe Martha can help you with the research."

Jake nodded. "Perhaps but really she is doing a lot already. I don't want to bother her with this until I have some concrete ideas and can write up a real proposal. For now, what we are doing in Oklahoma supports itself. But I can't afford to start another one without a little help with funding. I want to start out right."

After the rest stop and when they were back on the road again Glory said, "I am so ready to be home. It is hard for me to conceive of being on the road traveling a lot now I have a home I love."

"I know the feeling. I love the house in North Bend. I can't wait to be back home there and see what Jason has done with the house."

"I know and I'm eager to see the landscaping. Martha said Lori insisted they not send photos because she wants to see my reactions the first time I see the yard. Martha said our wedding will be in a perfect setting. She said to think mystic feminine and rock art as we drive up."

"I remember you mentioning rock art but I've no idea what rock art might be. I know that you, Martha, Lori and Emily feel like magical women. Anything you ladies set out to do, happens. I've never felt that so strongly with a group of women before."

Glory touched his arm. "This surprised me as much as it does you. I think I understand the feeling you are talking about. It is that way for the four of us. Something changed when we met Emily and then Lori. It was nearly like a physical 'click' for me, in my brain. If felt as though we were doing things together that destiny had planned all along. I had that same experience when we settled how we could be in Oklahoma and Washington. It feels like a 'click' in my brain. I've experienced nothing like it before."

"In a way," Jake said, "Your laying it out like that makes it easier for me too. There was a part of me, in the back of my mind that was saying for me to not move forward too quickly. My gut was telling me to not hesitate."

"I'm glad you didn't hesitate, Cowboy."

"Me too, Darlin'."

When they were exiting off I-90 at exit 34, Glory called Martha and said, "We are nearly home. We should be there in about five minutes."

"Yikes!" Martha said. "We will meet you at the end of the driveway."

Glory laughed. "We will be sure to not run over you."

After she hung up Jake said, "They are serious about you not seeing the house and yard without them leading the way."

"Seems so. It makes me even more excited to be home and makes me happy that they care so much."

"I think they love you nearly as much as I do."

Glory nodded her head. "I hope they made cinnamon rolls, Cowboy."

Jake laughed. "If they didn't, I'll go to the closest bakery and get you some, Darlin'."

As they turned onto Glory's street their friends were waiting in the cul-de-sac for their arrival. Jason stepped up to the driver's side of the van and told Jake to park the van at the edge of the street. Everyone wanted to walk with Glory and Jake to show them their new home. Glory got out of the van with Freya in her arms. Jake parked the van and joined her walking hand in hand to their friends.

Martha, Emily and Lori enveloped Glory with hugs and welcoming voices. Jason said, "When you girls are ready, we can show Glory and Jake their new home. Lori you lead the way until we get to the inside the house. You are the genius who turned this into a showpiece."

Lori blushed. "I was channeling Glory and Martha; it happened to be something special." She led Glory and Jake to the driveway and after a few steps she stopped. "First I'd like to say thank you for trusting me with this. You hardly know me but you've taken me in as if we were sisters. You said to create whatever felt right. I hope it feels right for you too."

She pointed out the fresh gravel on the drive but as they walked a few steps more Glory stopped. "I'm in awe of everything I'm seeing. The house is beautiful with that deep teal blue and the beautiful cedar trim but the most astounding thing is the gardens."

Lori smiled. "Thank you. Let's walk down the drive and let me show you special planters Jason made. In fact, the planters were his idea." There were five tall planters standing next to the drive. Each was about four feet tall with flowering vines over flowing down the sides. When Glory and Jake got close to the planters, they could see that someone had stacked cinder blocks to form the planter structures.

Lori asked, "Aren't they spectacular?"

"Yes, they are," Jake said. "I'd never have thought of something like this."

Then Lori led them to the center of the front yard. She pointed to the whore bush. "I decided in the spirit of Magdalen that this bush would represent goddesses."

Glory looked and saw that Lori had pruned the lower limbs up about three feet and beneath was a small pathway of bright-colored glass rocks with pockets of tiny violets and even a fairy house. "Lori it is delightful."

"Thanks. When the whore bush fills in a little more, I'll gradually raise the branches more."

Lori took Glory's hand and pointed to another part of the garden. "Here is a mixture of primroses of all different colors and Hostas with the laughing Buddha in the middle."

Glory clapped her hands. "This fills me with joy. And look, you've trimmed the big cedar. All the Oregon grape growing underneath is beautiful."

"I moved the hydrangeas in the house's front, so they stood in the middle and to the sides of two wavy bay windows." Lori said, "You'll really appreciate those more once you see them from inside."

Jason said, "I know you want to see the inside the house, but I really think you should let Lori show you the back yard. We did a few unique things I think you'll like a lot."

Lori grinned. "I am working hard to not giggle and dance. I love it and hope you love it too. Jason brought his art to create something unexpected."

Jake said, "Knowing the bed he created I can't wait to see the backyard." He held Glory's hand and was happy the Universe sent this woman and her friends into his life. He felt nearly overwhelmed with the delight of it all.

Lori led them across the front of the house and driveway, through the east gate of the side yard. There was a new fence with open meshwork on the top of the wooden solid fence. They stained it a dark cedar. The green shrubs with their flowers opened a path with cedar chip mulch and the fence framing the walk way. The smell of cedar was intoxicating to Glory.

When they entered the backyard Glory said, "This is amazing." The friends all walked fully into the yard, standing on the back patio, quiet letting Glory and Jake take in the landscapes. In the back corner where Glory had called it a swamp was a deck surrounding the large maple tree there. The flooring of the deck was in light and dark wood creating a yin-yang pattern. They walked onto the deck led by Lori. Glory took Jake's hand. "We are standing on Yin-Yang. Opposites working together."

Jake touched the carvings of the handrails. "The woodwork is amazing. I don't understand how Jason got all this carving and trim completed in such a short time."

Jason had quietly come up behind Jake. "The first day Glory told me she wanted a deck for special occasions and to sit in the evenings, this was what I thought of. I've spent my evenings creating the carvings. Putting it together took only two days."

Jake turned to Jason. "You are a magician with wood. Never, ever stop creating beauty like this. It is a blessing just to stand here."

Glory nodded. "And to know this is here for us, our children and our friends gives me overwhelming joy."

Lori, Jason, Glory and Jake stood for a few minutes and then Glory pointed to the garden walkway. "Jake, look at the path!"

Lori beamed. "The walkway is what I wanted to create with the colored rocks. It took time but every rock became a meditation for me. I thought of Martha and her love. I thought of you and your visions. I look at it now and it seems to pull me to come walk the path."

Jake nodded. "I feel that too. Let's go walk for ourselves."

Lori said, "I'll go around the other way and meet you at the end of the path."

Glory and Jake walked down from the tree house and across to the patio. Martha asked, "You see all the primroses?"

Glory nodded and smiled. "Is this a primrose garden path?"

Martha laughed. "Yes, it is. Lori said this is a sacred path but also a path of joy and love. She thought the tongue in cheek of 'walking the primrose path' was too much of an opportunity to pass up."

Jake laughed. "I like that girl more and more."

As they walked, the path both Jake and Glory pointed out different symbols. There were several goddess symbols but there were also birds and squirrels and rabbits in the rock designs. There was even a tiger and a horse. Glory laughed and pointed to a pair of cowboy boots. There were a few rock flowers scattered through the whole path and a few in the garden itself. Some were rocks with painted hearts in lots of different colors including a few rainbow rocks too.

Jake said, "I have seen nothing like this nor could I have dreamed up anything like this. I'll say it again, you women are magic, Darlin'."

Glory kissed him on the cheek. "Thank you, Cowboy."

When they got to the end of the garden path there were stepping stones outlined with patterns created from the old slate that had been the garden path. Lori had pruned the shrubs and trees. There were shade tolerant flowers and ground cover highlighting the path. Glory said, "What amazing work you have done Lori. I agree with Jake. This is more than anything I ever dreamed it could be."

Lori beamed. "I've made a few additions to the mediation garden, but it is basically the same as it was before you left."

They entered the meditation garden. Martha, Jason and Emily were sitting on benches waiting for them. Guanyin was in the center of the depression but now sitting on a platform of stacked slate. Lori had covered the ground beneath the slate with painted rocks of many varieties and colors. The spaces between the square stepping stones was filled with chips of slate and colored rocks. From the trees several small wind chimes tinkled in the breeze. "It is beautiful," Glory said.

Lori pointed. "If you follow the paths through the trees and ferns you will find you are walking a labyrinth that itself is a meditation path."

Glory and Jake walked through the deeper woods following the path. For Glory the world seemed to hold its breath. There were small bird baths and feeders scattered along the path and more of the tiny wind chimes. When they returned to the garden, their friends were sitting on the benches and waiting for their return. Jake and Glory sat and waited with their friends for a few minutes. Glory took Jake's hand in hers and leaned her head against his shoulder.

When a few minutes had passed, Emily took a deep breath and sighed. "If your senses aren't overwhelmed and when you are ready, we'd like to show you your beautiful home."

Jake stood and pulled Glory to her feet. He said, "This is the most amazing and spiritual experience I've ever had. Glory, will you marry me on that beautiful deck?"

She smiled. "Yes, and after I'll meet you in the garden."

•

Martha and Lori were both crying, and Jason held Emily close. Jake said, "I love being a part of this circle of friends."

Martha said, "We love having you. Jason, let's show the happy couple the home you have created for them."

Jason grinned. "I think you'll like it."

They walked back to the patio Jason and his crew had refurbished with new brickwork. On one side was a beautiful glass table with six chairs surrounding it. There was an umbrella in the table's middle closed up for now. On the other side was brick grilling area and Jason said, "You being from the south I thought you'd appreciate a smoker."

He showed Jake the smoker beside the grill and Jake said, "You, my friend, are a prince! I love this and can't wait to fire it up."

"Good," Martha said. "I bought a lot of steaks and salmon and shrimp to have a feast this evening."

"Hooray!" Jake said.

Jason opened the patio door and said, "Let's look at the kitchen and dining area first."

They walked into the kitchen Glory said, "This is perfection." Jason had used reclaimed Douglas Fir for the floor. The dining table was one of Jason's creations in carved maple with matching chairs. They painted the walls a light peach, like at Martha's house, and the edging was a rich antique ivory. Along the walls of the dining area were light oak shelves and chests. Martha had taken some of Glory's mother's crocheted doilies and decorated the surfaces with them.

Glory turned to the kitchen area. There was an island built with the same oak of the cabinets. They topped the island and countertop with peach, gold, gray and ivory granite. Oak cabinets surrounded the kitchen area. There was a new glass-top stove with double ovens, a microwave above the stove, a new refrigerator and freezer and a new dishwasher. "I love it all but especially the stove."

Martha said, "It is clean." Glory opened the oven door to be sure.

They all laughed and walked through the rest of the house. The living room was open, and light poured in the large picture windows toward the front yard on one end and toward the backyard on the other end. There was an entertainment center in the corner with a large television. Along one side was a bookcase. Jason had painted the walls with the same light peach and ivory. The ceiling was the soft ivory color. The room felt warm and welcoming and light.

Jason pointed to the corner. "The TV was the only furniture we purchased for this room. We thought you'd like to have some say in for furniture choices."

Jake said, "Thanks for that. I love this room. It is big and open and even without furniture feels welcoming."

Jason took them into the hallway where he pointed out the coat closet with light stained hemlock doors. He said, "All the doors in the house are this same wood and stain. Here's the washroom for when you have guests." It was small with only a toilet and sink but was painted a soft chocolate brown with ivory trim. The floor was tile that was a lighter brown and ivory swirl. The backsplash was the same tile with gold mirror accents. The mirror was oval with an ivory antique frame.

"I love this room," Glory said. "It is beautiful and feminine and welcoming."

Jason smiled. "Emily and I worked together to pick out all the fixtures and tiles throughout the house. She has great taste in color and trims."

They walked back to the bedroom hall. The main suite door was closed but the other two bedrooms were open. "We'll look at the main suite last," Jason said. "Let's look at the other two bedrooms. I made them twins of each other. I thought although you will have guests from time to time, for now I expect you'll need these rooms for children. I built these with the thought of two children in each room."

When they walked into the rooms, Glory said, "This is perfect! I love the color and the woodwork in here." The walls were a soft buttery yellow with bright white trim. On the long wall Jason had built-in side-by-side desks and in each corner of the wall were the closets. Opening the closet doors revealed drawers, shelves and hang up bars. Jason said, "I equipped the desks with stands for computer monitors and had electric plugs on the desktop wall. Above the desk top are book shelves. At the top are closed wooden doors."

Jake said, "These desks are great, but I can't see kids being able to reach those top cupboards."

Jason nodded. "You'll find these will be useful for storing things you want to keep but don't use often. Like extra blankets and pillows, holiday decorations. I built similar ones at Emily's house and she loves them."

Emily nodded. "Those cupboards really decrease the clutter. They lined the drawers and closets with cedar. Not only does it smell great it will keep moths at bay."

Glory said, "I love this room but the bay windows with seats are the best. And you are right Lori. I didn't understand the wave shape of the windows from the outside. From the inside it is obvious someone meant them for two children to each have their own space for sitting in the window."

Jake said, "I can see this being a room any child would love."

Martha smiled. "Wait until you see the bath between the two bedrooms." In the bathroom was a shorter than usual toilet and low sided bathtub with a dual shower head, one low and one high. They could use the lower one as a spray arm. The tile was white subway tile and the ceiling and walls were the same buttery color as the bedrooms. Glory and Jake walked through the bathroom into the other bedroom. Jake said, "I can't wait to see our kids playing and living in these rooms."

Emily said, "As long as you don't have over four kids, you got it made."

Glory said, "Well, for now we have one to plan for. I'll take it one child at a time."

"Well, Darlin'," Jake said, "We have twins in the family."

Glory laughed and said, "Let's not talk about chickens that haven't been laid or hatched."

Jake grinned and said, "We'll see."

The final showing of the house was the couple's bedroom suite. Before Jason opened the door, he said, "I furnished these two rooms. I also added a half wall in the sitting area to use what was the old closet in there as a nursery area until the baby is old enough to move into their own bedroom. I can easily take the wall out, but I think you'll like it."

He opened the door and led Glory and Jake into their suite. The half wall was actually an alcove created where the old closet had been. In the alcove Jason had built a baby bed with drawers underneath and a small wall extending a few feet into the room with shelves and drawers on the bedside of the alcove. Above were more storage cabinets like in the children's bedrooms. Glory walked over and touched every surface. She turned back to the group, smiling. "Jason this is perfect."

"Thanks. As I was building it, I was thinking of our children yet to come. I wanted it to be a space that was utilitarian yet beautiful and would keep the newborn close to mom."

Beside the baby bed sat Glory's mother's red rocking chair. She sat down in the chair and said, "This is perfect. I can hardly wait to rock her in this chair."

Jake smiled looking at his bride, loving the glow on her face. "You did a beautiful thing Jason."

"Thanks. Do you want to see the rest?" He asked.

"Yes, we do," Jake said.

"Here is the sitting area for you two," Jason said. "I can imagine you two sitting here watching Mt. Si in all her glory."

Glory stood up and walked to the sitting area. "I love the matching rocking chairs and the table. The leather on the chairs looks like butter and is so very soft. I love the choices you made. I also love the red shag rugs scattered around. Looking out at Mt. Si is exactly what I want to do in the mornings and evenings."

Jake sat in one of the rocking chairs. "I am overwhelmed with this Jason. The deck is beautiful, and this room will be where we spend a lot of quiet time, I'm sure."

They walked into the bedroom to find another surprise. In the bedroom's corner was a small bay window with double French doors that opened onto a small oval porch with steps leading down to a walkway that led to the back entrance to the meditation garden. Glory walked over and opened the doors. "This is such a great surprise and one I didn't expect. How were you able to build this without sacrificing the structural stability?"

"I had to talk with an architectural engineer. He helped me with stabilizing the corner with steel posts from the foundation up through to the roof. You see these wood jambs on each side of the doors? The wood is covering the steel posts."

Jake said, "That is amazing, and I love that we can go in and out of the meditation garden directly from our room."

"I have finished the closets and you will find there are lots of built-in drawers, shelves and hanging space."

Glory and Jake walked into the closet and Jake said, "I love this. Which two drawers do I get, Darlin'?"

Glory said, "Two? Do you really need that many, Cowboy?"

Chapter 40

"It is such a happiness
When good people get together —
And they always do."
—Jane Austen

Martha said, "You look beautiful in your grandmother's wedding dress."

"Thank you," Glory said. "It worried me it was so old it might be too fragile to wear."

"It is perfect, and you are beautiful, Glory. Are you nervous?"

"No, I'm excited. I can hardly believe how much has happened in such a short time."

"You're over the guilt part, right?"

"I'm good on that. I think Edgar would be happy to know how much good and how much love he has given a lot of people. I'm in the middle of saying goodbye to the old life I had and creating the new I've always wanted."

Martha smiled. "That's beautiful. So much has happened yet it all feels it is happening exactly as it should."

Glory nodded. "Yes, it feels right. It is almost as if the dam of anger, hurt and deprivation has broken bringing with it love, grace and abundance. I also realize that Edgar's money made some of this easier, but I know now, I could have gotten here on my own. All I needed was to know myself better and believe in me."

"I'm happy to hear you say that. I had faith in you," Martha said.

"I love everything that is happening and all because four women have learned that lesson. We will do great things. I feel blessed you, Emily and Lori are a part of my journey."

Martha hugged Glory. "It has all happened just as you said but with you at the center of everything. You spreading love and being who you are made it all possible. The money was just a sideshow all along."

"Yes, that's it exactly," Glory said and smiled at her reflection in the mirror.

"It's time to get you married. Are you ready?"

Glory took a deep breath. "Is Rob ready?"

"Are you kidding?" Martha said. "He is pacing the hallway back and forth. He is over the moon with joy to be walking with you to your groom and officiating the ceremony. Hugh said he hardly slept last night."

"I'm so happy he agreed to walk with me and officiate at our wedding. It makes today perfect."

"Have you and Jake decided on the last name?"

"Yes, we will be Pennington-Casey," Glory said, "He offered to take my name, but that didn't feel right. I told him I did not want to be subjugated by giving up my name and I did not want him to be subjugated by giving up his name. However, we both wanted to have the same last name. We thought about creating a new last name but decided we both loved our families and wanted to pass on all of our lives to our children."

"Sounds perfect," Martha said. "Take a deep breath and let's go. Get that knot tied before that kid in your belly is too big for your dress."

Glory grinned. "Here we go."

Rob walked beside Glory feeling love move them forward. He saw Jake in a very nice suit and grinned when he saw the cowboy boots. They were black and new but still made Rob grin at this incredible man who found Glory and loved her. His heart was full knowing the best woman he knew was marrying for love that was a miracle of life.

Glory looked up to see Jake standing on the top of the yin-yang portion of the deck. *Edgar, I love you more now, than ever before. I'm walking to marry Jake knowing everything in your life and my life has led me here. I want to honor you. I hope you are happy for me and happy with the start we've made to make your grandfather's legacy one of love and hope. Blessings to you Edgar and peace always.*

She and Rob walked to stand beside Jake. Then Rob said, "I walk with this woman who wishes, in love, to join with this man. All the friends and family who love her and love the man waiting for her, welcome them to the joining of lives and hearts. They are joining, this man and woman, in love and honor."

Rob stepped forward and turned to Jake and Glory.

Glory handed her bouquet to Martha and stepped closer to Jake.

He took her hand and said, "Hello, Darlin'."

Glory said, "Hello, Cowboy."

The

Beginning

Authors Notes

I love dogs and cats. I have always had a dog and occasionally a cat. Usually I have at least two dogs. I strongly believe with all the rescue dogs and cats needing homes everyone who can should rescue a dog or cat. There are lots of great rescue websites across our nation. My favorite one near me is PUP: People United for Pets in Issaquah, WA. Their website is: https://www.pupdogrescue.org

Because I love dogs and cats, I want them to be safe. They chip almost all pets in the United States. However, the chip is difficult for the average person on the street to read—most of us don't carry chip readers in our pockets! BUT almost all of us carry smart phones in our pockets. PetHub in Wenatchee, WA makes ID tags with QR codes on the tag. Anyone with a smart phone can scan the tag. Then the scanned alert goes to the owner of the pet and to PetHub to alert that the pet has been found. You can even call the phone number on the tag if you don't want to scan the tag. Their website is: https://www.pethub.com. These tags make great gifts for birthdays or holidays too!

A lot of the messages in this book result from my experience in learning to know myself from the inside out. My peak experience in this was because of the Feminine Power program I took on-line through Evolving Wisdom. The Evolving Wisdom website is: https://evolvingwisdom.com They have lots of programs for men and women that are always a great learning experience.

Beginning This Story

Beginning in 1987, when my daughter started college at the tender age of 15, I began my journey toward learning more about Life, The Universe, and Everything (cudo's to Douglas Adams) through listening to books and reading books. My first audiobook experience was driving through a Kansas snowstorm from Columbia, Missouri to Norman, Oklahoma. It was getting dark when I got to Kansas City and had another six hours to go. I had heard of audiobooks (on tape) and stopped at a shopping mall, went into Barnes and Noble to find a book on tape. I met a young man (sorry I don't remember your name because this was a pivotal night in my life) who was a salesperson in the store.

He asked what I was looking for and I said, "A book on tape that is stimulating and will keep me awake for six hours."

He said, "I just finished listening to Joseph Campbell's interviews with Bill Moyers. Have you heard of it?"

I shook my head and asked, "Will it keep me awake?"

He shrugged his shoulders and said, "It woke me up. Maybe it will you too."

I paid $60.00 for the set of six cassette tapes. Not only did it keep me awake and helped me survive the snowy drive, it woke me up. Literally. I wore out those tapes and bought another set I wore out too. Luckily by the time the second set wore out I bought the set as a mp3 audio download and still listen to those interviews from time-to-time. I saw a few nights ago that the video of those interviews is also available on Netflix.

This story of Gloriana and her friends began that snowy night.

Made in the USA
Columbia, SC
09 August 2019